Pity Warrick could not simply ask *where* the little Latin-speaking governess took herself off to each day. He hadn't seen her, not beyond spying her once with her charge out the window—which counted for naught.

Miss Prim, in whom his interest continued to brim, had not been close enough in days for him to see her smile. Had not been close enough to hear her laugh or make her blush. Nor close enough to contemplate a kiss.

Ahh, a kiss.

Something he continued to think about with monstrous consistency. So much so that he had tried, yet again, to bring himself off last eve.

To no avail.

His prick was having none of it, and the bitter reality had turned Warrick's mood sour enough he'd begged off all forms of entertainment this afternoon. Another turn about the portrait gallery? He thought not, heartily declining with a false grin, unwilling to be jostled again between burly footmen first *up* and then *down* the grand stairwell... The very notion was unpalatable in the extreme.

He wasn't a small man—six four, now reduced to about four six—and solid. At least he had been. *Before.* Before—

He wrenched his thoughts away from Spain. Returned them smack to thoughts of kissing her. What was it about those primly pursed lips and coppery hair that kept waltzing through his thoughts just before he drifted off at night? Why did he have to go and attach his interest on—

Forget her. Find your heiress.

If he could just have one more chance—

To what? Apologize? Kiss her? Slide your hand beneath—

He choked off wishes that direction, coughing into his shoulder.

And that's when he saw her. Well, not *her*, exactly. But definitely her well-worn slippers (practically threadbare over one toe) peeping out from a heavy brown hem, the remainder of the skirt just out of sight thanks to the most inopportune doorpost to ever grace a manor.

You knave! 'Tis your duty to save the estate! To ensure the title lives on. You must avoid courting scandal if you are to have any hope of a financially advantageous marriage.

A profitable, *proper* marriage could go hang.

Did he want to deny himself his last wish as his hours here grew shorter? His opportunities scarcer?

Could he help it, then, as laughter and noise and conversations swirled around him, above him, if his chair just happened to move? To rotate a few inches? To...roll...to a...stop just under the big bough of mistletoe?

Never would he be granted such an opportunity again.

Might as well avail himself of it—and her mouth.

A MOONLIT CHRISTMAS KISS

REGENCY CHRISTMAS KISSES
BOOK THREE

LARISSA LYONS

This one's for my readers...those with saintly patience. ;) Thank you for staying with me while I endeavor to make every love story the absolute best I can.

And also for Maria T. You know why. 😺 Magnas gratias tibi ago.

A Moonlit Christmas Kiss Copyright © 2024 by Larissa Lyons
Published by Literary Madness.

No AI contributed to this story; 100% human effort.

ISBN
978-1-949426-97-7 Ebook
978-1-949426-72-4 Print

First Edition, all formats: November 2024

DON'T BE A SCURVY PIRATE! Please respect the hard work of this author and only read authorized, purchased downloads.

All rights reserved, including the right to decide how to market this book. By law, no part of this publication may be copied, uploaded or transferred to illegal recipients. Please respect the hard work of this author and only read authorized, purchased downloads. All characters are fictional creations; any resemblance to actual persons is unintentional and coincidental.

Proofread by Judy Zweifel at Judy's Proofreading. Cover by Erin Dameron-Hill at EDH Professionals.

At Literary Madness, our goal is to create a book free of typos. If you notice anything amiss, please let us know. litmadness@yahoo.com

NO Generative or other AI uses Permitted.

Author and Publisher reserve all rights to this content, both text and cover. No person or entity may reproduce and/or otherwise use this content in any manner, including for purposes of training artificial intelligence technologies. With the exception of brief quotes in reviews (one to two sentences in length) no other use may be made of this content without the Author and Publisher's specific, express, and written permission.

CONTENTS

About A Moonlit Christmas Kiss — 9

PART I

1. A Squealing Introduction — 13
2. Burgeoning Awareness — 25
3. Christmas Joy? — 42
4. Overheard Curiosities — 54
5. A Bit of Wine and Whining — 69
6. Pins to Paintings...to Punishments? — 85
7. Propositioning a Pigeon — 98
8. Patientia infernum est — 110
9. To Hint at Dalliance, One Knowses, Is Not All Primroses — 124
10. Chastise. Sympathize. Scandalize. — 137
11. A Miserably Magnificent Mistletoe Kiss — 147

PART II

12. 1812 — 161
13. 1812 From Another Direction — 175
14. Kings, Knights and Other Siblings — 185
15. Four Months Later... — 195
16. Letters to Dazzle, Daze and Disappoint (part 1) — 203
17. Letters to Dazzle, Daze and Disappoint (part 2) — 217
18. Torture via The Tyrant — 229
19. Sensible Advice — 238
20. Another Letter or Four — 247

PART III

21. A Seasonal Surprise — 265
22. Shock of the Season — 276
23. 'Tis Morning and Memories Continue... — 287
24. Back to the (Naked) Present — 303
25. Coming Clean — 316
26. Abuse my Eardrums, Please — 329
27. Here, Have Some Meat (part 1) — 344
28. Here, Have Some Meat (part 2) — 354
29. Hardness. Softness. Contrariness. — 363
30. Falling For You — 375
31. That Moonlit Kiss — 388
32. More Falling — 399
33. Cuts Like a Knife — 412
34. Time for a Bath — 427
35. Duty Calls (er, Writes) — 440
36. Speeding Toward The End — 453
37. The List — 464
38. The Bewigged Hermit — 474
    Epilogue I - April 1814 — 485
    Epilogue II - Eight Years Later — 489

About Larissa — 495
Larissa's Complete Booklist — 497

A Moonlit Christmas Kiss

He needs to walk again. But he may need her more...

Lord Warrick lost more than the use of his legs on the battlefield, injuries crushing his expectation of an heir along with his spirits. But it's hard to keep a bawdy man down, so Warrick continues to entertain with outlandish remarks, denying his pain. But when he starts up a flirt with a most unusual female, he cannot get the Latin-speaking governess out of his mind...

Responsible for the most exuberant young lady around, Aphrodite Primrose has her hands more than full—so why do they keep aching to comfort the haughty yet haunted peer who crosses her path time and again at her employer's house party? Past threats to her virtue taught her some lords cannot be trusted, but this one...seems different. And it's more than his inability to walk.

Impossible hopes dare to beckon when they exchange a kiss under the mistletoe but common sense brings them crashing down. For there exists no possible way this unrepentant fortune hunter, responsible for more than just himself, can marry anyone but an heiress. Time passes, filled with both tragedies and triumphs, until their paths cross again.

This time? Warrick's determined to catch her, whether he can chase her or not.

A 120,000 word extended novel, *A Moonlit Christmas Kiss* is a sweet (with a hint of spice) Regency-styled historical romance containing lots of fun and sexy banter but very minimal actual intimacy on the page.

A Moonlit Christmas Kiss takes place over a two-year period, with Part I occurring during the house party that begins in *A Snowlit Christmas Kiss*.

All *Regency Christmas Kisses* books are HEA standalones.

PART I

If I could be assured that he never was so very wicked as my fears have sometimes fancied him...

—Jane Austen, *Sense and Sensibility*

1

A SQUEALING INTRODUCTION

December 1811

Ballenger Estate, Bordering the Midlands and Yorkshire

His right leg was useless. His left leg was too. And his propagator in the middle? Broken as well.

So Richard Andrew Martinson, eighth Earl of Warrick, sixth Viscount Tawton, not that long ago of His Majesty's 13th Light Dragoons, allowed his voice free rein.

"Here!" he barked, beyond humiliated, bilious with the up-and-down motion he'd endured across the formal gardens and toward the less populated lawn. "Stop with me here."

"But...Lord...War...rick," one of the footmen clutching and grasping to retain hold of his third of their burden panted, "thought...you—"

"Enough," he all but bellowed, uncaring if he sounded

ungrateful. Downright pleased if his irritation shone through. "This is smashing, I tell you. Utterly."

His misery, at this moment, could not be worse, his shattered carcass being carted about by three strapping lads he had met but seven painstaking minutes prior. Winded to a man, the trio drop-clanked his cumbersome ambulatory chair with every bit of the ungainly finesse they had used hauling his unwieldy arse out thus far. Considering how his lump-of-a-dead-weight self was in said chair, his body drop-clanked-*plopped* right along with it.

Strangling down the lashing he wanted to flay them with, he choked on the mortification rather than let it spew. It wasn't their fault Lady Ballenger thought it a grand idea to let "poor Lord Warrick, cooped up in that carriage for days, have a spot of fresh air before the temperatures turn bitter and he retires to ready himself for dinner".

Bah. He cared nothing about pleasing his managing hostess.

But he did care about Ed. About Frost. About the hell in Spain the three of them had endured—and barely survived—together. If he hadn't valued the boundless friendships as much as he did, it would have been an easy thing to tell Ed's future mama-in-law to take her unhelpful suggestions and shove them up her burgeoning stays.

Thank God and broken pricks *he* wasn't the one who had to put up with her the rest of his life. Nay, *he* was the one who got to salivate over the sour tang of embarrassment harsh upon his tongue when one of the men punched his shoulder to shove him rearward before Warrick's face planted itself among the lush grass.

His spine whipped back, slammed against the hated chair on a spike of pain. One hand clutched the grip; the other clasped the seat near his thigh. His head bobbed like a lure on a lake before he gained control again.

Control.

One second at a time, Rich, he reminded himself, although he heard the words in his mama's voice as the sharp breeze floated tendrils of hair in front of his eyes. *Hold tight for one moment more, dear boy. And then one moment more beyond that...*

He had held on. Fought. Made it out alive.

Unlike so many of his comrades, Warrick had made it back to England, although he couldn't claim to have stepped "foot" upon the shores of home.

"One second more," he reminded himself on a low murmur, exhaling through the agony that had rammed up his back at the clipped landing. Why could he *feel* so much torture in places and *none* in others? Sitting so many hours at a time couldn't be wise.

Nearly being toppled on your head didn't help.

So much pain, sometimes lingering, sometimes sharp, in his mid to low back, crawling up to his shoulders at times. But below his waist? Naught. A drought, on so many levels...

"My lord?" a footman asked, interrupting the negative fog wrapping around him in a tight smother. He glared through the strands, his vision blurred until it wasn't. The oldest one, yet still younger than Warrick. "Have you further need of us?"

He couldn't answer. Not yet. Another slow breath as the red-hot fire faded to pink, spreading upward and outward. But not downward. Never downward.

It will fade. Think of something lovely. His mother's voice again.

But nothing lovely interrupted the raw journey of the blaze still flaring low on his back.

One single aim for this week—his voice now—*hide your pain. The worry.*

There was precedent, after all. The eighth Lord of Warrick's presence was valued for a reason: he was *expected* to do the pretty, smile and laugh and jest about with others, to enliven any gathering he deigned to attend. But that had been before. Now? His first excursion beyond home or physicians since he'd been reduced to rolling about in a god-blame chair.

He had far underestimated how difficult that would prove once outside the narrow confines of his London townhouse, where he had holed up upon finally convincing Mama to return to her younger children—and cease hovering over him—sparse months ago.

Pretend all is grand.

No one must guess. No one must even suspect how dire things had become, both his estate and his prospects of siring progeny.

Not when his dear mother—and others—remained dependent upon him to find, meet and marry a mushroom's daughter. Some merchant's unfortunate offspring who would be sacrificed to line *his* pockets and bank accounts.

Lucky, lucky girl, he thought with every bit of sarcasm in his blighted soul. Trading her future and blunt for... Nothing. He had nothing to offer anyone and could not see his way to condemning another to share his miserable fate until he could find something, *anything* valuable to trade in exchange.

His one comfort was that his mother and half-siblings lived a modest yet secure life. It was only *his* birthright, the Warrick title and entailed grounds, that headed for sure destruction.

"Forgive me, my lord, I did not—uh—" blathered the

one whose knuckles were now imprinted in the hollow of his shoulder, "didn't mean—"

"'Tis naught." The words swift, hard. All he could get out. "Back to the house with you."

Straightening, he dismissed the men with a curt nod. *Leave me to wallow in angst, to wish my hand held a tumbler instead of these infernal controls.* Once they were beyond hearing, he banged his fist against one of the two handles that turned and propelled his chair. *Leave me to try and forget the last few miserable moments.*

"Something god-damned lovely?" Pfft. He shook the lingering strands in front of one eye off with a swift turn of his head—and froze.

Devil take it! Blasted—

Rather than blast blasphemies until the second coming, he nearly bit the tip of his tongue off, until he could trust himself to speak.

"Might as well come forth," he said upon releasing his tender tongue, aiming his words toward the thick trees a few yards away.

A shrouded miss, bonnet and dress as dark as the shade she hovered in. Face obscured but posture not. The upright, stiff bearing one he recognized, could not halt curiosity over. He knew what caused his angst; what caused hers? "Your very stillness does you a discredit, unwavering against the rustling branches."

If he couldn't have blasted lovely, he would settle for *distraction*.

A FEW MINUTES PRIOR...

"Primmy! Here!" Lady Harriet, the exuberant twelve-year-old known far and wide for her love of what *she* considered fun, handed off the squirming, squealing piggy into the unsuspecting grasp of her governess.

Her governess, Aphrodite Primrose, who feared this week would only become more fraught as any number of titled lords and ladies of rank continued to descend upon the Larchmont home where she worked (valiantly) to impart manners, knowledge and decorum to her charge.

Over the coming days, Lady Harriet Larchmont—the youngest daughter of Lord and Lady Ballenger and Aphrodite's energetic challenge—would be leading her a merry chase, testing Aphrodite's lauded patience as she attempted to moderate the child's natural exuberance into something less loud—and less likely to offend.

And while guiding her charge was something Aphrodite excelled at, proper, sedate governesses were no match for mud-slicked hoglets.

The scuffle to control the squirming bundle of pink-and-brown porkling (brown thanks to the sludge, not something *else*, she dearly hoped) was lost. The slippery creature sliding from her frantic grapple to coast down her dress before scampering off toward its siblings and the promised safety of its pen. At least the gruntling ran *toward* Lady Harriet and not the formal gardens and milling guests.

"Why, oh why," Aphrodite muttered, looking at her customary day dress with naught but dismay, and speaking to the woman at her side—the elder Larchmont daughter, Lady Anne, "do I ever expect a visit to the barns to elapse without Lady Harriet or myself needing to change and scrub?" She looked up, rueful grin in place, to see Lady Anne suppressing giggles. "Or should I say scrub and change?"

"Oh, Miss Primrose!" The forthright blonde, within a year or two of Aphrodite's age, lost the battle to stifle laughter. "You have been with us long enough to know better than to hope for such a miracle. Take this." The other woman held out a handkerchief, then quickly whipped it back. "Wait. Let me help remove your gloves first."

Lady Anne considerately muddied her own, peeling Aphrodite's gloves back by the very edge, leaving at least Aphrodite's hands free of grime, though the rest of her reeked with it.

Plucking the soiled gloves from her companion, carefully holding them by the edges, she accepted the clean handkerchief with thanks.

The comfortably cool hour after nuncheon had seen the three of them casually walking the grounds, ostensibly to expend Lady Harriet's energy, but in truth, Aphrodite suspected, both she and Lady Anne wanted to avoid the visitors who had begun trickling in this morning on the grand carriages she'd heard more than once since escaping outside, rambling around the manor, heading for the stables and carriage house.

After a fruitless search for a goose she considered more pet than was appropriate, Lady Harriet had turned her attention to the swine pen, giving Aphrodite and Lady Anne a few moments of adult-oriented privacy. Privacy that now wallowed beneath the wet filth and sour stench of her dress, she feared. Though conversations with Lady Anne were never overly familiar, the easefulness with which they occurred was something Aphrodite looked forward to.

"I will remain with Our Trial," Lady Anne offered, sharing a quick smile over her sister—Aphrodite's *only* responsibility since joining the Larchmont household not quite a year prior. The responsibility who managed to necessitate the care of governess, elder sister *and* their mother. Yet the boisterous child's antics could somehow manage to elude them all at times. "Go see about washing and changing. Take a few moments for yourself before your unceasing duties begin in earnest."

Aphrodite bit back a sigh. "How long is everyone staying, do you know?"

Guests, a myriad of them, coming for the Winter Ball that very evening and staying for the house party intended to celebrate the pending nuptials of Lady Anne herself.

Guests. (Which might as well have been *gnats*, as welcome as Aphrodite considered them.) Invading the normally quiet—if one discounted Lady Harriet's environs—estate Aphrodite had come to appreciate as the weeks and months went by without incident to threaten her well-being.

But no more, not in the coming days, while she would be exposed to any number of arrogant, titled men—and their dangerous whims.

"Longer than either of us might wish, I daresay." In private, Lady Anne had made little effort to disguise her plaguesome doubts about the arrival of her intended.

Childish giggles and a couple squealed *grunt-grumphs* flew toward them on the breeze, prompting a shared, indulgent smile. "At least someone is excited about the coming week."

"Three someones." Lady Anne's humor faltered. "Make that *four* someones. Harriet, our parents *and* Lord Redford's mother."

Lord Redford, whose yet-to-be-realized arrival boggled with all its uncertainty, and now with tonight's ball? All waited for him perched uncomfortably on edge.

"No sense in you being disordered over my absent

betrothed." The smile returned to Lady Anne's suddenly drawn features, full of insincerity. "The longer he delays, the more I find a life of spinstry beckons." Her expression eased upon voicing that. "Best you go tend your dress before Harriet returns with another *porcellum*."

"Very well." Chuckling over the Latin, Aphrodite nevertheless hesitated, uneasy about crossing the grounds, currently peopled by a few strangers, on her own. "I shall run up to my bedchamber and return posthaste to—"

"No running allowed, Miss Primrose." Lady Anne gave a light laugh, one that quickly turned rueful. "What sort of example would that be for my sister? Nay, walk at your leisure, take ease in the respite. For we both know the coming days are likely to be fraught."

Fraught, which emphasized her own disquiet, the unease knotting her chest as she made her way back to the manor house. Hoping to avoid encountering anyone, she took a circular route around the formal gardens, coming up through the line of trees that had been left wild along one side of the manicured grounds.

Only to stop short just before exiting the copse upon spying three footmen laboring with a most unusual burden.

"Might as well come forth," the burden barked at her endless moments later, his voice a dangerous growl. "Your very stillness does you a discredit..."

Caught.

The rest of his sentence lost beneath the instinctive panic. Though her feet twitched with the need to retreat toward the familiar, toward safety, Aphrodite kept them firmly rooted. Maintained her wits. Squeezed her muddied gloves in one palm and Lady Anne's clean handkerchief in the other.

It was daytime. She was not alone. Not locked in her room, trapped.

The rustle of evergreens comforted when a pleasantly cool wind gusted forth and danced the fall of sooty black hair about his face. She cautioned her rapid, not-quite-panting breaths to calm. Bade her heart to quit jumping.

Simply one of the guests, newly arrived. Others walked the formal gardens, could be seen from the edge of the trimmed lawn. If she were to scream, her cries would be heard. Although no one—save herself and the seated stranger—existed in their immediate environs.

But after what she had stumbled upon? What she had seen? Haughty lord or no, her slowly settling heart went out to this particular guest.

To not be able to walk must be a trial indeed, unlike anything she could fathom. To realize someone had witnessed the near catastrophe of being topsy-turvied onto one's head? That must be a crushing blow that smarted beyond the moment.

She remained where she was, amidst thick evergreens at her back and sides, though apparently not concealing her front. Noticed, as the urge to sweep his thick hair off his forehead and out of his eyes grew, how the limb-stiffening fear freezing her in place slowly receded.

Which made her daft. To allow her closely held guard to slacken, even for a moment?

But today's circumstances were nothing like the other two. Nothing at all.

She wasn't the one being restrained against her will. Wasn't being forced to accept the hard thrust of a tongue —and threatened with worse.

Nay. She was free. Could walk away—or even run—if she chose. But he could not...

"I would bid you to show yourself." The command in his deep voice drew her back to her quandary: 1. Turn and flee with calm restraint? 2. Race swiftly past? Or... 3. Remain? "Why hesitate? After witnessing that harsh struggle, 'tis the least you can do—give me a moment to spew *something* redeeming."

She almost smiled. But didn't, oddly wounded at how his softer, almost cajoling tone was now tinged with unmistakable chagrin.

No wonder. She had no doubt the limits his body placed on him rankled, had not yet been met with acceptance. For defiance was written in every raw line of his body. From the muscular arms that had to be straining the seams of his fitted midnight-blue tailcoat, to the way he ruthlessly shoved his knees together when his legs splayed apart at an abrupt jostle. To the slightly gaunt, angular planes haunting his features beneath that sweep of black-as-sin hair.

And when do you think of sinning, missy?

"Come now. I lose patience at your dithering." He was back to being brusque. "You are ill-disguised, standing there all agawp."

Before she had quite made up her mind, she was charging from the blanket of trees. "I am not gawping!"

"Oh no? What, then?"

"If you must know, admiring your hair," she practically spat at him, stomping to a stand far beyond his reach. "'Tis longer and thicker than I am used to seeing and—and—" Her fingers squeezed tighter. "Oh! That was such an inane thing to say. Why did you propel it from me?"

He gestured toward his chair and the smooth, narrow wheels, inept, she was sure, over the pebbled walkways and lush grass carpeting the Ballenger estate. "I propel *nothing*, the least of which are your words. But I do bid you to entertain me further. Please."

Entertain him? *That* was his wish?

Please.

How silly of her, to be flattered by the ridiculous request. He wished her attention but for a moment, to ease his own embarrassment?

She could do that, surely...

2

BURGEONING AWARENESS

I BID YOU TO ENTERTAIN ME FURTHER.

Anything.

God in heaven, Warrick would prefer *anything* pull his attention from the uncomfortable heat swirling through every limb (that still possessed feeling). Knowing someone had watched that disgrace? Beginning with nearly falling out of the ponderous contraption as the men hoisted him up and stumbled down the patio stairs, and ended with him almost kissing the grass? It was not to be borne.

She remained far enough away he did not have to angle his head to an unpleasant degree. For the most part, his distraction appeared rather average. Average height, average figure—average face, what he could see of it, her plain bonnet shielding more of her features than he might wish.

Several loose coils of glorious sunset hair nudged him toward reluctant admiration. Anything but average, the mix of bronze and russet, amber and deep copper had his fingers itching to knock the bonnet askew so he could behold the rest.

But her dress? Gah. Her dress! He'd seen better attire on beggars.

No female under 200 would so much as be buried in something that horrid. Thick and stiff, as though she wore armor instead of cloth. And the color? One could be forgiven for thinking they *stepped* in it, so repulsive was the hue, somewhere between cat cascade and...

Better not be.

"Come closer," he demanded, not a modicum of doubt he'd met with a servant of some sort.

She held her ground.

"Please," he pried from lips not used to uttering such. "Only a step or two." He just needed her out of the shadows and close enough to—

Satisfaction roared through him when she moved.

Bracing one hand on the knobs that topped the vertical controls on either side of the chair and keeping the other locked securely behind him, he leaned forward. Inhaled down to his unfeeling toes. Then did it again.

"Sir! What in heaven's name are you doing?" She sidled aways and frowned at him, that prim little mouth—visible above the stubborn chin—pursing with more plump to it than he'd expected. "Are you *sniffing* me?"

"Only your dress."

For some absurd reason that seemed to calm her, and she came forth another stride. Just in time for him to rear back. "Tell me those are not fartleberries adorning your gown."

"Fartle—?" An adorable squeak of outrage emerged when she realized he'd accused her of wearing shit. "Nay! You inappropriate lout. I will have you know 'tis naught but... Swine-slick."

Swine-slick? A scratchy sort of an elegant snort came from his throat. An unfamiliar tickle had him knocking one fist against his chest twice. Was he laughing? "Why, miss, have you been tumbling about in Ballenger's bacon pens?"

"No more so than you have been tumbling about the grounds," she said with more bite than he would have expected mere moments ago.

Irritated with her for the reminder of what he sought to forget, he barked back, "Grounds I would prefer *never* to have seen. Not today nor the rest of this godforsaken sennight."

"Then why attend? If you intend to crank about all week?"

He had done it solely as a favor to Ed. (Not to mention Frost's nagging—in the form of hauling his liquor-addled self outside and shoving him into his carriage). "I am often prized as a guest." At least he had been. *Before.* "'Tis quite the boon for Lady Ballenger to gain my attendance."

Waving a muddy hand his direction, she made a dismissive sound in her throat.

"You do not believe me?"

"It matters not what I believe. What do *you* believe?"

"That aside from the last two minutes, I regret lending my presence to this forsaken endeavor with every cell of my being."

"Forsaken endeavor?"

"Here." His glower encompassed everything either of them could see. "This ball. House party, holiday, what have you."

"That's honest. And rather—"

"*Pathetic? Pitiable?*"

"I was going to say heart-rendering." With the hand not muddied, a slim thumb rubbed absently over the clutched handkerchief, the sight twisting something in his stomach. "You are here," she continued, drawing his gaze back to her bonnet-hidden face, "why not bring about a different attitude? Attempt to make the best of things?"

"The best of legs that don't work?" He had no wish to be reasonable. "The best of burdening *three* footmen who clumsily traipsed through the garden just to plant my sorry arse outside for a bit of sun?"

At *arse*, she hissed in a breath. But instead of calling him to task—or retreating—she only glanced overhead at the thick clouds that had covered the sun since morning, considerately askewing her bonnet for him. Gave him a view of somewhat winsome features and her still shaded eyes, now narrowed at him. "Lamentable you have not achieved your aims, then."

"Nay, it would seem I have achieved much more."

"More?"

He couldn't tell her how sparring with her enlivened his being more than anything save copious brandy in weeks. So he floundered about for something... "I would have you know I am counted something of a wit."

Idiot. That's what you come up with?

"Oh? I would have thought you were counted arrogant."

"Would you now?" Though her skin had pinkened upon uttering that, she remained in place, simply held his gaze.

Bold for a servant. He liked it.

"I will accept that..." He gave her a nod, wishing for the first time in several weeks he had taken the time to trim his overlong hair, wishing he'd made more of an effort before making the arduous journey here. "For despite losing feeling in half my body, it would seem I have not lost my touch."

Her sunset brows flew skyward. "You *like* being considered a touch arrogant?"

"I would like it more if I could feel *your* touch."

"For shame," she hissed, the pink on her cheeks turning nearly red, but still she retreated not.

He liked her even more. "You wouldn't possess brimming accounts hiding at home, by chance?"

"Why would you ask such a thing?" As if he had stones for brains. "Nay. But I could find myself in possession of a stick. One to poke you hard enough with that I daresay you would feel that."

He laughed out loud, felt his chest and stomach muscles moving with the motion. Ah, but it had been a long time since anything made him laugh so hard. "I would tell you to go find your stick and make good on your promise, but I would regret to lose the delight of your company."

"You would?"

At her wide-eyed disbelief, he laughed even harder. "Do not sound so surprised, my dear. Why would I not enjoy our flirt, when all my enjoyment—rare though it is of late—shall soon come to come an end, should I heed my mother's wishes?"

Is that what they were doing? Flirting? It was completely out of her realm, but the ongoing prickle of awareness he brought about, the prickle she could not deny made Aphrodite think it likely.

Never before had she bantered about with any *man* (young boys, much her age, a decade ago counted for naught), much less one with a title. *But he's seated, and likely to remain so*, some contrary imp nudged.

Which made it easier to step a bit closer and speak with more candor.

"Mother's wishes?" He had spoken of accounts. Which was unheard of: to discuss such in the presence of others, much less in the hearing of a servant. "Is your own engagement in the offing? To be announced at tonight's ball?" As was the expectation for Lady Anne.

And why did that notion sadden her every bit as much as the glimpses of devastation he'd revealed during their short exchange?

"Not if I can help it." His hard tone slammed the door on that topic. Beneath his furrowed brow, blue eyes glinted, their color so dark it made one think of midnight. Of things that *happened* at night.

Made Aphrodite hold her breath, waiting for the terror. That still didn't come.

So take your leave. While all is well and safe. Which seemed oddly unpalatable, so... "How are you acquainted with Lord and Lady Ballenger?"

"I am not, but the man who they wish for a son-in-law, have arranged for their eldest? He, I am friends with. And my estate resides not terribly far from here."

Why did that make him frown? Glower? Would he not be happy to be near a good friend? "And your estate—it brings you...displeasure?"

He glared at his kneecaps. "Much brings me displeasure these days." He looked back up to her then, from the top of her bonnet to the tips of her worn but comfortable walking boots, his expression inscrutable. "While I am here, you could offer to arsey-varsey that for me."

He wished her to turn his displeasure into... Pleasure?

Watch him now. Lest he become as dangerous as the others...

One breath, though. One single exhale and the instinctive tightening of every muscle eased. *He* was the one trapped now. He posed no threat, certainly not to her virtue.

But your common sense?

Pish and poh, an on-the-shelf maiden of four and twenty could do with a little less sense and a little more nonthreatening flirtation. "And how might you expect me to do that, my lord?"

"Please. Do not *my lord* me. After nearly ten years with the dragoons, with naught but rough men for company, that is not how I am used to being addressed." He scraped the thick, inky hair off his forehead. If she touched the strands, would her fingers blacken? Itching to find out, her rebellious hands tingled. She coiled them tight.

"Nor is it what I seek from you."

He could not climb the stairs and threaten her tonight. "Oh?" *Flirtation.* "So, pray, what is it you seek from me?"

Danger again—if the glimmer in his glittering eyes was anything to go by. "Let me keep that to myself, lest I invite your departure with more haste than I might wish."

So he did wish for something *beyond* further banter?

Before his rakish ways could tip her on edge, she offered, "I applaud your restraint. And if you were to suffer being bandied about like a shuttlecock to reach your current position, you could choose to take heart in not being spilt from your chair. That and the beauteous, mild weather."

"Please halt with the infernal optimism. You remind me overly much of my mother."

Which seemed safe enough. "Your mother? Is she here?"

"Nay. She is off with her other family."

Other family? Rather than give in to the cork-brained notion of asking what he meant, she kept silent.

"I admit, my conversational skills are likely brusque. You are the first female I have spoken to in weeks, not counting my mother and her close crony."

Which all but begged for details... "Are your injuries recent?" Inappropriate! "Forgive me. 'Tis overly forward of me to ask. You need not—" *Answer* got swallowed when he did.

"May last."

Seven months? "Recent enough, then."

"Which means you are also the first female that I—" He halted, looked down and scowled at his feet, lolling inward from his splayed knees until he wrenched them together, his tall boots snapping with the rough motion. He lifted his head and snared her in place, the depth of his hard stare roiling with unnamed emotion. "The first genteel female to see me being carried about like the invalid I am."

"As you are a guest, and I am a servant," she assured in her best governess voice, the one that brooked no argument, "what I witness is of no import. I shall blink away the memory in a trice if you wish."

"Do it."

Do it.

The glare in his gaze obliterated the pain from seconds ago, his anguish evaporating even as the way he looked at her did something unfamiliar and not wholly unwelcome to her middle.

"Do what?" *For shame, Aphrodite. You know full well what he means, and here you claim to seek no attention from men? Especially titled ones?*

"Blink away the memory, if you would." His deep voice scraped over nerves gone suddenly raw. "I would have it erased from your mind ever more."

Swallowing the trepidation her body's response

wrought, she gave him a sincere, if tremulous, smile and closed her eyes slowly, blinked twice. Opened them to find his, still burning. Still intense, upon hers. "There now. I have no recollection of—of..." 'Twas far too easy to allow bewilderment to suffuse her features. "Of what were we speaking?"

He grinned. "What of that sludge upon your skirt? If you were not rolling about in the pens, how did it slick you up all over?" And why did those simple words that sounded anything but lewd have her blushing again—and not only her face?

She aimed a scowl of her own toward the barns on the opposite side of the grounds. "Please do not ask."

"Alas, I have. And now you must answer."

"Must I?"

"Of course. For you are a servant," he said, sounding the most lofty yet, and drawing her attention back to the angular planes of his face, "lest you forget, and I am the lord here."

Her cheeks hollowed as she fought a laugh. "Rid yourself of that haughty look. If you were my charge, I would rap your knuckles for that sort of insolence."

She wouldn't, not really, had never rapped knuckles, not once. But he need not know it. "That, or assign you a thousand-word essay on The Evils of Arrogance." Holding his stare with her own, amazed at her ability to do so, she finished with, "To be composed in Latin."

One side of his lips tilted and there went her stomach again, topsy-turvying itself in ways better left unknown.

"Are you quite certain you are not an heiress in disguise?" The airiness of their exchange, the strange lightness invading his deadened limbs, had the words bubbling up and floating free before Warrick could call them back. "I could selfishly see myself settling for you."

"You rotten fiend. *Settling?*"

Grateful 'twas not the "selfish" part of that sentence she chose to question, he said, "Of course. In exchange for my title. Is that not what every young girl dreams of?"

"So many things I could say in response. But I doubt that an arrogant wit such as yourself is prepared to hear them."

His hands flexed on the handles, tensing. Because he wanted to jump from this chair, grab hold of her muddy skirt and haul her closer. "Do you not see? You illustrate my point. Without question I would be bored to Bedlam with some cherub-cheeked chit too young to recall the turn of the century."

He could not fathom living with some immature, martyred female whose sole purpose had been to snare a title to satisfy her father. To stare at her over breakfast every day, for the rest of his life? Without passion to tie them together, nor the promise of children? For both their sakes, "Better to die a pauper than suffer that fate."

"Did you not mention your mother? Her *other* family?" she said now, all traces of humor fading. "Do they not extend to you? *Your* other family as well? I would think it would be a source of pride, if nothing else, to carry on what you can of the title, even if—"

"What would you know of it? Of the demands placed on an earl?"

"Absolutely nothing, except there ought to be more good lords such as Lord Ballenger and less like Lords Tate, Paulson and Verdell."

Those were audacious words from a servant. Unfortunately, they bore out the rumors circling around Tate, which must be legion indeed, for Warrick to have heard of them, given his lack of extended residence in London prior to the past few months.

"You are talking with obscene freedom in front of me as well," she argued—when he had yet to say a word. "But that is to be expected. One of your ilk and all."

"My *ilk*? Pray, do enlighten me."

"An attractive peer, with beautiful hair, devastatingly blue eyes and an abominably outrageous manner. As though you *intend* to be beyond the pale. Strive for it. Why, even my charge behaves..." She gave a hard shake of her head as though to erase everything just uttered. "Never you mind about that."

And there he was, laughing again. "You were about to say I behave *worse* than your charge, but halted? Oh ho, that is one lass I must meet."

You do not question her over your "devastating eyes"?

Assuredly not. For that lovely distraction he would focus upon the next time pain held his body in thrall.

As to Lords Verdell and Paulson, he knew little to nothing about them and chose not to form an opinion based on one alluded-to accusation. So he prompted, curious what else she might reveal. "You claim to have had dealings with Verdell, Paulson and Tate, sufficient to know their character?"

"I claim nothing. But I know *fact*. And if any of them are boon companions to you and Lord Redford, I hope Lady Anne, for her sake, disavows any formal engagement between the two of them as her reticence has hinted."

What ho! This was news.

He knew Ed was reluctant. (Else why would he still be absent, still delaying at the Warrick hunting lodge or mayhap the gamekeeper's cottage, both of which Warrick had offered the use of when they spoke last week in

London?) Yet, admittedly, not a single thought had he spared for his friend's intended.

"You're a bit gossipy, for a governess."

She laughed—actually laughed outright. "Forgive me. That strikes me as more preposterous than anything you could have said."

"Why is that?"

"I grant you would not know it, given the last few moments, but I am the *least* person I know given over to rumor. Nor do I ever, *ever* engage in conversation with—"

She cut herself off.

"Engage in conversation with? Men?" he hazarded. "Guests? Men guests in Merlin's chairs?"

"Ah... None of that. *All* of it." The blush threatened to flare again, as she started to wave one mud-coated hand in front of her face, only stopping when a clump hit her in the cheek. "I know not what it is about you that causes my normally idle tongue to waggle."

How he would like to claim 'twas his wit that now held *her* in thrall. But he knew better.

Devastatingly so.

Comport herself differently with him than she did with other males? He was back to clenching fists and gritting teeth. At this rate, he would crush them into powder. "I know exactly what it is: Seated, unable to rise, you see me as beneath you, not worth your deference—"

"Nay, that is not it."

"Liar," he challenged, curious. Still miffed, though it only showed weakness of character. Which he would blame on his damn weakness of limb.

"All right, that is *exactly* it—*mpfth*!" As though surprised at the admission, she slapped both palms to her cheeks, mouth open, eyes aghast. "But it is not—not *why* you think."

"You have no inkling what I might be thinking."

But he had an idea. A fairly accurate one, given the talk that swirled about Tate and his proclivities. Had she been governess to the baron's children before coming here? If that rot had been her example of men, it was a marvel the moment he addressed her she hadn't upended his chair and sent him tumbling onto his head.

"Inkling... Thinking." Her lips pressed inward, over her teeth, before she loosed a shy smile. "And you just rhymed. Oh glory, and I just spread *mud* over my face. Heavens!" Features dismayed, she dropped the soiled gloves and ducked. Muttering to herself, she lifted her long skirt and scrubbed at her cheeks, leaving them both reddened and gently streaked.

More delighted than he could explain, he waited until she straightened. "Can we not claim equals? At least when we are alone?"

"Equals?" she squeaked. "Alone!" Her glance took in the expansive lawn and majestic gardens, much of both visible from their position, where more and more others milled about, all far enough away to not be privy to a single syllable.

"I know, 'tis unheard of. But there you have it, I am—now—a most unique earl."

"I should say so. You are attempting a compromise, much as I would if I had come to an impasse with Lady Harriet."

"Were we at an impasse?" he mused, his restless fingers flittering about the wooden handles, as he fought the strange urge to brush them beneath her eye where a smear clung far too close to her lashes. "Regardless... Compromising with a servant. I must admit, this is new for me."

New and insane. You are in no position to dally, even should she be amenable.

Which she wasn't. He knew. *Knew.*

But could not seem to help but wish... That he was a different person. With a different past. That she might be too.

Never could he recall being so increasingly aware of the joy to be gained from naught but reviving conversation. Nor could he deny how her countenance had gone from plain to interesting to inviting in the short span of their discourse.

But 'twas past time—exceedingly so—he returned inside and saw to the mundane. The necessary.

How to see her off, then? When he very much wanted her to stay?

"Compromising with a lord." The wonderment in her tone matched that marching uncomfortably through his chest. "This is new for me as well."

"I would offer my hand to shake on it, but yours are still swine-slicked."

BLUSHING UNDER HIS STEADY REGARD, Aphrodite knelt to retrieve Lady Anne's handkerchief and gave her hands a faint swipe. "So...you have been ordered to find an heiress?"

It seemed prudent to remind herself.

"Which does not mean I shall comply."

Why did her silly heart skip at that?

Silly heart? *Nay, silly widgeon! For continuing to dither about when you have no reason to.*

A distant shout, a girlish shrill, carried their direction. Whether it was Lady Harriet or another youngling, the sound proved an uncomfortable reminder, prodding her departure.

But he was so different than what she might have predicted. And, no matter how inappropriate, her awareness of him and the depth of their forbidden exchange, she could not stifle her heartfelt, "I *do* wish you success. In whatever endeavors you may attempt."

"Ah, then I would like to stride back to the manor—on my *feet*, mind, not wheels." His words were just this side of bitter. "Order about Frost's carriage and depart for home."

And why would that cause a pang in her chest? For the pleasant skipping to stumble? *Halfwit!*

"I do not wish to be anywhere I cannot move about independently, with the sole effort being my own and not that of others."

"We all must lean on others at times."

"Ah, but leaning is a world away from *prostrating*. Like a babe, hither and yon." Definitely bitter. "Dependent upon others for every damn thing." He lowered his volume, barely muttered that last bit, but it came through clear enough. It and his keen frustration.

He swung his head as though shaking off the self-directed pity, flinging hair off his forehead and grinned—a somewhat evil grin, to be sure. He released one of the handles and flicked his fingers toward the house. "Now be off with you. I need to find a chamber pot."

A chamber pot?

...

A chamber pot!

...

"And take a good, long piss."

...

...

...

Words. There were simply...

…
None.

He would dare utter *that* in her hearing?

As though *she* were the one imposing? And after *he* begged for her company? Termed their exchange a *flirt*?

That he would be brazen enough to say something, *several* things, so vastly inappropriate? And in a female's presence—in *her* presence—showed Aphrodite more than anything that despite his earlier claims, he *did* think her far beneath him.

Far, *far* beneath.

Unworthy of his respect. Unworthy of his restraint.

Which meant he was completely unworthy of her time.

She brushed her hands together with vigor, pretended it was his head in the middle of her palms being ground into dust. The mud, now more dried than not, went flying, might have blown toward his face, to her satisfaction.

Without another glance, she whirled and gave him her back. Forget changing. Forget having an hour or two to herself. She *needed* the diversion of responsibility, so started trampling directly *toward* Lady Harriet and the pit of mud the child and her squealing, porcine friends had likely deepened.

As to the corrupt guest whose gaze bore heavily into her back? (Though, the way her flesh seared made her suspect he stared *lower*, the fiend.) As to him?

Her heart may have gone out to the injured earl, her mind may have delighted in their friendly exchange, but no more! She refused to muse over the monstrously rude lord. Would *never* think of him again. Ever.

Not a second more.

Not even for an instant would she recall how his manner put her at ease yet excited her too, how her fingers twitched at the tempting sight of his hair, how her body had responded to the twinkle in his dark eyes, the tilt of his lips—

"Aph-ro-di-te!" Her lungs heaved, given the mad stomp she craved across the grounds.

The stomp that had moderated into prim, proper feminine paces after one single outraged stride. Because, for a governess hired to teach decorum and calmness of nature, appearances were everything. So she plastered an inane smile across her lips, avoided glancing at anyone directly and continued on, outwardly perfect. Railing inside, *Never! Never again!*

3

CHRISTMAS JOY?

NAY! CHRISTMAS COMPLAINTS

"Do you really think you need another, and so soon on the heels of the last?"

The question came from about two feet above a sitting Warrick's left shoulder as soon as he lifted his empty glass, nodding to a passing servant to indicate he needed another. Though the deep voice rumbled quietly, the criticism behind it only made Warrick want the requested beverage more.

His hand tightened around the one he held, in a grip so crushing, 'twas a wonder it didn't shatter.

Late that afternoon, "sitting" in Lord and Lady Ballenger's beautifully decorated drawing room brimming with fragrant and colorful reminders of the season should have brought Warrick a measure of joy.

It didn't.

Hard to be joyful when one's legs were broken.

Nay, broken would have been an improvement. *Useless.*

Incompetent. Weak. Not, at the moment, worth the space they occupied.

Gripping the glass, he glanced beyond his torso, at the two thighs—withered and worthless—covered by buff pantaloons, and then angled his head three inches forward to look beyond to see his feet—aye, useless (utterly so), the pair of them—encased now in dress shoes. Dress shoes for what was supposed to be a jovial occasion.

Firming his lips against the sneer that threatened, he leaned back in the hated ambulatory chair he'd been confined to ever since the battle and craned his neck to meet Lord Frostwood's grim gaze.

He scowled at Frost, pitching his voice as low as he could. "Counting my beverages? Now that's the sort of thing I would expect from Ed, not you."

"Ed didn't journey with you the last four days." The excruciatingly long—he meant leisurely—jaunt up from London in Frost's fine carriage. Long because Frost proved a solicitous traveling companion, refusing to rush what should have taken a mere two days and fidgeting more over Warrick than even a paid nurse until finally, Warrick threatened a boxing bout if Frost needed to be reminded he still had some strength *and* the wherewithal to care for himself. (Which was an absolute clanker.) "I, more than most," Frost continued, "know the pain is still there, but do you think smothering it with brandy is the best path?"

Sometimes he wished the pain was still there.

It wasn't, though; couldn't feel a damn blasted thing, not below his waist. Made taking a piss horribly uncomfortable. He could watch it come out but never quite knew when he needed to find a chamber pot—or a field while traveling—so he had a tendency to relieve himself as frequently as a breeding female.

He grunted. Didn't tell Frost he'd switched to his host's rich port.

Gave Frost a grimace that could have, another time, passed for a smile. "Are we not to celebrate? Was that not the purpose of our arduous, if uneventful, journey here?"

Raising his empty glass to his well-intentioned, if irritating at this moment, friend and fellow soldier, Warrick bit back the vitriol he wanted to spew. After chasing off the little governess, his mood had turned more downward than his south-facing prick.

"Glance around, Frost. What do you see?" After unclenching his grip, he placed the glass on the table alongside his chair, put there for his use no doubt, and answered before Frost could attempt a reply. "I shall tell you. You see smiling, laughing, holiday-minded folk engaging in banter and seasonal beverages while waiting to be called for a dinner that promises to be every bit as spectacular as the decor."

Ribbons, tied about candleholders, bowed throughout swags of greenery draped over ornate frames and the paintings they housed. Mistletoe, nauseating heaps of it, threatening to sag the ceiling where it hung, strewn through with more red and gold ribbon.

Frost shifted, peered down at Warrick. "What of it? I do not see anyone else becoming tippled before dinner even commences."

The servant neared with a tray and Warrick all but snatched the new glass to down the contents before the man had made it half a dozen steps away. He brought his empty fist up to his lips, knuckled away the remnants of port—no seasonal tulip-arse wassail for him.

"Nor do you see any other soldiers," he stated. "Any other stalwart fellows who served their king." *And paid for it dearly* didn't need uttered; it still echoed between them.

Three seconds passed, then four more. Warrick and Frost each nodded at others as they walked by, many on their way to greet their hostess, Lady Ballenger. Once their assigned corner, the one that had been cleared for Warrick and his bulky conveyance near the drawing room door, emptied of other guests, Frost knelt—in a smooth folding of muscle and sinew, hearty bone and unblemished flesh Warrick envied so much he hated himself for the very thought.

Past the burgundy of his superfine tailcoat that now strained at the shoulders, given the months of maneuvering his entire body with naught but his arms, Frost's strong fingers gripped his forearm. "We know not what trials others have borne. Not everyone's sufferings are visible. I know that likely helps not at all for what amounts to your biggest, if not your first, foray back into society."

With Frost's reminder of invisible hurts, he felt lower than sewage. Selfish sewage at that. Though he knew that wasn't his friend's intention, regret slammed into his middle every bit as hard as he hit the floor any time he attempted to use his useless legs.

While his memories after the fighting ended had been a blessed murk of pain-and-angel-riddled insensibility, Frost had braved returning to the battlefield to search among the bloodied fallen, the destroyed, looking for Warrick, unwilling to retreat without ensuring his friends returned to England as well. And to hear Ed retell it (which he had, countless times during their months of convalescence), the agony Frost experienced seeing the aftermath up close—digging through piles and parts of people—compounded with a vehement argument with their field surgeon when the man wanted to cast Warrick aside to spend his time on others with greater chances. An argument whereupon Frost proved victorious, else Warrick would have surely perished back in Spain.

He pressed his eyes shut, ashamed. With an audible sigh, he faced his friend and, with his free hand, clipped Frost on the upper arm, a silent nod to all they'd been through, and were still learning how to cope with.

And then, as though he had just offered naught but holiday felicitations, Frost smiled—an uncommon, almost scary visage, that—and returned to his feet. A quick squeeze of Warrick's shoulder and Frost retreated, giving Warrick a few moments alone while he approached their host and hostess and engaged the couple responsible for tonight's gathering.

The ball to celebrate not only the return of his and Frost's friend and fellow soldier, but also to commemorate the arranged betrothal to Lord and Lady Ballenger's eldest daughter, remained in question. For Ed—Lord Redford—severely injured at Albuera (the same battle that felled Warrick) had yet to show his scraggly face. If Frost was the overly serious of their trio and Warrick—pre-war—the outrageous charmer, then Ed was the best of both of them.

Failing to show or send word wasn't like the dependable man, and the hour marched ever closer to dinner.

Spying Lady Redford, Ed's mother, through a cluster of young ladies, he breathed easily for the first time since exiting his assigned room. The wounded boy in him had responded to the maternal Lady Redford from the moment he'd met her at the regimental hospital months ago. Since then, she had proven her dedication to her son several times over, impressing Warrick and finding a place in his heart alongside her son.

Thank God and decent roads, she had arrived safely.

Through the unwelcome gaggle of giggling lasses, he watched as she was greeted by others. Though she avoided overly long conversations, she appeared to be traveling the perimeter of the room such that he could not catch her eye.

Tension rose in his chest and arms (it might have risen in his legs as well—that, he had no way of knowing) because he could not fail to notice how more than one of the irritatingly positioned females took turns glancing coyly over their shoulders, to seek out his attention only to turn back to the others and say something that spurred laughter. Louder giggles.

And he was bound by duty to find one of these brainless chits with a caravan of funds and woo her with his unresponsive frigger? *Pfft.*

Refusing to acknowledge them further, he angled one handle, turned his chair. Made no difference. Too many bits of fluff in their pastel best impeded his view. A light-colored skirt would shift, but a gloved elbow would block. A hip would cock just so, and he would catch a glimpse of Lady Redford, then another horde of giggles and a reticule upon a wrist would swing to obstruct the way once again.

If only he could stand.

He would tower over these impossibly young and cackling misses whose immature antics made him wish he could kick them right out the French windows. Already, their cloying perfumes battled with the more subtle allure of outdoor fragrances gracing the room's horizontal planes thanks to the plethora of greenery placed about in honor of the season.

His heart beat harder, faster.

Dread assailed, leaving a sour taste in his mouth. His face flushed, only seconds away from an unwanted luster of sweat. Tongue thickened as he knew what he had to do.

"Damn it all." The whisper scratched from a tight throat.

He had to draw attention to himself in order to obtain hers. *Would rather just shat myself.*

Nay. He'd rather return to earlier. To outside. To an unexpected flirt that—

Means nothing.

"LdyRd—" The garbled syllables didn't come close to the volume—nor command—he needed. He swallowed hard and tried again. "Lady Redford!"

That did it. Yanked everyone's attention—not just the startled misses—right to his corner. Right to him. Right to his deficiencies.

As though he hadn't just humiliated himself, he pretended ignorance of the stares he'd garnered and attempted to calm his disturbed breaths before she reached his side.

"Oh my dear boy." She greeted him as one of her own, the gracious welcome allowing him to focus on her whilst the rest of the room faded. "I saw you out of the corner of my eye, but didn't want to make a spectacle by rushing over."

"And here I made a spectacle of the both of us." Hidden at his side, his right hand fisted around an almost dry handkerchief, retrieved from the grounds, brushed clean and rinsed in his washbasin. "My apologies."

"No apologies needed, Lord Warrick, never you fear." She placed one hand on her chest. "I confess, the moment I realized you were here, I wanted to hug you." The warmth from her greeting now battled the heat in his cheeks. "I know that isn't the thing, not at all. Not—"

"I would welcome a hug." Shoving the wrinkled fabric in a pocket, he held out his arms, stopped bothering about what others might think and accepted the caring concern of the woman who had practically become a second mother to him the last few months.

For Ed's mother and his had joined forces to create an impenetrable barrier between their sons and death, doing everything they could, from seeing them moved from the common room of the regimental hospital (where the Army had stashed them along with other wrecked soldiers), and into a private residence, to hiring hand-picked physicians and nurses to see to their care.

As she bent down and wrapped her arms about his neck, he curved his around her waist, if awkwardly, and breathed in that subtle maternal scent that seemed to cling to mothers the world over. He thought of the last time he'd seen his. Just five days ago, right before Frost showed up to whisk him from London, when he and Mama had quarreled. With thunderous results. At his city townhome, not at her cottage in the country, thank goodness, so at least his half-siblings were spared the barrage of ruffing words that blasted between the two of them.

You have all but given up! she'd cried. Literally cried, streams tracking down the gently aging face that was usually wreathed in laughter and smiles. Much like his own had been, *before.*

He'd thrust his jaw out and leaned forward until he nearly toppled off the rolling chair. Before pitching groundward, he whipped back, wobbling in place, infuriated all over again. At her. Because she was convenient. But in reality, maddened at the world. At God. The king. At that vile louse Napoleon who thought he could overtake every country for his own...

Nay! I have not, he'd gritted out between clenched teeth, hands coiled tight at his side so he wouldn't bang them against the hated chair. *What do you think I have been doing for months?*

Trying until his will had just worn down. No progress, no feeling, no movement.

No hope.

But, Richard... She'd startled him with his first name, so seldom heard since he'd inherited the title—and everything along with it—before his ninth birthday. *You do not understand. There is more at stake than either of us realized.*

More at stake than ever walking? he'd spat. *Ever swiving?* he'd dared yell, expecting her to slap him for speaking thus in her presence, only to watch more tears slide down her cheeks as she slowly backed away.

The title. Is that what you think of? All *you consider?*

Of course it was. That and sinking deep into a welcoming woman, one who wanted him for himself and not just the brash charmer always eager for a rousing time. But now? He had nothing to sink. No working twanger to help win the right woman to his side and heart.

He had nothing but years and years in front of him: sitting. *Sitting* on his numb arse while he watched others walk. Ride. *Dance.*

Dancing. Something his mother ensured he learned at a young age, something he had always, *always* taken pleasure from. Dancing with a smiling lass, even with no intentions of aiming for more, had brought joy to his soul. And now? Now his soul felt mired back on the battlefield while the rest of him—the shell—pretended all was well here in England.

It hadn't been until the second full day of his and Frost's journey here that what his mother hadn't said penetrated his garret: his younger siblings. *That's* what concerned her beyond the title—and what tempted him to drink like a man deprived: *his siblings*, and how he had given no thought to them, nor their future. At least not verbally, not with his mother the last months. Nor had he once given thought to how their lives had changed since she rushed to his side, leaving them with their father.

Neither she nor her second husband had any living siblings. So as the eldest of her children, not to mention the title holder, it would fall to him to be the dependable, elder brother throughout what he hoped was their long lives. Older brother? He'd failed at—

Lost in the past, it wasn't until the second, softly voiced "Dear boy" reached his awareness that he loosened the embrace that had, so very quickly, brought back everything he sought to forget.

Lady Redford kissed his cheek as she pulled away, allowing him to see the moisture glistening in her eyes. "I did not expect to see you here. I daresay Ward will be as delighted as I am that you made the effort."

Ward. What she called her son, Edward.

"Thank Frost." Who had adamantly refused to accept Warrick's irritable refusal. Who had practically packed his bag, his needed-but-hated wheeled chair, and then his complaining self straight into the carriage, ordering the coachman to be off before Warrick could load a pistol and bargain, threaten or cajole for his freedom. "He's to"—*blame*—"thank."

"And Ward?" she knelt to whisper, bracing one hand on his for balance and keeping the question between them. "Have you word of my son's arrival?"

Nay, he did not. But could not help but notice the worried expressions and quiet murmurings between Lord and Lady Ballenger when they thought no one was watching (or listening)... *Where was Lord Redford? Should he not have been here a week ago? Surely by yesterday. Had tragedy befallen the recovering soldier and new viscount now betrothed to their daughter?*

"I believe I may be to blame for his tardiness," Warrick admitted. "Forgive me, but I dangled the use of my hunting lodge to Ed, knowing he was anxious about the betrothal. About the gathering..." After indicating the throng, he gestured to his right arm, the one Ed no longer possessed. "I believe we can both understand his reluctance to appear in society."

For it is taking every shred of bravery that wasn't stomped out of me in Spain to appear here myself.

Blinking rapidly—to contain the moisture he suspected—she gave a nod. "I do. I can. Especially since even his remaining one"—she flexed the fingers of her left hand, giving rise to the image of the distorted mangle his friend had come home with—"still causes him significant difficulty."

"Worry not, for if he doesn't show his ugly face by the dancing hour, Frost and I will travel to my estate"—only a few hours away, but not something he had visited since returning to England—"and collect him posthaste. He may have simply neglected to mind the calendar."

"Or he could be hurt, needing—"

"We shall go now." As soon as he touched the controls to move his chair, she stopped him with her gloved hand over his.

"Nay. I worry overmuch. A hearty meal may put things to rights. And we both know traveling in winter without the moon is asking for calamities, something none of us need court. If he isn't here by morning, I shall go with you, if I may?"

"Absolutely." If Ed wasn't there by nightfall, he might learn firsthand just how much strength working this blasted chair and hauling the weight of his unresponsive lower half about had given Warrick's shoulders and arms, for worrying her so.

Warrick caught Frost's attention when he turned from their hosts, gave a tilt of his chin, indicating he was fine, and spent several more minutes in conversation with Lady

Redford—but only after he'd summoned a servant and requested they bring her a chair.

A while later, after she moved off to chatter with an old friend, he and Frost exchanged another, more deliberate look, Warrick now making clear his goal of escaping.

Despite Frost's frowning countenance—his customary expression, holidays and battles not withstanding—he understood Warrick's need to vacate the crush before they were summoned to dinner. Understood his need to seek out seclusion, where he could fumble in private with his chair and the blasted chamber pot.

4

OVERHEARD CURIOSITIES

"Oh, Primmy!" The youngling fidgeted beside her in the narrow corridor outside a little-used sitting room. "*Must* I?"

As the long day approached the dinner hour, Aphrodite Primrose knew three things with utter certainty:

1. She was fortunate indeed, to have landed such a post earlier this year, being governess to Lord and Lady Ballenger's youngest. No older brother "lordlings" assuming she was theirs for the summoning. No nose-hair-sporting arrogant Lord of the Manor creeping his way into her attic room at night. Aye, she was most fortunate. Most relieved. And likely the most appreciative governess in all England.

"But, Primmy," the whining continued (something she suspected had gotten the child her way in the past), "the other does not fit nearly as good. It—"

"As *well*."

"As *well*." Accompanied by a stomp from one slipper. "The color might be grand, but I cannot tolerate how it…"

Briefly shuttling her attention away from the childish excuses, she continued through her list.

2. Quickly now, she needed to devise a better way to chastise and discipline her energetic charge when the girl behaved in a manner unbecoming. Aphrodite approached her ninth month of employment and neither reasoning nor cajoling nor threats of meals withheld had the least effect on the exuberant girl.

"We were not even outside an hour this time!" That same slippered foot now *kicked* the wall twice before Aphrodite, wincing at how loud the *thump*, managed to take the girl by her shoulders and spin her around. "I am so addled I could scream!"

How was it her toes didn't ache after that abuse against the wall? Had she put metal tips in her slippers?

"Lady Harriet!" Stern and forceful, for all that her words were nowhere near a scream, Aphrodite ordered, "Compose yourself this instant."

"But, Prim*my*! I barely had time to look—"

3. And she absolutely, positively *hated* how Lady Harriet thought it amusing to address her as *Primmy*. Given not only her position but also the years between herself and the child, aside from the repeated requests, she should have been known solely as "Miss Primrose".

Most certainly *not* the near-rhyming epithet similar to that which England's Prince Regent had been saddled with: Prinny. At least *he* had the expectation of the crown to run alongside it; she had naught but boring brown dresses and a pleasant room in the attic—one with a sturdy lock she was thankful for every night.

Even tonight? With broad shoulders and haunted blue eyes, what if the—

She slammed that notion against the wall with more force than Harriet's foot and wrenched her wayward attention back to the girl.

"—for Lancelot. He needs me!" The vivacious youth glanced over her shoulder, back toward the little-used way they had come, Aphrodite doing all she could to keep the state of Lady Harriet's dress hidden from the girl's mother, Lady Ballenger.

"There will be plenty of time to search for Lancelot tomorrow. As to the other, there is no question: you *will* be changing before dinner. *Again*," she told the girl on a resigned sigh, granting her shoulders a firm squeeze before releasing her.

Not apologetic in the least, Lady Harriet continued to bounce in place, unable to ever sit—or stand—still. She would complain until she got her way if Aphrodite didn't halt things posthaste. "Though you managed to obtain permission to attend the gathering tonight," she told the girl, still in awe at that feat, "a sludge-spattered, feather-bedecked dress is no way to greet guests nor partake of your first meal with the adults."

Lady Ballenger had lost a wager to her youngest, and instead of paying the total sum—nearing an exorbitant 300 pounds, or so the story went—had agreed Lady Harriet could sit down to dinner with the guests, and only retire to the nursery once the adults abandoned the table for the ballroom.

"But Lancelot... Sir Galahad!"

What was it with her charge and her affinity for animals? Fur or feathers, skin or scales (Aphrodite shuddered at the last), it mattered naught; Lady Harriet adored them all—sometimes to her detriment.

With this most recent disastrous excursion outside, the hoglets had been exchanged for geese. "How you managed to soil two dresses in one day is a feat not to be repeated."

Intelligent, precocious children were both a joy and a trial, and though teaching the headstrong, forthright Lady Harriet tested her will and her wits, Aphrodite wouldn't trade her job for anything.

Except, mayhap, a family of her own.

Which wasn't likely, she knew. At her age, even the only child of a scholarly father married to the daughter of a baronet's sixth son who wed against her parents' wishes had little hopes of matrimony. Not unless she wanted to marry a widowed man far too many years her senior and already endowed with a herd of unruly children in need of a mother.

Alas, she was already quite devoted to her unruly charge...

Before Harriet's tears could start in earnest again, Aphrodite asked, "Are you not excited about this evening and the next several days?" The ball might be tonight, but the house party was intended to last the entire holiday week or more. "Have you yet met any guests near your age?"

"*Pffft.*" Lady Harriet wavered back and forth, showing a rip near the hem, the sight of which—in the new gown—made Aphrodite's stomach pitch. "Babies, one and all. The oldest one of them is *eight*. I will be thirteen soon, *so* much closer to an adult than one who belongs in the nursery. With the *children*."

"Shall I accompany you upstairs?" she asked, biting down a smile. "See that you attire yourself in that pretty scarlet—"

"The red one?" Lady Harriet groaned, her normally happy expression turning harried. "It bothers me—here." She tugged on the fabric near the crease of one arm, spreading yet more mud on the blue frock Lady Ballenger had selected for the evening, not realizing Harriet would put it on early enough to slip back outside. "Simply let me have this one washed."

"Out of the question." Aphrodite leaned back to better study the damage. "Is that a goose feather? I thought we brushed those off before entering. Never you mind, I do not want to know. Upstairs, please, lest your mother see the stains and chastise us both."

"Fine, I shall change"—the mutinous tone was only slightly less so—"and you do not need to assist. If I cannot do it myself..." Her charge was surprisingly independent for one raised with indulgence. "Then, Primmy, I shall ring for the maid."

Ugh. Primmy—*again*.

"There *are* two guests I admit curiosity over..." Lady Harriet said, plucking what was most definitely a goose feather off the front of her dirty smock and delaying her retreat upstairs.

What followed was more discussion, more bargaining, and more precious time keeping her charge occupied—and not outside...

After coming to an agreement—of sorts—about the hated nickname, they conversed briefly about the two military men arrived just that afternoon—friends of Lord Redford, Lady Harriet's soon-to-be brother-in-law. While Aphrodite pretended great ignorance of either gentleman, busying herself with tidying her hair after looping the chin ribbon of her bonnet over her elbow.

Then they talked again about Harri's ill-timed fascination with Christmas dinner which finally gave Aphrodite insight into today's aberrant behavior.

Once sufficient time elapsed that the grime began to dry and another feather to fly on the once pristine blue gown, and Aphrodite feared more flaking off—leaving a trail straight to her charge's chamber, which would not do, not at all, not considering what a catastrophe Lady Ballenger would consider the dirty and torn gown—she directed Harri up to her bedchamber. "Remain in your room until I join you—"

"When will that be?" A mulish bottom lip thrust out.

No matter what expression she wore, Lady Harriet managed, to everyone's consternation, to remain *adorable*. One reason why disciplining her proved such a challenge.

In a few short years, Aphrodite feared adorable would turn to *beautiful*, and what manner of trouble might her unrestrained charge get into then? Even when she pouted, the smile didn't leave her face for more than a moment. Today was unusual. So much whining; not at all typical for her charge.

"You need not wait long. I will freshen myself as well. Then locate Lady Ballenger to explain the change from blue to scarlet, and be along."

Grumbling beneath her breath, Harri sauntered slowly down the hallway in a weaving path and trudged up the servants' stairs as though an execution waited instead of a new dress.

Aphrodite turned the opposite direction, knowing Lady Ballenger would be in the main part of the extensive home, seeing to her guests and ordering servants about.

Yet she walked even slower than Harri's unhurried escape, knowing the longer they dawdled, the less time the girl would have to dirty her only other appropriate dress.

Are you certain it isn't because you fear seeing your flirt *again?*

MOMENTS PRIOR...

THE FIERCE *THWAP-THWAP* landing right behind him caused Warrick to flinch. Nearly caused the sort of chamber pot mishap no one ever, *ever* wants to experience.

He bit back an oath, watching things slosh for several seconds before balancing back to an even level, then ever so carefully he returned the pot to the covered shelf where he'd found it. A servant would no doubt empty it later.

Earlier, when he'd asked a footman about the most remote water closet to be found, the servant had informed Warrick that his chamber had been readied on this, the main floor—unlike the others that were all one or two levels above. After being shown the way, his chair rolling and creaking at an abysmal pace, the man had opened the door and gestured him inside, closing it only once Warrick assured the helpful footman he didn't need further assistance.

He'd been situated in an airy sitting room converted for his use, the original furniture scooted to the far side and nestled tight along one wall. A bed had been brought in, certainly not as large as what he would have found upstairs but neither as small as what the servants made do with. Several tables had been placed about with strategic care (a couple of shelves added per the scent of fresh paint) and his belongings brought in and kept within arm's reach, instead of remaining in his bags or a trunk on the floor.

Taking up a goodly portion of the corner nearest the door was a screen for privacy. Behind it, paraphernalia for tending to one's bodily functions. The open spaces surrounding and in between everything generous enough to accommodate his Merlin's chair.

The Ballengers' thoughtfulness should have been touching.

Really, attempting to keep him independent and ambulatory, and not reliant upon servants to haul him up and down the stairs several times a day was truly thoughtful. He should appreciate the considerateness. The effort they had expended.

Instead, it was one more thing to be humiliated over—causing the servants more work. Both before *and* after his visit—setting things back to rights.

And since when do you give servants consideration?

When I now burden them constantly with every little request:

Giles, can you dip into my trunk and retrieve my dress shoes? They are stashed somewhere near the bottom, I believe. Warrick certainly couldn't do it; not without unbalancing himself and toppling his chair, careening both of them onto the floor in an ungainly heap. (He knew. For he had done that more than once.)

Giles, I'm not able to reach that volume of (he could insert any number of enjoyable books one might wish to peruse); *get it down for me, would you?*

Giles, my apologies. I had a...erm...bloody-prigging-self-damning mishap in bed overnight. Please see that one of the maids tends to it posthaste.

By now, just the thought of everything that had gone on in the early days was enough to make his arms and neck tense. Make him glad he no longer held the slosh.

As to Giles? Warrick's new valet had been hired by Mother, as he'd not had need of one since purchasing his commission. Soldiers and officers learned to be independent and self-sustaining; yet another reason depending upon others proved frustrating.

And with Mama choosing Giles, the servant wasn't someone Warrick felt at liberty to lower his guard with, assuming the man had strict orders to report every little effort—or lack thereof—which would have kept Warrick on his toes, had his muscles the wherewithal to get him there.

Up till now, he'd ignored most of the quiet murmurs coming from the hallway that had started up scant moments ago, too busy concentrating on not making a hash—a horrifically humiliating mess—of things. But now?

Now?

"Primmy! I am so frustrated I could scream! We were not even outside an hour."

"Lady Harriet. Compose yourself this instant."

"But, Prim*my*! I barely had time to look—"

Upon hearing the strident complaints—and gentle yet stern admonitions that followed—a curious lurch in his chest telling him who might be on the other side—he rolled closer to the door...

Lancelot? Sir Galahad?

Primmy?

Curious and curiouser...

"...Lady Harriet—"

"Please, Primmy. I *much* prefer 'Harri'. I keep telling you *Lady Harriet* just makes me feel as stuffed up as Miss Fairfax's nose."

He muffled a snort at that.

"So, you would rather be called Harri?"

"Did I not just say that?"

"And I would prefer *not* to be called Primmy. *At all.*"

Another slight whine reached his ears.

"Shall we make an agreement?" His governess proposed this. For by now, he had deduced exactly who argued on the other side of his room. *Yours? Tut-tut, man.* "I shall use *Harri* when we are in private and I become Miss Primrose, for you will refrain from referring to me as Primmy in front of anyone else."

"But I can still do it when we are alone?"

A very adult groan that time. "May."

"May what?"

"May. *May* I still do it when we are alone?"

"Of course you can." The entertaining Harri kicked his wall again. "Is that not what we just said?"

Was that a sigh he heard? Then a laugh. "Harri, you claim you need to learn Latin, correct?"

"If the *boys* are going to know it, I must know it too." Smart little chit.

And the governess knew Latin sufficiently to *teach* it?

Unusual. Rather impressive too.

Miss Primrose, now that he had a name for her. Whom he knew wasn't quite as prim as those around her might suppose…

"We will not continue your Latin lessons until you work to be more accurate on your English grammar."

A few seconds of silence, then, "I forgot. Might not have been attending when you imparted that. Repeat it, please?"

"Of course. It is not *can* I do this or that. It is *may* I do this or that."

"Of course you can. I mean *may*. You are the governess, after all. I am just a child."

"The most contrary child imaginable."

"Mayhap so, but I still do not want to change into that blasted red dress—"

"Harri! Language."

"What if I used Latin instead? Is there a good Latin swear word you know?"

"As if I would teach you that!"

"Perhaps I will ask one of the guests."

"Whoa-ho! You do that, young lady, and I fear you would bury your poor mother in mortification."

"I do not care." The girl had turned mutinous.

"That is a harsh thing to say. What has happened? You are not usually this..."

Obstinate?

Entertaining?

Both applied to Lady Harriet; thank heavens *his* sisters didn't behave quite so outrageously.

How would you know? You have not spent time with either of them.

"'Tis Sir Galahad. It is Mother's fault he's gone."

"Oh, Harri." Was she comforting the girl? Hugging her? Her voice had turned soft with understanding, and for some reason, it made his heart yearn. "You truly befriended the goose after all? Did I not tell you—"

"I know. I *know*." A loud sniff. "Beatrice is for petting; the geese are for eating."

He gave a silent grunt. Bah. His heart wasn't yearning, not for a hug or anything else.

And if it were? Well, he quite needed to meet this *pettable* Beatrice. His handle might be broke, but his hands worked just fine...

"...If I cannot do it myself, Primmy, I will ring for a maid. Although, there *are* two guests I admit curiosity over," the boisterous Harri said, stalling, he suspected, at having to change into the detested red dress.

"And who might that be?"

"Lord Redford's friends."

He stiffened. Swallowed hard. Debated scrambling, rolling the wheels backward and escaping the rest... For that had every bit of ease that had seeped into his muscles the last few minutes drying up like a parched desert.

"Lords Frostwood and Warrick? What sort of curiosity?" The even tone of the yearned-for Miss Primrose stalled any retreat.

He needed to know what this Latin-speaking governess might say about him. Especially after he'd chased her off.

You want your already debilitatingly low self-worth trounced further?

"Over every*thing*! What is war like? How does one fight on a horse? They are part of the dragoons, you know. How do you pittle when you are in the middle of battle? What if one's horse needs to...scumber one out?"

He slapped a hand over his mouth so fast the *pop* of skin on skin reached his ears. His chest started shaking. Lips trembled beneath the firm clasp of his fingers as he fought a ferocious battle of his own not to howl with laughter.

The governess was silent. Fighting laughter as well? Or restraining herself from giving the lewd little lady a reprimand and that threatened rap across the knuckles?

"Harri. Wherever did you hear such a thing?" she asked with remarkable restraint.

"Near the kennels, where the hunt servants tend Papa's hounds."

"Please, *please* promise me never will you say such in front of your mother. She would likely dismiss me at once."

"She would not!" Another—milder—kick to his wall.

"I would not stand for it. For you are exceedingly better than the last two miseries they hired to teach me."

A muffled snicker, then, "Thank you for that. But you and I both know I serve at the whim of your parents, not your own. Now, as to Lords Warrick and Frostwood... I fear you forget yourself, dear. Children are not to initiate any manner of conversation with adults not relatives. You know—"

"But they are practically family! To hear Papa speak of Lord Redford's father and the friendship they shared at school? To hear Lord Redford's own mother speak of him as she visited with Anne the last months? Speak of both her son *and* Lord Warrick. I am curious over each of them. But since Lord Redford is marrying Merry Anne, why, I will have forever to ask him questions. But Lord Warrick? He will not be here beyond the holiday."

Another groan reached his fascinated ears. "It is a shameful fact that you cannot study law, for I vow, you could sway anyone to your viewpoint. All right, since your mother agreed you could dine with the adults, *if* you have questions that absolutely cannot wait and you have the perfect and convenient opportunity to speak with either gentleman, mayhap you simply *ask* them? But, mind, *only* if you can moderate both your curiosity and your tongue. No inappropriate sallies about personal matters, equine or human! A young lady does not speak of such things in company. Or out of it, really."

"Then how is one to ever learn?"

The governess had no answer to that.

"And what of Lord Warrick, himself?" He lowered his hand, his mirth evaporating, tension increasing.

"What of him, dear?"

"Do you know if he will walk again? What happened to confine him to the Merlin's chair?"

"I doubt whether he would want to share *that* with you. It is truly none of our business."

"But could I ask him?"

"Harriet. Dear. There are times I truly do not know how to answer you, and this is one of them. It would be better to ask him than to speculate or gossip, that I know with certainty, but neither do I believe it appropriate for you to voice such a thing."

"What if I were to engage him in conversation that had nothing to do with his legs?"

Much as her governess accomplished earlier?

"Then if you can avoid everything to do with...scumbering"—her voice near lowered to a whisper—"I think that would be fine. But *only* if you find him not surrounded by others and you can mind your volume as well as politely inquire if he would like to visit and converse. If he says *nay*, be off with naught but a smile. Can you do that, do you think?"

He didn't hear the chit's answer, so very surprised by the response, the one not heaped in sympathy nor mired in disgust, simply common sense.

If he was alone, *ask* if he would like a visit.

Why could others not do the same?

His thoughts turned to the cackling horde. The staring. The tittering. The nauseating blaze that had flared through him knowing he was under discussion—and likely not a complimentary one.

A difficult and uncomfortable position for one who had never before worried what others thought, certainly cared naught about what they might be gossiping about.

He idly rubbed one fist over his chest.

"I will freshen myself as well," said Miss Primrose. "Then find your mother and explain the change from blue to scarlet and be along shortly."

Silence ensued as the chatter ended and the whirl-blast blew upstairs.

But strangely, he found it not awkward for once. They both had been so very forthright about his condition. No titters nor tittle-tattles nor excessive pity that made him want to claw something. Mayhap his unfeeling legs?

The door was right in front of him. He could not help but turn the knob and use his fingers on one side of its frame to pull himself forward several inches, just enough where his feet and knees poked out and he could safely lean forward to glance both directions.

Satisfaction blossomed, for he was in time to see her slim figure as she departed, no longer swine-slicked but once again encased in what looked like—from the back—a mourning shroud...

Leaving him oddly comforted by the overheard exchange. More than a little curious about Miss Primrose herself. And somewhat sick at the thought.

For he, crippled and committed to that unknown, unfound rich wife, had no right to be staring at the slim rumple hidden by the heavy material.

No right to notice the fabric nipped in at her waist just above the curved flesh he could not help but admire.

And certainly no right to study the inviting hair tied at her nape, no longer hiding beneath a bonnet, and wonder what those sunset strands would look like down, around her shoulders, upon his sheets...

5

A BIT OF WINE AND WHINING

I<small>T SHOULD HAVE BEEN A SIN</small> to study someone so closely without their knowledge.

But 'twas surprisingly easy. Servants, after all, were invisible to nobility—at least the sort that didn't seek to attack or abuse for nefarious purposes.

So, during the candlelit dinner that very evening, with most all the guests arrived and gathered round the long, formal table, Aphrodite watched.

Observed from her quiet, unseen place standing on the other side of a decorative column, disguised by its shadow at the farthest end of the table, awaiting the moment when Lady Ballenger summoned her to escort Harri up to the nursery.

Aphrodite waited, she watched, and she ached. For the strong man who suffered at the hands of war.

For, by now, while waiting to speak with Lady Ballenger earlier and being privy to a horrid, if insightful, blather between three of the younger females, Aphrodite knew:

1. Lord Warrick had the well-earned reputation of Accomplished Flirt and Brash Entertainer.

So that (and perhaps more importantly),

2. He was known for his wildly inappropriate remarks and yet still welcomed by many.

And most important of all,

3. The three "ladies" were conniving, and wagering over, which one would enter his chamber before the sennight expired, to catch him unaware and snare themselves the title of *Countess*.

The fiendish, immature trio cared nothing about the marriage itself (or the man), only the *title*, the titters about arranging for their chosen *cicisbeo*, a multitude of peccadillos already planned! (Which jolted her far more than shock over the wagers.)

To be treated as such? Disregarded? As if your wishes mattered naught to others? It could not help but remind how she had been treated twice upon a time, as though *she* didn't matter. And to realize how his inability to walk had reduced him, in their eyes at least, to someone only to be used brought back uncomfortable memories. But this time, for an entirely different reason.

For though Lords Frostwood and Warrick, and Lord Redford if he ever deigned to appear, possessed what most everyone dreamed of—a birthright, no doubt beautiful and immense homes, and ample funds to care for themselves and their loved ones without worry—they were also burdened by tragedies others never considered: the memories of battle and the ever-present wounds of war, whatever form they might take.

You really ought not be thinking of them.

She wasn't, not really.

She was thinking of *him*—only one of the three—

To what end? Why waste a moment's thought his direction? You cannot fix him!

But how she ached to try.

Were his injuries of a permanent nature? Or might he, in time, recover some use of his legs? Were they simply weakened from a severe wound? Or completely paralyzed? Might her uncle—

Aphrodite! Behave thyself!

She closed her eyes, attempted to think of *anything* other than the broken bit of masculinity mere feet away...

Heard the steady hum of a multitude of conversations. The metallic clink of tableware hitting porcelain as an especially aromatic course was served. Tried not to notice the hollow in the pit of her stomach.

That's what you get for not eating a bite since early that morn.

No, that's what came from gathering greenery with Harri and Lady Anne directly after breaking her fast so many hours ago. Greenery that Harri insisted they place on every available surface upon their return, the swags and wreathes they'd coiled prior to returning outside for more and being distracted by piggies and peers. The fresh branches wafted the outdoors throughout, tickling her nose with the bracing winter scent that eclipsed the candle smoke but not that of heavy perfume worn by some.

She tucked her hands behind her at the small of her back, fingers straight, palms pressed into the wall and tried not to sniff the food. How she wished her curiosity could be tucked away as easily.

How long until her boisterous, twelve-year-old responsibility disturbed the peace sufficiently for the awaited summons?

Her ears searched for Lady Ballenger's voice only to be greeted with the tune being played in the ballroom by the string quartet hired for the week, as they rehearsed, the sounds muted but airy.

Deep laughter delivered her eyes and attention to where they ought not to dwell: Lord Warrick.

The scandalously tempting man, with his black-as-midnight hair and inviting smile that showed both teeth and dimples, had just spouted some quip that made those near him lose composure. One poor fellow started hacking a cough.

Oh, to have been a guest seated nearby. To hear what tickled them so...

She'd not known the seating arrangements planned for this eve.

Had not known when she'd silently scuttled to her (mostly) hidden position before dinner was announced that she would be left—drat—in full view of the three or so people seated at this, the far end of the table. Had certainly not known she would be stationed mere feet away from Lord Ballenger, who had proved a surprisingly kind and lenient employer, and next to him, at the far corner of the narrow end where his Merlin's chair could position him closer to the table, Lord Warrick.

How could he not consume her thoughts?

Especially after having glimpsed the anguish on his features more than once this day, when he failed to fix his expression. To seemingly hold everything within your grasp, only to have it stolen away must be a trial indeed.

So observe she did, beyond befuddled when a mere second later he lifted his glass, in the guise of drinking what never met his lips, and made it a point to snare her gaze with his.

Expression inscrutable, intensity unacceptable.

She blushed—for absolutely no reason at all. Her cheeks flamed to life and she demurred, lowered her chin to study her toes, grateful she at least wore decent slippers tonight. The newer, stiffer ones and not her favored pair (the ones with a hole near the big toe worn right through).

Despite the blaze of self-consciousness blistering her skin, some imp made her abandon all that was proper and she gathered courage to meet his heated stare once again.

Have you more to say to me? she silently challenged, feeling one eyebrow arch quite without intent. *Mayhap you have need of a...chamber pot?*

'TWAS CONSIDERATE OF LORD BALLENGER to direct him toward the head of the table, citing a more informal arrangement than usual and granting the extra room needed to maneuver about in his chair. Considerate, but not what he would have chosen if given a say—easily visible to anyone who chanced to look down the table's lengthy expanse. Coupled with Frost being a good shout's distance away at the opposite end, seated near Lady Ballenger and her daughters, Warrick chose to ignore most of the guests and braced himself to deal only with the individuals on either side.

Though he did spare more than one, hopefully comforting, glance at Lady Redford, seated near the middle, his expression indicating he was aware of his promise to travel forth if needed to track down her tardy son.

So he sampled his beverage—no getting tippled now,

not if the dreaded jaunt to his estate was in the offing—and attempted to appreciate the food. All while avoiding any hint of acknowledging any of the scornful gigglers.

The meal proved an utter trial.

So he made every attempt to appreciate his place between Lord Ballenger and the sneezing Miss Fairfax (he hadn't cared sufficiently to determine which one, only ascertained that the young female seated closest to him wasn't one of the giggling gaggle from earlier—a definite point in her favor).

Attempted to appreciate the easy, intermittent, conversation flowing between him and his host, whose attention—and remarks—were more often than not focused on his daughters, and wife, at the far end of the laden table.

Though courtesy dictated Warrick engage the pleasant-enough lady seated on one side in conversation every bit as much as he spoke to his host on the other, 'twas easier to let her and Sam Gregory banter, offer the stray—if pithy—comment and let his attention wander...

Until he narrowed in on one of the large room's equally large paintings. Then he startled. Snorted into his glass and covered it with a muffled cough. What, ho!

A surprised chuckle emerged as he quickly inventoried the other paintings. Checking...

Confirming. Shoulders shaking with silent laughter, until he glanced to the next painting on his right, over the slender shoulder of Miss Fairfax (bent toward her lap as she sneezed into a handkerchief), and spied the slight figure stashed just beyond a decorative column.

Likely out of view of 98% of the people present. But 100% visible to him.

Well now. He straightened his spine, more invigorated than he'd been since dinner began.

Miss Primrose, of the red nose, thanks to the instant

pink coloring her cheeks when she became aware that *he* was aware.

She wasn't quite in shadows, but nearly so. Though flagrant was more his style, he studied her without seeming to, unwilling to alert anyone else to his interest—

Nay. His curiosity.

No bonnet indoors, thank etiquette, so despite the evening light, more was revealed. And study her he did, as surreptitiously, and as intently, as possible.

A slim oval of a face, her complexion neither porcelain nor bronzed. So she spent time outdoors, yet used a parasol when she had to?

A pert, not quite narrow nose; plump, not quite prim lips (those he already recalled—and more than he ought); mounds of hair, severely scraped back—despite the few wavy strands that escaped and wafted near her face and shoulders.

Tut, tut. Something that thick, that potentially lush should not be so confined. He needed to see it down, unkept. Needed to allow his fingers to sink into the strands, lift them to his nose and inhale.

The fine hinterlands he'd already admired; didn't need to see them now to remember the allure (good thing, too, as they were flattened against the wall). He'd been overly distracted by the rest of her earlier to note the average bosom above the slim waist—he was a man, after all, if not one in prime twig.

But it was two other things that fueled his growing fascination:

She wore yet another absurd dress of heavy brown bombazine, and—even more compelling—the serene study of her eyes on him had yet to waver.

The unmistakable, unmissable flare of awareness between them could no longer be denied.

Oh? You fool yourself if you believe you have denied it thus far.

He couldn't help it. Even more than the glazed pigeon on his plate (which was quite divine), *she* was the most delectable thing in the room.

Since when do you dally with servants?

Never. Well, never, not once—not since he was a brazen lad, soon to be birched and taught better by his stepfather.

A lift buoyed his spirits.

How refreshing. To think of something from his past—something rather painful, mind—with an elevation of his spirits and not a stomping of them.

Ever since that decidedly uncomfortable lesson, never had he been curious about the help. Never studied them more than he ought. Never really even noticed them.

Until today. Three times now.

Seemed as though simply the change in elevation—his attention lowered between twenty and thirty inches, depending upon what he was seated upon—made him more observant than ever.

Blast him, made him more taken over this one than he could remember feeling about a female since long before Albuera stole that handful of feet from his eyesight.

Even with that reminder, he couldn't help the smile that curved his lips.

Couldn't help but delight when hers curved in return.

As though she, too, experienced the growing sense of camaraderie and attraction, she licked her lips, mashed them together and looked away to the side—all that was demure and proper.

He absently accepted another drink after all, keeping his attention on her. And was rewarded, when only scant seconds later she glanced back at him.

So. 'Twas as he'd suspected.

Though she might try to pretend otherwise, Harri's little Latin-speaking governess had some spunk to her. Was able to look him in the eye without appearing either overly bold or excessively embarrassed? And after how he'd run her off at his vulgar (not quite) best? He instantly liked that about her.

What he didn't like was her dress. Or the fact that she had to stand up against the wall, in hiding. Watching everyone else as they ate.

LOOK AWAY. LOOK AWAY, *you brazen hussy.*

But the braised pigeon looked so divine.

'Tis not the pigeon you stare at, you peagoose.

Was she not allowed the teeniest, tiniest flirt? To enjoy the disordered bubbling in her stomach at the realization a man had actually noticed her?

Noticed?! every hair on her head seemed to scream in outrage. *Noticed? Why, he's rendering your dress gone and you naked with naught but a look.*

'Twas about time.

What? Now her nails squawked at her. *Have you not spent the last years seeking to* avoid *lecherous looks?*

But nothing about Lord Warrick *felt* lecherous. Nor did his obvious interest—and, aye, *accomplished* flirting.

For she knew it could never be anything more.

And so it went, course after course, her heels, back and shoulders leaning against the wall, the rest of her in shadow, her ears attuned not to the hum of conversation, but to Lady Ballenger and the snap of her fingers. Aphrodite's focus unerringly trading between the inviting pull—and naughty thrill—of meeting Lord Warrick's heated glances and that of studying the ceiling, her slippered toes, and on more than one slightly embarrassing occasion, the skin at the bottom of two nails that desperately needed trimmed.

How is it he makes me burn with naught but a glance?

How is it you have reached the appalling age of four and twenty without—voluntarily—knowing a man's touch?

Forcing her hands behind her once again, her shoulders shuffled upward and back in a stretch constrained by her stiff dress.

At the other end of the table, Harriet seemed to be causing both laughter and angst, her repeated (and wholly inappropriate) whines about Sir Galahad the goose and his fate growing in volume and frequency.

Aphrodite slid forward to peer around the column. Lady Ballenger was speaking with the guest next to her and not looking at her daughter, nor for Aphrodite, so she stepped back. Felt warmth brim over her body and face yet again when she found Lord Warrick, that flirty fiend, lifting his glass to her and giving her a slight nod.

Then he toasted the painting to her left, tilted his head that direction. Inviting her to look?

Peculiar.

Her action hidden by the column, she turned her head, saw the heavy gilded frame surrounding one of Lord Ballenger's prized hunting paintings. The particular one inherited from an ancestor and huge—eight feet wide and six feet tall, at least. Her employer had hired an artist to come in and paint over the dogs this past summer, making them look like *his* hunters instead.

She couldn't see the painting now, only the frame, but she knew by memory nearly everything visible in the public rooms, had enjoyed walking the halls, exploring each wall table and shelf, studying the art and knickknackery, enjoying the freedom to do so at leisure and not having to cast glances over her shoulder or fear being trapped anywhere she might happen to trod.

Seeing nothing amiss, she turned back to Lord Warrick and lifted one shoulder. *What? I see naught beyond the ordinary.*

He pinched his lips and shook his head at her, as though vastly disappointed. Then he casually aimed one finger behind his shoulder—directing her to inspect the painting on the wall opposite? The frame was graced with heavy swags of greenery, much like all the others, Harriet draping what she could from the top corners of every frame thick enough to hold it, winding greenery around the balustrade, coiling the wreaths around busts of philosophers she fortunately hadn't asked Aphrodite to name.

Another course was brought out, servants exchanging empty plates for full ones. Her middle squeezed at the new scents, but her attention stayed on the painting, this one of Lord Ballenger's great-grandfather and his family: wife, seven children, three dogs and a cat, all sitting or standing clustered around a settee, their likenesses captured forever enduring daubs of color.

But then she saw it.

Harriet's handiwork.

Each dog "wore" a red ribbon bow—pinned? glued?—upon its neck. The cat's was gold.

Aphrodite bit her lips against a giggle. *Oh, Harri, you will be reprimanded for this. Severely, I fear.*

How many paintings had she...?

Aphrodite jerked her head back to the left, toward the wall parallel to her position, took one tiny step forward to see beyond the frame surrounding the hunting depiction. A muffled squeak escaped as she looked closer through the shadows on this side of the room, most of the candelabra and wall lamps concentrated near the guests.

Gracious punishments indeed.

Little red and gold ribbons stuck out from the canvas, their positions matching what she remembered of the exuberant canines racing across the hunting fields. She whipped back, shushing laughter by biting on one knuckle.

Couldn't stop herself from seeking out *his* gaze. While conversation—and another of Harriet's whines (followed by a wail of her mother's)—swirled around him, he somehow managed to study Aphrodite while appearing to stare through his glass.

This lord, his eyesight positioned differently than most, had seen what others had not? Why did that fill her with admiration? Impress her every bit as much as the sacrifices he and his friends had made as part of the dragoons?

More laughter from the other side of the room tried to interrupt their silent communication. Even Lord Ballenger, from practically right in front of her, joined in, offering something that had the entire table chiming in with good spirits. But another screech from Lady Ballenger told Aphrodite she didn't have much time.

These brief, all-too-surprising moments with a member of the titled class would be over all too soon. Never to be repeated.

She widened her eyes and twirled her finger, indicating the entire room. *All of them?*

He gave a single, decisive nod. *Aye, every single one.*

Punishments aplenty, then.

By now, her palm covered her mouth and chin as she sought to regain composure that had fled. *Oh, Harri.*

Harri, who must know beyond doubt that with this

action, she had exceeded the bounds of behavior that even her understanding parents would tolerate.

Firming her stance against the wall, she pulled her hand from her mouth and gave him a slight nod, acknowledging the shared secret.

He gave her another heated glimmer, pleasure emanating from him now that she'd recognized what he'd already seen.

And there went her belly, circling and swooping.

Totally inappropriate!

Nay, totally thrilling.

Her toes curled tightly toward the floor. Her nails practically scratching the wall at her sides as she strove to remain outwardly calm.

He took a bite of the latest dish and chewed slowly. E-x-c-r-u-c-i-a-t-i-n-g-l-y s-l-o-w-l-y. To fend off any attempt of his seat mates to engage in conversation?

After he swallowed, the tip of his tongue slid over a small part of his upper lip.

But 'twas more than sufficient.

For his actions sent hers to tingling. Her heart to thrumming.

Oh my. My oh my. This was no way for an employed, sedate female to behave: nearly giddy and out of breath from the illicit attention. The shared knowledge of painting defacement.

How she wished they could talk. Truly talk. No table between them, no other guests vying for his attention. No responsibilities claiming half of hers. No—

What do you anticipate would come of it? Is not courting privacy with him simply courting the sort of danger you take pains to avoid?

If only they could meet in the garden—

'Tis near freezing outside now.

They could sit up on the bench, exchange—
A bench? What of his invalid's chair. His legs do not work.
What about the rest of him?
Mayhap she need not fear—*do you not mean thrill to?*—the notion of him ascending the staircases up to her room and barging in.

Of course she didn't. Lord Ballenger's guests wouldn't do such a thing.

Lord Warrick certainly couldn't do such a thing.

Drat.

And there it was—the imminent summons heralded by Lady Ballenger's near skreak of outrage toward her youngest.

My apologies, my lord, she told no one but herself, *I must be away.*

With nothing more than a regretful inhale, a swift blink—that did nothing to erase his compelling attention or features—and a reluctant step, Aphrodite pushed off the wall and clasped her hands together at her waist. On silent slippers, she made her way around the perimeter, ready to remove her charge up to the nursery before Harriet's scandalous holiday adornments were discovered.

How much damage had the child caused? Could the paintings be repaired? Or would some damage remain visible, regardless?

Lady Anne rose and accompanied Harriet from the room, mere moments ahead of Aphrodite.

Doubtful even the engagement of Lord and Lady Ballenger's eldest would save their youngest from their ire. That and dire consequences.

With every second that elapsed, every inch she traversed, longing deepened and sorrow strengthened. For she'd had no chance to bid *him* good evening.

Are you a fanciful loon? 'Tis not as though you owe the titled lord anything.

No, but she *wished...*

In vain, she knew.

Escaping out the dining hall, Aphrodite had to fist her fingers to keep from slapping her forehead.

WITH A CRAVING HE'D NOT KNOWN himself capable of mere hours ago, Warrick watched the little governess fade back into the walls. Her silent exit unnoticed by all—but him— left him reeling at how those few moments of shared mirth reached inside and clouted him in the gut.

How he wanted to call her back.

To shove the snuffling Fairfax chit out of the way and order a chair brought round for Miss Primrose, she who didn't constantly snivel her nose, so she could sit beside him and—

And what? 'Tis not as though you can do anything about it. The attraction. The desire.

Of course not. She was a servant. He shouldn't even be noticing her.

And you cannot do anything about it even if she wanted to.

A squawk from Lady Ballenger and loud round of chuckles drew his attention toward the end of the table closest to the exit as Lady Anne escorted her sister away.

Despite the unfamiliar ache gnawing at his gut, he managed his own chuckle. Doubtless misery coated Frost like his namesake, as he suffered the jubilant spirits of everyone around him—especially since his stalwart friend hated everything to do with the holidays. One of those "secrets" a good man let his fellow schoolmates and soldiers keep to themselves, knowing that if Frost were privy to the truth—that those closest to him saw right through his attempts at falsity—'twould wound his pride most heartily.

Let Frost blithely go on thinking Warrick and Ed didn't know that his own personal tragedies had hardened Frost against even the most minimal amounts of holiday merriment.

For Warrick now had his own holiday horrors to contemplate: lusting after the *illictus* governess.

6

PINS TO PAINTINGS...TO PUNISHMENTS?

VOICES FILTERING IN FROM THE GREAT HALL moments later heralded Ed's long-anticipated arrival.

Warrick's cheeks lifted, his heart buoyed on a relieved inhale that brought peachy heaven sailing toward his nose as he sought out Lady Redford's relieved gaze halfway down the table. Flushed with joy, she scrambled to standing, inadvertently colliding with a tray-carrying servant dispensing the blissfully awaited compote of peaches and sugared nuts.

Warrick tensed his thighs—or tried to—ready to jump to her aid when knocking into the tray askewed her balance. But all he did was lurch into the table, as his bottom half denied his top half's instincts.

Damn legs.

"Let us all remain seated," Frost said by way of a command, immediately doing what Warrick could not and coming to her aid after the embarrassed servant scuttled back. "Allow Lady Redford and her son a moment of privacy before bombarding him with greetings."

"Hear, hear!" Lord Ballenger echoed heartily, then turned to Warrick. "*Where* the devil has he been?" his host asked, voice hushed, brow pinched and face ruddy. "More than half suspected he meant to cry off."

Warrick knew Ballenger had been responsible for the arranged betrothal between his daughter and the son of his closest childhood friend, even if the original agreement had been not for Ed, but his older brother.

"I do not believe so. 'Tis just that..." A slight shrug of Warrick's shoulders, a grit of his teeth, his hands hovering beside the mechanisms that moved his chair before he jerked one arm toward the other, made a chopping motion and watched as understanding dawned.

"Ah. Forgive me, son." The bristling Lord Ballenger noticeably smoothed his ruffled feathers upon recollecting the most obvious loss his potential son-in-law had suffered. "Have been selfishly worried about my Anne, not giving considerate thought to the challenges that you both —all three of you," Lord Ballenger added as Frost approached, "must now become accustomed to."

"Thank God," Frost said, his frown not easing despite his words. "Now that Ed's accounted for, we need not search him out among the icicles and shadows."

Moments prior...

Still sensing *his* eyes on her, like a tangible touch buzzing over her skin, Aphrodite crossed into the Great Hall aside Lady Anne and a chattering Harri.

"If you wish..." Aphrodite indicated the stairs. "I shall see to Lady Harriet from here."

"Why do you not *both* come with me?" Harri proposed, gaze alight now that she was no longer under her mother's watchful presence. "We can shuffle off to my room and play hustle cap, for you are both ever so much more entertaining than the babies in the nursery."

Over the head of the child rising up and down on her toes, Lady Anne gave Aphrodite a conspiratial smile. "I will take Harri up and stay with her. Have you eaten? Take thirty minutes for yourself and rejoin us when you're ready."

"But *your* dinner," Aphrodite protested. "Has it not already been interrupted?"

"Not nearly enough," the other woman muttered, then louder, "I insist. Please, take some time for yourself."

The hollow in her belly relished the suggestion. "You are too kind."

"Too selfish, I confess," Lady Anne confided. "In truth, I shall savor the distraction."

Bobbing up and down like a bouncing ball, Harri gave an exasperated sigh. "Adults. Too boring by half."

"When we are not entertaining your whims, you mean?" Aphrodite surmised. "Mind your sister, now."

"When do I not?"

"Every other minute," said Lady Anne and the women parted on a shared laugh.

No sooner than her feet aimed for the servants' hall and kitchens below, a sturdy *clunk* of the door's knocker sounded.

The missing betrothed?

Just out of sight, Aphrodite paused. Ears perked.

For if Lady Anne's espoused *had* arrived, Aphrodite would no doubt be tending her charge after all.

Another double *thump-clunk* reverberated, even louder than the last.

Wilson, the Larchmonts' longtime butler, balding and brandishing a napkin, barreled up the servant stairs behind her. "Pardon... Ms.... Primrose."

The poor man nearly panted as he scurried by, trying to race, chew and swallow at once. "Pitiful timing, my lad," he grumbled. "Could...not have... knocked...ere or aft?"

My lad?

"I will get it!" Harri trilled, announcing to anyone and everyone within the house. A veritable whirlwind, she rushed ahead of both footman and butler to whip the heavy door open.

"Who are you?" she demanded.

"Lord Redford, at your service," a firm voice intoned. "Come for the Twelfth Night Ball, if I am not mistaken, though a few calendar days early by my count, but here I am, dates notwithstanding. Do you require my written invitation?"

"What happened to your arm?" Harriet demanded—manners notwithstanding either—and Aphrodite slapped her forehead. "Where's the rest of it?"

The rest of it? The man's arm?

Aphrodite gulped. Hunger pangs turning to horror pains. Had she taught the child nothing?

"Harriet!" Lady Anne gasped.

"Lord Redford." Wilson stepped into the breach. "'Tis beyond good to see you again." *Again.* So Wilson's "lad" was Lady Anne's intended? "Come in, my lord. May I have your coat and hat? Your gloves? Er, apologies. Glove?"

"Think nothing of it, Wilson." Lord Redford crossed over the threshold and began to remove his outer garments (seen because, by now, Aphrodite could not help but edge forward, only to glimpse, mind).

A notable presence, Lord Redford was only an inch or two shorter than Lord Frostwood's impressive height and every bit as broad through the chest and shoulders as Lord Warrick. The rugged lines of his face crinkled easily into a smile as he spoke. "'Tis war, after all. Each of us must adapt and accommodate for change."

It wasn't until first his coat and scarf and then his glove (singular) was removed with Wilson's assistance that the misshapen fingers were visible. He stretched them forth, opening and closing his hand several times as though to return warmth—or work out the cramped soreness, now free of the heavy travel trappings.

"Your hand," Harri persisted, hovering between the adults as Lady Anne stood by silently, face ashen. "Did you lose it fighting Napoleon?"

"Aye. Left it in Spain, I fear."

"Lord Redford!" The stout Lady Ballenger scurried in, the long feather protruding from her turban bobbing like a sail. "Welcome! Welcome! I see you have already met Anne. Your mother will be along—"

"Anne?" His gaze swung from Harriet to her mother to Lady Anne's pale countenance. Lord Redford's forehead pinched in a frown. "*Lady* Anne? Not Mary?"

Mary? Oh! *Merry.* What Harriet had been calling her sister all month: Soon-to-be-married Merry Anne. But why would he be surprised by her honorific of *lady*? And when would he have heard the other?

"*Where* at in Spain?" Harri cried on an excited screech —trying to rival her mother? "Did you see it afterward? Your hand? The rest of your arm? Terrifically gruesome! How much did you bleed? Did your claret splash out? Or only trickle?"

Aphrodite was going to be sick. Not at the words, though fairly gruesome in and of themselves, but that

Lady Harriet, whom Aphrodite had been drumming manners and decorum into from the moment her employment commenced, should be asking—

Asking? Nay, *peltering* the gentleman with such discourteous things.

"Did you scream when it happened?" Harriet's enthusiastic barrage showed no signs of wavering.

"Terrifically gruesome," Lord Redford responded. Admirable, his patience with the girl. "As to the, er... *spatter*, I am not certain that is a subject fit for genteel company."

Bile crawled into her throat. Surely she would be shown the door soon. Would her efforts at least garner a reference?

"Oh, but you can tell me!" the girl encouraged, heedless of the destruction her every word wrought. "I am ever so curious about—"

"Harriet Jane!" Lady Ballenger's screak shook the chandelier and sent the mistletoe to quivering.

"*Lovely* to meet you, Lord Redford!" Harriet called out, fighting against her sister's valiant tugging. "You can tell me more later!"

Much closer to Aphrodite than the front door, Lady Anne wrenched the child around and gave her a sharp shake. "*Shhhht*. Not another word—do you hear me? Not until we reach your room, you frustrating hoity-toity."

As the pair ascended the stairs with all the haste Lady Anne could muster from the reluctant Harri, Aphrodite faded back toward the servants' quarters. Toward the meal and granted respite, with three thoughts at the forefront:

1. The minutes, which had now dwindled from thirty to twenty-three.
2. The meal, which in no conceivable way could her roiling stomach begin to partake of.

3. Her position, which if she wasn't bidding adieu to by morning, she would count herself among the most fortunate of governesses ever to walk the globe.

She refused to think on *secrets*.

The ones she suspected might exist between Lady Anne and Lord Redford.

The ones she herself shared with Lord Warrick.

Nay. Not contemplating either.

A deep sigh puffed from her lips as her feet dashed down the stairs. Forget servings of holiday fare. She needed to find a wall. A private one.

To bang her head against.

"Oh, Harri."

"Do not look at me like that." Standing there, in the lamplight some time later and *not* looking as guilty as she ought, Aphrodite's charge crossed her legs.

Then uncrossed them. Stuck out her bottom lip and swung one leg back in front of the other, the toes of her foot practically perpendicular to the floor in the most convoluted of positions as the girl rocked back on her heels, tugging at the fabric beneath one arm. "I *know* you are mad at me. Can it not wait until tomorrow? Un*merry* Anne has already railed at me. To a *copious* degree."

Back in the bedchamber of the ever-entertaining young lady, Aphrodite sought to subdue, not crush, the child's vaunted spirit. But after Lady Anne took the youngster to task over her tongue's ill-advised laxative greeting toward Lord Redford, it now fell to Aphrodite to address the other, egregious, error of the day.

Her dratted stomach persisted in tingling.

Worry over being cast out in the coming days? Penance

for the few sparse bites she had managed to consume, after all (enough to quell any audible rumblings)? Certainly, the disturbingly delightful sensation could in no way be related to the illicit, if wordless, interlude shared with Lord Warrick.

One palm pressed to her traitorous middle, Aphrodite approached the bench at the foot of the bed. "Can you be still long enough to sit with me a moment?

"Please?" she encouraged when the child made no move to join her.

Balancing up on her toes twice before straightening her legs and moving toward the now-seated Aphrodite, Harri joined her with a light *huff*. "What?" She pulled up the skirt of her dress and started picking at nothing, avoiding Aphrodite's eyes. "I did not mean any harm, only thought the ribbons *belonged* on the dogs."

And the cats.

And some children.

A couple of birds.

And even upon the nose of the long-deceased fourth Earl of Ballenger, Aphrodite had seen to her dismay, upon her return upstairs when she chanced to inspect every painting in the emptied-of-guests dining room.

"It made me laugh," Harri continued. "It was—*is*—festive and funny and I see no reason why—"

"Halt." Abandoning her own distractions, Aphrodite placed her hands over the twitchy fingers of her charge and gave a light shake, until Harriet's gaze met her own. "Festive? Mayhap. Amusing? That might depend upon who you ask. But, Harriet, inconsiderate in the extreme. Completely out of bounds. Rude and thoughtless toward your parents, especially your father—whose family many of these paintings have been in for generations. You may have destroyed several priceless—"

"Destroyed?" Harri cried, bounding to her feet. "I did no such thing!"

"Oh?" Aphrodite shifted to keep track of the girl as she stomped across the floor. Thank heavens the musicians had started playing lively and loudly. "Tell me—how did you affix the bows and ribbons?"

Harriet just looked at her, mouth half open—silent for once. Then she slammed it shut and shrugged, stomped off the opposite direction.

"No more of that, now." Surging to standing the next time Harri drew near, Aphrodite snared the girl's shoulders. "Halt. Answer me."

"I couldn't get pins to go through them without falling out." Aphrodite cringed. "I tried sewing them on, but it was too hard with the paintings up against the wall," Harriet all but whined—as though the canvases were at fault. "So I used paste."

Smothering a groan, Aphrodite tugged Harri to her, her chin coming to rest on the top of the child's head.

"What?" the youth murmured, not fighting the embrace. "Why are you not still yelling at me? Bemoaning my 'vexing and troublesome nature'?"

Something Lady Ballenger had exclaimed more than once.

"Is that what you want? To be railed at? Do you think enduring a barrage of critical words is sufficient punishment?"

Harri eased free, looked up, her countenance—finally —burdened with guilt. "Perhaps?"

"Not even close. And some things cannot be resolved by yelling. Some things, you will learn in time I pray, hurt someone enough, cut deeply such that mere apologies of sorrow or regrets cannot ever make them right."

"You tr-truly think I *ruined* the paintings? For *ever*?" Her lower lip quivered.

"I really have no idea. But I do think, the moment your parents discover what you did—or someone brings it to their attention—you will be in more trouble than you ever have been thus far."

"*Gawp.*" The strangled sound emerged. "*Ever?*"

"Mayhap. I surmise that their reaction alone will be sufficient for you to understand the egregiousness of your—"

"I don't know what that means. That eee-gree... thingummy."

"*E-gre-gious.*" She let each syllable sit alone. "It means the severity of what you did. How very flagrant—intentional—your actions. How—"

"I know. I know!" Harriet gripped the top of her head with both hands as though she could hold in some of the sense. "I am in full understanding of how poorly you think I behaved. You need not berate me further."

"Very well. I know not what sort of punishment your parents will demand, but as for myself—"

"*You* are going to punish me too?"

"You give me no choice, Harri. My entire reason for being here is to see to your education. To see that you mature in such a way you shine a positive light on your family and toward your future. To ensure that one day, you may have your own family and behave in such a manner you bring about respect for yourself and those in your household, not ridicule."

The girl had no answer for that. Had even lowered her hands and was now occupying them by yanking on the sides of the dress.

But how? *What* might finally reach through the impenetrable, stubborn skull of her student?

A thousand-word essay on The Evils of Arrogance, to be composed in Latin.

The answer echoed in her ears as though she had spoken the words aloud seconds ago, instead of half a day and a world away. "Despite the merriments going on this week, I expect you to compose a three-hundred-word apology to—"

"*Three* hundred? Are you—"

"A *five*-hundred-word apology"—Aphrodite altered at the interruption, hoping to suppress any others—"directed to your father, explaining what you did and why, and expressing how you feel over the matter." And if regret and remorse were not included, there would be consequences indeed. "For your mother, you will compose a four-hundred-word apology telling her how you seek to make reparations for this act. Reparations—how you seek to make it better."

A single nod—despite a mutinous gleam.

"As to the rest—"

"There is *more*?"

"Much more. You will write three hundred words, intended for my eyes only, explaining your complete disregard for my position in this household and your understanding that through your actions"—and words—"I might be dismissed. Then—"

"You cannot be! Mama and Papa would never turn you off. I won't allow it!"

Pray, should things become dire, the Larchmonts would listen to their youngest's wishes, allowing Aphrodite to retain her position in their household. "Though your fierce defense is flattering, neither of us knows exactly how your parents will respond."

"Is there any more?" Harri's vibrant tone had dulled, the seriousness of her actions reaching through the beautiful wall of energetic happiness and thoughtless selfishness that truly needed tempered.

"Aye. Lines. The one thing we have yet to try. You shall write 'I will think upon how my actions and words affect others; I will refrain from selfish, destructive acts.'"

"All of that?" she questioned in mayhap the quietest voice Aphrodite had ever heard her use. "Is it not... absurdly long?"

Aphrodite allowed her sad smile to show just a hint of satisfaction. For Harriet, thank heavens and beribboned paintings, now seemed to understand the full import of what she had heedlessly done. "It is long. And between now and Twelfth Night"—which gave the girl a good ten days—"you will write it seven hundred times."

"*Gawp.*"

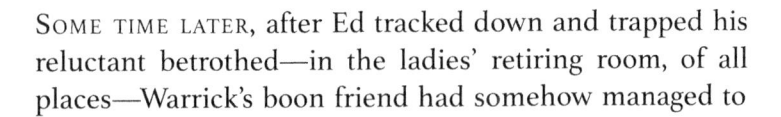

SOME TIME LATER, after Ed tracked down and trapped his reluctant betrothed—in the ladies' retiring room, of all places—Warrick's boon friend had somehow managed to turn the lady's misgivings about their engagement into elation over their coming nuptials.

Exuberant celebrations were in order (or so claimed the young Lady Harriet, returned from upstairs with only a slight mitigation to her natural enthusiasm), ushering everyone in sight into the bowels of the ballroom where the blame dancing had already commenced.

From the crush edging the equally crowded dance floor, Warrick concentrated on the conversations that swirled above him—or tried to. Tried to calculate how long since he'd last relieved his bladder and wondered how long the revelry might go on tonight.

Those hovering near at least shielded his sitting self

from any of the too-young, too-rude gagglers from this afternoon. *Since when do you care what anyone else thinks?*

Since I cannot get out of this infernal contraption!

He rubbed the back of his neck. Pinched the muscles on the sides and over his shoulders. Gah. How was one supposed to look up for hours without their neck screaming a protest?

How was one to suffer watching others flit, jump and skip their way across the dance floor when one had no hope of ever joining in?

7

PROPOSITIONING A PIGEON

Late, late that evening, much had been accomplished.

Not only had Harriet completed the 400 words dedicated to her mother (chosen to start with "because it is the second-shortest one you are making me do *and* the one I most dread"), but she and Aphrodite had nearly run holes in their slippers:

1. Jointly traipsing down to the ballroom ("only for another peek—pleeeeeeeeease").

2. Visiting the card room, Aphrodite waiting by the door as Harri flitted inside ("but for a moment to hug Papa goodnight—*before* he learns of my eee-*greeee*-gious behavior and forever banishes me to live in the stables").

3. And, most recently, subsequent to completing the first fifty-seven of her lines, Harri had crossed into her mother's bedchamber after scratching at the door and being bid to enter, while Aphrodite waited in the corridor ("not to leave the punishment note, not yet. Only to ask if Merry Anne truly did accept Lord

Redford's suit—which means I shall have a brother at long last! But also to make sure Mama isn't yet aware of the Ruinous Ribbon Atrocity and to tell her I forgive her for eating Sir Gal"—huge sigh—"a"—and another that wafted the fallen curls near her face—"*had*. Which I do not, in truth. But I shall pretend I have, so on the morrow, mayhap she will not be *quite* so angry with me." "Oh, Harri.").

Talk of big sighs heaving forth. From both of them by now.

Though they had interrupted scant minutes of writing (accompanied by an abundance of whining) no less than three separate times to satisfy, what was in fact, both their curiosities, for Aphrodite, naught had been becalmed.

Not appeased, pleased nor remotely satisfied. For a certain flirtatious gentleman remained least-in-sight.

Oh well. If wishes were horses, she still had no saddle to ride.

Though her duties typically ended far earlier each day, the plethora of guests, the boundlessly unique presence of musicians and the official announcement of Lord Redford and Lady Anne's engagement, added to the revelrous season, ensured that today and the ones that followed would be anything but typical.

After Harri's lady's maid, the one shared betwixt the sisters, assisted the girl out of her finery and into her nightclothes, Aphrodite spent a few restful moments, more friend than teacher, as she and Harri took turns reciting their favorite parts of the day.

Once the quiet murmurs, that went on far longer than she'd anticipated, wound down, Aphrodite let herself out of Harri's chamber. Walking down the corridor toward the lesser-used back stairs, she passed the maid (now awaiting Lady Anne's eventual summons); they shared a few quiet moments of conversation before both went about their business.

Heart and mind equally full, stomach just this side of hollow—perfect for sleep—and still twinging with the odd tingle of losing her job. (*Not* at the thought of black hair and gleaming eyes, of broad shoulders and—)

"And stop that right now," she chastised herself, trailing her fingers lightly against the wall as she descended the narrow staircase, "else I will set *you* to writing lines."

I shall not covet nor think of nor remember anything about L— About a certain man I must forget.

Must forget.

If she had any hope of a settled stomach.

AT SOME POINT during countless hours and drinks, Warrick stationed himself *outside* the ballroom. Not quite obscured in a small nook where, earlier, servants had traded full glasses for empty ones upon their trays before rushing off to either wash and refill or to deliver the full ones to those making revels inside.

Mulled wine or warmed wassail, even weak whiskey, he cared not as long as it was wet and within reaching distance.

As the hour grew later, closer to morn than midnight, some guests retired while others retreated to the card room, exchanging sore toes for partners at whist. Most? It seemed to him, and his inert feet and unresponsive legs, that most continued to delight in dancing about. *Damn them.*

Somewhere around his fourth or fifth glass since rolling off to ruminate alone, he'd aimed his wheels toward his room and emptied his bladder. No kick-*thump*s this time, so no dangerous sloshing—but no intriguing conversations to overhear either.

After debating bed for but a moment—hell, no. Not nearly tippled enough to sleep, not after that silent dalliance over dinner—he'd rolled back to his nook only to discover it void of servants, trays and booze. Blast it.

How was a man to get bosky enough to blot out all the horribly happy dancing within without a fermented or distilled beverage in hand? How was a not-quite sober—

"Ah." He heralded a passing servant. "I shall have another, if you please."

And…twenty minutes later, "Another!"

Watching everyone dance had just invited sorrows, encouraged regrets and welcomed the dismals to take hold. All things he did not need.

At least his head now floated pleasantly. Too bad his feet couldn't do the same.

Or mayhap his soul. Some days, the burden of disappointing his mother, of not being able to carry out the responsibilities of the title on his misbegotten shoulders and broken body weighed heavily.

Mama had been gnawing, cajoling and irritating him to visit some newfangled doctor she knew of. Irking him until he finally agreed. So he had that to look forward to upon his return to London. Another doctor? More poking, prodding and pronouncements of "Never will you walk again".

How blissful moments await! his mind trilled with more mocking melody than his talented fingers could ever pull from a pianoforte.

"Putrid. Pigeon. Dress. Miss. Prim. Rose…"

The unexpected rumble stopped Aphrodite's feet as though she'd stumbled into a boulder. A boulder intoning her name as Moses might before casting forth the Commandments.

"You need not fear me," the rumble continued, speaking from the shadows. "Anything shared between us will no doubt trickle from my memory before it can gain hold. But really, your attire galls. *Who would not dance until he could not stand, that had a sweet pigeon by the hand.*"

Pigeon? The last was recited like a verse, but none she claimed familiarity with.

Astonishment held her in thrall as both eyes and mind grappled.

Had her rebellious, not-to-be-subdued thoughts conjured temptation? For here sat Lord Warrick, in a seldom-used recess, more than half hidden in shadows where he would have gone unnoticed—had he wished.

Every bit as compelling as earlier—though instead of half a dozen feet distant, only two or three separated them now.

From exchanging clandestine secrets over dinner, with nearly a hundred others present, to engaging in a private, one-on-one rendezvous? Dare she be so bold?

Without quite meaning to, she edged toward him. "Lord Warrick," she acknowledged, relieved her voice conveyed not how her entire body had taken to thrumming with an odd heat. "Is there something I might assist you with? Are you lost? Need, mmm, help getting somewhere?"

His laconic posture straightened. "Perish the thought. I reside exactly where I wish to be. Nay," he said quickly, when she fidgeted, debating whether or not to heed the proper urge to leave, "stay. Visit with me a moment?"

Before she could accede or decline, he steepled his fingers beneath his chin and stared at her, his intent gaze appraising her from toes to nose. As her vision adapted to his dark nook, she saw him more clearly than was wise.

"Aye..." he mused, "beneath the pigeon wear, lurks the beauty of a peacock, I do believe. One might wish you were another sort of female." His shadowed gaze inspected her as though she were on display—and for sale—like a piece of ripe fruit. "I daresay, if you *were* that other sort, I would be remiss if I did not entice you to sit upon my lap."

Cursed compliments.

There was so much to contemplate in his racy words. A peacock? Her? A beauty? No one was supposed to see beneath the tightly pulled-back hair, bound breasts and heavy, unadorned attire. Even given their earlier, most unusual...*accord* outside and then again during those near magical moments in the dining room, this sort of verbal "greeting" only *proved* that beyond his appealing exterior and astute mind, Lord Warrick boasted horrendous manners and appalling behavior.

Just like those *other* titled lords.

But unlike those two others, attention from *this* one didn't send her scampering as it should have.

Sit upon his *lap*? Another sort of female?

How would she sleep a wink the next sennight, contemplating either?

Nor did she know what to address first. "You, Lord Warrick, appear deep in your cups."

"Decidedly so. And you, Miss Primrose—traipsing by stiffer than a hedgerow—appear deeply stuffed into your dress."

"I liked you better silent." A lie.

"Pity, for I find your spirited responses *worthy* of my lap indeed."

Worthy? His lap again!

"Do stop pinching your face, Peacock. 'Tis quite unbecoming. Unnecessary as well, for did I not admit I am likely tippled beyond recollection? Ergo, you may keep a poor cripple company without concern over your reputation. I assume you haven't ruined it yet?"

"Or had it ruined for me?" Her tart reply surprised them both.

"We shall be eminently grateful neither is the case."

"*We* shall?"

"Aye. I will join with you in valuing your reputation."

"You will join with me not at all!"

Smile-inducing laughter barked from him. "Yet with every sentence, you make me contemplate it more."

Knowing she should find everything he said disagreeable and offensive, but oddly...not, she sputtered, "I do believe your mouth would be better served glued shut." There now, that sounded appropriately disdainful. "As each time it opens, more inappropriate drivel babbles forth."

"Inappropriate, eh?" The wicked Warrick appeared flattered by the insult, giving a low chuckle that did *only* inappropriate things to her middle. "Are you unaccustomed to the silver tongue of an admirer?"

Laughter burbled from her then, self-directed more than not. *Admirer?* "What taradiddle! You had best halt—Ack!" Quickly did she step aside, to avoid the reach of his hand, when he maneuvered the chair closer with the opposite one. "Come now," she said severely, "do stop trifling with me."

"Miss Primrose, in whom my interest only grows, a *trifle* does not begin to approach how I think of you."

Hearing voices exiting the ballroom, as the music grew in volume until being abruptly cut off once the door thumped shut, she scuttled past, hiding herself in the deepest part of the shadows surrounding him, pressing into the corner and sucking in her stomach as though to make herself invisible to anyone who might chance by. Bending toward his ear, she gave a harsh whisper, "You should not be thinking of me at all."

He turned his head until his lips were but a kiss away. "*Merciful powers,*" he intoned in a very stately manner at odds with how many servings of spirits she suspected he'd downed. "*Restrain in me the cursed thoughts that my lusty nature might bring about. Stifle—*"

"Nay, you stifle and stubble it." She gave the side of his head a light shove, nearly groaning when her fingers fisted against the urge to delve through his thick hair. "Misquoting *Macbeth* in the dead of night? You should feel a double portion of shame for that, my lord."

As she straightened, he lightly clasped her nearest arm, trailing his fingers down until they brushed hers. "Would I not have to feel a single portion of shame first?" Her fingers fluttered against his. "Which I assuredly do not."

Lusty lords and midnight mayhem, her saner side asserted, *get thyself away from this one lest you be tempted further by what his naughty nature might bring about. Before your willing nature has you falling prey to his.*

Right. A proper governess—a moral woman—would be protesting. Ah, but an immoral one—

Aphrodite!

Reluctantly, very much so, she retrieved her tingly fingers, wrapped her other hand around them and squeezed. "Why waste your time dithering about with me when you should be"—her eyes glanced beyond their shadowed, private nook toward the ballroom and card room beyond where the season's revelries continued—"in *there*. Discoursing and such."

He stuck out his tongue and blew on it.

The sound, loud and childish, surprised a laugh from her.

"Aye," he huffed. "Because one on jolty, creak-laden wheels *belongs* in a ballroom full of dancing debutantes."

The scorn in his tone vanquished her lingering smile.

"In truth, my dear..." His voice growing hushed, intimate, he "jolted" and "creaked" closer again. This time she stayed in place, curious, interested, *attracted*, despite every reason why she shouldn't be. "I would much prefer to dither about with you. Come to my chamber later?"

He had not just proposed a tawdry tête-à-tête between them.

He had *not*.

This wounded gentleman, though she was coming to realize the term *gentleman* scarcely applied...this astute, amusing, possibly anguished man, one she admitted to vast curiosity over, one who had nearly lost his life fighting for England and freedom, had just doused any dreams she might have foolishly nurtured.

Because, upon uttering that last sentence, he had moved beyond ribald flirtation into downright insultation.

She bent at the waist and glared in his face. "With that, my lord, you have stepped over and beyond any bounds of propriety that you might have held on to by a mile. Were—"

"*Stepped?*" One haughty brow arched to a point, a move she was certain he had perfected in a mirror. "Nay, my shrouded peacock, for I step nowhere these past months. Which is why you must rouse yourself to step—preferably hasten—toward my room this eve." The scoundrel gestured toward his lap. "Whilst I apply myself to *rousing* other things just-for-*you*."

How could he so ruthlessly destroy any remaining hint of girlish infatuation? Of preposterous dreams? Ones she had been relying on to entertain and comfort (if not arouse) every time she closed her eyes for weeks to come?

She hated him, then. *Hated.*

"Were you not seated indefinitely," she said in a harsh whisper approaching a shriek, "a clout it is I would deliver, and hard to the side of your face for speaking thus to me, servant or no."

Her breath heaved when she finished, and it had naught to do with the scents of wine and wassail that invaded her nostrils from his proximity. She hauled back, upright, constricted breasts protesting each painful inhale, her feet rooted in place though they should have already fled.

Because she fully expected him to summon his host—her employer—and have her chastised if not outright dismissed for speaking to *him* so.

Instead of taking offense, of being abashed, ashamed or appalled at his own behavior, the rotten lout only smiled. A devil's smile. A tempting, sinful smile full of sadness and, yes, yearning—which made her *want* to hate him more.

A smile that reached past the bonds tight across her breasts, reached past the ugly brown fabric that made her perspire more often than not, reached beyond the practiced air of serenity she wore like a cloak every waking moment and *touched her soul*. Blast him.

"Ah, but were I not seated in this chair—indefinitely—I would stand on my own two feet and whisk you within my arms and *into the ballroom*. I would sweep you onto the floor, so we could move as one to the music of the season, scandal-mongers be damned.

"And if retribution was to be had? A clout from your flesh to mine?" He brought one hand up from his chair and clapped it resoundingly against the side of his face. "I would welcome it from you."

His voice grew ragged, as though confessing so much at once wore on him. "Would welcome the touch of your skin—even in anger—upon my own. Should you, perchance, see your way to changing your mind and altering your opinion of me, my door shall remain unlocked."

"Do not," the warning hissed from her unbidden. "Lest you desire a wife by scandal, one you have no say in, you will not leave your door unlocked at any point during your stay."

He acknowledged her words with a hardening of his expression, a nod of understanding. "My thanks."

He angled his upper body as though intent on leaving, only to jerk back toward her. "Lest you be concerned for your virtue, dear one..." His voice lowered, grew not bolder but instead now lacked the bravado she'd heard from him thus far.

He gave a mocking laugh and angled the chair away from her, guiding it slowly away from their alcove and toward the inner reaches of Redford Manor, requiring her to follow on slippered feet in order to hear the rest of his softly spoken words. "Do not. I vow, you would leave as chaste—or nearly so—as you arrived. For you see before you a seated man with a broken prick. I would bid you *au revoir*"—he cast a brief look at her over his shoulder, and she could see a hint of red above the bristle on his cheek where he had slapped his own face—"but after becoming so intimately acquainted with French blades, bullets and cannon blasts, I cannot. For I can no longer tolerate *anything* French at all. Goodbye."

Goodbye.

So very final.

It should be a relief.

Why was it, then, when *he* was the rotten, filthy-mouthed inappropriate one... When he was the one rolling off in a creaking Merlin's chair—rolling *away* from her...

Why was it *she* was the one who stood there, mired in place and trembling in the aftermath of their encounter?

8

PATIENTIA INFERNUM EST

"Good day! Might you wish for a spot of companionship this afternoon?" The bold urchin with the sable curls slipped in between the heavy ballroom doors.

Knowing the room to be empty (for who would be in here when everyone else took advantage of the warmer day out on the lawn playing games?), Warrick had shoved his way in long enough ago to make his way across the barren floor where he looked out the French window. The one that gave him a soul-crushing view of ladies and lads gadding about on happy, functioning feet with laughter lighting their faces.

He directed his chair away from the view and rolled several feet forward before stopping.

"I saw you creep in here," his visitor continued, making sure the doors latched behind her, "and decided I should follow suit and sneak in here as well."

"Oh? Do you seek to avoid detection?" A more probable thought occurred. "Or do you play a seeking game?"

"Nothing of the sort." She approached without hesitation. "But my hand, you see?" She raised her right hand, and flexed the fingers open and closed several times. "'Tis plumb worn out from doing *lines*. Hordes of them. I decided my fingers were due a respite and, since you are quite alone, concluded greetings are in order."

Charmed despite himself, he gave her a genuine smile.

"And who are you?" Warrick inquired, even though he knew full well, still in awe of the youthful excitement coupled with wonder in every word he'd heard her speak.

"Lady Harriet Jane Larchmont, youngest daughter of Lord and Lady Ballenger. You are friends with Lord Redford, the man who is marrying my sister."

"I am indeed. The closest of friends." At least he had been, before he'd started letting irrational jealousy consume him the last couple days. Jealousy that had grown worse with each new thing others participated in that he could not.

Knowing that Ed's loss rivaled that of his own, though in very different ways, he had no business avoiding Ed and the other men, but he continued to do so. Only Frost, it seemed, understood the level of strain Warrick endured, seeing so many clustered around while unable to join in, unable to be the center of fun and frolic as he had always been before.

As Lady Harriet approached, her gaze locked upon his knees, he tensed. "May I inquire," she began, and for once her voice didn't exude confidence, "about your injuries? Or is it best to keep mum?"

"It would be refreshing of you to ask directly, rather than speculate or rumor about. Would that others might do the same."

"Well then." She plopped to the floor at his feet, her dress of bright scarlet—the hated one?—straining to cover her crossed legs. "Did you get injured fighting Napoleon at the same time Lord Redford found his arm de-capped?"

"Decapitated?"

"Aye, just like that poor French lady—or was she a queen? A princess? I confess, I was not attending lessons that day—but the same thing happened to her. Only it had been not her *arm*, but her *head* sliced clear through!"

She accompanied this with ye olde slicing motion and he struggled not to laugh, the tightly held strain easing from his muscles. "I did at that, both Ed—your sister's intended—and I felled at Albuera in Spain."

Losing interest in his kneecaps, she captured his gaze. "Will your legs ever work again?"

He couldn't stop the sigh that heaved from his lungs. "I wish I could say. Physicians claim 'tis doubtful. My mother would tell you yes."

She grinned at him. "Mothers always *think* they know everything."

They shared a quiet laugh.

Until she idly pulled at the top edge of one red sleeve and asked, "But what do *you* think? Are your legs apt to walk again?"

"What do I believe?" That it was likely time he stopped wallowing. *If only I could.* "Time will tell how much"—if any—"use of them I regain."

Giving the sleeve an irritated glance, she released it to tug beneath her arm. "I confess, I am *very* impatient. It would make me crazed to have to wait. Especially not knowing and all."

"On that, Lady Harriet—"

"Call me Harri."

He hoped his own lingering despondence over the matter didn't show. "On that, dear Harri, we are in accord. Waiting is a sorry state indeed."

She glanced at the door—ensuring they were still alone?—and then turned back to him, placing her arms straight behind her, palms on the floor, as she leaned back to lengthen her legs, toes pointing to and fro in an alternating fashion. "I almost wish my sister was marrying *you* instead. You are easy to talk to. Not like *some* adults..." The way she emphasized that indicated she had attempted to chatter about with a grand number who wanted nothing to do with her. "I so wish to converse with Lord Redford about his arm, you know. The missing one, not the other."

"I gathered that."

"Yet my sister is *forever* in his company now that she has decided they will suit." The toes still danced, her feet as lively and energetic as the rest of her.

Ah, how he missed that. The freedom of childhood. Just being near young Harri reminded of it, brightened his spirits a good deal more than the sunshine outside. *Then why do you not spend more time with your siblings? They are much an age with this one here.*

And *boom*. The sky darkened once more, heavy clouds pressing in over his head and upon his shoulders. For thoughts of his own siblings only reminded him of responsibilities, and how very ill-equipped he felt now to handle them.

"Ed is good company," he told her. "I know that to be true. If they are to be wed, one must understand their desire to spend time together."

"But every *minute*? I vow, they spend so much time together one would think they must share a chamber pot!" He snort-laughed into one fist. "I spoke with Lord Redford upon his arrival, and it was grand, but now? Merry Anne refuses to count—um, count..."

"Countenance?"

"Aye, that. She will not *coun*tenance me inquiring

further. Claims he has already 'tolerated quite enough of my badgering' this week."

"May I let you in on a secret?"

"Always!" Lady Harri scrambled to her knees and clapped twice. "I adore secrets! And I vow to keep any you share solely to myself."

"Ed, Lord Redford, is a better man than I. He shall make your sister a fine husband. And if you find him in a quiet moment, I wager he would answer your questions sufficiently to satisfy even that inquisitive mind you boast."

She started pulling on the dress near her waist, wrenching it downward with both hands. "I really hope you walk again. I shall put in some extra prayers for just that."

Standing, she heaved at the sides of her bodice. Yanking the material with a vengeance.

"Difficulty?" He fought against a smile. "Ah...with your dress?"

"Very much so. It is *most* disagreeable. The"—*tug*—"horrid"—*yank*—"thing!"

Rrrrriiiiippp!

She groaned, her vivacious face pinching as she frowned down at the maligned frock. "Imbecilic thing! I do not have words to describe how much I hate wearing the blasted—" Hearing the curse come from her lips, she gasped. Looked more determined than contrite. "You did not hear that."

Oh-ho. Something the infamous Lady Harriet regretted uttering? From what he had seen—and heard—a rare occurrence indeed. "Wretched uncomfortable, is it?"

"You have no idea. Though, in truth, I am to blame." Her eyes rolled heavenward as she minced out, "*For dirtying my other and then, once clean, tearing it anew.*" After the credible imitation of her mother, she glared down her front at the wine-colored velvet. "If it were more comfortable, I wouldn't hate it so. As it is, I would curse it if I could."

"Mmm. You could try *ruinosus veste!* Or perhaps *stultum veste.* No, wait! *Horridus rubrum veste. Est infernum!*"

"*Infernum.* Hell?" Her eyes grew round. "Are we swearing in Latin?"

"Close enough."

"You are my *maxime ventus* person this week!"

She was approaching one of his most favored as well. "*Gratias.*"

"*Satis grata es.*"

Having naught else to do with his time, knowing he couldn't ask after her governess—the one he hadn't seen since that first day and night—he offered, "Bring me thread and needle, and I shall mend both this one and the other you 'tore anew'."

She stared at him as though his severed head had rolled right back onto his neck. "You cannot."

"Why not?"

"Men do not mend—"

"Aye, they most certainly do. Does your father's valet not see to his clothes?" Her nod came slowly, after thought. "I assure you. I do not mind wielding a needle and thread. A soldier learns to be self-sufficient."

"Then I am doubly sorry you remain in the Merlin's chair. For it must pain you quite *profunde* to be unable to do for yourself."

To his very depths?
It did. It cut to his soul.
Est infernum.

"Have you found yourself beneath the mistletoe yet?" she startled him by asking.

Hadn't everyone? For the sprite had seen it hung everywhere. "Aye, but never with an unmarried lass beneath it with me."

He wouldn't burden a single female here with having to bend awkwardly to give him a kiss. Nor could he, he knew because he had failingly tried, even attempt to stand to offer a buss at the proper height.

He refused to acknowledge the spike of disappointment that slammed into him at the painful reminder, for growing up, Mama always ensured mistletoe, and its accompanying traditions, remained a lively fixture in their home.

"We could conspire to make it happen." Lady Harri beamed at him, the detested dress all but forgotten. "Who would you like to kiss?"

He knew better than to answer that. "Should the question not be who might be amenable to kissing *me*?"

Are you really discussing kissing to a child?

She started it!

"Everyone agrees you are handsome." She gave him a conspiratorial grin. "Only you and I know you are witty in English and *also* in Latin. Even without the working legs, I am quite sure any number of appropriate females would be in alt at the notion of sampling your kiss. I shall see what I can do."

Why court danger?

True to Miss Primrose's grudgingly offered warning to keep his door locked, he had awakened, twice now, to scrabbled attempts to gain uninvited entry. It appeared she of the pert yet kissable nose was correct: the lure of *countess*, for some, did win out over unworking limbs and rumors of dust-laden coffers.

"Thank you for the thought," he said now, "but I think not—"

Ah. So much for declining any assistance in the mistletoe realm, for his excitable visitor was already off, scurrying away—once again yanking at the hated *rubrum veste*.

'TWAS BLISTERINGLY COLD. Thanks to the biting wind, the kind of cold that chapped faces and napped words. That made fingers numb and lungs ache.

Warrick didn't care.

Halfway through this days-long house party, the walls and ceilings had all but closed in. With the aim of alleviating his growing agitation, he'd suffered the humiliation of being carried—at his behest—down the steps, deep into the garden and placed upon a bench beneath some winter-dead brambles that formed an arch overhead.

Bundled against the cold—rather braced by it, in fact—he sought to flick his thoughts far away. Away from everyone else's jaunt into the nearest town for shopping, and skating if the lake had iced over, after the pleasant weather of yesterday had been obliterated overnight.

While he, unable to keep up, unable to participate, to laugh and entertain and wile the hours away—being all that was pleasing and pleasant as did all the *walking* gentlemen—found himself alone.

Alone and sitting outside—legs as dead as the brambles, wrapped in a blanket nevertheless—his bare hands firm upon the cold stone bench to ensure his sorry arse didn't topple off, he sought some measure of peace.

Thick clouds hid the sun, but also kept the temperatures just *this* side of bearable if one craved numbness.

A couple of determined birds picked at the hard ground near the base of some dried-up, scraggled plant. Watching their antics, 'twas several seconds before the methodical climb of someone approaching from the forested area abutting one side of the estate altered his focus.

An angel come to earth, swathed against the elements, materializing from the evergreens moments later his reward. An angel not with blond, ethereal hair and feathery alabaster wings, but one sporting strands of sunset hair escaping a winter blue bonnet, no white wings upon her back, but a light brown muff about her hands.

Angels. A multitude of them. Filling his sight. Flying in on those tremendous wings, ready to swoop him away...

He blinked. Blinked again, because of a sudden, his vision no longer beheld the frozen garden and potential company who made his heart take flight, but instead, he was back on the battlefield...

Unable to move.

Mired...

"Warrick!"

Slick mud coated the side of his face: cold, thick and wet. His arm felt wrenched from its socket, twisted beneath the weight of his torso.

Richard Andrew Martinson.

He tried to pull his mind free of the sludge, never mind his face.

Who called him? Who?

For no one ever, ever used his entire name.

What was that? Nagging at his thick head? His pain-buffeted brain?

He'd forgotten something. Forgotten to be somewhere...

But where?

Richard Andrew.

The voice soothed the jagged edges of his burning flesh. But how could that be? How could fire exist where only rain and—and—

Soldiers! Where soldiers existed? Mounds of them, piled alongside, heaped on top, smothering him deeper and deeper into the mud.

He tried to raise his arm, wipe the grime from his mouth, but couldn't move. Pinned in place.

The distant sound of retching attempted to gain his attention but failed, his nose suddenly assailed with the stench of blood and death, vomit, piss and shit. He gagged. Gagged again, as though his body would cast up all the evil smells—and the memories that hit him at once.

Following orders and riding into battle, despite the storms covering the land and combatants. The spike of energy that flowed through him and his horse—

Wait. His horse? Where was—

Richard. It is time to take you from this place.

What? Who?

A gentle, gossamer touch across his brow, over his shoulder. Through eyes squeezed tightly shut against the fire blazing through his shoulder and down part of his back, he saw wings. Majestic, beautiful angelic wings.

Richard. It is time.

For what? he thought.

And was answered though he hadn't given voice to anything.

Time to escort you—

To heaven? A snort-whimper escaped then. *We both know that's likely not the direction I'm bound.*

Another nebulous touch; this time he felt his body moving, rolling over on its own. He sure as certain wasn't doing anything to propel it.

Beyond the soothing presence, wind howled, gusted forth the taste of destruction and decay.

He shuddered, sickened down to his bones as the memories of the last hours flooded in: the piercing screams that clawed their way inside one's head and wouldn't leave; the shrill of clashing swords, of booming cannon shot; the unforgettable sight of broken men and horses, flying backward or crashing to the ground. The howls of anguish. The—

Richard Andrew. One of the many angels spoke— without moving their lips. But he heard it through the growing agony all the same. *Think naught of the past. Come with me and embrace your future.*

Wings flapped silently, casting a glowing warmth over him. Banishing the riotous memories. Calming the increasing torment. Creating a soothing, protective shield that made him feel as though he floated.

Now that was lovely.

He relaxed his closed eyes. Let the air lift him. His shoulder stopped hurting. The gnawing pain in his back faded.

Hell's bells. Gup! 'Pologies, angels. But I feel smashing. As though soused just this side of sleep...

Wait until his mates heard this one! Ed and Frost were as likely to believe him as if he'd spied a flying fox jiggling on the breeze with their foxed Regent. Thinking of... Ed? "Saint Nick?" Where were his friends? His horse?

Your horse no longer suffers. Be at peace with that. As for your friends—

"Warrick!" The deep shout tried to pierce through his

drifting, contented haze. "You damn reprobate! Where the hell are you?"

Are you ready? To leave and come with us?

Leave?

"Oh, thank God in heaven. Good Lord, man! You are covered—" More retching. More curses. More jostling around him, but none of it mattered. Not when he felt so light, so very grand.

"Where are you injured? Can you move? What— Oh. Damn, damn."

Something jerked his torso. His heavy eyelids fluttered. Saint Nick. Frost. Filthy Frost. Warrick snickered. For his immaculate friend 'peared grossly disgusting. Mud and blood and filth covering near every inch—

Richard Andrew Martinson. It is time.

"I say, naggin' Nicky-boy," he managed through a thick tongue. Had to share. Wanted to drift some more. "Angels, I tell you. Flappin' those glitt'ry wings... Can you see? Think they're 'bout to float me off."

If I go, he asked his angels, and his tongue wasn't thick anymore, *what of them? My mates? Mother? The siblings?*

"Angels? Pah." Frost cursed again. What was he doing? "Apple-fed pigs would be more likely to cart off your burdensome carcass. Pray to your angels, man. I need some aid."

What of it? Can you help my friend?

Do you wish to remain?

I can choose?

This time you may. For not all exits are decided. Some come with choices. If you choose to remain, it will not be easy. There will be challenges ahead, ones you do not anticipate. You cannot walk off this battlefield today. Perhaps not ever.

Ever? Walk? What were they trying to tell him?

The path to your future will take effort, more effort than you can conceive, and much patience. But time and perseverance will bring unimaginable rewards.

Rewards?

Happiness. Joy.

Happiness? Oh, how he like that. Loved laughing, making others smile. Loved dancing and—

It is time, Richard. You must decide. Shall your future be decided by coming with us? Or remaining here?

If I stay, I will have that? A future? A happy one?

Eventually. With your own angel.

Now that sounded lovely. Almost as lovely as floating some more. *All right. Aye, I wish to remain. To—*

The warm, comforting presence was gone. Evaporated. Vanished in a blink.

The pain returned, rioting forth like a hundred enemy soldiers, ready to batter him to ribbons.

The smells, the memories, the strange burn—dulling now, in the lower part of his back but growing in his arm and chest—gnawed at him, competed with the damp, miserable chill and abrupt, exploring grip from Frost who knelt. Gripped Warrick's torso against his bent knees and started fumbling with his clothing.

"Blazes, Nick... What the devil?"

"Where are you injured? Can you stand? Show me—"

"Can see naught but you getting pert with my groin and pizzle." Warrick scrambled, tried to push Frost's hands away from his falls. "I don't conjobble that way, man. Or are you tryin' to help me piss? God *damn*—'pologies, angels—but I can't feel—"

"Help me, damn you," Frost grunted. "Got to get you back up on my horse, for I have no hope of carrying your heavy arse—"

"Not t'day, you crank of a commandin' officer. Angels

said I could fly with them. *Fly*, man. Or wait. For you. Your tardy hide. No walkin' today. Maybe... Never?" Moisture wept from his eyes, blurring the mud and battlefield into a jumble that haunted him in the coming days and weeks every bit as much as the loss of his angels.

Of his legs.

9

TO HINT AT DALLIANCE, ONE KNOWSES, IS NOT ALL PRIMROSES

A CHILL SHUDDERED THROUGH WARRICK. Shook his whole body. He gripped the bench hard, harder than he had before, felt a piece of the carved stone crumble beneath the clench of his fingers. Sweat broke out on his brow. His heart thundered. Breaths came swift and fast as he blinked even faster.

Brambles.

Arch. Garden.

The Ballenger estate.

Each recognition eased the fierce panic gripping every muscle and galloping through his chest.

Hell's bells and devil take it. He had not thought of that day, of those moments—his angels?—in months. Had nearly forgotten. (Or tried to.)

Until a glimpse of a winter "angel" brought it all back.

His? His angel?

The governess? She was his promised angel? His heart tried to float at that. Till reality shot it down. *Of course not, you fool! Not when you are destined to marry a fortune so you may care for your siblings. The estate.*

Utter rot and rubbish. A man should be able to make his own way, care for siblings without sacrificing—

A walking man mayhap. A man able to work. Not a titled man strapped to debts and family.

Pushing the unpalatable thoughts of his miserable future aside, his desperate gaze sought out—

And found. A gentle peace wound through him, deepened his next inhale.

Navy cloak about her shoulders, plain winter bonnet disguising the fetching hue of her hair, his earthbound angel scuttled up from afar.

"Miss Primrose!" What *was* her first name? Though she attempted to maintain that "prim" demeanor, he knew much more lurked beneath.

At his shout, she stumbled, angled his direction but didn't spy him immediately. "Might you scamper closer," he invited, "and bring a ray of sunshine my way?"

Had he really just *yelled* for her to join him?

Spotting him amongst the brambles, she stilled. Exertion pinkened her cheeks and inflated her lungs.

"Please?"

After an inner battle, or so it seemed, she gave a slight nod and plowed through the light smattering of snow that had fallen overnight.

"What takes you afield today?" he inquired. "You did not accompany Lady Harriet into the village?"

As she came within talking (not shouting) distance, she pulled one gloved hand from the fur muff held tightly between them to tuck a few stray hairs back beneath her bonnet. "Lady Ballenger declared a holiday from lessons."

And *lines?* he could not help but wonder. "At Harri's urging, I'd wager."

She tucked her hand back inside the muff. Up close, he could see what was likely cream or white when new had become brown with use and time. Did it, mayhap, match yet another brown dress beneath the cloak? "Harri?" She frowned at him. "Is that not presumptive? Even for you?"

"She invited the diminutive." He gestured to the space beside him, more than enough for her trim frame and lightly flared hips. "Have a seat, if you would."

"I think not." She took one step away.

He gave a sardonic bark of laughter. "You scamper away as though you expect me to give chase. We both know the chances of that happening are naught."

She glanced around, took note of the dried leaves and dead flowers, the rose beds dormant until spring; the house a good distance away; before turning her attention back to him. "Where is your conveyance?"

"Inside." Where the grit, grime and goodly amount of dirt found outside wouldn't find its way into the chair's gears, making it even more challenging to use.

Beneath the shadow of her bonnet, on this already cloudy and bleak day, he saw her brow pinch, so closely did he watch her. "Then how did you..."

"Gain my current position?" He gave the bench a quick slap of one palm. "Carried." He gave her a grim smile. "Carried by the burliest Larchmont footman to be found."

"I am certain that grievously injured your pride."

That went without saying.

He wanted to cross one leg, prop his right ankle on the opposite thigh and lean back, appear the gadabout rake she thought him, but nay. He could only coil his fingers around the edge of the bench, hope he appeared to be at ease, and pray he didn't fall off.

"You wound me. Miss Primrose, skittering up through

the snows, coming the way the wind dost blow. Wound me quite deeply."

"Oh?" She was wary, but not enough to avoid his presence, cautiously approaching as he imagined a fawn might if he sat there long enough. "How so?"

"My lonely, ah…" He made an obvious show of looking toward his lap before facing her again. Couldn't halt the lift of one eyebrow. "*Self* awaited your arrival for hours my first night here."

"Hours?" she scoffed. "Does not a soused man sleep soundly—and swiftly?"

"Ah. Not-quite soused enough to slumber without thoughts of you."

She grew bolder, took two steps toward him and he had to fight not to show his pleasure. "Thoughts? Pray, shall I save us both the fuss and bother, slap you posthaste?"

He chuckled. "Please do not. For I am desirous of your company and therefore will keep my potentially *bother*some thoughts to myself. Shall I tender my apologies?" Not because he would necessarily mean them but because he truly wished her to remain. "I will, you know. For everything uttered at our last encounter, if you so wish it."

"Mayhap. But not for *every*thing."

This time, he couldn't keep the gloat from showing as satisfaction flowed from her pert response straight through his body. "There now. Your eyes shimmer and cheeks brighten."

How lovely she was, angel or no. Even covered head to snow-tipped toes.

"Should you not be frozen clear through? Simply sitting here—alone? For I at least have had my rousing walk to—" As though she heard herself, she blushed deeper. "Your fingers look iced. Shall I summon—"

"Do not dare. And you accuse *me* of being frozen? Cast thine eyes downward. The bottom of your dress shows the sort of treatment one might expect from Lady Harri, not from her respectable governess. Your hem near dragging icicles, madam. As to myself? I may sit here through the day"—and he would, if he didn't need to go in and piss at some point—"because I can *feel*.

"I welcome the sting of near-frozen fingers. The air's cold bite within my lungs. The nip of the frosty breeze upon my skin. The strain of muscles too-little used these past months as I—"

No. She need not know the effort it took to balance right now. Gah. How had he let sitting in that chair make him so weak? Though his shoulders and arms might have grown bigger from hauling his deadweight carcass around, they had no stamina whatsoever.

"How long have you been outside?"

"It matters not."

"It does if you have let your blood congeal into shockles." She thought his blood would turn to ice? Never. Not with her presence to warm him. "I do not wish to return inside. Too oft, it feels a prison." Bitterness dripped from his mouth like melt off the branches. "Nor do I wish to be carried about like in infant." *Especially not in front of you.*

"That is understandable. Eminently so. This past May is not yet that distant. Perhaps in time, things will improve."

He grunted. "Enough distant to frustrate."

She gave him a comforting smile, one that made him want to reach out and pull her down to sit beside him so he could bask in her closeness every bit as much as he had once clung to his angels. "At your home, can you smooth doorways?" she asked. "Build inclines your chair can climb? Mayhap even install a rope pulley for your arms to work your chair across distances faster? Give yourself some manner of independence?"

"You steal my breath." And she did, on so many levels. But at the moment, 'twas her enterprising suggestions that invigorated something inside him that had been dormant for too long. "I vow, Miss Primrose, of the reddened nose, you should return with me, prod my body into healing."

"Return?" To the house? *To your estate?* He could all but hear the disbelief.

"Aye." His gaze dared her. Beseeched her.

"Should you take *that* attitude—your fixed determination to entice me upon your lap—and use similar perseverance to take strides toward healing, I wager you shall be rising on your own before long."

"Tell that to my legs. Pardon. My *limbs*, would you?"

Absurd, that a man wasn't supposed to utter the word *leg* in front of females.

"I know someone who might be of benefit..." She gestured toward the useless limbs which only made him wince, ready to abandon the topic. "Someone who might help restore—"

"Spare me, please. These last months, I have burdened more physicians—and they me—than I care to recall."

"But my uncle—"

"Nay. Tell me of *Miss Primrose,* of the brightly glowing nose—"

"You scoundrel!" She rubbed the red tip. "For pointing it out."

"Then, Miss Governess of the Latin Vocabulary, teach me something about yourself. Let me learn more of you—so as to take my thoughts away from your...cherry-red nose and frost-nipped toes."

. . .

MUFFLING A LAUGH, lest he continue his absurdities, she glared at him. "I would wager my last quarter's earnings 'tis not my nose nor my toes that occupy your wicked thoughts."

"Shall I tell you more? Perhaps, Miss Primrose, we could plan another coze? For which I could prepare any number of wickedly alluring odes?"

Still fighting it, she finally released the laugh. "You are a trial."

As though he considered it a compliment, his eyes gleamed. "And should you not share something of yourself..." He brought one hand up to rub his chin, considering. "It is to your elbows, odes I shall compose."

"Stop! Stop, you fiend," she giggled, completely out of character.

He gave the dark slash of his brows a double wiggle. "Best you disclose..."

She sobered, thinking. Share of herself? Easier asked than answered.

But he sat there, confident, cocky and waiting.

What did he expect her to say? That her breasts hurt from being harnessed so tightly? That she hated wearing the "hide-me" pigeon dress he accused her of? That all week, she'd watched other females, not excessively much younger, flourishing in pastels made of frothy fabric that glided about when they walked instead of *clunking*? Should she tell him that she'd pulled her hair so tight this day, she'd given herself an aching noggin? Or that, contrary to what she might wish, he'd occupied an indecent amount of her thoughts as well?

"Come now," he prodded, returning his hand to the bench, where he had both curved about the edge, alongside each thigh. His feet, encased in tall boots, propped on the ground directly in front of him, remained as still as ice. "The last time we spoke, you showed no such hesitation in bantering with me and voicing your thoughts."

"The last time we spoke, you claimed to be tippled beyond recollection." Yet his intent, devil-may-care glint made her suspect he remembered every word.

He proved her right when he immediately cracked, "Pretty as a peacock, I do believe. *If you were another sort of female, I would ask you to sit upon my lap.* Alas, you left both my lap and my heart empty that night."

"Your heart? Your *bed*, you mean." She pierced him with her best disapproving, governess glare while inside the snug confines of her muff, her fingers tangled.

Why could she not be rid of him? Why must he, of all the men she had met (which actually weren't *all* that many) since leaving the Young Ladies Improving Academy and striking out on her own, be the only one who provoked her fancy? *Because you know he, of all of them, poses no threat?*

No threat? He might not be able to give chase if she said nay, but he could threaten her heart indeed. "If you would devote yourself to working your *limbs* with half as much effort as you do at being shocking, I daresay you could dance by May Day."

"And if a May Day dance is not what *inspires* me to *work* as you so despairingly phrase it?"

"Then determine what you care about sufficiently that will stir you to action. That is not something anyone else can do for you."

"Will you meet me under the mistletoe?" he drawled, completely ignoring the gust of wind that buffeted them both, scattering his thick hair into disarray. She clenched her fingers tight, lest they be enticed to smooth it back. "Doubtless I could find something to *stir* me in that."

"Mistletoe? Me? Nay. I am not bound for such trivialities. Nor is my place here—bantering in the garden with a rake..." She *should* glance toward the manor, see if anyone witnessed his nonsensical claims. But her attention couldn't be swayed from the movement of his lips, of the wind rustling his hair. Of his strong, bare hands perched so temptingly near... She shook herself. "My place is shepherding and teaching young, impressible—"

"Is it now? Then why do you remain? Here? With me?"

There is nowhere else I would rather be. No other place as compelling.

The brisk, solitary walk meant to enliven now excited instead. Made it far too easy to discard the distance she'd protected herself with.

After living in the Larchmont household for the last months, and being treated with a combination of respect and indifference from Lord Ballenger, the constant wariness she had worn like travailsome armor these past years had begun, just a bit, mind, to wane. But certainly wasn't gone.

Being caught unaware by the younger, visiting brother of the wealthy viscount who had previously employed Aphrodite to shepherd his two young daughters... Being held immobile and forced to accept the hard thrust of his tongue—and the rest of his unwelcome body against hers despite her struggles—and forced to listen silently when he slapped his fingers over her mouth and uttered taunting promises of how he'd ensure her compliance, his restrictive grip only easing when a handful of maids came bustling in, wet and laughing from the rain that had chased them inside early after their half day off, had taught her early and well how certain men could not be trusted.

And that had been the least of her two awful encounters with the peerage. (Which, to sometimes calm her rising apprehension, she had begun secretly thinking of collectively as the *pukeage*.)

For once, instead of the dreadful memories hovering, she had to yank them forth, remind herself how very dangerous—

"Do not retreat."

"I have not—" But she had. Had taken two steps backward.

Traitorous feet.

"If bantering is not to your taste," he blurted in a low rumble that topsy-turvied her stomach, "then let me confess I desire a kiss. Should not a brave and wounded soldier rate such a small token?"

"Well," she huffed, determined to thwart what his request—and those lips—persisted in doing to her. "I desire my father safely returned to me and to know my mother's embrace again, neither of which will ever occur. Despite petulant wishes, we do not always gain something simply because we desire it."

He gave a low whistle. "Damn me, Miss Primrose, poetry to whom I must endeavor to compose. You surprise me, not something females often do. You have depths blazing from beneath that ugly shroud. *Profunde* ones. I would so find satisfaction in uncovering them. Ah! There it is. That lovely flush upon your nose. Miss Prim—"

"That is quite enough! Not another ludicrous rhyming word about my red nose, slippered toes or—"

"Banishing your clothes?"

A garbled scream strangled her throat. "You are the outside of enough!"

She whirled toward the big house.

A sharp pull on her cloak, accompanied by his deep curse, and he was hauling back on the bench and bringing her with him.

She toppled, practically into his arms—into his lap!

Attempting to ignore the strength of his arms, the welcome scent of his neck, where his scarf had loosened—something outside-fresh, kitchen-spicy and virile-male musky—she fought the urge to kiss his skin. To inhale him. To thread her fingers through—

Aphrodite!

She scrambled to her feet. Reared back, shaking hands on trembling hips, and employed the tone that brooked immediate (or nearly so) obedience from Harriet. "My person is not a trifle to be dallied with at your whims. Please leave off haranguing me so I may return to my charge."

"Tut, tut. I did not take you for one who would spout clankers. We both know your charge went into town with everyone. So harangue you, I must. I am duty bound, you see."

Calling on every ounce of temperate behavior she exercised in front of others, she barely avoided stomping her foot. Instead, gave him a patently false yet serene smile. "Duty bound to annoy me straight inside. Good day!" That was too polite. She bent toward him and fairly growled, "I misspoke. I bid you a rotten day!"

Aphrodite! For shame.

He makes me feel things. Far too much.

She hadn't been this riled in... In... Ever!

Before she could flounce off, he lunged and snagged her muff, right off her chilled hands.

"Miss Primrose, pardon." He held the muff between

them in a manner that might indicate surrender to someone more foolhardy than she.

Her father had given that to her mother when she was young. She refused to leave without it. She gripped one worn end and tugged. "Return that to me."

"Not quite yet." He tugged right back.

Several seconds elapsed, neither of them giving an inch. Her riotous breathing finally evened out. Skin flushed hot at his proximity, almost making her wish she could do away with her cloak and bonnet. She gave another, halfhearted tug.

He held firm. Practically drew her forth until she stood right in front of him, her long skirt brushing against his knees and all but obliterating the sight of his boots.

His head up-tilted, his eyes steady on hers, he allowed the jovial, half-bored mask to slip "This I tell you true: were I in a position to *dally*, you would not need fear me. Never so. For I have yet to attempt seducing the help since I was fourteen and received a birching for my effort."

She did not know what to say to that. Just as well, for he wasn't finished, rearranging his hold on her muff until she stood so close, his knees bumped into her trembling legs. "Alas, Miss Primrose of the petite, adorable nose *and* burdensome clothes, you behold before you a broken man. No dancing nor dallying in my future. So you see, promising me a kiss beneath the moonlight—"

"Mistletoe."

He gave a sad smile. "Can you not see? Granting me either would be a singular act of charity to one so grievously injured. One who has naught to excite his thoughts. What occupies them is only dread, knowing that *next* Christmas will arrive with my *legs* and body still confined." His rakish air had crumbled. The pretense of roguish gallant vanished on the vapor.

Without conscious thought, she placed light fingers upon his shoulder, needing to comfort. Trembled more when they slid to the warmth of his neck. "Come next Christmas, Lord Warrick, should you present your boots—or dress shoes—beneath the mistletoe, whether standing or not, I will grant you a kiss."

The thought of doing just that had more than her shaky legs aflutter.

He gave her a hard stare at odds with the half quirk lifting one side of his mouth. "And if I decide I desire a moonlit kiss as well?" He covered her fingers with the strength of one hand. "Mayhap from the position of *our* limbs entangled upon my bed—"

Oh my blazes!

She plucked her hand free from beneath the dizzying thrill of his, whipped her muff from his loosened grasp, and slapped his outstretched fingers when they reached for her. "Then, my lord, I consider it my duty to remind you that I am a servant." Hell and drat. "*Limbs entangled?* There are *mistresses* for that sort of thing."

The idea of their naked limbs—legs—rubbing against each other's? Of her, hated dress gone, sprawled upon his mattress? Of him, sprawled there with her? Her hair, loose and down...his strong fingers feathering through the tangle... Him, rising up over her—

"You wretch!" she cried, mayhap out of proportion to his toysome banter, but not to how she responded. Craved to respond even more. "Evil, loathsome fouling! How dare you go and put such imagery in my head!"

Heart fluttering like the wings of a poor fledgling flicked from its nest, she bolted. More *stirred* than she'd ever been in her life.

10

CHASTISE. SYMPATHIZE. SCANDALIZE.

"By all that's holy and blessed..." Ed began after everyone returned from their excursion to town several hours later.

With most guests retiring to their rooms, to rest, change and ready themselves for dinner, Warrick and his friend stole a few private moments in Lord Ballenger's study, where Warrick had gone to thaw his body—and cool his ardor—after the heated exchange with Miss Prim (his new name for her, if she wouldn't permit him to cast about for appropriate rhymes anymore).

"What?" he prompted when Ed remained silent, curious over his companion's tense posture, especially given the relaxed air between them both for the last hour or more.

After exchanging superficial pleasantries over first port and then snuff, and then back to beverages, Ed now stood by his future father-in-law's desk, his one hand clamped, white-fingered, around his tumbler.

"What has you in a dither?" Not accounting for unexpectedly inheriting the title—and the betrothal—when his two older brothers met their end in the last year, Ed was generally the most calm, congenial of fellows. But now? "You look like you want to cuff someone."

"Aye, you."

Incredulous over that revelation, Warrick set aside the snuff tin he'd been idling with. "Explain yourself."

"Tell me I need not be anxious over you imposing upon of Harriet's governess."

Caught. "Imposing?" Stalling? "Whatever makes you say such a thing?"

"I saw you both." Ed scowled as though he'd swallowed the snuff instead of only inhaling it. "In the garden late morn. When I rode back to retrieve some giggling chit's cloak and scarf as the carriages rolled on."

Well and truly caught.

What did one do once across enemy lines and threatened with capture? Running was out, so it fell to deflection. "That little annoyance?" Warrick spat remarkably well, given the hard, anxious thump of his heart. "I don't know what you think you saw, but I simply bade her to summon a footman or two, to see me returned inside."

Ed's craggy face remained inscrutable. "And you needed to clasp her hand for that?"

Damn. Absolutely caught. "What of it? She has a lively mind. We discussed Latin." Had they? Ed looked understandably doubtful, so he added, "Talked of my injury and some physician her uncle knows. And May Day."

"May Day?" His friend's skepticism knew no bounds.

And mistletoe and kissing. And me seeing her sans clothing. "And something of her parents." What had she said? "She misses them dreadfully. There was nothing untoward about it."

Liar.

"Hmmm." Ed shifted, brought his port slowly to his lips but stopped just shy of drinking. "And her batting away your hand?"

"She took umbrage when I— When…" Warrick rubbed his fingers over his lips. "When, ah…"

After a slow swallow, Ed lowered the glass. "When you spouted something inappropriate?"

Shame threatened to warm his cheeks. He clenched his jaw against it. "Well, it isn't as though I can *sprout* anything inappropriate." Like a serviceable prick. "Despite your advances toward marital-bed occurrences, *words* are all I have left."

Ed placed the drink on the nearest glass-top table and took four strides, until he knelt in front of the despised Merlin's chair. "Richard."

Ack. His name. The one from school when they were boys. "What? To consider anything about her diverting… Any curiosity is inconsequential. Nothing can come of it." He spared a dark look toward his groin. "You know that."

"Then why trifle with her?"

"I wasn't trifling!" Without intent, the words exploded. "I cannot *sprout* nor can I trifle. We both know I cannot. I am destined to buy some rich mushroom's insipid daughter with my title. Not that I can do the faceless unfortunate any good either."

With his ever-strengthening hand—the one that remained—Ed gripped the flesh above one knee and squeezed. Warrick knew because he saw Ed's fingers move. Not because he felt anything.

"What harm can come from a mild flirtation?" Warrick asked, sounding both defensive and subdued; the ache in the question surprised them both.

Ed moved his hand to grip Warrick's where he'd fisted

both near the hated handles that directed his chair. This he felt. Warm comfort from the best of mates. A stern squeeze of chastisement as well.

Ed sighed, as though surrendering—but not before asking, "What harm, Rich? Have you stopped to ask yourself what harm courting *anything* between the two of you might do to her? Or, more importantly—more selfishly, to my thinking, since you are the one I care about—what it might do to *you*?"

"Ahhh, Warrick. Wassail?" Lord Ballenger said the next night with a heavy dose of disappointment, once the men relocated to his study after dinner and before some games began, noticing the glass Frost had just handed him. "No need to keep drinking that here, ladies not present and all that." His host gestured toward the sideboard where an array of bottles awaited his preference. "Especially as there exists more than sufficient port and sundry others."

Knowing surrounding eyes were on him once again, Warrick did what he did best. He entertained. He sought smiles. Sought to direct attention away from himself and back into the rumpus of the others.

"One cannot top well if one is tippled, you know. Hard to seduce when one is in their cups." That brought the anticipated chuckles, and kept him on the path of being his outrageous self.

Until he could escape. Roll off somewhere that promised solitude. Where he didn't have to present loud joviality when all he really wanted to do was knock down a bottle of brandy and knock out a wall, or mayhap two.

For, ever since the forbidden governess took herself off (directly after a few recitations of *You evil, vile wretch!*—

among others—that echoed behind her fleeing form, gonging about in his brain and bringing guilt), seemed all his mind wanted to do was wallow.

Wallow in regret—that he wasn't standing. That his accounts and pockets weren't brimming with blunt. That he hadn't had a chance to apologize, sincerely this time, because he *did* regret offending Miss Prim's prim sensibilities during their not-quite tryst in the garden. Most of all, Warrick regretted that *he* wasn't, even remotely, in any state to follow her or give serious attention to continuing their flirt.

The familiar anger that had ridden him constantly during the weeks after they landed on English shores had roared back with a vengeance. Sadness and the beginnings of acceptance had been trampled under the rage.

After sucking down the few remaining swallows of wassail, he handed off the glass to Frost and shook his head: *Nay, do not hand me another, lest I should crumble and crush the glass within my grip, having not a care of slicing or shredding my flesh further.*

As though you need more injuries?

What he needed was the ability to sit a horse again. To march out of this happy holiday home, coax forth and catch up a horse, saddle it and swing up without care. Without any bloody assistance. To race off toward London and his bachelor townhouse—not his family estate, nor toward his mama (and siblings) which lay in opposite directions.

What he needed was to escape back into his private bedchamber and the bottles his servants would bring without censure lining their expressions.

For their wages, at least, he had continued to pay.

Despite one brief—very brief—illicit (only because he'd been told to leave her alone and engaged her in flirtation anyway), moonlit encounter with Miss Primrose in the ballroom during the deep hours of last night, melancholy had replaced his morose turn of mind by the next afternoon.

But failed to herald much improvement. Because the seasonal, celebratory visit had eclipsed by both in a blink and with excruciating slowness. And here he was, saying goodbye to Ed and his mother, Lady Redford, as they prepared to depart Redford Manor, along with Lady Anne who accompanied her new intended and future mama-in-law.

Most of the guests, including his ride Frost, were bound here another day, with plans to depart in the morning at first light. Shocking, that—that ol' Saint Nick had managed to endure the revelries this long. About the only thing bringing a smile to Warrick's face today was the scowl on his friend's. Still wallowing, he took a perverse pleasure knowing Frostwood was, in his own way, just as miserable.

And what kind of man does that make you? To revel in the suffering of others?

A petty, petulant one whose peevish prick still refuses to poke properly.

All thoughts of pouts and penises vanished when Lady Redford bustled over, seeking him out amidst those present and standing around (would that he could), milling about in the Great Hall near the entry, witnessing the spectacle of a couple of grand carriages, containing other guests, depart.

"Dear Richard, do your mother and I proud. Eat, stave

off imbibing too much." She accompanied this gentle harangue with a fierce hug so of course he could take no offense. "And listen to that surgeon your mama found for you. She wrote me, in alt over stories she heard about him. He's had notable success with others injured severely. He—"

He—Warrick—had endured enough. More hope? More promises? More *disappointment.*

Crushing disappointment the more it occurred.

So he cradled her hands, pressed her frailer, feminine ones between the strength of his, and forced a smile. "You know I will endeavor to do my best. I meet with him later in January."

"Good. Good." A kiss to his cheek and a "I shall see you both, and your brothers and sisters too, this summer" and she was off.

Leaving him disappointed, once again.

This time, from bidding her comfortable presence goodbye. Also from the small sliver of hope she'd left dancing about his head.

Perhaps when he and his family visited Lady Redford in six months as promised, he'd have some sort of progress to show for the dreaded, forthcoming visit with this lauded, crack-brain of a doctor.

Damn that sliver of hope.

LATE THAT EVENING, Aphrodite trod down the backstairs once seeing an exhausted Harri tucked safely to bed after an energetic day where the child sought to visit with *everyone.* To do *everything.* Her antics entertaining those around her, her enthrallment with everything from discovering Sir Lancelot (brother of the already mourned Sir

Galahad, with neck still intact) out near the lake to her giggling delight over a finger-singeing game of snapdragon.

Aphrodite's feet ached from use. From darting after her bouncing charge throughout the manor house and over the estate gardens...

The gardens. Which she pointedly refused to think about. For to do so only courted scandalous enticement she could well do without.

She forced her mind back to Harri and how the girl had laughingly led Aphrodite on a merry chase today:

1. To the lawn for shuttlecock.

2. Up the stairs to the portrait gallery to regale the remaining guests with stories of "the pompous ancestors of Papa's who deserved to be pasted or pinned with bows". (By now, not only did everyone know of her exploits with ribbons and subsequent punishment—only because Harri herself freely shared—but her parents had quite given up trying to confine their youngest to the nursery.)

3. Back down to the card rooms for whist—"Does anyone care to wager me?" (They did *not*, not after learning how soundly the child had trounced her mother, while *learning* the game.)

All in all, this—the last full day the Larchmont home would overflow with guests—had been a mix of high spirits occasioned by deep doldrums. "Everyone will be gone t-tomorrow," Harri had cried against Aphrodite's chest moments ago as she sat with the girl before sleep claimed her. "And I shall be *all* alone once more!"

Oh, the trials of youth.

Leaving the back stairwell for the hallway, she dabbed her handkerchief over the shoulder of her dress—slightly damp from Harri's recent tears. Let the girl cry while she was still young enough to do so, for the more years one gained, the less one was allowed to indulge in tears and the deeper the hurts cut.

Though she would deny it outright, Aphrodite suffered lassitude over the coming quiet as well. In the last sennight, she'd grown rather used to the bustle, to the morsels of news gleaned from London and abroad.

What you have, missy, is grown rather used to dodging a certain gentleman relegated to the main floor and his fixed—if inappropriate—attention.

Affronted at the very thought, she lowered her arm and tightened her fist around the handkerchief. *I am sure that need not be dignified with—*

And there he was—in a circle of others, so easily spied the moment she reached the end of the long corridor, despite the number of men milling around his seated form. She stumbled two steps back. Then inched forward yet again.

Why had she thought to drop by the kitchens below, to enjoy a cup of tea before retiring to her attic room?

Because, you daring hussy, you hoped to gain another glimpse of the inappropriate lord. To entertain a further flirt.

Nay, I—

Deny it no longer, lest your fingers ache from lines: I shall not covet a man above my station. I shall not think of him, dream of him, yearn for—

A silent groan strangled up her throat. For it was true. She had avoided him with stellar success the last fifty some-odd hours and knew she'd not be granted this chance again.

The chance to see him one last time.

Lout or no, fiend or not, she could not deny he fascinated.

"Warrick, when are *you* going to make use of the

mistletoe?" someone asked, which only made her lips tingle.

"The next time a good opportunity arises." His deep rumble of a voice easily carried her way though she'd retreated to a halt just inside the doorway...

Carried right through her ears and fairly swept her off her feet.

11

A MISERABLY MAGNIFICENT
MISTLETOE KISS

"The next time a good opportunity arises." Warrick's quipped reply brought a round of good-natured jostles and ribald words of encouragement.

Lord knew he still wasn't. Rising, that was, on his legs or otherwise, despite wishes to the contrary.

Numbers only slightly smaller, given those who had left for home earlier, the fellows had decided to indulge in one last evening of cards and stakes during the remaining few hours. Lord Ballenger promising his wife a new dress —or something of the sort, mayhap curtains for the drawing room?—if she would make the ladies absent so the men could drink, wager and whinge about politics without having to mind their manners, or their mouths.

Liquor had flowed as freely as deft hands dealing cards, as had their not-always-fit-for-company conversation.

Everyone, it seemed, reluctant to let the night, and the holiday, come to a close. As the hours elapsed, eyelids grew heavy and more than one person yawned behind their hand (or bemoaned reaching the bottom of their pockets due to good—their opponent's—or bad—theirs— play), tumblers had been drained, cards and vowels collected, and the group as a whole (save Lord Ballenger and a crony of his, who remained behind to deepen their play), escaped the card room to congregate in the area that led both up to the bedchambers and down to the kitchens.

The old Warrick would have reveled in the evening. Rejoiced at spending such lighthearted, carefree hours before the journey homeward that began early tomorrow. A journey he was not looking forward to, because the respite of the season was all but over.

Upon reaching London, he would face not only his dearth of finances, but also the dread of more doctors. More disappointment. And more familial responsibility he felt ill-equipped to handle.

He should be commended, though. For his stage skills had grown: he'd not made public his personal angst toward his future, simply played where the cards took him and moderated both his beverages and his betting. Frost should be so proud.

As to Ed? If his friend had any inkling of the voluminous time Warrick had spent thinking of the Larchmonts' not-to-be-found governess since that stern talking-to Ed had delivered, his friend might not have been so swift to return home with his mother and bride-to-be.

Pity Warrick could not simply ask *where* the little Latin-speaking governess took herself off to each day. He hadn't seen her, not beyond spying her once with the young Lady Harri out the window—which counted for naught.

Miss Prim, in whom his interest continued to brim, had not been close enough in days for him to see her smile. Had not been close enough to hear her laugh or make her blush. Nor close enough to contemplate a kiss.

Ahh, a kiss.

Something he continued to think about with monstrous consistency. So much so that he had tried, yet again, to bring himself off last eve.

To no avail.

His prick was having none of it, and the bitter reality had turned Warrick's mood sour enough he'd begged off all forms of entertainment this afternoon. Another turn about the portrait gallery? He thought not, heartily declining with a false grin, unwilling to be jostled again between burly footmen first *up* and then *down* the grand stairwell… The very notion was unpalatable in the extreme.

He wasn't a small man—six four, now reduced to about four six—and solid. At least he had been. *Before.* Before—

"Mayhap he's too particular," one of the nearby gents put in, recalling him to the moment, the last few pleasurable hours, where nearly everyone was seated. The monies he'd managed to maintain in his pocket, neither gaining nor losing a significant amount throughout the evening.

Ah, yes. Lucky him.

His useless legs might not be under discussion, but his under-used lips were (to his dismay) the talk of the moment.

"Or…not interested?" another suggested, motivating him to perform as expected.

"Not interested in gratifying myself with a delightful kiss beneath the mistletoe? Perish that thought. Of course I am," he said with all the bravado he could muster. "Only the best for these lips. Alas, where's our commanding, managing sprite?" Everybody laughed, as Lady Harriet had earned the nickery Lady Commander, after running around for days, capturing a fellow with one hand and a lady with another, dragging them both until they met beneath the mistletoe.

He palmed the bristle lining his cheeks at the late hour. "Ought to tell her 'tis time to find *my* mistletoe lady before my stubble turns grey."

More smiles, as they left off haranguing him and started in on Sam Gregory who had stolen one of the most talked-about kisses of the season.

There now. Joviality returned to all.

Except himself, it seemed.

What was it about those primly pursed lips and coppery hair that kept waltzing through his thoughts just before he drifted off at night? Why did he have to go and attach his interest on—

Forget her. Find your heiress.

If he could just have one more chance—

To what? Apologize? Kiss her? Slide your hand beneath—

He choked off wishes that direction, coughing into his shoulder.

And that's when he saw *her*. Well, not her, exactly. But definitely her well-worn slippers (practically threadbare over one toe) peeping out from a heavy brown hem, the remainder of the skirt just out of sight thanks to the most inopportune doorpost to ever grace a manor.

Richard! As though Ed, Lady Redford *and* Warrick's own mother chastised him all at once, he heard gasps of imagined outrage. *You knave! 'Tis your duty to save the estate! To ensure the title lives on. You must avoid courting scandal if you are to have any hope of a financially advantageous marriage.*

A profitable, *proper* marriage could go hang.

Did he want to deny himself his last wish as his hours here grew shorter? His opportunities scarcer?

Could he help it, then, as laughter and noise and conversations swirled around him, above him, if his chair just happened to move? To rotate a few inches? To...roll... to a...stop just under the big bough of mistletoe?

Never would he be granted such an opportunity again.

Might as well avail himself of it—and her mouth.

"Frostwood? Nay," Lord Warrick responded to someone's question as she dared peek beyond the corner of wall and plaster shielding her from discovery. "No mistletoe kisses for that frigot, not this year." Had the entire group come a foot or two closer? Or was that simply dangerous hope? "He's out in the stables or carriage house, checking with his groom and coachman, readying all for our departure come morn."

What to do? Go back upstairs—sans tea and warm belly (not to mention additional glimpses of that Dangerous Hope)—or ease along the opposite side, staying in the shadows—

"What, ho!" one of the men on the far side of their loose circle called loudly—and pointed at her! "Warrick, you need not go unkissed this week, for there awaits an available lass."

Every Jack one of them turned toward her.

A *swooping* sensation rolled up through her middle and crashed into the back of her throat. Rendered speechless, she tried to give a tight smile and move.

But nay, her useless feet had decided to grow roots.

"What good fortune!" another gentleman exclaimed, lifting his glass first toward her and then at the seated man in their midst. "Each of us have had a turn or three beneath the mistletoe. Past time we let you have yours."

Feet shuffled. And there he was—in the middle of the standing others, Lord Warrick's piercing midnight blues fixed upon her. Stealing sense. Capturing the air from her lungs.

Her body blazed as though sun instead of dwindling candles shone down. Her face flamed. Heart practically sang in her ears, its chaotic, drumming beats drowning out everything but *him*.

His gleaming gaze held hers and he spoke a veritable volume with naught but a blink:

Please, his eyes said, *I seek your forgiveness.*

Then they heated, as though the flame burning through her caught at him too. Narrowed. One of those eyebrows quirked. *Though, I confess, a kiss wouldn't be amiss either.*

How did his glance sever those roots, freeing her feet —if not her breath—and propel her toward him? One slow, excruciating step at a time…

You did promise me one. His smoldering look tried to hurry her along.

Not until next year!

Ah, but now, Miss Primrose—I shall kiss you even wearing clothes—do not cause an injured man undue humiliation in front of his peers. Even you cannot be that cruel.

Blast your peers. I am a servant!

But then she was at his side, her breath now coming in pants. She was lightheaded with the wonder of it—her first kiss freely given! (The forced, messy ones counted not.) Her entire body thrummed, fingers and toes started tingling. *Quickly now, get this over with.*

The order came from her saner (slightly scared) side. The side that claimed the tingling was from the lack of air.

But the part of her that was all woman—yearning, curious woman—just wanted to linger now that she was this close.

Wanted to caress the back of his neck, where a small section of hair remained tucked beneath his neckcloth. Wanted to breathe in his heady, musky scent, the one that she remembered before those last disastrous moments in the garden. Outdoors. A hint of something spicy. And all man.

But years of cultivated propriety proved impossible to banish. That and self-preservation.

She was surrounded by a horde of titled men. Who knew what sort of invitation others might assume her willing participation meant?

So she bent her knees and leaned over a few inches to chastely press her lips against his cheek. To have the matter over and done with posthaste.

With every intention to escape to her room. The tea she would do without.

What about the damage to your reputation?

When she hesitated, he tilted his chin up in challenge. "Oh come now, Miss Prim, you cannot let me be the only hapless fellow who is neglected beneath the mistletoe."

Was he in his cups? She couldn't tell.

The group was loud enough, one would suspect so, but his eyes didn't convey that shiny, somewhat dazed look so often associated with an over-tippler, and his words, both the ones overheard and those now, were crisp, not at all sluggish.

As to the others? She did not know any of them; they were all of an age, each possessing twenty or thirty years, and a handful beyond. Where were all the ladies? Already abed? Perhaps having their own late-night, last-night coze?

Where would the harm be in a simple—and quick—Christmas kiss?

What she never expected, when she gave in to his coaxing, to her own desires, and bent the last couple of inches to reach his cheek was the scrape of short whiskers across her lips as he swiftly turned his head.

What she couldn't have anticipated was the glide of his tongue across the seam of her mouth that startled her to gasp and it to open.

What she never—well, what she really *should have*—expected, was how one strong arm wrapped around the back of her thighs and tugged, until she toppled over sideways into his lap.

The bawdy laughter surrounding her plight was expected. Even the scurrilous comments that flew back and forth, a few quite escaping her comprehension.

But the heat of his thighs beneath her bottom? The breadth of his chest against one arm...the lingering press of his mouth against hers? His lips warm and mobile and devastatingly welcome?

Those, she never, ever, not in a myriad lifetimes could have prepared for.

When his tongue brushed across her mouth again, accompanied by her needy groan, the chuckles around them turned to awkward snickers, a couple of muffled coughs and knowing *Mmmm-hmmmms*.

But she paid them no heed. How could she? For his taste, the sinfully sublime taste—

Just as his tongue slid fully against hers, and the hollow space deep in her woman's core contracted, a familiar sound—screech, really—met her eardrums.

"Miss Primrose! How *could* you?"

Lady Ballenger!

Aphrodite scrambled. She pushed at the strong arm holding her in place until it loosened. Nearly fell to her arse, so quickly did she twist free, needing to escape.

"Oh, my lands and Lord!" Her employer. Shrieking wrath and disbelief the likes of which were usually only reserved for her wayward daughter, but now directed at Aphrodite. Another screak or four, while the matron forcefully herded and shuffled the others, amongst feminine squeaks and squeals, back into the room from whence they'd come.

"No harm done," one of the men drawled in a tone that indicated he would revel in watching all night. "Holiday spirits and all that."

Her stomach sank so deep it practically reached the pits of hell. Would Lady Ballenger wait until the morning to dismiss her? Or cast her out tonight?

When she regained her footing, Lord Warrick snared her wrist and kept her from fleeing.

The squeak of shock she made quickly muffled by laughter—*his* (to the devil with him) and that of those surrounding them—when he brought the back of her resisting hand to his lips, pressed a kiss to the air above it and said, "I daresay, if my sisters' governess had kissed so sweetly, I might have kept the snake *out* of her bed—instead of putting it there."

More laughter. Raucous, this time. Accompanied by a couple slaps to his back, one of them hard enough it jarred his hold and she wrenched her arm back to her side. Took to the shadows as quickly as she could, praying they could make her invisible.

How could he have kissed her like that? With such... Thoroughness? With such *passion*?

The fiend! She'd wager *he* had a snake—in his falls. And the way his eyes glinted at her now? Followed every frantic step of her feeble retreat? She'd wager that snake (the one in his trousers) might have found its way to the governess's bedchamber after all.

The inconsiderate degenerate. To kiss her like that in front of others! To speak such within her hearing! To prolong this unending, mortifying moment?

"Even in the dead of winter, I vow..." His brash words halted her already stuttering feet. "Miss Primrose—of the blushing red nose—grants delightful kisses quite inviting of peccadilloes."

He nodded toward her, to make sure everyone saw, and *winked*, the lecherous, fiendish oaf! The brute whose snake she was now thinking of severing.

But he wasn't done, not yet. "Come now, Miss Prim. Prim*rose*. Dare I wonder—flushing pink beneath your clothes? Allow me the chance to lure you back upon my lap..."

WHAT THE DEVIL WAS WRONG with his mouth?

Why couldn't he stop? Stop making it worse? Stop tasting her, by damn. Stop wishing...

'Twas his lower half that was broken—so why was his upper story determined to wreck, ruin and destroy *everything*?

Wreck the moment—which he feared he'd never raze from his mind?

Ruin her reputation? By continuing to draw attention to her retreating form.

But more than anything, why was he compelled to *destroy* her memory of him?

Ah. There it was. Self-destruction.

If she hated him with every cell in her being, would he stop this wretched craving for what could never be? Would his boundless curiosity about her wither to naught?

If that is truly your goal, take care ere you gain your wish.

For the winsome, primly fierce lass now glared his direction as though his was the boot that kicked her kitten and stomped her heart.

Ludicrous. Insane. Preposterous!

His damned foot kicked naught. And he shouldn't care what she thought.

Shouldn't have treated her that way.

Shouldn't wish, even for a trice, that Frost had left his cracked carcass back in Spain, on the battlefield.

Sure as shat shouldn't wish he could race after her and apologize with every truth in him, share everything in his trampled soul.

Not when his wounded, petulant side chafed at being thwarted by the interruptions. Infuriated by his lot in life.

Not when his mouth was opening again...

Vexed at not kissing her long enough, tasting her deep enough...

Provoked beyond reason and restraint at the loss of her. At the loss of her respect (not that he ever held it to begin with). Devastated by losing any chance of what might have existed between them...

He winked at her broadly, blatantly. Crushed the thin fabric of her handkerchief into his palm—the second one collected off her this sennight. And spoke the damn truth after all. "I declare, if I could only get my twanger to work, I might just stay beneath Ed's mistletoe till someone finds us a parson."

PART II

...very far from happy himself. He was suffering from disappointment and regret, grieving over what was, and wishing for what could never be.

—Jane Austen, *Mansfield Park*

12

1812

FISTICUFFS GO SOLO

AT HIS MOTHER'S BEHEST, in January Warrick visited with her maggot-brain of a doctor. Or should he say, the man visited him? Rather than hauling his wrecked body to Bath, Warrick agreed to an exorbitant sum he could ill afford so the codger would travel to his London townhouse.

Only to tell Warrick, after a cursory glance, that his injuries were severe enough, and still fresh enough, not yet a full year since, that he shouldn't expect miracles. Well, what in blazes was he going to waste his time for, then?

"I don't need a *miracle*," he told the man with thick silver hair and kind eyes. Eyes that turned hard when Warrick finished with, "What I need is for my damn legs to work again."

Silas Arbuckle then evaluated him so thoroughly Warrick grew uncomfortable, awkward heat running through him until it took everything he had not to show the fidgets. To halt the doomed endeavor ere it began.

Finally, the man stepped away, allowed Warrick privacy to redress himself before they spoke again.

Giving him an indecipherable look, Arbuckle cleared his throat. Then again. "The majority of fellows I have worked with thus far are not of your station. Not titled." There was naught to say, so Warrick just held his breath, his muscles taut, and waited.

"Are you willing to do all I request for a chance at that? For your 'damn legs' to work?" the surgeon wanted to know.

"A chance?" Air and frustration burst forth. "Can you promise me I will walk again? Ride?" A horse. A *woman*. But he couldn't say that. "*Dance?*"

"No, sir, I will not. I will tell you that I can give your legs more strength than they possess now and teach you how to do that yourself. Once any lingering inflammation has waned, and your nerves have time to recover, we just might—*might*, mind—be able to get you up and on your feet. Beyond that? It is entirely too soon to say."

"Then be away with you." He flicked his hand toward the exit. "For I do not have time to waste piddling about."

With a tight nod, the man was gone. And to Warrick's way of thinking, not a moment too soon.

Despite his mother's disappointment, he refused to reconsider or to visit her and his half-siblings in Thropmoor. Better to remain here, to keep his bachelor door barred to most visitors, and his heart barred to hope.

IN MARCH, HE IGNORED MAMA'S TWO LETTERS, asking if he

felt well enough to vacation in Brighton with her and her husband and their boisterous brood.

The letter about Warrick making an effort to meet "suitable" brides he might find in London as the season commenced?

That one, he answered.

Briefly:

Not yet.
—W

As to the "spy", Giles, his mother had hired as valet?

No quarter wages had seen the annoyance on his way soon enough, leaving Warrick to make do with Shieldings, whom he preferred anyhow.

Nearly thirty years his senior and in his employ as long as he could recall, Shieldings was the son of a soldier and a former enlisted man himself. Stationed at the Warrick London townhouse as butler a good many years, Shieldings understood an employer's right to crank about in his own home. Didn't go reporting every little (or not so little) mishap, spilled beverage or spat with a surgeon to a man's mama.

For 1812 had brought nothing to look forward to, thanks to Arbuckle's disheartening January pronouncements, and as the date of Albuera approached, only a rousing need to *not* look back motivated Warrick.

Ample drinking helped accomplish that.

During May, both Warrick's mother and Ed's came to London. For a visit.

Oh, capital.

Thank heavens and his filthy home she'd sent round a note ahead of their arrival. The scant few days provided the necessary time to have his butler/footman/valet/and everything else (the only male servant Warrick had retained in town as the months went on and he chose not to go out) confer with his likely overpaid housekeeper/cook/laundress (the only female he still employed, and the wife to his butler). Gave the two, Shieldings and his missus, the opportunity to hire and oversee additional staff to give his townhouse a thorough cleaning—and his self as well.

After his home was tamed, Warrick suffered his man's serious scrub down, shaving of the heavy beard he'd grown since winter, trimming of his nails, his hair and—a slight—trimming of his liquor consumption.

So that by the time his mother and Lady Redford were handed down from Ed's borrowed travel carriage and entered his domain, Lady Redford gave him a joyous smile and remarked how much better he looked. Not as pale as she'd expected. (He owed his housekeeper a thanks for shoving his lazy arse out into the small vegetable garden in the back—and the sun—while she commanded the cleaning efforts.)

Even his mama complimented how well he controlled the newer chair he'd scraped down one account to purchase. "Why, if one did not know any better, they might think you enjoyed skittering from one room to the next."

Likely he'd given her that erroneous impression when he'd accompanied his spins and rolls with utterances of pretended glee and, "Weeeeeeeeeeeeee!"

Of course he *acted* as though everything were absolutely ripping. He couldn't walk, by damn, had no idea if he would ever swive again. He already railed at himself to a sufficient degree, he didn't need anyone else bleeding for him.

I know not whether you will ever leave the Merlin's chair, but you are alive, man. Take heart from that. Per Frost, one night when Warrick had turned overly maudlin about the future.

"Oh, my sweet boy, you remain the light of my life," said his keenly optimistic mother now, during their visit on the one-year anniversary of the battle. May 16th. "And will remain so."

My sweet boy.

Was it selfish, that some part of him reveled, hearing that? Warmed. Even knowing she'd left her other, younger children home with their father so much this last year, so she could travel to London and be with him during the early days?

'Twas late. Lady Redford had retired, his servants as well (both Shieldings and his wife, and the ones recently brought in), so it was just he and his persevering, always-smiling mama.

"Boy?" He felt one side of his mouth quirk—his attempt to match her happy expression, but falling short, landing somewhere between sardonic and self-pitying. "We both know that appellation has not applied for some decades."

She reached across the table to cover his hand—the one holding several cards—with hers. He suspected she'd dealt herself a ruinous hand this last round, hence the slightly solemn turn to the night. "You are, you know. It matters not that I have two more I love dearly as well. It matters not if I were to have two hundred more. You are my first, my eldest—the one who let me practice and fail and *learn* how to be a mother, the one who turned out beautifully despite all my mistakes."

"Beautiful?" He all but snorted at that. "Do you not mean brash?" She knew of his bent for spouting whatever licentious remark came to mind, whether in suitable company or not.

Tut-tutting at him, she slid from her chair to come round the table. She leaned down and hugged his neck, giving him a chance to inhale her always familiar, always welcome scent, some floral mix or other. He never knew what it was; it didn't seem to matter. Whatever fragrance she wore, she always simply smelled like *Mama* to him. "You are, Richard. My beautiful boy. The laughter of my life. The light of my empty lantern sputtering about—"

"I am sure that is *not* how it goes," he told her, chuckling now, thinking she sought to quote some poet or another. "But I appreciate the sentiment even so."

She released his neck, but kept one hand on his shoulder as she leaned back to meet his eyes, her deep blue ones, so like his own, looking more tired than he liked to see. "Give yourself, your limbs, more time to recover. Do not abandon all hope," she advised. "They've had a blow—"

"You believe so?" he responded with brutal sarcasm, ignoring how she flinched.

How quickly she forgave and continued on, that soft smile lighting her features as always. "—and just as with any injury—to head, heart or body—'twill no doubt take a measure of time before you are ready to heal. But I have no doubt that you will, my love. For you still have grandbabies to dawdle about upon my waiting lap. And at the end of your foot, hmm—just like your father did. Once it's stronger, of course."

The last part wasn't a question. It was a statement. A fact. She expected his foot to get stronger, ergo, it would.

He wanted to believe in *her* belief—of him. Wanted to

trust in her faith. But he knew better. Doubted, after a year, anything would improve beyond where it already had. But still...

Still...

The imagery she created, despite his resolve not to buckle beneath her hopes, made him long for that as well: for children, a babe *and* a wife. A family of his own.

Because he *did* remember how his father used to cross his legs at the knee, place a toddling Warrick upon his top foot, angled upward to create a cradle at his ankle. Whereupon Papa would bob his leg up and down, holding on to his small son as they both made—very undignified, very loud—neighs, whinnies and snuffled snorts, more than sufficient to do any self-respecting horse proud.

IN JUNE, the surgeon dared reach out again, offering to meet with him once more, but only if Warrick traveled *to him*. Not hardly.

Not when, by now, he had given up the inapt life of a hermit, had begun inviting a few mates around and was indulging in his love of cards. His love of decanters. His love of wallowing.

BY AUGUST, knowing that the swelling had long since receded, that the scarring was as good as it would ever be, and that to further delay only made him feel weaker than he already knew he was, he stopped avoiding the injuries.

Started exploring the damaged skin low on his back. Swallowed down bile and let his hands and fingers reach where they could, survey along either side of his spine, and behind and over his shoulders, where some of the canister shot had fragmented and embedded itself below the surface.

Much of it had been removed early on—especially the pieces that trapped fabric, pinning his clothing into flesh beneath the metal. Leaving small hollows where things had been pried out or worked free.

One ugsome little crater behind his left shoulder—the deepest—poked at him and bothered him more than most (well, more than everything *except* the destruction of his damned legs).

Every time he took off his shirt or ran a wet cloth over his body or just felt like berating himself for something other than an inopportunely broken penis, it was that particular crater that suffered his rough treatment more than the others. He had a habit of digging the tips of two fingers into that one, to test not only the ridged, scarred-over skin beneath his fingertips, but to experience the dulled bite of his nails...

To remind himself that he could no longer *feel* as much as he used to. Not his legs. Not through the burnt, thickened skin. Not with his heart.

He worried that spot, pricked it over and over with his nails to remind himself of all that was missing *beyond* his flesh.

IN AUTUMN, he made an effort to move past the malaise keeping him mired in London. Knowing that continued denial, and avoidance, would only make the realities he must eventually face worse, he dragged himself back to the estate.

'Twas past time to assess losses and damages—and, he

discovered, *thefts*—thanks to his extended absence abroad and the ill management of the steward he'd not supervised sufficiently.

But the rare visit north proved a boon (of sorts), for upon hearing the prodigal Lord Warrick had returned to the area, Ed stopped by on his way to London.

Only to find Warrick more disheveled than any self-respecting peer had a right to be—and morosely deep into his cups. Due certainly, to the rachitic ruin his estate had become, but even more so to the latest—and most unexpected—letter from his mother.

His friend set himself the task of sobering Warrick up with hearty food (that he brought) and copious, if not overly welcome, tea. Gallons of it, it seemed. Ed also set about a loquacious trattle informing Warrick of every little thing he might have missed since Christmas last.

He shared that his mama, now the "elder Lady Redford", delighted in her new status as dowager ever since Ed had married, his widowed mother relocating to the guest wing (to give the new couple more privacy), and often to Bath, where she visited a friend (that Ed suspicioned might be male).

The jolious Ed had spoken of everyone—his lovely wife, Anne; the outrageous Harri. He talked of his new parents-in-law; of Lord Ballenger's convivial, stalwart presence and how he—Ed—surmised that Lady Harri had inherited her loud and lively side from her zestful father (who had learned to mitigate it as warranted). He spoke of Ballenger's clamorous wife, who sometimes shrilled overly much at their youngest (he said this last in an aside, though no one else was around to hear).

But Ed uttered not a word about Lady Harriet's governess.

By now, the gin-induced euphoria—and escape—had

waned, such that Warrick was, regrettably, clearheaded enough to ponder... To yearn to inquire...

Should he? Ask? At the notion, his breath quickened, upper body leaned forward—

But nay.

He leaned back. Pinched his lips shut to prevent them from uttering a syllable of curiosity over Miss Primrose.

What had become of her?

The governess he was forbidden to see? To even think about.

Since when do your contrary thoughts cooperate?

That had been his bargain with Lord Ballenger, once the Great Hall had cleared and Lady Ballenger's piercing screaks had faded to grumbles: Warrick would take himself off, never to return, if Miss Primrose would suffer naught.

"Miss Primrose was in no way at fault," Frost had gritted from his tightly held mouth—aiming extra scowdering toward Warrick since Frostwood had returned from the stables just in time to see the mistletoe-induced mischief.

"Correct," Warrick had concurred, swift to stand with Frost (metaphorically speaking), as earnestly as he could manage given how his crazed lips were still buzzing at the all-too-brief contact with hers. "My inflated masculine honor was at stake, being prodded by the others. Blame *me*, the abundant mistletoe and revelrous males all tippled into ill-judgment, *not* Lady Harriet's governess." *I implore you.*

That last part went unsaid. No need to appear desperate. Or smitten.

"Never has Miss Primrose given any indication of loose behavior," Lord Ballenger mused, drumming his fingers over the waistcoat concealing his growing paunch. He stared down at Warrick, even though he seemed to be angling toward and addressing Frost, the only other male currently within hearing distance.

"Hmm. Hm." The man rocked back on his heels, released Warrick's gaze to glance toward the hallway where his wife had harried and hustled all the other ladies like kippers in a jar, then he turned toward the stairway where Miss Prim—oh, Warrick regretted how she must hate him—had flown.

"I see no reason to doubt her now." Lord Ballenger pinned him again, as though evaluating the truth and Warrick's sincerity. Made him feel smaller than he was already—thanks to his useless legs. "Especially if..."

"If we were to remove ourselves posthaste? Say... *tonight*?" he proposed quickly, because Lord Ballenger, miraculously it seemed, appeared to be leaning toward leniency. And perhaps the lack of Warrick's presence might mollify Lady Ballenger? "Not to return?" he threw out hastily, sober enough to recognize how his rash action might penalize her unduly.

"Aye," Frost chimed in, coming up behind him to curve his hands about Warrick's shoulders—tight enough to pinch, as though ready to push him *through* the closed door and right down the front steps. "We could be off in moments, would it...ah... Assist in calming Lady Ballenger's chagrin."

Their host *tsked*. "Regardless of any soothing actions we might take, Lady Ballenger's vexed feathers are likely to remain in a ruffled state." Lord Ballenger grunted, but mirth shone in his eyes. "Thanks to Harriet, a calm Lady Ballenger, my friends, is a rare occurrence indeed."

He sighed now, admitting defeat and letting the agreed-upon constraints go unchallenged. He would not ask after her. He would not inquire. He would attempt *not* to remember...

Miss Prim, how he wished his memory of her would dim.

Ed was the closest thing to a non-blood brother he had and he wouldn't risk damaging their relationship by pursuing his inane fascination. So he stretched his arms out to the sides, shook the tension loose. Unclamped his lips. Told his fiercely beating heart to slack, his breaths to even.

He swilled more tea. Enjoyed more stories.

And tried...to forget.

As the hour grew late, so dwindled their reticence to converse over more solemn matters.

Soon things turned more honest than comfortable.

What followed were stark confessions, honest admissions of pain and fears. Both of theirs.

Ed confided that his wife had recently lost a babe from her womb. How that had shaken both he and Anne, had made the time they spent with each other more precious.

Seeing the grief on his comrade's face, hearing it in his voice, a close mate who had suffered—both physically *and* emotionally—but who was not rolling around in his misery as Warrick had been wont to do these many months proved the kick to the arse he needed. *I hereby promise to honor your visit, your loss and sorrow,* Warrick vowed to himself while holding Ed's craggy yet wholesome face in view, *I vow to reduce my liquor indulgences from bottles per night to mere glasses.*

A single nod as though his earnest, silent pledge had been heard, accepted.

And before Warrick knew what he was about, he was

babbling aloud his deepest fear; the one he usually compressed into a box so small it fit in a thimble's dimple, never to see dawn's—or drunkard's—light...

"What female, of child-bearing age, with a father who possesses enough blunt to buy her a title would settle for mine?" He gestured first at his run-down surroundings, the sparse furnishings, pale squares on the walls where art had been sold, and then he pounded his lap with his fist. "Would settle for *this*? Would shackle herself to an invalid with *four* children yet to provide and care for, to see raised well into adultage, yet without any hope of her own?"

That wasn't entirely fair. Nor completely accurate.

As the parent, one might say the responsibility for his siblings fell upon his mama's slender shoulders. But nay. She had already done so much. Suffered so much...

He was the one resisting his mother's attempts to foster a relationship with his half-siblings, and *she* was the one who cared for them, all of them, now...

But Warrick knew his duty.

As the title holder, the *elder* sibling (no more of this "half" rimble-ramble), it fell to him to ensure the rest of his family flourished.

Then why are you not doing that, man? Why are you lolling about, either as a recluse or idling your time with soused shirkers?

"Warrick!"

Why are you thrashing your helpless groin?

Was he? Still?

He felt nothing.

Stared down at the blur of his clenched hands hitting his lap and couldn't feel a damn thing. So after shoving the vertical controls aside, he hit himself harder, bringing the full thrust of his arms and fists down on his useless prick. "How in blazes can I expect some wealthy, young female to tolerate this? This flaccid, unresponsive lump of flesh? She *wouldn't*. Of course she wouldn't. *No one* will…"

And then to his great bewilderment and shame, he broke.

Heaved tears like a baby. His shoulders quaked. Breath stuttered in ragged gasps. His wobbling, quivering lips became slick with salty tears as he finally released, not anger, not mocking irreverence, but the gut-wrenching truth that scared him more than facing Frogs on the battlefield: the soul-shriveling terror of facing the future *alone*.

"Rich! Stop that!" As Ed wrenched Warrick's hands away from their assault and scrambled past the metal rods to haul Warrick upright, to embrace him fully and hard, holding him up while pounding his back with comfort and shared grief, Warrick allowed the months of stifled and suppressed tears freedom. He cried at losing his father as a mere lad. He cried at the state of his coffers, thanks to the debts his father inherited before him, compounded by that swindling steward.

He cried for his defeated body.

For his half-siblings who had just lost their own father to a tragic accident. He cried for his mother, who had now buried two husbands.

He cried because he could. And because he hadn't.

And he cried because he knew he would never do so again.

1812 FROM ANOTHER DIRECTION

A BEACHED WHALE AND OTHER TALES

BALLENGER ESTATE, ENGLISH COUNTRYSIDE

As the promise of the new year came upon them, scant days after the house party—the kiss—that threatened to alter her very existence, Aphrodite Primrose knew three things with utter certainty:

1. She was fortunate that the Christmas Incident, which is how she thought of it, had not jeopardized her livelihood. To her surprise, both Lord Ballenger *and* Lord Redford came to her defense. Lord Ballenger the following morning and Lord Redford, upon learning of the contretemps (through chatty, related butlers or some such), who had returned to Larchmont Hall posthaste, claiming the entire—inappropriate—event lay firmly at Lord Warrick's door, and "most certainly *not* Miss Primrose's".

Emboldened by the unexpected support, Aphrodite nevertheless suspected it was more how she dealt with

Harriet—not to mention the child's threat of "dire mutiny" should they assign her yet another governess—that extended her employment. And if Aphrodite noticed Lady Ballenger eyeing her occasionally, with a slight pinch to her brow and sour pucker to her mouth? Well, 'twas likely no less than she deserved.

2. As the eventful year went on, Aphrodite became increasingly confident in herself and her comfortable position in such a pleasant household (discounting the occasional shrieks). Thus, she found her rigidly held wariness of men continued to mitigate. Along with a lessening of the constant tenseness with which she had become used to guarding her surroundings and safety, she slowly stopped trussing herself up so painfully tight every day. Had considered, though not yet acted upon, the notion of exchanging her heavy and uncomfortable garments—both inner and outer—for something less...restrictive... Mayhap even something slightly more becoming?

3. Though she valiantly tried to stifle her wayward thoughts, her mind—and other aspects—persisted on returning to a certain, totally indecorous, lord—*and his lips*. Blast him and his hold over her memories.

What she remained completely ignorant of was his fate, after their fateful encounter. She'd not seen him again. Had awoken to learn of his and Lord Frostwood's precipitous departure. Of a certainty, she could not inquire. Could *never* inquire.

For after being caught *in flagrante* upon his lap, any curiosity must forever remain unquenched.

Drat.

ALL THROUGHOUT FEBRUARY, Aphrodite remained exceedingly grateful she still had a generous position in a kind household. While she still bound her breasts, to minimize their unseemly size, she did so with a little less vigor. Laced her stays with a little more care. Could breathe easier as a result of both.

———◦◦———

IN MARCH, her charge proved once again that while lines may work in helping curb Lady Harriet's wayward behavior, they certainly did not stop it altogether.

Take Note—The Beached Whale Incident:

Aphrodite stood outside Lady Ballenger's personal morning room (cluttered with a plethora of valued ephemera handed down from her mother and grandmother and the like), waiting until her charge was dismissed.

Though she could not, at this moment, *see* anything beyond the beach idyll framed on the wall opposite the door, she could hear every word…

Lady Ballenger huffed before she ranted anew. "Wilson *might* be losing his hair as he ages"—this sufficiently loud that now every individual within the manor walls knew about poor Wilson's departing hair—"but one does *not* offer up in company that their family butler's balding pate looks much like the underside of a *piglet*."

"'Tis the truth, Mama. 'Twas not meant to hurt. I *like* piglets when they are small and adora—"

"*Harriet Jane!*" Ah. There it was. For the fourth time this particular session: The Screech. "Nor does one state their father's *gaping* belly resembles that of a *beached whale!*"

Aphrodite bit back a snicker. One of several since the utterance in question.

Lord Ballenger, not feeling all the thing, had lazed about in the gardens one pleasant afternoon, with tea and a volume on hunting. He'd had the misfortune to fall asleep whereupon his loosened clothing had gaped—er, edged—open to reveal the…um…pale, rounded belly now being compared to that possessed by its much larger mammalian brethren.

"But—"

"Nothing!" Screak number two. "But *nothing*! How would you like it if Lady Fairfax or one of her impeccable-mannered daughters remarked how *my youngest* has the manners of a rantipolish chuff and the tact of an *axe*? For that is what you do when you spout hurtful things without any consideration for anything other than hearing yourself speak!"

That ironic observation brought about another chuckle, barely suppressed.

"Mama, I do not mean to be vile or hurtful. Can I help it if words just venture forth quite before I know they are on their way?"

Dear Harri. The piglet and whale comments had resulted in two missed dinners and lines—assigned by her mother this time.

Eight hundred each:

I will not demean the servants by comparing them to farm animals.

and

Father is deserving of my respect and admiration, and I shall not compare ~~his belly~~ any part of his body to aquatic, airborne or beached creatures.

Seated at her desk, Harriet looked over her shoulder. "Does that mean I *can* disparage Papa's belly with terr... Mmmm, terrer..."

With a sigh, Aphrodite stopped organizing the newest acquisition of books and learning materials and approached. She checked the watch dangling off the chain at her waist. *Mmm.* Harri had managed to remain mum for ninety seconds this time.

Leaning over to inspect the first few lines, Aphrodite grimaced. (Eleven of eight hundred? At this rate, they would be here all month). "We have barely begun and already you seek to delay and disassemble?"

Bright hazel, always mischievous, eyes slid over to hers as Harri grinned, mouth closed *for once*.

Aphrodite tapped the page. "Continue—and no, you may not compare your father, or any part of his anatomy, to ter*restrial* animals either."

"Pity." Harriet re-inked her quill. "Have you not noticed how his smile is similar to Jollyboy's?"

"Harriet! Shame. Your father in no way resembles his favorite hound." But then she considered the canine's slightly off-tilted "grin", with just the tip of his tongue hanging out. "All right. I concur. *When* Lord Ballenger is tickled. But never shall either of us speak or think of this again!"

Harriet turned back to her punishment and started humming a gay tune as her pen skipped across the page.

"And, dear," Aphrodite said with her own self-satisfied smile and mischievous twinkle, "do not start feeling overly complacent, for when your lines are complete, you will be composing seven-hundred-word apologies to both your father and to Wilson."

"Primmy!"

Several splotches of black ink marred the page after that.

IN JUNE, Lady Harriet had the pleasure of meeting her new music tutor. A pleasant gentleman, only a year or two older than Aphrodite.

While her charge embraced these new lessons with enthusiasm, Aphrodite feared the girl might never be inclined toward musical giftedness, as her mother fervently hoped. ("Something pleasingly temperate to counter your monstrous mouth," Lady Ballenger had told her youngest.)

Mr. Matthew Phillips, whose musical gifts seemed boundless, proved both amiable and appealing in a fresh, unspoilt way and—to Aphrodite's surprise—took a fancy to her. While the lean, sandy-haired gentleman remained in the area, instructing several of the nearby lords' progeny (along with ongoing attempts to unearth a modicum of proficiency from the Larchmonts' youngest), he continued to make his interest known.

So that by August, she agreed to step out in the gardens with him more than once—always remaining in sight of the house, aware of how vital maintaining propriety was (both for herself and ongoing employment, and as an example to her charge). Twice, they walked to the village, chaperoning Lady Harriet and one of her friends—and managed to brush hands, intentionally. Three times, they picnicked on the lawn, while Harriet gamboled about with any four-hooved, -pawed, -clawed—

or any beaked—creature to be found. (Harriet, who shocked Aphrodite into the next shire upon proclaiming after one such excursion, "Oh, *this* small tear? Do not fret overmuch about that. I can repair it myself.")

By the beginning of September Aphrodite decided to abandon her chest bindings and horribly heavy gowns altogether in favor of a new, appropriately fitted corset and medium-weight day dresses. ("Oh, my. Primmy! Who knew you could look like something *other* than stuffed-and-burnt duck? But must you still wear *brown*? 'Tis quite tedious, I will have you know.")

By the middle of October, Aphrodite and Mr. Phillips kissed. Four separate times.

Before the end of October, she wondered...

What *if*...?

Yet as November marched on, inexplicably toward the first anniversary of the season where so much—inside her —had changed, she could not help but pine for what might have been—with Mr. Phillips.

Why did she not hold more affection toward him?

You do. You like him.

She did, true.

You look forward to spending time with him. Until he touches you.

And there it was.

Affection and desire were two very, very different things she was discovering.

Liking and lust. Mayhap they did not always go together, even when one found the exterior pleasing and the interior kind.

But the tall, slender musician with the quick smile and clever manner did not cause her heart to race or her breath to quicken. The idea of exchanging kisses (which they had) or *more than* kisses (which they definitely had not) caused not a thrill in her breast, but instead...a chill to her chest.

For despite everything that was sensible and sane, 'twas not the musician's fair face and courteous demeanor she thought of at night.

By all that was holy and horrid, 'twas the face of a devil, with, at turns, soulful and laughing eyes or cutting, tortured ones that proved her last awareness each night. 'Twas the deep and mocking rumble of playful—and lewd —remarks that danced through her dreams... ("Sit on my lap... Without *clothes*, Miss Primrose.") 'Twas a strong yet weakened, ill-suited but suitably tempting, positively outrageous lord whose fading memory still managed to keep her warm at night that prevented Aphrodite from being able to contemplate more with the affable musician.

Bless that flirty fiend's hide to France and back.

Nay!

Not back to France—or Spain or Portugal or any of a dozen or more unsafe places where life might deal him any more blows.

She wasn't sure his ragged spirit could take any further strikes. For certain, his battered body could not.

By December, she knew. With utter certainty and disheartening conviction, Aphrodite knew.

"No matter how much I admire you," she told Mr. Phillips, after he asked what she had both anticipated and dreaded—for her to consider resigning her post and accompanying him when he left, "and I do, it is with true regret that I confess I do not see any manner of future together."

He gained his feet with grace, leaving the blanket

where they, along with Harriet and her friend, had enjoyed a lengthy walk and picnic on this surprisingly warm day. The girls frolicked in sight, but far enough away they could not overhear, playing with a stray puppy that had sniffed out their meal of lamb and cheese and invited itself over.

Mr. Phillips stepped back, clasped his hands behind his waist and gave her a gracious nod and an even more polite smile—but she saw the hurt in his eyes. "Alas... It is my loss," he began slowly and she felt core rotten for spoiling the afternoon. "If I were given over to carping, I could say I *hope* it is your regret, but—"

"But we both know you are not *that* sort of fellow. The one to wish harm upon another."

"No, I am not." His jaw tightened and flexed as he glanced toward the girls before meeting her gaze again. "Though I *will* miss you, I confess I will *not* miss hearing Lady Harriet destruct music with so little effort."

A sharp breeze swept between them, as though ready to usher him on his way. "I do wish you happiness," she told him, surprised at the heaviness weighing her heart. She'd not expected her distress over saying goodbye. "I thank you for enlivening my summer and fall." And in a blink, every moment they had spent together, his consideration, his kindnesses, the intelligent conversations and shared laughs swirled about her as well. "Oh, Matthew, I *am* sorry. If—if I *could*—"

"You think I cannot tell?" He stepped closer, lowered his voice. And suddenly the look in his usually carefree eyes seemed both older and...desolate? Had he really cared for her that much? "I know you do not feel for me as a potential lover, as a potential wife should, even though I can envision it quite plainly. I knew I would berate myself if I did not inquire. It will be *my* regret, that I do not possess whatever you need to make your heart *want* to be mine, but that is the way of things, is it not? We chance across many people during our lifetimes, a few become special. A rare few, even special more." The more he spoke, with civility and wisdom, the worse she felt. "But those we can see ourselves spending our lives with—joining our lives with? Those are even fewer still."

THE FOLLOWING MORNING, the talented Mr. Matthew Phillips collected his fee and prepared to take his leave once and for all, proclaiming his efforts with Lord and Lady Ballenger's youngest had quite reached a standstill that even his lauded abilities could not overcome.

Mr. Phillips would be taking a stage to his next post, leaving Harriet nowhere near where her mother had aspired on the pianoforte or with anything else. He had, at least, managed to teach Harri how to read music and how to properly hold and handle several various instruments, but she never managed to coax *anything* halfway pleasing from a one of them. Aphrodite's ears, of a certainty, were relieved to bid him *adieu*; perhaps now Harriet's pianoforte pounding, harpsichord flaying and woodwind screeching would come to a blessed halt.

Yet Mr. Phillips's absence would be leaving the rest of her lingeringly sad…

For she *had* attempted to have warmer feelings toward him, had been flattered by his notice and grown more confident in herself as a result. But after the first kiss, she had questioned; after the third, suspected; and after the fourth had realized convincedly she could participate no more, for they left her unsmitten.

Unsmitten and—insanely—yearning for another pair of lips. Another sort of kiss.

14

KINGS, KNIGHTS AND OTHER SIBLINGS

December 1812

Warrick Estate, English Countryside

"Bertram! Climb down ere you fall and break your back." The Lord and Lord Warrick knew that way lay misery.

Warrick watched his fourteen-year-old half-brother (one of a matched pair) scale an old ladder straight up the wall to the highest painting that had hung in the same spot since as long as he could remember.

'Twas a marvel it hadn't been sold off yet—probably because no one wanted to climb up and retrieve the monstrosity. "I mean it. Bertram—"

"Told you to call me *King*!"

A racket overhead showed another ladder and another brother (the other half of the set) balancing precariously on a stool propped on a chair placed on top of a table— God save them all—as the boy fought with the chandelier.

"Beaufort, you too," Warrick practically growled, feeling as inept as ever, unable to launch from his seated prison and retrieve the obstinate boys himself. "Get down from there!"

"I'm not *Beaufort* any longer." The glum, amber-green eyes he'd grown used to seeing the last few hours spared a moment to gleam down at him. The boys very well might tumble to their demise, but at least they were smiling. For now. "I'm *Knight*. Did you forget—again?"

A hard exhale—because neither boy listened a lick, Bertram draping a thick evergreen swag over the neglected painting and Beaufort straining the chair-stool-table muddle, grasping for the chain so he could tie on a pathetically large conglomeration of mistletoe. Both things the boys had gone out hunting for earlier.

"I want to be Queen." Sophia hauled on his shirt sleeve, tugging his attention from the overhead tomfoolery to his second-youngest sibling. The frowning one who had whined of being famished thrice in the last quarter hour. "Can I be Queen? *Queens* have chefs and servants aplenty. I wager *they* do not wilt from hunger and maltreatment."

Maltreatment? He grunted, shoved his knees together. At least the girls were getting a decent education.

Little Julia had reverted to sucking on her thumb, tears rimming her eyes. She was the only quiet one of the bunch. The baby of the family had tucked herself beneath a blanket on the chaise several feet from where he sat in his trusty invalid's conveyance splat in the middle of the room, attempting to gain some semblance of control and failing spectacularly.

How did his mother deal with this day in and day out? Oh wait, she didn't. The twins—Beaufort and Bertram, currently known as King and Knight (or was it Knight and

King?)—spent the majority of their time off at school, when they weren't home for holiday, that was.

The girls? Six-year-old Julia and nine-year-old Sophia? They usually had their governess, one his mother had ~~foolishly~~ generously given her own extended winter holiday (too kind by half, his soft-hearted mama), and a number of servants running around who could assist—but why she'd left the bulk of them at her home three hours away in Thropmoor, he hadn't thought to ask. And with the already stretched staff at Warrick Manor dwindling every month?

Well, things were as bleak as they looked. As bleak as they felt. The tightness in his clenched jaw should have chipped a tooth or two.

"Can I?" Sophia prompted with another yank. First to his sleeve, then another on the hem of his trouse, sharp enough she dislodged one foot off the wooden beam affixed to his chair. He glanced down, almost surprised his seams had held thus far.

As Warrick bent to lift his lower leg, bringing his foot back onto the slat, one of the twins corrected, "*May* I, poppet."

Bringing to mind another *Can I-May I* conversation that prompted a smile—and then a wince, as he recalled how Ed's house party culminated in mistletoe and Warrick's own impudent actions making a spectacle of both himself and the beguiling governess. Twelve long months and he still knew naught.

Was Miss Prim still residing at the Larchmont home? Had she, perhaps, contrary to what he hoped and assumed, been ousted from her position by the complaintive Lady Ballenger? Or did she persevere, mayhap, in teaching the young Harri manners becoming a daughter of her station?

Dare he selfishly hope the opposite? That she had been ejected?

Might Miss Prim have need of a new post?

He could not help but ponder as he watched the sullen, hungry child yanking hard enough on his trousers 'twas a wonderment they hadn't slipped free of his hindquarters and fallen to the floor. As he listened to the two boys on the cusp of manhood arguing over where to place the ugliest, most uneven wreath he had ever beheld, once each had completed their current, singular efforts.

The other child, the wee one, still on the chaise alone. Eyelids fluttering, tears still leaking. Reddened cheeks hollowed as she practically made a meal of her thumb.

Alone. Apart. His growing kinship and affection for little Julia caught him unawares. Made more than his clenched jaw ache.

Turmoiled his heart. Pertroubled his entire chest.

Damn, but he needed a governess. And not just for his sisters.

"Warry? Can I? Be Queen?"

Warry? Might as well be *Worry*.

W-O-R-R-Y. What he was trying with valiant effort *not* to do.

With their mother off for part of the holiday, the boys had declared they would bring Christmas to the "bleak" manner, to surprise her upon her return.

Warrick? He had been agazed with the duty tasked to him upon obeying his mother's summons, the one couched so very sweetly in a deceptively congenial letter, coaxing (and compelling) him back home, to his misbegotten estate. Telling him how his siblings wanted to get to know him, had so many wondrous things to share—both things he doubted. And how she needed to discuss some financial matters with him—one thing he did not.

Just twanging. How he anticipated that conversation.

Did the cottage in Thropmoor need thatched? Had the boys' tuition increased? Whatever it was, he should be there for her. He'd been an abysmal son of late.

Guilt. Guilt is what brought him back home so quickly after his brief visit in October. After collapsing in Ed's arms that night, he couldn't face the stripped-down walls and neglected, empty air of the cold, unwelcoming manor. The unpalatable idea of staying had chilled his already frozen soul and had him departing directly after Ed announced his intention of forgoing his planned trip to London and returning posthaste to his wife.

But now? With Mama gone naught but a day, leaving that very morning after breaking her fast, he was ready to carve his hair out by the roots and crack open a bottle with his teeth.

The boys had already scaled the balustrade. Slid down to more *whoops* and blasted hollers than a man of his, ahem, mature years was used to hearing at home—or anywhere else. After they plucked the grounds and returned, arms laden and dragging a limping, overflowing cart behind them, they disappeared again.

Only to haul in old ladders—found where? The attic? The stable?—that would take them up to the ceilings of every room on the first floor. Had practically dangled off the faded curtains doing what they claimed Mama did *every* year back home.

Where the girls and Mama lived year-round now; where the boys had grown up and came every holiday away from school: the modest two-story cottage Sir William Feldon had offered Warrick's mother, along with his fervent avowals of love, after Warrick's father had died.

"Warry?" A hard pull on his sleeve brought his attention back to the little ones and the surrounding disorder. "Answer me!"

He'd invited the use of Richard. The boys still called him Warrick. Little Julia? Nothing at all. This fractious sprite? Warry, worry.

"Why not?" He forced his jaw to loosen and grinned. "*Queen* you shall be until Mama returns. Boys, *down*. Heed me this time. The last thing any of us need is you cracking your heads open." Suspecting they were only going to disregard his wishes yet again, he turned his chair around and found Julia watching everything. He offered the youngest a soft smile. "And what would you like to be called?"

Julia just stared at him, those big, dark blue eyes, swimming in tears. Looking at her now reminded him of what he saw in the mirror on the rare occasions he chanced to look anymore. Not the tears, so much as the color they'd both gotten from Mama...and what brimmed from them: so much sorrow and melancholy churned together.

A good, rousing cry sounded just the thing. For both of them. She didn't know him. She thought his mother—nay, she thought their—*her*—mother had abandoned them just like *her* father, who had died unexpectedly a few weeks ago after his horse tangled with a carriage.

And he—Warrick? Gone the past decade or more, he had never taken time to form bonds with the girls. The boys? At fourteen, they at least knew him, from before he'd joined the dragoons.

The soft, rhythmic thumb-sucking seemed to soothe the child, and he hadn't the heart to chastise her. Sweet, solemn Julia, with the prettiest light hair, still baby fine. Sophia, darker like him, the heavy black hair and brows not doing the girl any favors at the moment.

And the twins? Somewhere in between, varying shades of chestnut hair, depending upon whether they were studying or skipping out on classes to spend the day sunning around a fishing lake. He knew their competitive spirit already had one planning for Cambridge, the other for Oxford. Thankfully, their father had provided for them, so at least Warrick need not worry that direction.

"Seems we have a king and a queen," he told Julia, still seeking a response, "a knight—"

"*Ewww!*" squealed Bertram. Finally giving up on making the spruce-and-holly-berry bough even on both sides, he started to descend the rickety ladder. "King *and* Queen? She's our sister! *Blegh*."

Instead of rolling his eyes, Warrick used the controls to spin and roll his chair until he faced Bertram. Just when he got into place, the boy jumped the remaining four feet to the ground, bypassing one of the missing slats.

The hard landing made Warrick wince, but his brother popped up as though it were naught. "You are *all* from different countries," he told the lad; if they were going to pretend, might as well do it up big. "There is no need to balk at Sophia being *Queen*. Now, Julia, what would—"

"I'm still hungry." The soft whine came from near his knee, the urchin newly dubbed Queen plopped on the floor, barefoot, heedless of the winter temperatures only because he'd had the fire maintained in this one room during daylight hours.

"I have no sympathy for you," he told Sophia. "You chose to pluck at your food and not take a single bite. That is on you. Not me."

"But it *would* have been on you," Beaufort trilled overhead, pulling Warrick's concentration back to the atrocious hunk of white berries and thick, sage-colored leaves his brother still wrestled with, "had she eaten more than a bite. She cannot stomach fish and who knows what else. Cascades all over the place if she's forced to eat it."

He glanced down at Sophia and then over at Julia.

Julia. Silent, crying Julia. Who only nodded. *Aye*, the child seemed to say, *sister vomits*.

Twanging again.

What was he supposed to feed them? And why in blazes had Cook served that? Had his mother not informed his cook before she left? Was Mother trying to force some sort of test upon him?

"I told you to get down," he ordered Beaufort in an impressively mild tone. "At least until Jims returns and can assist." One of three remaining male servants—the one who worked where ever needed—while one of the others concentrated inside the manor and the other focused more on the grounds and remaining two horses. This last one had accompanied Warrick's mother and her maid on her jaunt to visit her oldest and dearest friend (since he no longer had an official coachman in his employ). Two servants in town. Three men and two females here at an estate that should have been staffed by fifty—at a minimum. A ragged sigh dragged through his chest.

"In a minute," Beaufort said, "and my feet are sound, never you worry," which sounded way too much like *wallow*. "We shall be finished in a trice! King—catch!"

A pair of scissors sailed overhead. Bertram ducked and they clattered against the wall.

Warrick's heart skipped several beats. How very awry that could have just gone. He squeezed his eyes shut for two long breaths. If they weren't going to be the death of him, they would be the death of each other. A stern reprimand—if not outright discipline—was in order the moment he had the boys alone.

If he unleashed his frustration and fury at that

dangerous act in front of the girls, he feared Julia might trip over her blanket in her haste to run and hide. Silently, where he couldn't find her, while she starved. Also silently.

Why again had his mother not brought the girls' governess?

Ah, but *he* knew an excellent governess. One who even taught Latin.

Do not ponder going there. Not in your mind—or in your carriage.

A huffed whinge brought Warrick's thoughts full circle, away from last Christmas and back to this one.

To the persistent, not-quite-petulant sibling near his knee with a fascination with dismantling his attire. "Halt that, now," he told her, twisting his arm to free his sleeve from her grip. "I am considering. Give me a moment."

Now—tasked with seeing all the mischief-makers safe (failing on that one), contented (failing with Julia) and fed (failed—Sophia) and determined to do better, he speared Sophia with his most serious look, brows flattened, jaw grim. "Will you bring me the calendar?" She didn't budge. Didn't blink. Amazing, nothing ruffled this one. "It's in the study. Either on the desk or in the top drawer."

She got to her feet, wiggled those tiny, bare toes but didn't move an inch beyond. "Will you feed me?"

"Are you going to bring me the calendar?"

"Why do you want it?"

To count the hours until Mama returns to manage your brothers, comfort your silent sister, and feed your little contrary arse.

"Sophia." Did he try for a fatherly tone? Or a commanding, elder-brother one? At a loss, he exhaled and strove for serene (though had doubts as to his success). "Would you, please, retrieve the calendar from the study? And bring it here?"

Her amber eyes narrowed at him. "Are you going to feed me?"

By Jove, the defiant imp had taken after him.

He remembered just such conversations with his father when he was younger than she, always willing to assist with any task—*if* he could gain something for himself.

He laughed.

Laughed hard enough he had to grip his chair lest he slide out and topple groundward.

Laughed with abandon and surprised not only himself but everyone else, as all four pairs of eyes in the room swiftly turned to him. Julia only wiped a couple tears from beneath one and rubbed her nose. Sophia glared at him, but he saw the start of a smile.

Knight and King looking so startled by the unfamiliar sound, it prompted another laugh.

Aye, it would take some effort, but befriending these four would be worth it.

Thank you, Mama.

15

FOUR MONTHS LATER...

...HIS WORLD TOPSY-TURVIED YET AGAIN.

WARRICK SAT INSIDE THE LUSH CARRIAGE that smelled of lavender and grief, body tensed, heart sickened, mind as numb as his nose. A biting breeze slapped his cheeks as he stared out the open window of Redford's expensive equipage with glazed eyes at the newly carved headstone addition in the family plot off a tree-lined, overgrown section on the Warrick estate:

Here lies Richard Joseph Martinson of Warrick
who departed this life the 28th day of September 1791
Aged 32

Also his Beloved wife Elizabeth Martinson Feldon
who died the 9th of April 1813
Aged 48

Forty-eight. Too damn young.

His teeth cut into his lips, so tightly did he bite down to stop their trembling.

He scrubbed at his eyes so he could read the rest.

*Cherished wife of Sir William Feldon of Portsmouth
and buried therein
Delighted mother to Richard, Beaufort, Bertram,
Sophia and Julia
"I love thee all with love everlasting."*

He'd argued with Beaufort over that last line of names—said it was ridiculous to carve so much, that the stone would be bursting to house them all, but his brother was adamant. Upheld that Mother told him her wishes once, and that as the eldest Feldon—if even by twelve minutes—he had been entrusted to see them carried out since her true eldest—Warrick's carcass—wasn't around. And by then, Beaufort and his brother had ceased being Knight and King; had practically stopped being children at all.

"Did she know?" Without moving his head, Warrick braved asking the only other occupant in the carriage, Ed's mother, the Dowager Viscountess Redford. "Did she know she was sick?"

"She…did. Confided to me last year, that she suspected something might be amiss when you boys first arrived in London." *Boys.* As though he and Ed, both possessing upward of thirty years, were still in leading strings. "She was determined you wouldn't know, not until the very end. Not with your own struggles."

His…struggles, to use her word. Adapting to non-military life in England, after years in the army.

Adapting to life *without legs*.

Grief had been hard on his mother, aging her a dozen

years in the last handful of months since her spouse's riding accident and burial.

Much became clear: her nagging insistence for Warrick's presence; her determination he would foster relationships with each of his siblings. Why she'd taken three brief trips recently, ordering his grumbling arse to the estate each time, though she and the children lived elsewhere...

She had been saying goodbye to friends. Keeping him close to his siblings—keeping them close to him—whether any of them were aware of it or not.

It explained why she'd looked so vastly wearied these last weeks—not just worry over him, and mourning her husband as he'd presumed. Nay, his mother had been *dying* and he had been too blind, too wrapped up in his own bloody problems to notice.

He swore. Didn't have it in him to apologize for the foul language dirtying the air between him and the one person approximating parental caring and wisdom who remained in his life.

"Rich, you see now why she remained such a staunch advocate of Mr. Arbuckle, do you not?" The elder Lady Redford's serene tones filled the carriage. Over the last week, all formality between them had vanished; he was no longer *Lord Warrick* to her but Rich, just as his mother had called him. "She was determined you grant him a true chance to see what he might be able to do for you." Her gloved hand met his shoulder and squeezed. "For your family."

And that was the crux of it.

What *mattered*: his family. The family that he was now the sole support for. Given how none of their parents had siblings who lived past infancy, he was the lone, "mature" adult shepherding four innocent souls.

His family. The sum total of his remaining blood relatives here on earth: two brothers and two sisters.

And he was responsible for them all?

What a disaster.

Dizziness assailed him. As though everything must be resolved that instant, the swirling plethora threatened to batter about his brain until he dealt with every myriad decision to be made.

What of the cozy two-story cottage in Thropmoor where the children had lived their entire lives, up until these last days? What of his dilapidated estate? Both of them drowning in debt, he'd been dismayed to learn, having previously been under the erroneous impression that the children's father had modest but sufficient monies set aside to fund their educations and dowries. Monies that he'd just learned did not exist, thanks to a numbing solicitor's letter found amongst his mother's personals.

His mind spun till he was addled. Gut churned till nausea paraded about like an old friend. What in God's name was he going to do with two sisters, each far too young to suffer the loss of *both* parents? Far too young to ship off to a women's improving academy, not after these great losses. Definitely too young for *him* to care for.

What did he know of little girls? He and his—before Albuera—rollicking ways?

Do you not mean you and your rolling ways?

His hands started to shake.

And what of Bertram and Beau? Two brothers, old enough to realize what challenges they faced but young enough to expect Warrick, as the eldest, to know how best to deal with them.

It was up to him. Everything.

All-encompassing accountability for every aspect of their lives. The vastness of it smothered all that nausea into a tangled knot that swelled in his throat. Threatened to choke off his air as the water rushed over his—always seated—head.

So easily could he drown under the crashing waves.

But nay. He knew how to swim.

He looked down and unclenched the white-knuckled, still quivering, hands in his lap. Were his arms not stronger than ever before? Could he not find a way to use his strengths to his advantage?

Going to roll yourself down to Cornwall, take a go unloading pirate ships with those strong arms of yours?

Again, he let the nagging doubts go unheeded.

Richard Andrew Martinson, eighth Earl of Warrick, sixth Viscount Tawton, who felt ill-prepared and ill-equipped now had to take his beggared title and debt-riddled estate and find a way to provide a home *and* a future for the only remaining family he could claim.

One day, he promised himself—

Then stopped. Clapped his palms together, steadied them and his raw nerves, both.

Swallowed that hard knot and said it out loud. *Proclaimed* it. "One day, I vow, I will step foot out of this carriage and *walk* over to that stone myself. One day, I will pray over it, for her"—*for my father*—"and the rest of us."

But not today. Today, he had to suffer—

Nay, not suffer.

He sat up straighter, lifted his shoulders, tensed his brawny arms—the ones that had gained such strength since Spain. Today, instead of suffering anything, he would *brave* it all. Brave the humiliation of being lifted out of the carriage and placed upon his chair. Brave the embarrassment of being carried about whenever stairs were involved. Brave meeting with townspeople and merchants his estate owed money to. Brave facing neglected tenants that had worked his land for years, and the past twenty or so without any in-person appreciation, or *any* appreciation at all, for that matter. How many of them were even still around?

Since her decline and swift death, no longer able to hide behind his mother or his idling ways, he'd learned the soul-crushing extent of how very much Father's old steward had stripped what little remained of the coffers and the dignity the Warrick title previously claimed. He'd known it was bad. But had assumed when he was ready, he could apply himself and make *something* of what was left.

But when the only thing left was dust and mouse dung? Easy to imagine dunking one's head in a latrine and never coming back up.

But no more.

No more wallowing. No more excuses.

Instead of acknowledging mortification over his weakness, he would begin by being grateful that he was still surrounded by people willing to cart his sorry hide about. He would be grateful that he had a home to go to, a beautiful one at that (if one discounted the worn and barren aspect cloaking every room).

Most of all, he thought with a strange pang hitting his heart and thickening his throat anew, he would be especially grateful that when he and the elder Lady Redford arrived home, he had four siblings to embrace and comfort through the grief they all shared.

Well, three, depending upon whether Julia was hiding or not, still very much withdrawn and wary. Worse now than before, understandably so. Barely had she begun to thaw, to grace him with a word or prized grin when her mother disappeared into the ground. Leaving the distraught sprite a silent shell of a child.

But after he exchanged words with his brothers and sister Sophia—and a hard candy for a prayed-for half-smile from Julia—his first order of business? Time to pen and post a pleasing, *pleading* letter to the ornery, cantankerous yet supposedly skilled Mr. Arbuckle.

A slight touch across the back of his hand startled him. "Rich. I can..." Lady Redford breathed deep, the ragged sound loud in the quiet carriage. She removed her hand, swept one bent finger beneath her eyes, drying her own grief. "If you would like, I could share the list of appropriate ladies, the one your mother—"

"Nay! Please, not yet." He could not stomach the thought of staring at a piece of paper in his mother's hand listing names of pitiful females that might be constrained to life with him—a life of serving him and his useless legs, wanting for things he could never provide; children, not the least of which.

If he could not discern the proper way forth from here, a way to save either home—not to mention himself—then he had no business seeking a wife. None whatsoever. Better to let the title die with him than to sentence an innocent to death by dearth of love. And with four precious souls to care for, he no longer had a dram of love to spare.

"We will revisit this in a few months," he told her, postponing any argument. "I will not shirk my duties any longer; not those to family nor to land. But neither am I ready to pursue shackling myself to someone—or them to me. Not quite yet. I need to heal my fractured family before introducing another into our lives."

What he needed to do was find a way to make Julia feel safe enough she would start talking again.

"When you are ready and whatever you may need, I am always here for you." Her fingers returned to his, granting a brief "hug". The quiet yet unwavering strength in her presence was a balm to every jagged edge cutting his insides. "Ward, Anne, all of us, Rich—we are willing—

"Nay, we remain *compelled* to help you and yours *any* way we can." Her hand slid away and she retreated to the opposite side of the carriage, settling back against the squabs and giving him a few more private moments to mourn. To accept.

As they sat there, hearing the occasional, hardy bird chirp, feeling the slight lurch to the carriage whenever an impatient horse stomped... As the sheen blurring his sight grew thicker and the sting from the breeze sharper, she waited until he re-fastened the window and knocked on the carriage above his head, indicating to the coachman that they were ready to depart.

Neither spoke as they *clip-clopped* toward the others, who had gone ahead to the meal waiting—thanks to generous townspeople and, no doubt, the younger Lady Redford's efforts—at home.

Home. Would the cold, desolate rooms of the Warrick estate house ever, *ever* feel like home again?

"I may not spend much time in London," she said quietly as they approached the front drive, "but I still have my lovely cronies from my early Seasons; ladies I remain quite close to and communicate with regularly."

Ladies. Mature ones, no doubt, with knowledge of rich, desperate Diamonds or mushrooms' daughters—with equally desperate papas—ready to say vows and become his countess.

"Whenever you are ready, my boy, I remain ready to assist. Whenever *you* are ready."

The knot turned into a rock. He made a strangled grunt.

Acceptance could only take him so far.

LETTERS TO DAZZLE, DAZE AND DISAPPOINT (PART 1)

———◦———

W‍ARRICK E‍STATE, E‍NGLISH C‍OUNTRYSIDE

M‍ISERY HAD NO SCHEDULE, it seemed.

Two months later, Warrick's being still ached with loss. With love, with remembrances of his gone-too-soon mama. His body still sat—when he wasn't sweating under The Tyrant's orders—broken.

Little did they know it, but his brothers (now back to Knight and King, at Warrick's prompting) savored their last few weeks at school. The third term expired shortly and tuition funds had become extinct; telling them they would not be returning in September when first term began was not a conversation he relished. One reason he'd encouraged them in their make-believe—fanciful imaginings in the here and now to soften the blows that were to come.

His own fanciful imaginings, to think that anything

would mitigate the death of their dreams of Oxford and Cambridge...

He'd thought to relocate with the girls to the Feldon cottage. Less staff needed there. Less money to heat... But nay, for after the burial, both Sophia and the twins had insisted Mama had told them all her desire for them to remain with "Richard" at his estate.

It was the *Richard* that had done it. Had convinced him the children spoke his mother's wishes true.

Sophia still thwarted him at every turn, but kept him —mentally, at least—nimble, anticipating both her protests and her persistent bargaining, something he appreciated, looked forward to even. Not that he would share that with her—his joy gleaned from their verbal sparring. Didn't need to give the rebellious lass any more ammunition in her already wickedly mature arsenal.

But as to Julia? Sweet, silent Julia?

Some days he thought 'twas she who made his heart ache most of all.

Progress, of a sort, had come from an unexpected quarter, when, just last week, she had silently slipped around his wheeled conveyance and climbed into his lap. His lap! Her curled fists clenched around a dirty blanket—one she refused to relinquish for a washing. Lips clutched around her thumb, she had scaled his unfeeling legs and pressed against his chest, allowed his arms to encircle her delicate form, and she had sighed. Sighed loud enough to reach through the astonishment holding him in thrall and hard enough to ruffle the open neck of his shirt.

Cradled against his chest, it took her but moments to fall into a heavy sleep. Her sucking motion slowed, stopped. Mouth went lax and damp thumb slid free...

With the unexpected action of her complete and utter trust, her confidence in his broken self to keep her safe, with the single event of her wondrous, innocent little body warm and solid against his own, she had wound herself so deep inside his heart, he knew he was forever slain.

"Precious girl," he murmured, blinking the sudden moisture from his eyes. He kept his embrace about her shoulders and back intentionally loose, couldn't frighten her with his relief, his dismay.

He may not yet have earned her words, but somehow, his patience and gentle coaxing had earned a modicum of her trust.

For now, that would do.

Warrick Estate, June 17, 1813

Miss Primrose,

Selfishly, I pray this letter finds you, and not completely satisfied in your current position.

Unselfishly, I pray with all sincerity this letter finds you still gainfully employed at the home of Lord and Lady Ballenger.

Though I have no doubt Lady Harriet would still benefit from your care, I have now found myself in possession of a pair of "daughters" (half-siblings really, but given our age disparity, and the emotions they both engender within me, well, I cannot imagine worrying over or loving them any more were they my own in truth).

Without cavilling about, let me state my earnest request:

Should you in any way be amenable to coming to either Thropmoor, and the Feldon cottage there, or to the Warrick estate, not horribly distant from where Lord and Lady Redford reside, as a governess in my employ?

Upon learning of some deplorable tactics recently used in the chastisement of young Julia, I relieved their most recent governess of her duties with haste and now seek a much more competent and caring replacement.

Have you any willingness to consider my request, please know I will move heaven and the moon to make it a reality by acceding to whatever stipulations you may have.

Yours,
Warrick

She need not know this was the third governess he'd dismissed. Well, the *first*—the one that the girls knew and who had been with them in Thropmoor, had quit of her own accord, affronted at the very thought of "spending a single night under the roof of a known reprobate."

Ha. Seemed his rollers for feet did nothing to improve his reputation in her eyes once his mother's shielding presence was gone.

Although, he surmised her real reluctance to continue on might have more to do with rumors of his light purse than fear of him lifting her skirts.

He'd cared naught. Only sought to find a suitable replacement.

Yet, their second governess since the April burial that had changed so much? The immediately available one he had found upon scrambling to do so, the daughter of a local merchant. And though she claimed proficiency in teaching incomparable embroidery and impeccable manners, he found her more interested in surveying the silver and relieving the estate of whatever valuables she could easily carry.

Which brought him to the third governess...

Only the second week of the wretched woman's employ and Sophia had confronted him in his study the day after his return from one of Arbuckle's London torture sessions. "Warry, I need you to follow me. Posthaste and without carrying on."

He looked up from a huge desk overflowing with reports on both his estate and the Thropmoor property. School tuition bills. Unpaid accounts. A burgeoning list of things still in arrears. Another of tenants visited. Of complaints lodged. Repairs needed. More invoices, both old and new, demanding funds he didn't have—

"Warry!" The dark-haired sprite pinched his forearm through the fabric of his shirt sleeve, his dress informal after the recent handful of days' travel, of sweat and frustration.

"Hmm? What was that?" He yanked his attention away from his notes, pulling hard to get his mind off the ever-worrisome future to pay attention to the present. "Follow you? Where?"

"To Julia's chamber." Stated as though he could simply rise and walk there without a thought.

"The one on the second or third floor?"

"The third."

He scoffed. Might as well ask him to fly to Jupiter.

Here at the estate, now that warming rooms wasn't as dire, he'd given all the children their choice. Sophia and Julia shared one chamber on the second floor, but each had also claimed a spot in the nursery, for "playtime".

He hadn't seen either of them yet this morning, rising early and cloistering himself in his study. But that was odd, he realized now, glancing at one of the few hardy, comfortable pieces of furniture still inhabiting the cavernous study, well over half the shelves barren, volumes either stolen by the colluding steward or long since sold off. In general, little Julia kept him silent company most morns. But she wasn't ensconced in the big leather chair, occupied by nothing more than thumb and blanket, staring off into space or his direction. As though to keep an eye on him, to make sure he didn't disappear as her parents had.

Cowardly, he had taken to leaving early each morning of his biweekly London trips, long before anyone else awoke. Unable—or unwilling—to see the look of betrayal fill her teary eyes when she knew he was about to be off. He didn't just disappear on her, nothing of the sort. Always spoke with her each day and evening before a trip, pointed out on a calendar the days he would be gone and when he would return… Yet the youngling could still fell his determination with a single, guilt-inducing glance.

Had he not been so whelmed by everything before him this morning—the twins' school tuition bill upon the top of what had arrived during his brief absence, he would have noted hers. The fact that he hadn't brought guilt storming up from the depths of every cell.

His gaze swept from the empty, worn burgundy leather to Sophia, impatiently staring him down.

The typically somber child looked more solemn than

usual. He relinquished his pen, grabbed hold of the chair controls and moved a few rotations away from his desk, taking care not to intersect with her bare toes. "What are you not telling me?"

She grimaced. "'Tis something you need to *see*. Before Trugmoldy awakes from her 'repose'." The last was sneered.

Miss Tuckett, who had come highly recommended from the London agency that had sent her.

Miss Tuckett, who now "reposed" as she lazily did every day after nuncheon.

He'd worked through the mid-day meal? And still hadn't noted Julia's absence?

His conscience cringed. Clamored that he make this right.

And by calling the woman *Trugmoldy*, Sophia had just labeled her governess, Miss Tuckett, a whore.

It was more than troublesome, that the just-turned ten-year-old knew such a term. But what was more bothersome, to Warrick at that moment? How the determined, vocal youngster continued to barter with him—for *everything*. The fact that she wasn't now sank dread into his chest.

The two remaining male servants were outside, repairing the simple cart he'd been using to visit tenants. He wouldn't call them back in. He stretched his fingers, then clamped them tight. Flexed his biceps. Rolled his shoulders up and back. Clenched every muscle in his arms. They were strong. As strong as they'd ever been.

His legs now? Annoyance made him slap one withered thigh. Despite the recent weeks of torture by Arbuckle, and his own determination not to give up, naught had changed.

Could he do it? Was he strong enough?

The fact that he hadn't outright told her *nay* told him he was about to gamble—on himself.

The back, servants' stairs were more narrow. But would give him a modicum of privacy not afforded by the grander, primary staircase, should the hired governess rise during his efforts. For he knew she had taken to using those deeper, broader ones herself (without seeking permission).

So the servants' staircase it would be.

Would he fit? Could he attain that third floor on his own?

By damn, he would give it a go.

"All right." He nodded, saw her surprise.

And determined he would climb those damn stairs or turn insensible and fall into a fainting fit before he abandoned the effort.

Dragging his useless, floundering legs behind him, ignoring the dull ache burgeoning low in his back by the second landing, Warrick tensed his jaw. Gritted his teeth and clawed his weight up each tread behind the darting child.

The first series of stairs he'd accomplished easier than anticipated. The second? Became twice as difficult.

But now that he rounded the wall of the tiny, second-floor landing and stared up at the slim corridor, riddled with far narrower steps he had to surmount before reaching the third level? Doubts didn't creep in. They surged. Swamped. Threatened to call a halt to his efforts thus far.

Breath heaving, he blinked. The contracting staircase loomed over him, blurring.

"Warry?" Sophia whispered, her slippers silent as she

turned around and came back down the half dozen treads to where he rested, muscles burning. Lungs bellowing.

"'Tis dire, I promise. You need to see before Trug wakes." She knelt beside him. Bunched the hem of her dress in one hand and lifted it to wipe his face.

'Twas only then he realized the sweat dripping from his nose and into his eyes. Slicking his shirt to his chest.

Pathetic. That such a puny effort rendered him spent.

Nearly spent. Keep going.

"Thanks, poppet." The gruff words were out the moment she stepped back after dabbing his face. "Lead on."

HE'D ARRIVED LATE LAST NIGHT, long after the girls were already abed, thought Julia had just been too slumbered to greet him properly, even though she'd hummed in welcome when he nudged open their door and whispered, "I am home now," before rolling in.

She'd murmured a second sleepy, wordless welcome but dozed on as he'd approached the bed, her face hidden by thumb and blanket. Until she'd wiggled to face the wall. Away from him.

A light palm to her back and a retreat before he awoke Sophia, who slept deeper than them all.

Despite the hour, he had insisted on leaving London as soon as he and Arbuckle had completed the last of the trio of appointments and ordered the hired coachman to drive straight through, given the clear night and moonlight. If it meant pissing in a can but arriving to the estate, and back to the girls, hours sooner, the inconvenience, the discomfort was worth it.

At least he no longer need worry about soiling himself. The sensations heralding the need for relieving oneself had returned during the first half of 1812. Something to be thankful for, at least. Less laundry. Less humiliation. A fraction more independence, and as the months went on with his arse confined to *sitting*, he would treasure every iota he could find.

Once he'd been carried to the second floor, he'd stopped by their chamber before retiring to his own. He'd taken to keeping his older Merlin's chair on the sleeping level, giving him some semblance of, albeit limited, mobility. Easier for the servants that way, to carry him bodily up and down only twice a day, morning and night, and be able to go about their business during the interim without attending to him. Let them focus on the other duties they graciously continued to do for the pittance he could continue to pay.

Some days—hell, some weeks—he wondered why he willingly tolerated Arbuckle's torture—ah, *treatment*—given the utter lack of any changes. But after—literally—prostrating himself, beggaring his pride, to get the man to agree to treat him once more, Warrick had aimed to do everything the man commanded, though admittedly through copious sweat and swears.

But now? By the time he gained that final landing, the lower half of his back on fire with the effort, even his hair protested. Long enough he had taken to tying it back like an ancient rather than suffer the inconvenience of regular trims, it now fell about his face, damp strands dripping. Mocking the difficulty, the preposterous picture he must make, seal-walking (or should he say *lumbering?*) his exhausted self down a thankfully flat passageway until he reached the locked door where Sophia stood, one impatient toe tapping, but the rest of her demonstrating the opposite: calmly waiting for him without chiding nor rushing.

How he must look, through her eyes, flashed in his mind. From one arm-clawed "step" to the next, he saw it clear as day. Oddly, though, for once, pitying emotions didn't clatter about. Not disgust. Nor embarrassment. Nor that impatience shown only by her toe...

For once, just as though following the example of the —unusually—behaved child before him, he simply saw how things were. More difficult for him, than most, when it came to moving about. Something he finally accepted, it seemed, and now could move beyond.

Move beyond as well as he was able, because when he reached her, she pointed overhead.

The key, strung with twine, hung over the door, well out of Sophia's reach. 'Twas but a moment to lift her confidently with his strong hands curved about her stiffened legs, braced around her calves, and raise her overhead until she grasped the key and tossed it down. A second later, he dispatched the lock and flung the door wide from his perspiring, nearly prone position on the floor, to see a shocking sight.

For his old nursery, the one that should have been filled with remnants of life and love...a stray tin soldier fighting across an imagined field...a chipped block, paint worn, tumbled among its brethren...colorful marbles clustered in a jar...was naught but a barren, senseless void. Nothing in the vast room save for scuffs from sold-off furniture, dust from little use and a silently crying, brutally shivering child in the far corner. No blanket to console. No thumb in her mouth, for her arms were bound behind her. Lips *glued* shut.

The rage he felt could not be expressed.

"Oh, sweetheart." His already fractured heart, grieving over the loss of so much, split clear in two when he saw the bruises surrounding Julia's lips. "Is this why you turned away when I saw you last night?"

A tumult of black and red, of hate and regret thundered through him until he roared loud enough to wake the dead, certainly a reposing prostitute of a governess.

"She started pinching her," Sophia informed him after he ignored the fire blazing in his back and scrambled through the doorway.

As to the six-year-old? The moment she saw it was him, despite his roar of rage, she charged forward until she slammed into his chest, painful whimpers emerging from her compressed lips. Bound, she could do nothing but burrow into him.

He fought the shambling trial of rearranging his dead limbs, until he could rest against the wall thus freeing his hands. He tore through the pitiful ropes holding her prisoner, hauled her small body off the floor and held her close to him as secure as he could convey. Her tiny arms gripped tight around his neck. Tugged on the hair at his nape, that which had not yet escaped the tie about it.

"Hold on, sweetheart," he murmured, petting the back of her head, patting her back, the sight of those bruises about her lips slamming into his heart. Rocking her from side to side as he clung tight and provided what shelter he could. "We'll get your lips unglued as soon as we can and nothing like this will ever, ever—"

He bit down, cut off his words before he started spewing oaths no child should witness.

"When pinching didn't make her talk, Trugmoldy started locking her in here. Told her that silent girls were a nuisance, and if Julia didn't start speaking, she would *make* her." Beneath that dark cap of curls and contrariness, Sophia's cheeks flushed with ire. Her brown eyes hopping mad. "I hate Miss Tuckett. Hate her."

The stalwart young guardian paced between him and the open door, hands flying as fast as her words, as she mimicked punching someone. "I hate her for Julia and I disdain her for myself. The unconscionable tyrant." Disdain? Unconscionable? Some errant part of his brain thought, *At least her vocabulary was increasing...* "Contemptible bitch."

Whoa. Pride over her vocabulary and intellect gave way to embarrassed amusement. "Who have you been listening to, to learn *that*?" Against him, Julia finally ceased her shivering as his neck grew damp from her tears. Every muscle he possessed either ached with emotion or screamed from exertion. And today wasn't even half over. "Soph, whatever we might both think of Miss Tuckett, calling her a bitch is not something appropriate nor allowable. Not out loud, anyway." She shot him a grin at that allowance. "Keep that to yourself, hmmm?"

How miraculous. How marvelous. How bloody astonishing that he could be seething with anger far beyond anything he had known before, yet possess the wherewithal to actually *parent*?

"Very well. But you will dismiss her, correct? Not let her harm Julia again?"

And you? he thought to ask, but didn't. *You saucy, stubborn minx. What has the vile governess I never should have hired done to you? How can I ever make it up to you?*

"Soph," he swore with more satisfaction than he should have, "that contemptuous bitch who thinks herself a teacher won't spend another night under our roof. Nor will she ever find employment in these environs again, I guarantee you that."

The clutch around his neck loosened; the weight against his chest deepened. Julia of the bruised, reddened mouth and chapped, swollen lips had fallen blessedly asleep. How in blazes was he to get them both down the stairs without waking her?

How the devil would he get her lips pried apart without hurting her?

"Will you take us with you when you travel to London?" Sophia asked in her direct way. "Promise not to leave us with another governess?" He'd been going every other week, to see Arbuckle, the trips both arduous and expensive. Not something he could legitimately continue, not now, with the girls back on their own, without sufficient nor trusted servants to see to their care.

It came down to either taking them with him, to London for his appointments—out of the question. Or Arbuckle traveling here.

But would he? Would the contrary, grumbling surgeon who had never really wanted to treat a peer in the first place trouble himself to travel once more, and repeatedly?

Warrick had strong doubts on that front.

17

LETTERS TO DAZZLE, DAZE AND DISAPPOINT (PART 2)

Ballenger Estate, June 25, 1813

Dear Lord Warrick,

I admit to surprised (and aye, dismayed) delight upon receiving your letter and offer of employment. That you would entrust your girls to me, whether siblings or a semblance of daughters, renders me both touched and flattered. Honored, even.

It is with complete honesty that I admit to my continued, and appreciated, employment with Lord and Lady Ballenger. As you have surmised, Lady Harriet continues to present a great challenge, one I like to think myself equal to.

Should you have an interest, I could recommend one or two others whom, depending upon their current circumstances, might be interested in the position. Please advise.

With greatest sincerity,
Miss Aphrodite Primrose

With Harriet and her parents visiting Lord and Lady Redford for the day, Aphrodite had ample time to review her response, deem it perfectly amiable, completely acceptable, and crease the pages with impeccable precision as she folded the note into the squarest of squares.

Why did you not simply include the names of other competent governesses in this letter? Save him both time and the trouble of a reply?

Because, try as she might, Aphrodite could not deny the welcome fluttering in her chest at the sight of his bold hand, not to mention the true offer of a position within his household.

But not exactly the position you crave, eh?

Pah. As if a lord such as he would offer her *any* sort of thing to salve the yearnings she constantly strove to ignore. To forget.

You will regret not sharing names if he writes anew and Lady Ballenger becomes aware of your correspondence...

Mayhap, but she didn't think so.

With time, a full year and a half now after the mistletoe scandal that had threatened to end her employment, with additional maturity and continued months within their household, came the confidence that she could do as she chose—within reason.

As long as she maintained propriety, there should be no reason why she could not exchange letters with someone who sought her services.

Even if she had no possible chance of ever accepting a position within his household.

Not and retain any hope of an *un*besmirched reputation.

It's done, man.

No snarling about or unwarranted embarrassment when we see you next, aye?

You know as well as we do they are better off there, even in their grief. Learning, drinking and carousing, fighting among their friends rather than having their young lives yarked about further. This ensures they can be boys for a few more years at least.

And I dare you not to concur.

Had the die cast another direction, you would have done the same, or more, for either of us—do not try to claim otherwise.

Now that's seen to, let me tell you Anne's latest…

The rest of Ed's letter was filled with ordinary pleasantries, humorous anecdotes of his pregnant wife's odd food yearnings and how his hand strength continued to improve.

Good for Redford. The same blast that blew apart Warrick's life had mangled one of Ed's hands and torn off the other.

But still…

"You bloody bastards."

Lords Frostwood and Redford, his closest comrades on earth, had seen the twins' school tuition paid forward through their graduation, three and a half years hence. Even arranged separate accounts to further fund the boys' university educations.

"Bloody God-damned bastards."

His eyes stung. Swam.

Realizing what he'd just muttered aloud, he wiped them dry with the back of one hand and snuck a glance at the leather chair facing his desk from a dozen feet away.

No hint of a smile.

No mischief at overhearing his naughty words upon her placid face, Julia's coiled fist pumped toward her mouth with the rhythmic suckling. Her lap overflowed with dingy blanket—he really needed to separate the two and see it laundered. Her other hand twined about the frayed edge.

"I know you heard that," he admitted. "Brother Richard—that's me—said bad words in front of a lady—that's you." He let the missive fall from his fingers and leaned back. "My apologies, dear one. I should not have forgotten myself thus."

Her shoulders lifted in a tiny shrug.

'Twas all he could do not to *whoop* with joy.

It was the first response he'd gotten from her in the days since dismissing Trugmoldy Tuckett—and ensuring her reputation preceded wherever her footsteps sought to take her. Mayhap Londonites condoned that sort of chastisement for their children. But it would not be tolerated here.

"I have a second letter," he told Julia. "One I am savoring the reading of." He reached for the folded missive and tapped one sharp corner against his desk. "I think it will be my reward, after I do my assigned motions from Mr. Arbuckle."

He waited, hoping for acknowledgment. A nod. A blink. A flicked-finger wave to *get on with it, then*.

But naught. Only thumb-sucking, blanket twining and sad-eye staring.

"Miss Julia Elizabeth Feldon Martinson."

A reaction. Slight, but a definite widening of her eyes.

"Aye, I know your name, sweetheart. Know you are named after our mother. And I have added mine after your father's as well. So you know you *belong*. You will always belong. Always have a home. I miss your laughter, little one." His chair gave a creak when he shifted, rolled an unasked-for inch before settling. "Cannot recall if I have ever heard it, you see. Wait—you did laugh..."

He grinned at the recollection. "Remember when Mama came back, right before Christmas, after visiting her friend? And we were in the Great Hall, Bertram boasting he could carry her bags in one hand and that damn—er, ah, blame—chandelier he and Beaufort had overburdened with mistletoe moaned? Remember how it groaned, warning us all back, and then dropped? Crashed right there in front of..."

As her cheeks lifted, partially obscured by her balled-up fist, he almost lost the thread of his tale, joy surging through him because she smiled. Mayhap not as much as she had then—at the astonished, shocked look on both boys' faces, but once Mama had started chuckling, they had all been done for.

As Warrick finished his remembrance out loud, memorizing that tiny lift of cheek and knowing he had helped bring it about, he heard Sophia banging back upstairs from her foray into the kitchens. And he savored something else besides the letter he saved for later.

He savored the smile. The acknowledgment of mirth.

A fragile shell surrounded sweet Julia now, but his instincts were serving him true: Patience and caring would bring her back to him. To the family.

They had to. Because to think otherwise was as intolerable to him as to accept he would never walk again.

Alone in her upstairs room, comforted by not more than the single candle she had read by, sadness threatening to swallow any hints of joy at seeing his penmanship, reading his words, Aphrodite stared down at the letter in her hand. Much, much longer than the first one he'd sent.

It had been hours and hours—most of the day, in fact—since it had first been turned over into her care...

Upon the servant bringing around the post that morning, pausing beside Aphrodite with a, "Yours, I believe," Lady Ballenger had arched an eyebrow with such a stiffening of form, Aphrodite could have been forgiven had she anticipated a staunch reprimand.

But the leisurely, late breaking of the family's fast, Lady Harriet and Lord Ballenger bickering happily at one end of the table, with Aphrodite maintaining her post, just on the edge of sight, must have made Lady Ballenger a bit more indulgent.

"Miss Primrose." Her employer beckoned her close, waved her fingers until Aphrodite held the letter up for the older woman's inspection.

"Lord Warrick is writing you?" The censure could not be mistaken, however couched.

Aphrodite shoved the folded, sealed note out of sight

deep in one dress pocket. She gave her best regal nod. "Yes, my lady. He inquires as to references for a governess, I believe. For his sisters."

When the eyebrow stayed arched and high, she elaborated. "'Tis the second such letter I have received from him." Might as well be forthright on that front, as the servants would have already told her. "It seems his other hires have been less than stellar."

Lady Ballenger gave a noticeable sniff. The eyebrow slowly lowered, but the suspicion remained in her tone. "It would not surprise me to learn he sought your services, Miss Primrose. Does he think to hire you away from us?"

"Primmy!" Harri chose that moment to listen in and instantly became distraught. "You cannot leave me!"

"Hush, child." With an exaggerated dose of irony, both Aphrodite and Harriet's mother shushed the child at the same moment.

"I have no intention of going anywhere, my lady. None whatsoever. As I told him, I am very appreciative of my post here with you and Lord Ballenger." And since Aphrodite had always suspected Lord Ballenger appreciated her efforts with Harriet far more than his wife, she made sure to include him in the conversation now. "In fact, my first reply offered Lord Warrick the names of others he might seek to engage."

"And you are certain that is all there is to it?"

"Absolutely. Lady Harriet, if you are finished, we have lessons to begin."

And as the young teen exited, grumbling beneath her breath, Aphrodite swallowed the flare of apprehension, knowing she was in no position—employed or not—to continue corresponding with Lord Warrick. However much she might have thought to continue.

For the rest of the day, she had bided her time, strained

her patience and waited until she retired to her upstairs room for the night, and complete privacy, before opening the received missive and reading...

Aphrodite?

A-P-H-R-O-D-I-T-E? <u>That</u> is your first name? How did I not already know of this?

Miss Prim, come now. You think to befuddle my thoughts with such foolery? Especially when we both know someone as stoutly prideful as your luscious self would never stand for such a flaunty name. <u>Never</u>. Nay, I am sure you came into this world, not kicking, screaming and crying as most of us, but with your tiny toes pointed, hands folded across your baby-rounded belly prayerfully, amber-hued eyes blinking open toward your mother past the astonished midwife assisting, insisting you be called Jane or Mary. Mayhap Alice. But Aphrodite?

Perish that titillating thought.

How was it, with naught but innocent jests over her name—and a remembrance of her eye color!—he brought heat to her cheeks, a simmer to her insides and a longing to be near him once more? Especially given how they had parted!

All right, Miss Prim, whose absurd claims now have my forehead furrowing grim, let me apply myself addressing two specific things (things <u>other</u> than your name absurdity):

-you offer up, in exchange for your services that you deny me the chance to engage, the names of one or two others

I decline. I do not want the names of others. I want you. Here, caring for my girls who need someone I would entrust with their lives. Which is what I would be doing, I realize, after the past and recent travesties of attempting to give that sort of trust to others who were in no way worthy of it.

Secondly:

-you stated you were both flattered and touched by my offer.

Hm. (Can you hear my grunt?)

Would that I <u>could</u> touch you. Could titillate your interest in joining us here by confessing that I am still in possession of <u>two</u> handkerchiefs taken off your person (though only one directly). Could express my curiosity about and consternation over whether <u>both</u> actually belonged to you, for according to my talented nose, it has found only one of them lingeringly sniff-worthy.

My naughty nose and thoughts aside, I needs must convince you how very vital I believe you to be to my household, especially for the sake of the youngest, Julia.

Ah. Dear Julia. Did I explain that she has ceased to speak? After losing both father and then mother in short weeks of each other, little Julia has withdrawn into herself (as well as drawn her thumb into her mouth, that no amount of coaxing can alter) such that I...

Forgive me.

I realize now, with (nearly) instant penance, how easily I fell into my old, former and irresponsible ways. I do beg your pardon. I should not have twitted you thus, not over your name—for Aphrodite is a beautiful name (even if I still have my doubts as to your sincerity over it). Nor over my indelicate thoughts pertaining toward your delicate handkerchiefs.

But I should, if not cast aside this effort and begin anew this entire response, at least express how my heart hurts. Stutters. Slams hard against my ribs each moment I ~~step~~ lean back and take a breath and evaluate the responsibilities laid before me now.

The other three children? The halfling twins, off at school (more men than boys, or though they would wish you to think), and ten-year-old Sophia? As rebellious and contrary as myself, I fear, the lot of them.

I know the boys grieve with anger. For their headmaster has written twice about their behavior. But given the staggering losses suffered, allowances continue to be made. As to Sophia? She has become something of a rock. I count on her to complain when it is time I see them fed. Time to see them abed. Time to see frocks changed and stories read...

Egad. It seems the mere thought of you turns me poetical, without intent.

Alas, I fear my little argumentative Sophia is bottling up her pain and hurt, and when it does finally erupt, the black cloud might singe the soul off anyone nearby.

But it is silent, unresponsive Julia that I need you here for, Aphrodite. Miss Primrose. Please. Julia needs you more than I—

The wicked, wicked man. Flirting in the same missive about touching her, yet threatening to crack her heart wide open with admissions of the grief-stricken younglings now in his care.

Quietly seething Sophia…

Silent, sorrowful Julia…

The wicked rat! To make her yearn—both for his touch, and to help heal the small children in need.

I confess to floundering about with the proper way to see her healed. I cannot vanquish her grief, no matter how I might wish. Nor can I, at this very moment, return her to all that she knew at her former home in Thropmoor, not given how the laborers there seek to repair the sagging, leaking roof. But that is not your concern.

None of this is, I do realize, your concern. And as I come to the end of the second side of this page, I realize how I have unburdened myself upon you in a completely inappropriate manner.

Though I have no doubt anyone you would recommend as governess would be adequate to the task, it is not adequacy I seek, but excellence—your excellence, should that be in doubt.

If you could but trouble yourself to consider my offer further, I would remain completely in your debt and at your disposal.

Yours, Warrick
(Richard Andrew Martinson, if you were curious. Nothing anywhere as provoking as Aphrodite...or Ares.)

How in blazes was she to respond to him now?

Not only had he laid himself bare, offering to do *anything* within his means to garner her assistance, the fiend had put himself as Ares alongside her namesake, Aphrodite.

Ares, the god of war, with whom Aphrodite not only bore several children, but shared a lengthy, tumultuous affair and tempestuous love.

Through the long hours of the night that followed, unlike many that had come before, she didn't just toss and turn. She didn't mourn for what wasn't, what could never be. She didn't dash away a silent tear for her own solitary state while furtively reaching beneath the bedclothes and raising her night-rail to touch herself before sleep claimed her—a touch she wished was granted by someone else.

Nay, that night, she cried.

Cried hard and long. Until her eyes stung and her chest hurt. Until her throat gasped and her emotions railed. Anger at God, at evil people, at chance, at Death.

Death that swooped in unexpectedly, claimed the unsuspecting and innocent, and left others in their place. Others oft ill equipped to pick up the broken pieces.

18

TORTURE VIA THE TYRANT

"Again."

Agony poured through him like lava over a blooming meadow... Destroying everything in its wake.

Sweat didn't just bead upon his brow. Lick across his upper lip. Dampen his face. Slick his shirt to his chest and arms.

Nay, it *bathed* him. Soaked his scalp and hair. Saturated the skin between his fingers, submerged that between his arms and torso. Dripped in rivers down the sides and front of his torso. Slid like a wave down his spine.

Yet still, The Tyrant wasn't satisfied. Nowhere close.

"Again, Lord Warrick. We are barely halfway through. Do not think to waste my time and effort by giving up now."

"Forty-seven," he gritted out, tasting the salt of his sweat when it slipped past his lips.

Forty-seven "seat to stands" that might as well have been 4700. That might as well have been a total waste of both their time—and Warrick's effort—given the lackluster difference in his lower half.

Yet using the specialized chair Arbuckle had devised, and the sets of handholds placed knee, waist and chest high, Warrick lifted and lowered himself time and again. "Forty-eight."

He swallowed past the salty sweat, shook his head—slinging more droplets about his shoulders and the floor—when the older man offered him a drink. "After."

After the torture was over.

That's when he would drink and rest.

The first few times he had met Arbuckle in London—the man who now preferred his smaller practice in Bath grumbling about the distance—had been spent on his back or his stomach, with Arbuckle maneuvering his body this way and that, stretching and shaping muscles that had either gone completely unused for nearly a year, or, conversely, muscles that had been overtaxed and tightened during the same time.

At every appointment, the surgeon first had Warrick disrobe, covered with a sheet (oh, the indignity, that!) whereupon he then put Warrick through a series of manhandled motions, more pokes and prods than any sane man wanted to endure, and a plethora of ridiculous little "tests".

Whether The Tyrant poked him with a needle, up and down his legs (unfelt), or along his lower back and up through his shoulders and arms (definitely felt), or squeezed his poor, withered muscles to a pulp, or angled Warrick's feet upon his chest, had Warrick himself hold the outside of his legs, at his knees, restricting their propensity to angle outward, Warrick using his arms to keep his knees upright and in place, and proceeded to push against his feet, cramming Warrick's thighs uncomfortably into his chest...

Whatever had been tossed his way, he had tolerated it. He had put up with everything. Every blasted thing. With such a small amount of complaint, Warrick quite thought he was due a medal, mayhap even another title from the regent.

No luck such as that. For what had he received in exchange? Only more orders, more nettling and more frustration and sweat than any peer ever wanted to experience.

More recently, though? The last handful of times Warrick journeyed south to London? At Arbuckle's insistence, they met three times over the course of three days, keeping Warrick from home at least two full nights, something that wore on him more with each successive trip, given the decline in his governess situation, not to mention the continuation of Julia's.

As to Sophia? It appeared she had charmed the cook he'd found willing to work for a pittance, as long as her son and his hound would have a home as well. Warrick had debated, counting pennies, but in the end decided feeding a growing boy of twelve who had interest in both animals and tending his mother's precious herb and vegetable gardens would be less expense than finding another equally agreeable servant.

With his clever sister in the kitchens more often than not, under the watchful eye of Cook, making lofty proclamations about what sort of food her belly would not tolerate—usually with her arms wrist deep in flour or snapping peas her new favorite servant had bartered for given the young age of the just-planted garden—that was one burden off his chest. 'Twas impossible to overlook

Sophia. If she needed attention, she was one to make sure it was known.

But still-silent Julia? The look in her blue-as-blazes eyes each time he told her he was leaving during the night for another trip nearly flayed him alive.

His lungs heaving like bellows, somewhere around sixty-three, Warrick paused. He might be "standing" but every bit of weight was supported with his upper body, hands clenched so tight around the waist-high handles he couldn't feel his fingers anymore. "Cannot continue… Travel London. Not working—" *for my girls,* he intended to finish, but couldn't, his dry throat swallowing against the effort of speech as he lowered himself back down.

Arbuckle—terrible tyrant that he was—had the audacity to snap at him to pop back up, all the while shaking his head. "On that we may agree, for neither can I continue to journey to London. It takes me away from my regular patients for too many days. You'll need to start coming to see me in Bath—"

"Impossible." It would mean more days, more nights away. "Cannot do that. Seventy-one."

"You seem to think, my lord"—the title only ever proffered with noticeable sarcasm—"that I should halt all other efforts and tend solely to you."

That was not true, not any longer. That might have been the attitude he had initially brought with him to London and their uncomfortable sessions, but as his own responsibilities had deepened, and he had allowed his alcoholic beverages to shallow, he had realized others had responsibilities too—ones they had not dismissed and ignored for years as he had.

Easier to fire back than agree, though. "Of course I do; I am likely the only earl in your care. Seventy-four."

"Pffft. Conceited peers."

"Cranky doctors."

"Arrogant rakes."

"Abhorrent tyrants. Seventy-five."

Arbuckle muttered a few more choice insults under his breath. Warrick let those slide right off his perspiring body. Took too much energy, to think right now, anyhow.

"Hold it there." Arbuckle indicated his current, arm-supported "stand". "Do not seat yourself yet. Well, sir, you are going to have to find a way, because my contract for leasing this building is up next week, and I won't be renewing it."

"Re-spon-si-bil-ities," he all but gasped. His entire body shook. Trembled like a frightened virgin on her wedding night. How was it that such stillness could cause so much sweat?

'Tis not the stillness, Richard. 'Tis the anger. The angst. The worry over those at home—and off at school—you perspire over, the—

"Responsibilities are something we all have," the good and terrible doctor interrupted his mental tirade, "though some of us manage them better than others. It is time I stopped abandoning those who rely upon me at my other office."

"Start to won...der..." Mortifyingly outbreathed, he had to pause, wipe sweat off his dripping brow with the back of one arm and swallow before he could take a deep enough breath to continue. "If things... Ever change... Both wasting our time?"

"Wasting our time, you wonder?" Arbuckle's brown eyes suddenly lit with an unholy light, a predatory, almost wolfish smile upon his lips. "Do you not realize what you just did? My lord, you are standing! Actually putting weight upon your feet without the full amount being supported by your arms."

Warrick immediately looked down, leaned forward, head bent, to see his widened, outward-pointing toes upon the ground.

And promptly pitched forward.

Straight into the waiting arms of The Tyrant. 'Twas embarrassing in the extreme, but he didn't care. He pushed off the older man's chest, away from the rescue, and gripped the handles once more, lowering himself before he fell again. "Did that really just occur?"

Arbuckle stepped back, reached for a towel and started blotting his face and chest—where Warrick's sweat had dampened his skin and clothing. "It did." The smile was still in place. "I know this has been difficult on you, mayhap not anymore than other patients I work with, but mayhap more due to your surrounding circumstances."

Surrounding circumstances. What a pithy way to address losing one's only remaining parent, gaining four siblings, two beggared properties (here, he thought only of his primary estate and the Thropmoor cottage, but in truth there were many others, all aligned with either the Warrick title or his family's ancestry, and all equally paupered).

"Up!" The Tyrant snapped and pointed his thumb toward the ceiling. "I believe you still have twenty-five more."

As Warrick took the proffered drink this time, swallowed down half in one gulp, his resolve firmed.

He had actually stood. His feet and legs had managed to hold his weight. It mattered not that the length was counted in mere seconds, even fractions thereof. What mattered was that it had happened. If it occurred once, he could make it happen again. Longer.

By the time he was counting out, "Eighty-nine," his mind was floating, body had passed through the strain and struggle, and if it wasn't quite floating, parts of him felt pretty damn close.

Arbuckle was talking again, and Warrick had to force himself to concentrate on the words. "Two things of note I want you aware of. Firstly, when we initially began working together back in May, your injury was two years old. I had no certainty that we would experience any progress, but you did write an impressively humbling note, to gain my cooperation—"

Not overly pleased with that description, even given the truth of it, Warrick grunted. "Ninety-three."

"Yet even that is not why I agreed. I agreed because of *Lady* Warrick"—his mama—"I knew there had to be good in you somewhere, having been reared by such a quality, determined female.

"What I did not tell you—I was saving it in my pocket in case you decided to become despondent or recalcitrant, and stop working as hard. But I admit you have surprised me, making every appointment we have made, and not slacking overly much in your efforts—"

"Overly much!" exploded from him. "Ninety-seven."

Another of those sly grins. "Around about June first, you were prone on your stomach, and I was going through my initial tests again—and you flinched. *Flinched* like a fiend when I pinched the bottom of your foot."

"Nay, I did not. That I would have remembered. Ninety-nine."

"You did, my man. That told me something—whether you could feel it or not, something in your body was responding. Because when I did the same test at our *first* meeting? No response whatsoever."

Somewhat dazed now, he leveraged himself up with a groan, muttered out, "One...hundred," and sank gratefully back down into his seat, every part of his body trembling.

Even his thighs, he thought on an odd spark of wonder, placing both palms atop his twitching muscles. "You said you had two things of note. Was that it?"

"That was the first thing—that *some*thing in your body is changing, so what we are doing *is* worthwhile. What *you* are doing is worthwhile. The second thing is this—if you will agree to continue accomplishing what I assign consistently and without complaint, I will allow you to take the equipment we have used thus far home with you this trip. I expect weekly letters as to exactly what you are doing: I want counts on everything; I want to know how you feel every hour of the day. Not your contrary thoughts—you may keep those to yourself. But how your muscles and nerves go on, that is the detailed information I seek. You do that—keep me apprised of everything pertaining to your body's strength, mobility and fortitude—and together, we will ascertain the best way to move forward from here. London is no longer an option. You refuse to travel to Bath. I am unable to travel all the way to your estate. But neither of us are imbeciles; something will present itself, of that I am certain."

While Warrick spun with thoughts of doing these sorts of "exercises" at home, without Arbuckle to ~~torture~~ encourage him onward, the man continued. "Additionally, it is of vital importance, in my experience, that your legs continue to receive frequent stimulation. Is there anyone there who can work the muscles for you as you have witnessed me doing so?"

Blotting his face with another towel left beside him for the purpose, he lowered it, and shook his head. "Nay, but I shall do it myself."

Arbuckle frowned. "Your thighs, your upper legs, both front and back, even sides, I agree that you can. But when it comes to your calves and feet? You are in no position to work them properly, not without more control and strength. The last thing I need is for you to be reaching for your toes and tumble about, blaming me over the whole fizz."

What popped into his mind was steely-eyed Sophia's stubborn chin and conniving ways. He was certain there was something he could trade the lass for helping him. But did she have the strength? "Can I get my ten-year-old sister to walk on the back of my legs?"

Arbuckle loosed a rare chuckle. "She would weigh, what? Somewhere around five stone? I see no reason why that would not help, but if there is an adult with strong hands, a coachman or stable boy, perhaps? Even better. What of your valet? You had one the first time we met. Does he not accompany you?"

Giles? After Mother's death, when faced with the true and dire state of all the finances, Giles had been the first servant Warrick released. Not because he disliked the man, for he had never given him a chance. Too humiliated by all he had requested the man do for him during those darkest weeks of his initial injury, made the valet difficult to face.

Last he heard, the man had found work elsewhere.

Shieldings, though? Warrick's trusted servant-of-all-work at the London townhouse? Mayhap 'twas time he asked Shieldings and his missus if they would relocate to the estate. Perhaps he could rent out the townhouse? Especially if he would no longer be using it for his visits with Arbuckle.

He grunted. "Aye. There is someone, a former soldier. He can pummel me about but good."

At least until I am able to do it myself.

19

SENSIBLE ADVICE

Ballenger Estate, August 14, 1813

Dear Lord Warrick,

Lady Ballenger is aware of our correspondence. So—dare I admit, <u>regretfully</u>, for I have enjoyed our brief conversance—this must be the last letter we exchange. Please honor that. Allow me to retain the job I have. And want.

Which does not mean I do not want to help you. I do. But I think it best from afar. And in the form of advice, if I may be so bold.

Of a certainty, this will not suffice for long, but at least through the end of the year, perhaps...might you consider governing them yourself? Not attempting to hire <u>another</u> to do the job for you?

I cannot believe I suggest such a thing. But I remember myself when, just a year beyond Sophia's age, I lost both my parents. I remember well. I found myself upon the doorstep of one distant family after another, all relatives of some sort yet none of them interested in another mouth to feed.

It was a fraught time, filled with excessive tears as I grappled with grief and the unknown, until Fortune shone its light upon me and I ended with the best possible parent imaginable, little did I know it at the time.

From the roundabout succession of governesses you describe, as well as the recent parental deaths in these dear children's lives, let no more excessive change burden their present. (Nor your own. Please pardon my neglect in not mentioning it sooner. I am incredibly sorrowed to hear of the early death of your mother. You mentioned her to me during our first conversation, do you recall? You indicated my "optimism" reminded you of hers. Though I do not believe it was ever intended as a compliment, I chose to take it as such and have felt an affinity toward the strong woman who would rear such an entertaining rake as yourself. I know how hard the loss of those closest to us can cut. I pray you find solace in time, and in the proximity of your siblings.)

Concerning your siblings... I believe you mention the boys continue at school, though with some questionable behaviors, outbursts, most likely. That is to be expected, I believe we can both agree.

Continue to engage each of them, both together and

separately, whenever they are on holiday with you and their sisters, and I daresay they will heal and their angry antics mitigate in time.

As to your sisters? Young girls far too soon without a mother...

Something in my heart tells me forcing a governess upon them, when the right one is yet to be found, is not the proper direction to take, not quite yet.

For you, ~~sir~~, my lord, you are the one constant in these girls' lives. The only consistency. The only recognizable paternal, authoritative "parent" they will know from here—

It dug at his craw, how she "my lorded" him. How she amended herself to do so. It mattered not that it was the appropriate address for a servant to one of his rank. It rankled, is what it did. Rankled quite uncomfortably.

I have allowed my sentiments to become far too maudlin, I know. As I try to explain why I believe there is no one better to care for them than yourself. At least until the worst of their grief has waned.

In truth, no matter that part of me is called, fiercely so, to assist you, Sophia, your precious Julia... I could never come live in your household and be governess to your girls without...

Without...

Without betraying who I am. As a person. One with

morals and ideals and thoughts about wrong and right, and my place. I know my place.

~~And~~

Lord Warrick, whatever you may think of me after reading this, it must be said—whether a <u>flirt</u> or something else entirely, something unnamed, <u>it exists</u> between us. And I cannot deny it no matter that I might wish to.

Selfishly, I cannot live with you as governess and watch you wed, which I know full well you must and will one day. Unselfishly, I cannot imagine extensive time would pass, if you remained a bachelor, and we lived under the same roof, when I would not give in to your prompting ~~and my own~~ <u>and sit upon your lap.</u>

We both know you take my meaning.

I could not make it any more plain nor blunt.

I cannot knowingly place myself in that situation—of being tempted because I suspect I would fall prey to it. To you. And that is not who I am (however a small—very small—shred of my being wishes I were exactly just so)...

His fingers turned lax, followed the fluttering page downward until it landed upon his desk, his eyes staring unseeingly toward the overgrown lawn through the study window.

"Not who you are, my Miss Primrose?" He sighed, flattened his fingers over the words she had written with such forthright honesty he was near floored with it. "Not who you are, indeed. And that is exactly why, despite every sound argument you present, you are the one I so desperately need to mother my children."

A tiny squeak, barely heard, of skin shifting against leather drew his gaze toward the thumb-suckling six-year-old staring at him with blue eyes, wide with wonder and curiosity.

His mind echoed the words he had just said—*mother my children.*

Begad!

"Ahem. *Govern* my sisters," he told the child with a wink he could not suppress. "Govern my sisters. That is you, dear heart. But alas, there are other things that prevent that wish."

Aphrodite Primrose, of the prim morals and distinctly fetching manner, thought he should abandon his governess efforts for the nonce, not shuffle the girls off on someone else. Not yet, not with grief still so fresh.

He sat back, buttocks and spine firm against his ambulatory chair. Then did something he had not yet attempted there in the confines of his study, something only previously attempted in the room housing Arbuckle's devices and set aside for what Warrick had come to think of his Torture Time, the daily rounds he and Shieldings put his body through after the children were abed and long before either of them sought their own.

He shoved aside the papers and pages, letters, notes, bills, reports... Moved everything to the edges, to give his fingers and then palms, strong purchase on the surface. The desk was massive, one of the few original pieces of furniture still within these walls, passed down for at least three generations, now. Kept because of its use and also the memories of Warrick's father associated with it. Good memories. Pleasant thoughts.

Facing the desk, he spread his fingers wide, shuffled his hands out just beyond the width of his torso and hips. Then realized he had forgotten to put his feet on the floor. Imbecile. He quickly righted that, lifted each thigh and swung his foot, nudging the calf as needed, until each booted foot met the ground just beneath the edge of the desk. His arms and fingers went right back to their prior position.

His forehead had already started to sweat. So inane. As though even the thought of the effort to come took a toll. A price he had to pay. One he would pay willingly. Would this work? Or was he about to end up, arsey-varsey, heels overhead, dignity abandoned?

The muscles in his arms and hands had already tensed. 'Twas but a moment to firm them and push upward. Took a bit more to maneuver the rest of him in the direction he hoped he would go, slightly up and slightly forward.

But a silenced grunt later, he was standing. Standing, by damn. Leaning forward more than he might wish, the pressure and reliance upon his arms keeping him slightly bowed, not standing upright, but no longer seated.

He wavered in place a moment, shifted his upper body, just a minim, testing his balance. There was complete silence from the other occupant in the room. Not a sound, nor a suckle.

His breath exited on a *whoosh*.

Warrick lifted his eyes from his taut fingers until he caught the staring gaze of Julia. Her thumb had slipped from her mouth. She stared at him, wide-eyed. Didn't quite give him a smile, but the slowly darkening blonde hair tilted when she did grant him a small nod.

"One."

He thought about slowly sitting back down, using his arms to maintain control, then had the lovely image of plunking down in his chair, the wheels skidding backward and him landing upon his arse after all.

He scanned the study. Not hard, with so few things still in residence. "That chair, Julia, the wooden one"—he paused to haul in air, more nerves than exhaustion, he knew, then indicated the small wooden chair he spoke of with a jerk of his chin—"over there behind the door. Are you able to bring that to me, lass? Is it too heavy? Or can you move—"

But she had already jumped down from the comfort of the burgundy leather, blanket abandoned for once, and raced across the room, skittering the simple chair across the wooden floor. It was of sturdy design, decades old, a basic wood frame with cushioned seat that some ancestor had replaced with a needle-pointed duck at some point, and some ornate carving work along the back.

She dragged it across the hard floor where one rug had been dispatched, over stains and neglect no amount of cleaning could take care of, and then bumped more silently over the rug that remained, closer to his desk. Without turning to watch, he listened as she abandoned that chair for the one he used on wheels, rolling it out of the way and placing the other right behind him.

"Like this?" The soft, feminine voice almost felled him. Nearly pitched him floorward in shock.

"Right up against my legs," he told her, shaking now not from exertion but sheer amazement. "Directly behind me. Can you stand there, hands on the chair, make sure it doesn't move??"

He yearned to hear the yes. Waited for it. But only received silence. He dared to angle his jaw over one shoulder, to watch her watching him, took a bit of solace from the confident nod, her small fingers gripped tight around the top horizontal brace of the chair.

Biting down on a small smile, because two words were more than none, he returned to face forward. Used his arms—and his legs, he thought—hoped—and gained his seat. Lifted his hands off the desk, stretched them out to the sides, felt the pull on his chest, the pinch in his upper back as he stretched them as far out as he could. Then he brought them overhead, mimicking one of the stretches Arbuckle had him do each time they finished. He stretched the muscles and skin down his sides.

"Let's do a few more, hmm?"

Silence. But a comfortable one, he thought.

And before that morning was over, he had stood upon his feet and gained a count of thirty before deciding that was probably enough without checking in—reporting, though the thought made his gaze roll skyward—with The Tyrant. If he was going to begin a session more than once a day, best not to overtax his muscles without seeking "permission" first.

He had taken to heart Arbuckle's experience, tales of sparse but miraculous success with certain people and injuries, and knew, given the state of everything within his household, he wouldn't risk falling on his arse and bungling any potential healing.

A decision he regretted not one whit, especially when, after a flurry of letters between him and The Mayhap-Not-So-Tyrannical man proved fruitful, as far as a "plan of attack" between now and the year's end.

Especially when both girls took to Mrs. Shieldings like the grandmother they hadn't had before, and Julia whispered something in his ear, one day a few weeks later. Only a handful of audible syllables, but ones cherished more than diamonds: "If you take steps, brother Richard, I will make more words."

With a promise such as that, he could deny the little sprite nothing.

So even when progress seemed at a crawl, or even nonexistent, he found unentailed properties to sell. Entailed ones to lease, and did everything he could to postpone the marital noose that wanted to slip around his neck and solve all his financial problems—while creating so many others.

20

ANOTHER LETTER OR FOUR

Marigold House, Bath, September 13, 1813

Dearest niece,

I hope this missive finds you well. I tender my heartfelt apologies for my lapse in consistent communication these last months. I have been devoting an inordinate amount of time to one very arrogant patient.

But alas, you need not hear of my travails or that of my persnickety clients. It is sufficient to say, when my bill comes due, I shall be adequately—or close to it—compensated for tolerating his irritating presence.

Aphrodite snickered at this. So rare was it for Uncle Silas to complain of a patient. She sat upon her bed, in her attic room, late one afternoon shortly before accompanying Harriet down to dinner. The letter had thrummed most pleasantly in her pocket since it had been delivered into her care earlier. Eager fingers had unfolded it and avid eyes scanned swiftly...

> *Dear, I confess I have been remiss in sharing some information with you, of a particularly delicate subject. It is to that end I would like to request your presence during the holidays. Are Lord and Lady Ballenger granting you a holiday this year as you mentioned they would? If so, I invite you to attend me here in Bath. We could celebrate as we did when you were younger, with roasting and baking, services and singing. If you don't mind my aging fingers pecking upon my sorely abused harpsichord—or if you would care to grace my little cottage with your <u>soothing</u> notes? All the better.*

Her "soothing" notes? His jest made her laugh, for talented, she was not!

> *Let me see, what else may I share? Indulge an old man, if you would—*

Old? He barely only now approached—but had not yet reached—sixty, still fit, even if she thought his height may have dipped a tad shy from the six foot two he used to boast of when she was young.

> *In recent months, I have met someone, I confess. An upstanding widow, somewhat wary of me (or mayhap all men?), so nothing overt has been said between us as of yet, but I admit to sharing some rather <u>speaking</u> looks with the lady in question.*

That made her smile.

She had first landed upon Uncle's doorstep as a sad, weeping child of eleven who had recently lost both parents.

Upon their unexpected deaths, she had been shuffled to her papa's favorite female cousin whose husband complained they couldn't have a crying, sullen child underfoot, so then Aphrodite was flicked from one strange home to the next as her tears failed to dry and the other myriad children, never-before-met distant cousins, wanted nothing to do with the sorrowful, remote girl in their midst.

After a few sparse weeks at each abode—sometimes only a handful of days—a note would be pinned to her cloak and off she would go on the next stage. *We have enough mouths to feed already. You take her. She's good for nothing but dampening cloths with her unceasing tears.*

Uncle Silas, the only son of her father's uncle's cousin or some such, had proved the lone stable and secure presence—after she'd been tossed from no less than four chaotic homes.

"Oh, dear heart," he'd murmured upon taking one look at her newly arrived self—and the battered note affixed beneath her wobbling chin and worn from several hours' travel.

She handed him the other, folded note she'd been told to share at each successive, and more disappointing home. That *and* the new letter that had just been added.

After perusing the contents within, frowning severely (at the second, new one), then wiping that free with a gentle smile, he held his door wide. "Come in, come in. You must be famished. Hermes is running around wild in the backyard. Why do you not set your things here..."

Her things, that by now consisted of one frayed valise that had belonged to her mother, so she gripped it even closer to her chest, not quite sure what to make of this kind-speaking man with the deathly quiet home and warm welcome. Nothing about him reminded her of her loud and always laughing father—except, perhaps, the bright, mischievous twinkle in his brown eyes.

"No, hmm? All right, keep hold of it, then. Hermes though. You hear him, do you not? He knows we have a visitor.

"Let us go outside and meet him, would you like that? He likes to bark. And whine. And sometimes it sounds as though he is gargling caterpillars or some other nonsense. Mind him not. He has the loudest mouth of anyone I know..."

Uncle Silas had allowed, if not encouraged, young Aphrodite to remain as quiet or solemn as she needed, to cry as hard and often as she wanted... Always ready with a kerchief, an embrace—or a serving of eggs—whatever she might need, but never forcing anything upon her.

Over the weeks and months, her tears had slowly dried. Though it had taken far longer for the gaping hole in her heart to mend, she had thrived in his most unusual bachelor household.

When she joined his family of one, his unusual "doctorship" had been broad in nature, as he tended to all manner of patients, always explaining out loud what he was doing or checking for, and his findings. His patients thought he was exceptionally verbose on their behalf, but nay. Uncle Silas and Aphrodite both knew he was talking *to her*, his unusually quiet niece hidden out of sight more often than not, either in a corner, beneath his desk or tucked away just beyond the door.

When he'd first spied her hidden self, while treating little Henry Johnston's broken arm, she'd swallowed her breath and choked silently, waiting to be expelled. Instead, her uncle's eyes had twinkled. Dimples appeared in both cheeks as he gave her a wink and turned back to his patient.

As she grew older? Expressed appreciation for all the knowledge she had gleaned, but confided not an ounce of desire in pursuing such work herself, he let her choose a ladies' finishing academy to attend and welcomed her home every weekend and every holiday, pleased to share his fascinating, ever-changing work—or not. Equally content to pore over *her* assignments, listen to the new wonders she had learned and indulge her love of Latin as much as any professor at university would have done for a male student.

Aphrodite had thrived in his care, and she knew it.

The only thing that marred her time with him had been the knowledge that 'twas most assuredly her presence that had kept him from finding his own lady love, interfered with him having his own children.

When she confessed her worry, he had only laughed and hugged her harder. "Never you fear, child. You have inopportuned nothing. The lass I once fancied now lives in Scotland with seventeen of her own." His eyes had grown wide in mock horror. "Seventeen? I certainly would not want *that* many children. How would I ever keep them all straight?

"Especially when half the time I call Mercury his predecessor's name? Poor pup's likely discombobulated by all the Hermes-Mercury mumbo-jumbo."

Mercury, the six-month-old canine they had chosen together after aged Hermes had barked his last the prior winter.

Ballenger Estate, October 3, 1813

Dear Uncle,

I hope this finds you as content and joyful as ever (possibly with overt words being spoken between you and your widow by the time this reaches you?).

I read your missive with great eagerness. (Whether delayed, inconsistent, irregular or anything of the sort, I welcome any letter that arrives with my name upon it.)

I regret to share that Lord and Lady Ballenger have requested my presence over the holidays at a house party being given by their eldest daughter, now Lady Redford if you will recall?

Her lying-in will be in early spring and we—Lady Ballenger, Lady Harriet and myself—are relocating to Redford Manor once December commences to help ready everything before the guests begin to arrive. More so, to keep Lady Anne from overstraining herself upon her (likely swollen) feet.

I admit to my curiosity being piqued by your pending news. Delicate? My oh my, that raises several possibilities. But I dare not speculate, knowing you will tell me in due time. (Also not having much time to speculate, as I continue to expend the majority of my waking hours keeping abreast of Lady Harriet and her latest outbursts—entertaining though some might be—and farm-related frolics. Though I admit the frolics are always entertaining, they are often accompanied by mud and rips which I daresay we both could do without.)

My charge has also now announced to one and all her desire to learn to play the cello! The cello, Uncle, if you can believe it. The broad instrument held betwixt one's lower limbs—widened at the thigh and knee to accommodate.

Well now. I am certain I do not need to regale you with Lady Ballenger's expected and emphatic reaction to that pronouncement!

As to the coming house party, with its myriad guests? It seems as though Lady Harriet is being bribed with a London shopping expedition if she maintains silence as to this new goal, thus avoiding shocking the guests with her latest aspirations at her sister's pending gathering. Enough about me and mine.

It warms my heart to hear you have found someone who makes yours beat with eagerness. I do hope things may progress for the two of you as you both wish. I would not be the capable, confident woman I am now without your love and care. I only wish for you to find every shred, speck, iota or modicum of happiness I consider your due...

Marigold House, Bath, November 17, 1813

...I understand. Commitments to one's employer must take precedence over frolics (farm-related and not). Aye,

do let us plan on meeting when next you have time off, if not spring, then by this summer at the absolute latest, may I hope? Who knows, mayhap a miracle will occur and I can present myself upon your doorstep at some point. But not now. Nay, for I continue to be quite busy with my cantankerous, aggravating lordling.

Lordling? What young, indulged peer had her uncle in a dither? Unusual, as Uncle Silas typically worked with laborers more often than not, sometimes former soldiers and seamen, but ever since abandoning his London practice solely for Bath, his patients tended toward gentry or fortunate tenants of generous employers—people who would rather their faithful tenants recover than have to find (and train) new ones to take their place.

I begin to think I may have but a modicum of the patience you, my to-be-applauded Aphrodite, continually exhibit toward your young charge these years past. If she argues even 1/10th as much as my oft-unpalatable laze about, then you, dear niece, should be among the saints. I declare, please remind me why I trained to become a surgeon, if you would? To willingly put myself under the commanding attitude of those with titles but not the responsible nature to go with them?

Please know you remain forever welcome upon my doorstep. Should your plans change, I would love to receive you at the cottage—and Mercury heartily agrees, with breath held and tail lifted. His old eyes may not see anymore, but his exuberance still outpaces my own, daily.

You asked of any progress with my lady. May I share

we have now stepped out a time or two (privately, but together)? Have discussed taking a brief trip at some undetermined future date... And here I am, putting ink to page completely beyond the bounds of an appropriate example for my exceedingly proper, favorite relative...

Exceedingly proper indeed.

If Aphrodite had *any* hope of laying claim to such a flattering description, she would not have been boundlessly disheartened upon learning that Lord Warrick would not be counted among this year's house party guests.

Although, how she would have managed to ever, *ever* look him in the eye after what she had inadvertently chanced across within Lord Redford's desk, when he bade her to retrieve paper one afternoon for lines Harri had just been assigned by her irate mother, Aphrodite could not fathom.

Unfortunately, neither could she seem to forget the words scrawled across a page in full sight when she opened the topmost drawer...

Words written in bold strokes she would recognize anywhere:

Warrick Estate, November 27, 1813

Ed, you rascally knave!

I am beside myself, recalling the words during your last visit. Pity I wasn't bosky enough to have them bubble from my brain after a night or ten of sleep.

What would your lady wife think of such an outlandish suggestion? You tempt me, man, I confess.

Tempt me with the immoderate thought: If the work on my lower limbs has brought some manner of feeling back to my legs (thank the Lord), however weak, would the same sort of attention work a miracle on my pizzle?

You are a fiend indeed. Because now that the notion has been planted, 'tis grown into a thorny bramble attacking my thoughts, poking painful hope back into my heart—and hammer—once more.

Alas, that brings me to why I must (most regretfully, I assure you), decline your invitation to visit Redford Manor throughout December and on into Twelfth Night. For I have made arrangements with my doctor to continue work on my legs...

Her eyes skipped to the bottom, to confirm the signature she already knew would reside there.

Please share my sincere regrets with Lady Redford (omitting any mention of my lonely prick), and I shall look forward, with vast eagerness, to your next visit or the time when I am able to join you once more of my own accord.

Warrick

P.S. It did not escape my notice that my siblings were included in Anne's invitation. Heartfelt appreciation, there.

Nor could she forget a word of the one discovered

beneath it when she shuffled it aside, seeking that blank paper, even as her loins threatened to catch flame.

Written in the same striking hand and dated only a week after the first…

> *Mistress? Good God, man…to suggest I gain a mistress for my dagger? And as a treatment to heal that portion of my anatomy?*
>
> *I can scarcely believe you would put that notion so plainly onto the page and into my head. For shame! What would your lady wife think should she know you had written thus?*
>
> *To bid me to find a mistress to handle—my handle? When my parts are still as useless as my legs? None more than the pizzle between them.*

Then Lord Redford's not-yet-finished reply…

> *Hold on to your newly not-completely-numb seat, dear friend, for it was my Anne who made the suggestion, thinking if time and attention had brought some semblance of feeling, however tenuous, back to your legs and feet, mayhap the same sort of attention to your manly anatomy would return feeling to your private parts.*
>
> *Would that not be wondrous? Think on it. For even if it should not have the desired results, well, would you not be desirous of the effort? The trying? Imagine that!*

Stop reading! her brain ordered. *Stop reading right this instant.* But she could not.

A mistress, one dedicated to your pleasure. Or, if not that, dedicated solely to your body. A woman you could avail yourself of any time you called upon her, eager and ready to pay attention to your muscles, the way you have described your doctor working your legs. But without the torturous aspect, with a more delicate touch instead? Feminine hands to work, to stroke—

I am halting now. I know not what else to say. (We both know I have already written too much.)

There you have it. My dear wife's thoughts upon the subject. Now you will have me blushing, do I not abandon this current discourse.

Oh! Here is something else you might find of note: Did you hear of the hunt this past fall? 'Twas the second one of its sort, for in addition to driving the foxes to ground, there was a new type of prey found in Lincolnshire last year...

His mistress. Lord Warrick's. Could that have been her? Had she accepted his offer of employment as governess to his girls?

Aphrodite, were you living under his roof, Lord Warrick would have had no need to contemplate Lord Redford's suggestion. The finding and housing of a kept woman. Because you would have been acting mistress to his muscles—one in particular!—long before now.

THREE WEEKS LATER, Lord Frostwood had presented his customarily scowling self at Redford Manor and had stunned everyone when he set out to woo Lady Anne's blind, if lovely, bosom friend, Isabella Spier. And, to Aphrodite's further surprise and personal delight, she and Lady Isabella had developed an amiable friendship over several intimate conversations upon the grounds.

Harriet, keeping her cello aspirations to herself, still managed to entertain most of the guests and outrage her mother on a continual basis, keeping Aphrodite busy as Christmas neared and days elapsed.

She could be forgiven if, every moment and around every corner, she sought the sight and sounds of another guest, met another year…

Early one morning, during Harri's daily lessons—the ones Aphrodite attempted to supervise through completion before their guests even awoke—Lady Ballenger swept in with the most startling announcement.

"Miss Primrose, did your uncle not invite you to Bath for the holiday? Eyes back on the page, young lady!" This directed toward her daughter, who had eagerly replaced her pen and scooted back at the unexpected interruption.

"Oh, Mama!" A loud scraping of her chair as young Harri returned to the table and begrudgingly re-inked her pen.

"He did indeed, my lady, but 'tis of no matter. You needed me here. I am content."

The bustling matron, never quiet or easy to overlook even at the best of times, marched forward, the bobbing two-foot-tall peacock feather tucked within her bright turquoise turban providing a great challenge to Aphrodite: Do not look above her forehead. Do not look above her eyes. Do not. Do not! *Do not!*

With a snap of her fingers (and a wave of that dastardly

compelling feather) Lady Ballenger presented herself at Aphrodite's side and knocked her knuckles against the desk. "Lessons are *over*. It was selfish of me to ask you to forgo your own family at this time of year. And it cannot escape *anyone*'s notice how Harriet has attached herself at the heels to dear Isabella. Would you still like to visit your uncle? The travel weather seems fair enough. And you already have your things packed."

Both were true enough. For she had packed for the month when they relocated several weeks earlier from the Larchmont home.

Aphrodite stood, relief now mingling with disappointment.

Relief that she would no longer strain her ears to hear the identity of any new arrivals. What if Lord Warrick changed course and decided to attend?

Disappointment that she might not be present to glean the latest on his condition. (Had he taken Lord Redford's advice and taken a mistress? Gasp! And of course, that was *not* a jealous gasp. Not one of envy. Of longing…)

Ordering her wayward thoughts to still, Aphrodite savored Harriet's enthusiastic hug, and then excused herself to ready her belongings. Upstairs in her room, she penned a letter to Lady Isabella, explaining her sudden disappearance and thanking the lady for her moments of friendship.

Aphrodite thought not of other letters, both those cherished ones within her possession and those that had gone unwritten. Unreceived. And *that* was an utter clanker, because she could not help but wonder, more frequently than one might admit, what else Lord Warrick would have said, had their correspondence continued. Could only wonder how she might have responded…

When Harri knocked upon her door late that evening,

wanting to share the season's delights with her governess (after only a several-hour absence Aphrodite couldn't help but release a warm smile over), she gave the folded letter over to her charge's care, with the request to see it delivered to Lady Isabella. "Of course I will! Oh, Primmy, whatever shall I do without you here the next two weeks?"

Whatever, indeed?

PART III

Love such as his, in a man like himself, must with perseverance secure a return, and at no great distance; and he had so much delight in the idea of obliging her to love him in a very short time.

—Jane Austen, *Mansfield Park*

21

A SEASONAL SURPRISE

LATE DECEMBER 1813

MARIGOLD COTTAGE, BATH

WEARIED BY TRAVEL, energized by anticipation, Aphrodite scolded not for the unlocked door that greeted her fingertips, recalling at once it was left thus whenever the healer who resided within awaited a patient, but locked after. Which meant she need not subdue her excitement.

"Uncle Silas!" she called out, eagerly stepping beyond the threshold of the home she'd gratefully called her own after her uncle took in a scared and otherwise abandoned eleven-year-old. Though she might have spent a number of years attending the Young Ladies Improving Academy, this old cottage, on the outskirts of Bath, would forever exude the warmest of welcomes. "Whoop, holiday! I made it for Christmas after all!"

Muffled thumps sounded beyond her sight. Then a

growl. And a snarl, which prompted a smile. Appeared as though her favorite relative and his elderly dog still liked to wrestle.

"Mercury! Uncle!" Dragging her heavy valise behind her, she looked around in surprise beneath the pushed-back brim of her travel bonnet. "Where is all the greenery? Not a ribbon nor wreath one."

When she'd written that she couldn't make it this year, had he decided not to go to the trouble of bringing the holiday inside? Something he'd always made such a point of—decorating their home—ever since their first holiday season together.

Attired for travel, she nevertheless shuddered. "My, 'tis chilly in here."

More noise filtered through the house; this time growling and a muted crash. "Uncle?"

After a moment's thought, she released her hold on her bag and bolted the door behind her. She'd hear if anyone knocked and Uncle must be away, having left in a hurry, else he would have heard her by now and responded.

What was Mercury into?

She hadn't seen the dog in close to a year, and though Uncle's letters hadn't alluded to anything dire, she sped through the sterile front rooms where he tended patients, toward the more relaxed ones in the back only stopping when Mercury raced past her just as she reached the informal family room, a wad of fabric gripped tight in his mouth, pale folds billowing out from either side.

Before exiting out toward the kitchen, the dog paused, sniffed the air and wiggled his hind end as he turned about until he brushed against her legs and gave a tiny *yip* around his mouthful.

Tugging off one glove, she knelt to pet the wavy,

uneven fur, enjoying the snuffled canine sniffs over her hand and forearm as she swiftly glanced from wall to wall, soft satisfaction brimming at the sight of the grey-blue paint she and Uncle had applied together, not to mention a trio of framed watercolors she had brought home from school one year, still hanging above a chaise. The flower-bedecked pond in the middle surrounded by more detailed vegetation on each side certainly not the quality one would usually find displayed quite so prominently. Nostalgia for the childhood he'd repaired brought an unexpected wealth of emotion and surprisingly watery eyes.

The dog's coat chilled her fingers. What manner of emergency had stolen Uncle from home for the house to grow this cold?

She reached around and hugged Mercury. "Oh my." Her nose wrinkled and any watering now only had to do with his pungent scent. "You, sir, need a washing posthaste."

Below the opaque black of unseeing eyes, his long snout angled up and down, as though agreeing. Carefree laughter met the dog's antics, the joyful spread of her cheeks so very welcome.

For *here*, was home. No young charge to constantly tend. No manner to mind, thoughts to subdue. Appearance to temper. Stress of mind and tension of body all fell away at the comfort of familiar surroundings and Merc's instant, enthused welcome.

But then a growl ruffled his upper lip and the dog lifted his nose in a quick jerk as though to say *hail* and *farewell* before he raced on, the tips of his claws clattering around the edges of a rug as he disappeared.

"You mangy mongrel!" The deeply jagged voice, raised in anger, wiped the smile free and brought Aphrodite to her feet. "You get your arse back in here, you thieving cur, or so help me—"

Another two thuds and a towering, disreputable man lurched in.

Messy long black hair in disarray, a week's growth of bristle upon his cheeks, the masculine body exposed before her was long and lean. Wholly shocking (and shockingly attired—or not). For most of all?

'Twas decidedly naked.

"L-lord War*rick?*"

Richard Andrew Martinson, who hinted at being Ares to her Aphrodite?

It couldn't be. Here? In her uncle's home? In her home!

He staggered. Braced bare, muscled arms against the doorway. "Prim?" Sinews flexed in legs and arms as he braced anew. "God-a-mercy. What in blazes are you doing here?"

He'd recognized her? After all this time?

"You—you're—you're..." Her hand flailed, indicating the center of the nude expanse.

You ought not be looking!

But look she did, fighting dual urges to stare even more intently, to apply her gaze—*everywhere*—and look till sundown (and even after), versus squeezing her eyelids tightly shut and retreating. With speed and distance. Retreating until her stunned and stumbling feet found themselves once again at the Ballenger estate.

Where all was safe.

Where nights were lonely.

He gave another heaved grunt that lifted his torso, midnight eyes upon her. Narrowed gaze unreadable. "I am...*what?*"

She looked *again*. As close as she dared from her (suitably) safe stance of ten feet distant. Circled the miles of skin and muscle, the scars and broad chest dusted with dark hairs with her flailing fingers. "You're here! And—and *unclothed!*"

The last barely squeaked from her tight throat.

"Astute of you." He grimaced. And it seemed that with every second that passed, that shredded her composure... that he regained his own. Her garret swam with dismay, mouth watered with want and heart threatened to pound out of her chest and into the next room as her serenity of moments before fled and his control seemed to strengthen.

He stood tall, even with both arms gripping the frame, one upraised to the timber lintel overhead, the other stretched to the side, firm upon the jamb. Not a shred of embarrassment or shame filled his posture—or gaze. The heat of it once again doing decidedly peculiar things to her insides.

"You are not going to run screaming from my vile, manly presence?"

"Vile? Whatever would make you say such a thing?" Especially after their exchange of letters not quite six months ago?

He was standing!

He was naked!

He was *standing naked!*

Oh my stars and stockings. She wanted to fan herself.

Nay, you want to climb up that brawny body and see if those broad shoulders are every bit as strong and firm as they appear. You want to sniff, lick along—

"Your l-legs," she babbled, wrenching her attention from the startling brawn in his thighs. Significantly more enhanced than what she recalled feeling beneath her during that wretchedly wonderful all-too-brief mistletoe kiss. "They are working."

"Working?" He gave a gruff laugh, no humor evident. "That is a matter of differing definitions. I am not walking, not without significant aid, if that is what you assume. Certainly not beyond a handful or less of hard-earned steps each day. But at least my legs manage to hold my weight now."

"Which is *wonderful*," she said, warmth brimming in her chest on his behalf.

"Again, differing definitions." He gave a rough shake of his head, dislodging overlong hair from his brow. "Though I do consider it an achievement."

"A *superior* achievement, make no doubt. One worthy of celebration. I am so happy for you."

"Happy?" He gave another light grunt, frown still in place. "What? That I can stand? But only with the help of my arms? When my doctor abandons me not to the care of that hairy hound, but tasks *me* with *caring* for it?"

His...doctor.

Everything became clear in an instant: why he was here; even why he now stood.

This was the indulged, spoiled "London lordling" her uncle had complained of? The "lazy arse" (Uncle Silas had attempted to blot out that last word and had replaced it with *rumple*, but it had made her chuckle nevertheless) who Uncle despaired of, given the peer's grudging reluctance to "comply with my directions" and "see his muscles exerted whether with help or on his own"?

And what might your uncle think when he comes home to find you thus? Agawp over his most "crabbedly difficult" of patients? Fair salivating over—

"You really ought not continue to stand there. Nude!"

He grinned at that. Taking pleasure in her exaggerated affront? "Can I not? What would you have me do, given how my unmentionables are in the filthy mouth of that misbegotten cur? Would you have me indulge in the 'healing waters of Bath'?" His tone mocked the very notion.

Though an air of fatigue clung to him and strain was evident in his tightly held, quivering muscles, his amusement was palpable. His firm, bristle-covered jaw gestured toward the corridor where Mercury had disappeared.

"Were I to *sit* here instead—still bare-arsed, mind—I can confidently assure you I would not be able to gain my feet again. Not today. So do not think to cast blame my direction for any missish airs I might have unintentionally offended." His mirthful expression turned to an all-out glower. "If that fiendish hellhound of Arbuckle's hadn't made off with my drawers after—"

His cheeks turned ruddy. His confident gaze faltered for the first time, as he glanced up to the ceiling and then down to the floor before meeting hers for but a blink only to scuttle away again.

"What embarrasses you *now*?" Now that she could not stop devouring the splendid sight of his body.

For shame! Look away, you hussy.

But she could not. For any *number* of reasons:

1. She was not an immature schoolgirl, without knowledge or awareness of the human form.

Injuries and scars might mar this particular specimen, yet she knew—her eyes confirmed it—she now beheld a beautiful sight indeed.

And no other simple viewing had ever affected her body in such a pleasurable, disconcerting way, had prompted it to—

This is no simple viewing, you brazen gawper!
Hush now.

2. Seeing the occasional bare limb of one of Uncle's patients, when she assisted by either comforting them or

helping him, had never affected any part of her. Not her breathing. Not her belly, nor hollow places lower. Hollow places that now heated, filling with the heavy, almost palatable liquid of desire. No other glimpse had ever engendered a want—or a need—to see more. *To touch.*

3. She had certainly never reacted thus, not to anyone; even the few early heart flutters with Mr. Phillips had *never* managed to make her feel so very aware—of not only who she observed, but of herself. How her body *responded.*

4. Curiosity held her in thrall. For a shifting, breathing naked human was so very different than a picture of a statue in a text or an illicit drawing shared amongst academy students.

5. When might she *ever* be granted such a chance again? To stare, at will, upon—

Him. Lord Warrick.

The man who haunted her nighttime hours.

You have gone beyond three.

So, so many reasons to stare. To commend this sight to memory.

Though the outside light had waned in the last minutes, rendering the inside rooms dimmer, she saw him so clearly. Every bit. So blazingly clear.

6. Their single kiss had commanded her daytime thoughts without permission for months. What might this boon do?

But the real reason she could not force her gaze elsewhere? He was standing! And... And...

7. The masculine contours of his body were undeniably beautiful. Not only the forbidden portions, but the more ordinary ones as well. The flexing, vertical tendons in the wrist of his upheld arm. The angled ones cording his neck, moving with each sway or tilt of his chin. The

shoulders, broad and wide that her fingers tingled to trace. Her lips to kiss. Not everything was smooth and pristine, nor anywhere close. This was a body that had known war. And it showed.

Despite the scarring edging around from the back of one hip and onto his abdomen and upper thigh... Despite the imbalance of the lesser-used muscles in his legs, even with the increase since she had seen him last, not in proportion to those bulging his chest and arms... Despite everything "wrong" with the picture, mayhap because of it, the sight of Richard A. Martinson, Lord Warrick, dried the moisture from her mouth, stole the breath from her lungs and infused her entire being with more longing than ever.

Longing to cross the dozen or so feet that separated them so she could touch, explore... Every fiber of her being strained to be close enough to caress. To heal.

"Had a mishap," he stated flatly when she remained silent and time stretched. "With the bedeviled chamber pot." His scurrying gaze met hers once again. Met and held. The look in his flame-blue eyes turning both irritated and intense.

He bit his lips, as though to prevent further profanities from blustering forth. Then, with a gusty sigh, he released them and continued. "With emptying it. Thanks to yon distraction"—he indicated the missing dog once more—"and my own weakness. Surprised you have not smelled the stench yet. Wrinkled up your nose and made haste away."

This last was accompanied by a shift of one foot and a hard glout toward his legs.

His legs. At the apex of which his penis, hanging loose against his scrotum, jostled. Swung from its resting position and then back. He looked up in time to find her attention fixed there before she jerked her gaze back to his.

"At least it tells me when I need to piss now," he said, sapphire eyes glittering with a touch of defiance. "Every damn time. That's an improvement. Another *superior* achievement to celebrate."

His tone was sardonic. As though *celebrating* the ability to know when one needed to pass water was the most ludicrous thought ever.

"So it is working." The words left her lips even as her heart pounded so intently she grew lightheaded. "Your... twanger? Shall I send for the parson?"

He blinked. Gave his head a light shake.

She'd startled him. Startled herself, more.

Why have you not retreated?

Because not once, not for a moment during this most peculiar of interactions had she felt any modicum of threat or danger. He meant her no harm. Not like the others.

And mayhap *time* had given her the confidence to believe in herself even more. That and her brief dalliance with Mr. Phillips.

Odd, how she'd not thought of him for months, yet twice in the last few minutes, he crosses her mind?

Only because you are relieved you did not pursue a life with him. Else you would not be here now.

Lord Warrick gave a loud bark of laughter and shifted again, bringing his overhead arm down as he leaned against one side of the doorway, still standing, still locked in place, gripping on with his other arm out to the side.

"I did say something of the sort."

"You remember?" Heavens knew she did. Every second of every encounter... Every word, spoken or written.

"But that was assuming you would remain on my lap while we waited for his arrival. Alas, you did not."

"Alas, indeed." She refused to lower her gaze. Refused to fan her flaming cheeks or perspiring forehead. Refused to apologize or be anything other than what she was: fascinated by him. Fascinated by her own responses.

He made a *pffft* sound. "Is it not the manifest duty of every... *Good virgin* when faced with a virile— Damn me. That jest failed. Turned upon myself, it did." He glowered toward his groin before looking back up to give her a forced half grin. His countenance grew harder. "Is it not the duty of every good virgin, when faced with a *non*-virile male to run fleeing and screaming?"

She couldn't fathom leaving. 'Twould be a travesty. But before she could answer him, his expression darkened to thunder clouds. "Or are you going to remove your bonnet and remain? Dispatch your other glove as well? Choose to court danger and scandal by associating with my wicked presence, virile or not?"

"Should not virility be in the eye of the beholder?"

Too bold by half!

22

SHOCK OF THE SEASON

MISS PRIMROSE? *HERE?* In the spawn of Satan's very own abode?

What manner of hell was this?

He'd not heard a thing over the mocking growl of the Canine Terror that had trotted after a snail-paced Warrick into his room—and proceeded to snap jaws around his drawers.

Through the ensuing tug and snarl, unwilling to relinquish his only clean, dry clothing, Warrick had traded balance for dignity and lost. The dog and its gleeful, material-brimming snout bumping their way past the partially open door. Giving chase (a total misnomer, given how unsteady and laboriously slow he was), wishing for the thousandth time he had his trusty chair, Warrick knocked into a painting hard enough it had fallen and cracked the frame—and somehow, he had wound up *here*.

Legs locked against tired, trembling, bare toes curved in a despairing bid to grip the solid floor. Desperate fingers clasping the doorway edges as his previously reliant vision played evil tricks upon his beleaguered brain.

Aphrodite. Only paces away...

Yet an impossible distance, all the same.

"Should not virility be in the eye of the beholder?" his apparition inquired with a saucy tilt of a bonneted head.

Virility? His?

What manner of nonsensical reality was this?

Miss Prim, *complimenting* him? And after having already referred to penises and parsons?

He had to be dreaming. Suffering delusions the toil of the last week had wrought.

"Clarify, if you would," he rasped, still doubting he was awake.

If you slumbered, 'twould not take nearly so much effort to remain upright.

"Why? So you can continue basking in your illicitly inappropriate posture?"

"Mayhap so I can bask in yours."

Though her face and the pale skin betwixt her chin and loosely wrapped scarf flushed peony, her attention remained impressively centered in the vicinity of his loins. "You wish me to clarify how one can find another...virile even when—"

"Aye. Even when." His voice rumbled through his chest before meeting his ears. So...if he could feel the vibration, he must be awake? "Especially as we both know your eyes do not discern *anything* virile before you now."

"Ah. Um." Upon her cheeks, those peonies bloomed anew. Her lips made a single smacking noise, then revealed with admirable certainty, "Because erect or not, you impress more than others I have beheld."

"Others? B*eheld*?" He could no more have stifled his chuckled disbelief than he could have stopped the sun from marching forth on its unwelcome journey to end his delightful roam to the Land of Nod. For sure, the moment it reached its goal, his slumber would stop. Dreams destroyed. But for the meanwhile...might as well savor the angelic vision visiting his sleep. "Why, Miss Aphrodite Primrose, you astonish me. Beholding penises and all."

"Books," she clamored. "Statuary!"

Before he could inquire as to her intriguing literary tastes, she straightened her shoulders and stiffened her spine (girding *her* loins?) and braved, "Assuredly so, you impress. Both in, ah, erm, length *and* breadth, if I am to be blunt."

Dream Prim thought his flaccid penis impressive? Both length and circumference? Strength surged through his trembly muscles.

"By all means, be blunt." *Please.*

"Proportionally speaking, that is. If one were to compare what is *there*"—she waved toward his lengthy, breadthy appendage, the one he wished would rise up and wave its own welcome—"with the rest of your...notable frame..."

An odd satisfaction soothed the wounds in his male pride that had pierced like thorns for years. He could not help but glance down, to endeavor to see himself as she did. Things still looked much the same as they had for months. But damn, if he didn't *feel* bigger.

Blast it all! He *was* dreaming.

Would that not explain the odd turn of events these last scant moments?

Moments that comprised a fraction of the hours and days he had spent in Bath, looking after himself in ways previously foreign, since rolling across the threshold mere days before Christmas...

But only after laborious travel and exhausted efforts

seeing not only to the twins' happiness, but also ensuring the girls were settled, secure and content ahead of his journey?

———————∋⊙⊂———————

A Sennight Prior

After navigating the narrow walkway that led from the road to the front door, his cumbersome chair bumping and lurching over the paving stones and trodden-down grass, Warrick had gotten inside the neat cottage with the help of his groom and coachman. Actually, Lord *Redford's* groom and coachman who had come with his friend's lush traveling coach, Warrick's own having been rendered unserviceable once he sold it.

"Take it, man," Ed had insisted when Warrick protested. His friend had given him no choice, arriving on horseback, carriage and servants in tow, a couple days before his planned journey. "With Anne and our guests to look after"—guests now descending upon Redford Manor for the holiday party Warrick had bowed out of—"I'm going nowhere for the month of December. If I have any need of a carriage, think you there will not be surplus at my disposal? If he can bring his surly carcass as promised, Frost's will be available should I have need of one.

"And the groom? He's a young man who loves horses, though his father is a valet, so he can assist you there as well."

It had been easier to accede than argue.

But that meant the servants with him had little allegiance when faced with Arbuckle's insistence—and unexpected bribery.

The doctor had been swift to dismiss Warrick's "staff",

practically before Warrick had wheeled about to face the three, telling both men to enjoy themselves the next weeks, that he would take care of Lord Warrick. The two servants were to see the horses and carriage cared for, find lodgings or frolic about. To Warrick's tolerant surprisal—at the time—the surgeon had handed each man a small pouch of coins. When they looked to him for confirmation, what could he do but nod? If the doctor wanted to indulge the servants, and spoil Warrick with those here, who was he to protest?

"Good, good," Arbuckle muttered, practically shoving them out the door. "Return in three weeks."

"*Two* weeks," Warrick emphasized, pleased when each man nodded before scurrying off toward the waiting horses.

"Three!" sing-songed Arbuckle. "Three shall suffice!"

"Two," Warrick growled at the frustratingly persistent man. *What did you expect? That his argumentative, trampling nature would transform into naught but clouds and bunnies during the holiday season?*

Bah. Of course he knew better.

Wondered where Arbuckle's servants had gone off to when the surgeon himself started dragging Warrick's heavy trunk past the open doors on either side down through a small hallway that led to a larger drawing-type room, then on past the kitchen, down another corridor and into the room pronounced as: "Yours, for the duration of your stay, Lord Warrick."

A tiny grunt of thanks, especially when his host offered to procure a repast, if Warrick would like to rest.

Over the next couple of hours, seeing himself washed and changed out of his somewhat travel-wearied clothing into the clean, half-dress he thought appropriate to the coming days of body and muscle work, of seeing the plain-but-filling fare quickly consumed, of seeing his tired body hauled from the confines of his ambulatory chair and onto the bed...

Of feeling not only his muscles, but his mind relax for the first time in memory...

'Twas to be expected, perhaps, that his thoughts, just before sleep stole his ability to think, might dwell upon the strange coincidences of circumstances that resulted in his presence in Bath...

How coming to be here proved a miracle of itself. Renting out his townhouse this past summer and moving Shieldings and wife to the estate proved near genius. Who knew the childless Mrs. Shieldings' sister lived not an hour away? And with grandchildren of her own—near his sisters' age?

When he learned a holiday family gathering had been planned for one and all—Shieldings extending the invitation to Warrick with a bit of a red face, indicating he did his wife's bidding, and at the behest of her sister's grandchildren who thought Julia and Sophia "smashing great fun", he had consulted both and received a nod (from Julia) and a *Whoop!* (from Sophia) and agreed they would attend.

Only to shortly after receive a note from King and Knight, telling him (not asking) that they were spending their school holiday with a mate in Birmingham and would not be home at all for the winter break between terms. Well...

When a stalwart Shieldings approached him again, the very night he'd received the twins' proclamation, betwixt a bout of perspiration and pain (seemed doing 200 seat-to-stands twice daily—without consulting Arbuckle —had not been the wisest decision). Regardless, his valet-turned-Tyrant-in-Training, remarked, "My lord, appears my sister-in-law's family are celebrating another birth and want the missus and I to come early. Not the sort of thing one asks of his employer, I know, but—"

"But nothing," Warrick *pffted* on a hard breath as Shieldings near hammered the muscles in his thighs with his beefy fives after the mere 120 they'd agreed upon. Didn't much matter what the soldier, more than two decades older than Warrick, might ask for; he would deliver it. Was the least he could do.

"When you indulged my selfish whims in eighteen twelve and beyond…" During the drink-filled, wallowing months following his injury.

"When you moved here and took up not only helping with this…" Warrick tried to kick one foot out; he got half a toe wiggle but naught else.

"When you, good sir," he told the servant with all heartfelt sincerity, "mucked out my stable and helped butcher those two hogs while Jenken was down on his back?" And had done it all without complaint, even when Warrick's own behavior had warranted it? Well then, "You, Shieldings, may talk to me any damn way you want. About anything on your mind."

Finished with pummeling the slightly more muscular flesh (Warrick thought. Hoped. Desperately prayed…) of one leg, the valued servant turned his attention to the other. The man inhaled—for courage? "Well, Lord Warrick, 'tis like this. There's more younglings at Millie's sister's than you can shake a stick at. Now they are planning a play. A theatrical performance. Two, in fact. Some nativity for Christmas services. But more than, some comedic farce the urchins are insisting on doing 'in secret' and performing for all the adults the last night of the gathering. January sixth or eighth or some such."

There was more. More uncharacteristic babble from

Shieldings. More not-quite-bruising of his tired limbs, until finally, Shieldings pulled back with a heavy sigh. "Sir. The heart of it is thus: Lords Bertram and Beaufort are seen to. Millie and I can guard Lady Sophia and Lady Julia with our lives. I believe they both want to go, and stay. Plan and participate with the other younglings. Lady Sophia told my Millie 'twas so. Seems to me that you have a fortuitous opportunity to heed your doctor's urging. Travel to Bath. Take the waters. Get these feet of yours up and walking."

Lords Bertram and Beaufort.
Ladies Julia and Sophia.

None of them were due any sort of honorific, not given their father's status as a baronet. But since coming to the estate, Shieldings treated his siblings as though they deserved every courtesy that could be bestowed. He and his wife treated both Warrick himself *and* the rest of his family with warmth and respect.

And by damn, if Sophia and Julia *did* want to spend days with their young friends—which he would confirm with them each—then mayhap he should go to Bath. Use the unexpected opportunity circumstances and serendipity dropped in his not-quite always unfeeling lap and acquiesce to Arbuckle's thinly veiled demands (and scrounge some coins to pay something toward his mounting bills) and travel to Bath...

Ergo, how he had come to be here. And at his continued silence, the tacit agreement he'd given that his borrowed servants could enjoy the boon of unexpected coins and time, Arbuckle spread his arms wide and damn near gloated. "After all, is it not the season of joy and generosity?"

Now that Warrick's travel companions had beat a hasty retreat, leaving Warrick, his traveling trunk—just the one, mind—and his finer Merlin's chair lolling in the entry, he was ready to begin. Begin the torture. Hopefully the promised, faster healing.

"What time do we start on the morrow?" Though fatigued, now that he had arrived, part of him perked at the idea of the upcoming physical exertion. His gaze slid to the energetic dog snuffling wet nose and tongue spit over every inch of his trunk alongside him and the surgeon. "When do we leave for the waters? Is that a daily occurrence?"

"It's not the waters I brought you here for," Arbuckle informed him, gloating gone. Stern expression back in place. "It's more that away from the bustle of home, a man's mind as well as his body tends to have more time to rejuvenate."

What? "So if I'm not here to take the waters"—*why in blazes did I travel this far?*—"what will I be doing all day?"

"You shall *be*. Take time to breathe. Watch a butterfly flit—"

"Butterflies? 'Tis December. Frost upon the ground many a morning."

"Watch a snowflake drift downward until it melts. See the sun rise—"

"I sleep till ten. Oftentimes till noon." Not really. Never, in fact. Not since the girls had come to live with him.

"Watch the sun *set* and the stars *rise*," Arbuckle said on an impatient huff at the continued interruptions. "Add in the exercises you have learned. The motions we have gone over both in person and in letters. Do them twice a day. Three times if you are of a mind. But not the same ones every day. Alternate. Change things up from one day to the next. Keep a reconciliation. At the end of three weeks, I daresay you will see as much or more progress as you have experienced the past three months."

"That's *all*?" Any anticipation that had invigored him since his arrival burst like an armour of fish bladder or sheep gut, bloated by breath and twisted until it *popped*. "What a bunch of drivel."

Part of him wanted to get angry, but the rest of him was too travel-tired to do more than protest by rote.

"It's more than you had two and a half months ago."

"No. I mean that's *all* I journeyed days for? Moonrise and exercise?"

The doctor chuckled. "That's quite good, Lord Warrick. You could try your hand at poetry, while you are here. Write a few sonnets or an ode—"

"An ode to my odious doctor?" He leaned forward and nudged the dog away from where it persisted in sniffing his foot, sat back and craned his neck to look into the larger room they had yet to enter. "Your house is not even decorated." Not that he cared. But at this moment, he was determined to nettle the man every bit as much as his unexpected pronouncement rankled Warrick. "You will land me here, in December *for the holiday season*"—*without my family, by damn*—"without anything? No Yule log? No greenery? No—"

The surgeon's palm thrusting toward his face brought the words to an abrupt halt. "I am a busy man, Lord Warrick. A man of my means and station has few-to-no servants. If you want your surroundings decorated, please be at ease to make the effort and see to it yourself."

Hang it all!

The decorations didn't mean nix to him, but he should be back home, overseeing the girls' efforts. Arguing with the twins. Not here, alone. With naught but the aggravating doctor for company. No waters? Why in blazes had he come to Bath? And why did the evil healer continue to insist on three weeks, instead of the two they'd agreed upon, mentioned in letters?

Gah. *A fortnight?* One that suddenly loomed like insurmountable challenge of scaling Egyptian pyramids in his wheeled chair.

"Follow me now," the surgeon said, bending toward his trunk. Gah again. Where were Arbuckle's own people? Had he sent them off with bags of coins as well? "I will see you settled for the evening."

Beyond exhausted from the long days of arduous travel, 'twas easier to retreat, marshal his forces and strength overnight (servants or no), and confront The Tyrant come morning.

ONLY MORNING BROUGHT more unwelcome revelations than the stark and glaring sunlight blustering into his eyes shortly after dawn, due to the uncurtained window in the bedroom he'd been given at the back of the two-story cottage.

23

'TIS MORNING AND MEMORIES CONTINUE...

———◦———

THE FOLLOWING DAY, after a deep and lengthy sleep that had rejuvenated both mind and body, the conversation that should have brought clarity, only confounded instead. For when Warrick roused not long after dawn, scrubbed his face with the plain cloth and tepid water from the basin, both found upon the dresser, and wheeled himself through the tidy home, navigating around furnishings not meant for ambulatory chairs, seeking his host...

The startling sight of a trio of bulging bags stationed in front of the door greeted him. That and Arbuckle himself. Already wearing a heavy cloak.

"Good. You awoke. I was beginning to wonder if I would need to leave a note."

"A note?" Warrick's mouth asked, as his brain struggled to comprehend what his eyes were starting to shout.

"I'm off."

"Off?" The shouting grew louder. "To where?"

Arbuckle was leaving? With packed bags?

The man *tsked*. "And what makes you think my personal business is any sort of yours? You realize you are not my only patient, correct? That would be foolish of me and conceited of you."

"But *off*? I only arrived—"

"And you agreed to stay for three weeks."

"Two." Uncomfortable angling his neck to keep the tall man in focus, Warrick rolled backward a pace or two. Noticed how the muscles in his thighs tensed (at least he thought they did), as though just being near Arbuckle primed them for work. "Two weeks."

"Three. Mercury will need—"

"Who?"

"My dog. You met him last night, lest you forget. You two will take care of each other, and I shall see you upon the new year. The week after Epiphany or thereabouts."

The week *after* Epiphany, which was the sixth. So... January *thirteenth*? Or *thereabouts*? This old fool truly expected him to remain here—by himself (dogs did not count)—for three blasted weeks? "Here now," Warrick began, "stop this bout of ludicrousness. That is impossible."

As if he had protested not, the man continued. "Mercury, now... Keep an eye on your belongings. He's a pilferer at heart. Blind as can be but still quite active." The dog, ever present at the doctor's side tipped his greyed muzzle up in a semblance of agreement.

"Given half a chance, he'll make off with your breeches, even if they are attached to your ballocks." Arbuckle rummaged a hook on the wall and tossed something into Warrick's lap. "Here's his lead. Take him out four or five times a day to—"

"*Four or five times?*" The protest reverberated off the walls. "As in *outside*? When I can barely stand? Arbuckle, your wits have not just gone begging, they have scattered to the ether."

"To take care of things." The surgeon continued as though Warrick had remained silent. "And three of those times, for at least *twenty* minutes." The man with ballocks for brains (mayhap his dog had made away with those too?) behaved as though he were deaf to legitimate protests, simply drew a long, dirt-brown scarf over his coat and wound it around his neck. Warrick beheld a sudden image of wrapping his hands about the edges and *p-u-l-l-i-n-g*...

"Keep any valuables beyond his reach, do your muscle drills and, if you at all can, simply sit—or stand—with your thoughts."

"Stop!" His voice whipped across the space. "What do you mean you're *not staying*? Was not the entire point of me traveling here to continue our work *together*? To hasten my healing?"

"And that is exactly what you shall do, my lord. Only on your own. Continue to regain your strength and independence."

"You cannot *leave*." And if his voice became a bit strident toward the end, a bit panicked? Not at all the tone a titled peer should engage? Well, that could be understood, given the untenable circumstances.

"Of course I can."

"You cannot leave me here. Alone! I forbid it."

"Oh?" The doctor glanced down at Warrick's slippered feet, lolling idle between the wheels upon the horizontal support of the chair he'd been confined to for the better part of two and a half years. "Can I not? I do not see you exerting yourself to stop me."

"And what does that mean?"

"It means, *my lord*"—the healer made a mockery of his

status—"that in order for you to truly get better, to the extent that I now believe possible, you must take pains to apply yourself *more* than you have thus far. You and Merc shall maintain things here whilst I take myself off."

"N-nay! You are not abandoning me to go g-gadding about," Warrick all but sputtered, his hands fisting helplessly in his lap. "I refuse to allow it."

"My lord..." Both the tone and sardonic smile mocked, damn the insolent man. "Perhaps you have not examined your accounts of late, but you have yet to pay a single invoice these last sixteen weeks. Not a single one." Another *tsk-tsk*. "That is suitably long enough for me to either cease assisting you or consider debtors' prison."

"As if you would dare—"

His words went unheeded.

"And as we have been working together for twice that long, I say you *will* remain here. You *will* feed Mercury, see that he is exercised thrice daily—"

As the impotence of his entire situation came crashing down, his temper flared. "Thrice? How in blazes do you expect me to walk a damn dog?"

The surgeon gave an indifferent, one-shoulder shrug. "I have no doubt you will manage, for *this* is how you will satisfy your account.

"In addition to caring for my sweet boy"—Arbuckle paused to rub the slobbering cur under the chin and around one ear—"you will take suitable care of yourself as well. You will bathe. You will dress each day as though expecting company. No wasting about like a drunkard in your nightclothes.

"And after your reminder last eve how I have been remiss, I have left some ribbons and candles and such on the kitchen table. Please see that they are strewn about in honor of the season. My only excuse for neglecting the task this year was that I invited my niece to join me as she always has, but alas, work kept her away."

What manner of work would a surgeon's niece be engaging in that would refuse her time off for the holidays? Blasted woman, he thought irrationally, but with no small amount of gleeful irritation—thankful to have a target for his ire. 'Twas all *her* blame fault. If she were here now, Warrick certainly wouldn't be.

"Regardless of her absence, we cannot let the season go unremarked, and so it shall fall to you, *my lord*, to attire my home appropriately, so that you will enjoy it while I am away, and I may upon my return. Christmas services are Saturday, should you choose to attend and—"

"Attend services? When I'm not even sure I can fasten my falls?" Of course he could. Had been since waking, finally sensible, in London. But his growing wrath toward the tyrant proved boundless. "You had me abandon my girls—"

"Fasten your falls?" the doctor repeated with an embarrassed cough. "Well now, Lord Warrick. That does seem the perplexing conundrum. One would think a man of your mature years would know how to secure his pants, whether that be breeches, pantaloons or trousers and *without* assistance."

Warrick's snarl rivaled that of the best fighting dog.

Arbuckle only smiled—this one with true humor, the contrarious surgeon.

The older man looped the strap of one traveling case over his shoulder and picked up the others. He turned and reached for the doorknob. "I shall see you—"

Warrick thrust upward. His chair clomped into the wall behind him. His palm slapped the door the moment the other man edged it open, the momentum from his body slamming it shut. "What the bloody blazes?"

He'd traveled well over 200 miles to come for: "*Private, frequent treatments. The healing waters of Bath.*" His voice dragged over the words like they were jagged gravel. "That's what you claimed when you proposed this hash."

The hand flush against the door helped him remain upright though his worse leg had started to shake. So he shook his opposite arm in the air, hoping somehow to fling the frustration out his body. And if he flattened the deceitful doctor or scared the thieving dog, so much the better. "I did *not* travel all this way to be a bloody, glorified bitch minder."

At that, Arbuckle frowned, took one step forward and got right in Warrick's face. "Mercury is male. And you are an arse. An arrogant, pious lordling who has done little to bear the right to the title you hold. You—"

"You shall not speak to me that way," Warrick protested more as a matter of habit, pride piqued more than out of real angst. But as it was, now even his better leg quivered. Neither should be trembling about, not this soon after waking. He blamed being cooped up in a carriage the last few days.

If he didn't end this soon, his slowly healing, but exhausted-from-the-journey muscles would end it for him. And he would end up a heap on the floor. "Do not forget whom you address."

The doctor's eyes, normally full of patience and perseverance, lit with a flash of indignation. "And do not forget within whose home you stand."

"I have yet to meet your servants." The words shot out from between gritted teeth.

"No servants. You will get along just fine without them. I do."

"I will not!" Warrick yelled, completely at the end of any resolve, control or courtesy. "I bloody well will not go on the next three damn weeks without a bloody servant to assist where—"

"You can *bloody* walk!" For the first time in their months-long acquaintance, Arbuckle placed his hand on Warrick in anger, clutching his shoulder in a strong pinch and jerking the muscles to and fro. "You *can*! If you will only concentrate your efforts that direction without allowing others to coddle you. To keep you from gaining strength and confidence on your own!"

Warrick jerked back, both hands falling limply to his sides. Never before had he heard the surgeon raise his voice. Never had he seen the doctor tremble with rage—and it was all directed his way. Unfamiliar with feeling the force of another's wrath (battle opponents notwithstanding), he stood there in silence, heart thrumming, beating hard against his ribs, as he clenched every muscle he could manage to remain upright, on his weakening legs, his exhausted feet.

As though surprised at his own outburst, Arbuckle ran one hand over his face, cupping his chin a few seconds before lowering it and resuming the calm nature Warrick had become accustomed to. "My lord.

"Have you walked unaided? At all?"

"Unaided? You mean without a cane?"

"No, I mean have you been able to take more than a step without your hands gripping furniture or a wall? There's no shame in a cane or walking stick, none at all."

"I know that," he said sharper than intended. "And nay, I have not. Look at my limbs. Do they not tremble before you even now?"

A level of understanding that had been heretofore missing entered the other man's gaze. "As your doctor, I am instructing you the best way I know how. Stay here.

Care for Mercury—and yourself. Give your body time to regain strength, and give your mind time to calm."

In seconds, the man opened the door a few inches and slipped through, with only a couple clunks and weaves, maneuvering himself and his trio of cases until he snapped the door shut behind him.

Leaving a stunned, sweating, sore-in-body, weary-in-spirit man clutching the closest wall for support—and crumpling to the floor regardless.

Bloody hell.

THE MOMENT HE WAS BEYOND sight of the door, Silas Arbuckle paused. Turned a corner and rested his back against his trusty abode.

His heart hammered painfully, making deep breaths a chore, one that might have scared another man—made him fear obliteration.

But nothing was wrong with his panter, he knew. His heart was as strong as an ox. As stubborn as a mule, much like the man he'd just left. Nay, it was confronting the confounding man now occupying his house that unnerved.

Was he doing the right thing? Badgering the earnest lordling so?

Warrick might have been an angry annoyance when they first met, a true tinder-box with unreasonable expectations, but time—and his mother's death—had matured the determined peer swift enough.

He wasn't nearly so irksome anymore. But still, 'twas a risk Silas took now.

If anything happened to dear Merc while in Lord Warrick's care—

Nay. He mustn't think thus.

Silas shrugged his heaviest bag up higher over his shoulder, firmed his grip on the other two as he firmed his resolve.

Had he not promised the ingrate's mother, Lady Warrick, the last time he'd seen her (mere weeks before the kind woman breathed her last) that he would do all within his power to help "her boy" if, Silas had stressed at the time, "the boy will agree to be helped"?

And while Silas had never considered himself a performer of miracles, he had witnessed near bodily miracles a time or two. Enough to trust. To pray. To hope.

Hope. Pray. Trust.

An inhale of crisp air to fortify both body and mind. "I *hope* you do not harm my dog," he muttered, starting off again, as his destination beckoned. "For if you do, lordling, I *trust* you cannot *pray* my wrath away..."

The brisk December wind buffeted his cheeks and forehead.

Ugh. "Forgot my hat."

His scalp tingled. For did not the lady he was on his way to see love running her fingers through his still-thick, now silvered hair?

She did, indeed.

And the anticipation of being with her again, if even in secret thus far, lent wings to his feet (Hermes and Mercury would be so proud) as he sped the scant distance toward the female awaiting his arrival.

THREE DAYS LATER, Warrick wasn't sure whether to laugh or yell. Rolling along the blame floor, embarrassingly slow at navigating the geegaw-laden abode, chasing a blind-arse dog who carried the sash of his robe between his teeth and growled anytime Warrick came close.

But though tired, as the antics continued, he was laughing, lighter in spirit than he expected, especially given how he'd felt this morning—or should he say come nooning?—after yesterday, feeling overly maudlin and missing his family, turning himself into a bingo boy with his host's brandy.

But as the hours and days had worn on and Warrick occupied himself with the dog, it seemed as though Arbuckle's unorthodox treatment had some merit. For the games betwixt him and the dog, their own versions of hide-and-seek and tug of war (once he located the noisy barker), along with the cessation of all his other responsibilities, had truly allowed his mind to do as ordered: to simply be, for the first time since Albuera. Mayhap for the first time in years.

And if he'd contemplated the ancient harpsichord occupying a rather prominent place in the drawing room a time or two? Wondered how poorly tuned it might be (dwelling with The Tyrant, as it were), then... He had yet to appease his idle curiosity.

Hadn't touched it. Not once.

Because playing whilst he was here did not at all fit his memories of the bawdry revelry, the evenings he would play whenever he and his mates could escape school for a wild night of fun and dancing. Lewd songs always upon his lips...

In this nearly silent abode, if one discounted the hound's clattering toenails and entertaining snarls, the slight squeak of Warrick's chair or its wheels, or the occasional gasp he made when he approached the end of his hundreds' count, forcing his body up and down, angling his toes or ankles (more like simply trying to and not accomplishing anything there)... In the charming if somewhat crowded cottage of his piously persistent host, touching the keyboard for the first time since the accident prickled at something in him. Made him decidedly uncomfortable.

So he strove to ignore it. Angled his chair and therefore his back to the instrument and wheeled out of the formal room and toward the kitchen. Time to wrap the twine he'd discovered—after poking his nose into Arbuckle's cabinets—around the dog's front legs and chest, sit at the doorway while the barker romped and pissed to his content.

SILAS ARBUCKLE NUDGED the heavy curtain aside, wiped condensation from the glass and focused his hand telescope beyond the one window that managed a glimpse toward the back, kitchen exit of his home. If he stood upon his toes, balancing most of his weight on his right foot and angling his head just so, he could glimpse the upper half of the doorway and a good portion of his rocked-in yard.

"Is he there?" The feminine voice behind him preceded two arms wrapping around his middle and a chin just barely reaching his shoulder and looking over.

"Not yet. It's past time. Mercury has to be howling by now."

Behind him, and her, the room exuded warmth, and no, it wasn't just from the past hours of exertion, but from the hearth that burned merrily. In front of him? The chill strode in from the glass now that the thick curtains no longer helped keep it contained.

Dawn was long since past. And, aye, Arbuckle had stood vigil practically since dark.

'Twas the first morning since he'd abandoned his cherished pup into the other man's questionable care that he'd woken early enough to keep watch, knowing his dog's bladder as well as his own.

He'd meant to check long before now, but had been, admittedly—and aroused-ly (real word or not, that's what came to mind, with a pleasurable, highly satisfied tingle near his groin)—distracted.

His distraction hugged his waist. "Give him time yet. He'll rise to the challenge, never you fear."

"I pray, with everything in me, that you have the right of it." His feet and calves tiring, he came down off his toes to rest on his heels. When his arms came down as well, bringing the telescope with it, his companion released her hold, took up the looking glass and scooted around in front of him, now standing on her toes to peer forth as well. "If not, too easily can I imagine either him—or my dog—destroying my entire home."

She made a soothing *hmmm* that managed to comfort, if not entirely vanquish his concerns.

He stretched his neck, his eyes glancing over the rumpled bedclothes in the small room they inhabited. 'Twas attached to an even smaller kitchen and not much else, in this, the tiny home where they met.

About the only compliments he could give it (aside from his companion's warm-and-welcome presence) was cleanliness and conveniency. When he first visited her here, after she leased it, he hadn't even realized the location of the tiny abode would afford him such a boon as to look toward his own.

"Wait! Is he coming out now?" Her voice held excitement as she scrambled to return the spyglass to his hands and move aside so he could look out.

And aye, the door that led into his kitchen had swung inward.

"Vi, bless you." He couldn't help the relief that breathed out on a sigh. "You have much more faith in him than I— Wait. 'Tis not him emerging." Every muscle tensed in surprise. Dismay. "But Mercury, alone!"

The coarse brown fuzz atop his dog's head, two floppy ears on either side, bounced out into the cold.

Silas watched with dawning horror as his blind, aged dog nosed his way right into the yard. No tall, lumbering man followed; no seated gentleman, within a jerkily moving Merlin's chair followed either. Nothing!

His hands clenched so tightly around his late father's spyglass the poor metal squeaked. "I will give him five seconds to join Merc and then I'm going over there..."

In silence, five seconds elapsed. Her soft but strong touch splayed across his upper back. Soothing, bidding him to patience.

But then seven more. And his dog was still alone— outside!

He shrugged out of her loose hold and tossed the hand telescope down on the bed. "I apologize, but nay. I cannot wait any longer."

While he found his outerwear and sat on the mattress to tug on first his trousers and then his boots, his actions harried and hurried, she had taken up his vigil at the window.

Standing, he reached for his overcoat, beyond ready to give that selfish, inconsiderate lord a scathing for the ages. Coat in place, he looked for his hat, only then recalling he had forgotten it.

"Silas. Leave off your inpatient retreat and return." She spoke quietly but firmly, that gentle tone full of strength. Convincing strength, did she but know it. Else, how could she have convinced him to sacrifice his home—and canine companion—for this trial?

"He's there. He's come." For the first time in nearly a minute, his chest didn't hurt when he drew breath. "Haltingly." She continued sharing what she saw. "Appears to be swearing up and down at the dog"—she dared to chuckle at that, which lightened his strain even more—"and cursing his legs, too, but he's there. Just lured Mercury back to him, with... With something in his hand."

Just as he was ready to rip the spyglass from her, she handed it over. "Ham?" she surmised. "I cannot tell."

But Silas could. He could tell that Lord Warrick remained on his seat, in one of the kitchen chairs he had dragged over. After yelling (seen, not heard), Lord Warrick used fingers wrapped around the door jambs to haul himself to his feet. Scowling, he leaned against the frame and held his hand out toward the circling dog. A hand holding a definite clump of ham. "Good God, that's too much for my boy. Mercury will choke on it going down."

"He shall be fine, Silas," she soothed, liberating the telescope from his grasp and turning him away from the window with a tug on his coat sleeve. "Both man and dog will be fine, I assure you. Now, what shall we do today? Because hours spent at that window, one of us practically falling on our side to see that sliver of yard will not suffice. I cannot let my monthly trip to Bath to see you elapse without some form of entertainment that doesn't involve being stript to skin and wrapped in your arms. No matter how enjoyable that might be."

TIME PASSED AND THE HARPSICHORD still tempted. Drew Warrick like times expired.

Though it was an older machine, with polished, gleaming burled wood about the casing, 'twas not entirely in its principal condition. At some point, someone had severed its original legs from its body and lowered it upon a base either meant for another instrument or made, perhaps, specifically for this one, but the wood that supported the body was different both in type, garnishment and stain.

Not nearly as ornate as the original. Much plainer, more serviceable. Not as visually alluring.

The black and white paint was worn in places over the slim, wooden keys. Someone had loved and played this instrument once upon a time

But now it sat, abandoned.

Warrick hated that he noticed such detail. Churned inside at the similarities he felt with the ignored instrument. Dust coated the exterior and the horizontal bench tucked beneath the manuals. A serviceable bench but not fanciful like what hovered above it.

With care, the masterpiece would have been stunning, but instead was dulled with age and time. Yet he could not stop his thoughts from rumbling over how someone, at some point, had taken time to take the instrument intended to be played while *standing* and lowered it, like the more popular pianofortes of today, enabling it to be played while *seated*.

It was a double manual, with one keyboard stacked atop another. Three choirs. *Three.* That was notable. Three separate strings per note…not simply the more common and frugal single string.

He knew because on his fifth day here, he had lifted the closed lid, propped it up and *looked*. But naught else.

The night of the sixth, found him staring at the instrument from across the room. Thoughts of plying his fingers to the aged instrument had him clenching them tight and he closed them into a fist that didn't unfurl until Mercury wandered into the room, sniffing...finding...and making his way over to Warrick's side. Panting softly, the dog nosed his legs and shifted, sat down upon his haunches and leaned against Warrick's right leg.

He closed his eyes, let his right arm drift down to sift the tips of his fingers through the coarse fur. Tried to determine if he really felt the pressure of the warm body resting against the side of his calf.

Or if he only imagined it.

24

BACK TO THE (NAKED) PRESENT

—⊃○⊂—

Returning to now...

His chair had gone missing two nights ago. He'd woken yesterday morn to find it *gone*. He certainly hadn't *misplaced* the blame contraption. Nor had the dog hidden it.

So where the devil had it gotten off to?

But at least its disappearance explained why, in his questionable murky-conscious state he now stood, trembling and bare, before the sunset-haired, freckled angel who persisted in haunting his deepest dreams...

Exhaustion. Pure, sheer, all-encompassing exhaustion.

Is that not what his hours had been the last forty-eight or more? Ever since waking with his trusty chair no longer beside his bed?

No wonder his garret conjured visions to nourish and succor.

Succor? Do you not mean suck the sense right out the gap between your ears?

True. To be imagining such…

Miss Prim? Whatever brought her here? To the Blasted Tyrant's abode?

"I could offer apologies for not greeting you properly," his dream self said now, "but you are the one who has burst upon me uninvited."

"Have you wed? Since last we corresponded? Or—or met? Your letters didn't say—"

"Why would you ask that?"

"I would—would stop looking."

"And shred my newly soothed pride? Please do not. And no, no wooing nor wife. No desire for either."

"Well. Good, then."

Good?

That confirmed it. He *was* dreaming.

Or dying.

Aye, *dying* would explain *everything*. Instead of laboriously making his way back to his room, he had never left the kitchen after the calamitous events of that afternoon.

The kitchen, where he'd been crossing to reach the outside pail he would empty that evening, the pail just beyond the door used during daytime hours for convenience. But he had not made it over the hard floor. Of course not, else he would not be having such visions now. He had, in fact, slipped in the sludge—spilt only when the damned dog jumped up from behind and knocked heavy paws into his back. Shoving him—and the bowl balanced within his hands as precariously as Warrick himself balanced upon his feet, into the table.

The dog had jumped. Knocked him askew.

Pot went flying. Or rather, dropping. Straight to yon floor, in a smelly, slick mess of broken shards and disgusting filth that needed cleaned. Cleaned swiftly—before the imbecilic dog pranced paws through it and dragged the stench through the house.

It mattered not that this was, if not the *first* disaster he'd dealt with during his week-long stay, then definitely the *worst* disaster he'd faced. It mattered not that he washed his hands (and feet), after removing shoes, and made his stumbling, slow and laborious way to his assigned room to scrounge his last remaining set of clean clothing before tackling the disparaging rumfoozle.

Mattered not that *he* had washed his other clothing, *all* that he hadn't donned that very morning, and had wrung them out and spread to dry—also in said kitchen. Even his great coat had been sponged of dog dander and opened outside in to dry and air.

At first, he'd tried to keep up heating fires in the two or three rooms he occupied. But had quickly discovered 'twas warmth or starvation. Food had won out.

At night, after a day chasing behind the dog—who liked to make off with *anything* near at Warrick's hand not cemented down (neckcloth, handcloth, sock, pencil, half-written letter to Shieldings and the girls, three-quarters of a letter penned to the twins, the last slice of ham upon his plate...ad nauseam...), it was all he could do to leverage himself onto the bed and sleep like the dead.

Which meant he hadn't kept up with heating the house, not at all.

He preferred to sleep shivering, but with a belly not gnawing at him in hunger, when not back-snugged by the damned dog. The dog who sometimes used the stealth and quiet of night to bang around the house, stealing things and making a general, audible, nuisance of himself until Warrick had trained himself to ignore the odd thumps and shuffles, if he had any hope of staying asleep.

He already put himself out to an extensive degree, caring for "dear Merc" during daylight hours, didn't need to add to his misery at night.

Already "walking" said damn dog twice daily (*thrice* had been out of the question from the moment it was uttered). Not when he also comforted the whining hound during more than one night terror that had woken them both. For the barker's sleep, when he deigned to join Warrick upon the bed, proved far less restful than Warrick's own.

You have your angels tending you in your misery; the old, blind dog has naught but you.

Pah.

It had taken days before the sound of Warrick's voice was enough to soothe the beast. He wouldn't admit it, but his heart had gone out to the mongrel. Must be difficult to not have the use of sight to help make your way. Especially when a stranger invaded your midst. And your trusted owner and constant companion abandoned you to said invalid.

The first two days, both he and the dog had whined and wallowed about. But Warrick soon took pride in every little accomplishment. After a several-hour bout of rain, unsticking the back door? Puffed his beleaguered soul up as though he'd won a prize.

Managing meals for both himself *and* his four-footed sightless friend? More accomplishments. More difficulties, yet more pleasure each time he provided full bowls and bellies for them both. Even if it was only once or twice each day.

And while he wasn't certain he approved of Arbuckle's recent and deceptive methods, Warrick had to admit being away from his already scant servants—and siblings, who he may have come to rely on a bit more than was wise (to fetch and barter with, whenever others weren't around, offering to assist with whatever he might need) had brought him an unexpected measure of both satisfaction and independence.

Despite his vocal complaining—first to Arbuckle, then to the sightless dog who seemed not affected in the least at any amount of growled complaints or curses—what mattered was that Warrick had done it.

He had survived this past sennight. In part on his doddering feet. Mostly with the use of his chair, until recent hours. He had fed himself. And the dog. Successfully emptied the blasted chamber pot—until today—and kept them both alive, if not necessarily warm.

But now that he'd slipped in his own spilt shite and obviously hit his head on the way down, likely cracked it open upon the hard landing, he was dreaming. That explained *everything*.

Dreaming. Dying.

Because why else would he—in his dream-induced state, no doubt—be clutching the door jambs and waving his limp prick boldly at the one lass he thought of more than any other not already family?

Already?

His head started to pound. "Tell me I'm dead, if you would. Either that or stitch back in any brain matter that still resides in the kitchen. For you look too inviting by half. And I have not the energy nor the will to fight...you...myself...imaginings...any..."

The room—and even Miss Prim, whose startled smile grew dim—sped by in a haze as his body gave out and he wilted to the floor in one fell, painful *swoop*.

Splat.

And that was that.

. . .

"Your chair! Where is it?" Aphrodite all but screeched, in stunned panic when the strong and powerful man before her just *dropped*. Wilted.

His face turned white as curd, eyelids flickered and *whomp*, downward he sank.

Pushing past the dog—mouth now empty of its prize—she raced forward, arms outstretched, knees hitting the ground as her dress slid over the floor in her haste to reach him. "Did you hit your head?"

Groaning, he turned and faced her, blinking, forehead rumpled above dazed eyes before they drifted shut. "P-prim?"

"Answer me!" She brushed her hands over his head. No bright blood, thank heavens.

"Blazes if I know." His voice was weak, weaker than expected, given how he had bantered with her the last few moments.

"You don't know if you hit your head? Or you don't know where your chair is?"

Could a man shrug while lying down? His shoulders seemed to lift, as did his upper torso. Blazes was right! His chest. Her nails cut into her palms as she resisted the urge to pet him. To feather her fingers over not just scalp and hair, but *skin*.

You must get him off the floor!

"Your chair! Where is it?"

"What...I would...like to know."

She couldn't help it. She smoothed his brow.

With a sigh, he seemed to sink even deeper into the floor.

"What? You could not have *lost* it."

"In full...agreement, but there it is." His lashes fluttered open, that startling blue gaze catching hers before they slammed shut again. He moaned. She couldn't tell if it was in pain, or perhaps more of *his* style of flattery and flirtation (only suspected because of how he seemed to *rise* into her touch). Either way, the sound reached toward her stomach and *twisted*. "Or *not* is. Gone. Stolen? Ask Mercury."

Mercury? Who now snuffled about the fallen man's legs.

His words weren't very clear. Exhaustion? Or had he conked his noggin in truth?

"Heathen dog"—that was clear enough—"likely snuffled it one night, bartered it for an hour with a pretty bitch."

She snickered. Found she had somehow scooted beneath his head, drawn it into her lap and now cradled the sides of his face with her palms. Her fingers testing the bristle of his chin. Her thumbs brushing over his temples and toward that black-as-sin hair. "That is not the least humorous. He's ten or twelve by now. And—and—"

His lashes flew open, eyes looking clearer than they had just seconds ago. "You think time would dull my desire?" *For you* might have gone unsaid, but they both heard it plain enough. "Because it wouldn't."

She swallowed the knot that had lodged in her throat. His hair was like silk. She tried to concentrate. To think.

Because *Get him off the floor* had turned into *Save yourself and your sanity!*

"Still adept with the ribald gallantry, I see."

Swifter than she might have expected, he grasped one of her arms, coiled his fingers around her unsuspecting wrist and stroked his thumb over the delicate blue veins just beneath the surface. They both watched the motion until he lifted his head, leaned up on the bent arm that wasn't holding hers captive, and met her gaze straight on.

"Is it flirting if 'tis the truth? If it isn't something said to shock or entertain?"

The knot was back. Bigger than before. Making it difficult to breathe. "Lord Warrick, I—"

"Richard."

"R..." Her voice faltered at the intimacy he'd just invited.

The husky tone of his voice made it seem later than it was. Nearing midnight instead of merely the dusk of evening approaching.

His eyes gleamed. "Aye. My name. Rarely heard since I became the earl before I gained even nine years on my plate. I would have you use it."

"I..." Her lashes swept downward, hiding the depths this man made her feel.

So bloody dangerous, Aphrodite.

"I... Mayhap. But not now. Not when you are on the floor and...and—"

"Naaaaaked?" 'Twas a droll, elongated sound.

"Aye, that," she squeaked, feeling her face flame anew. "Now, while you have me looking like a roasted tomato, let us get you upright, back on your feet and to bed."

"I *adore* seasoned, roasted tomatoes. And we might have to skip over upright. Do away with further ado and seek ourselves straight to bed—given how my limbs shake even now."

The truth of that, the gritting of his jaw, the single, fast clasp of his fingers—warm and strong—about her wrist before he released her all that kept her from chastising him.

Well, that and the sight of his large, hardened, scarred body as he shoved the inquisitive dog aside, rolled to his stomach and used his arms to drag himself toward the passageway that led toward the sole sleeping chamber on this, the ground floor.

Breath labored from the entire encounter, fingers fizzing at the remembered texture of his hair, she followed a pace or two behind—trying, unsuccessfully, to keep her gaze off *his*.

His *behind*. Blazes and blazing fires brimming in her belly. The flex of pale, smooth muscle fired through her—

But then she gasped. Choked. Slapped a hand over her mouth to smother the sounds. But 'twas too late. For he flinched as though struck. Paused. Angled sideways until he captured her gaze and froze her in place, his eyes heated, as though she hadn't near strangled upon seeing the mash of mottled skin and sickening scars that knotted about the base of his spine.

"You are beautiful to me. More stunning tonight than ever before. What happened to make it so?" His forehead creased, head gave a hard shake. "Naught but a vision, I know, but still so very welcome. I will see myself to bed. Do not follow."

A loud sigh. A frown, and he rolled back to his stomach. Several more surprisingly smooth shuffled steps of his strong arms and he disappeared from view.

Leaving her more disordered than she had ever been in her life, and taking into account a couple of her encounters with titled men and their relations, that was saying something.

"I'm not seeing the log pile go down. Not for a while, now."

Viola, Silas's lovely companion, made this remark with definite concern. No surprise as this day had grown colder than any other and now marched decidedly toward nightfall.

Concern which made him feel lower than he wanted to admit. "We know he hasn't frozen through. Does he not open the door several times a day, lure poor Mercury out with a haunch of meat, tied to a blasted string, and lazily wait before reeling him in like a deuced fish?"

She made a murmur of agreement, for one of them had seen just that at least once each day.

Silas swallowed the rock her worry had grown in his throat. "Fret not about the wood. Likely his belligerence keeps him warm."

"You gruff about him often enough." She spoke toward the window, where her face was in shadows, leaning forward as though she could melt through the glass and go order a fire built—if not to do it herself. "But I think you have a fondness for him."

"Pah," he disparaged, determined to ignore the nagging uncertainty that grew every day he didn't see his most irritating patient "walk" outside, or at least lean, upon his feet, against the rock wall while dispensing his canine duty.

She abandoned her stance at the window and came over where he had been tidying his notes for the last week's appointments with various patients—or at least pretending to, his mind certainly not on the task as it should have been.

He might be visiting them this month, especially ones he had been seeing for a spell, instead of requesting they come to him, where he had equipment and instruments they might not, but in truth... With most families occupied with each other this time of year? With the cold that had climbed into this southern part of England? Between fact and the short daylight hours, meant he had precious little to occupy him outside of her cherished companionship and troublous thoughts of the stubborn lord who, it seemed as time went on, truly might not be able to walk.

Viola smoothed the rumpled paper from his grip, the pencil from his clutch. She drew him up to standing. "You do. Else he would not be inhabiting *your* home."

"My home *and* my garret, more's the pity. Would rather be thinking of you and naught else."

She gave him that siren smile, the one he never would have expected, not in a trillion years, to have directed his way, the first time they met. "Come now, I will ensure you have no thoughts of anything but me..."

WARRICK AWOKE WITH HIS HAND fisted about an erection.

Shock quivered through him like an electric charge. Blasted through his mind like a lightning bolt.

Shook his frame, clenched his fingers—and then was gone. Vanished in the stark light of late morning that blared through his window. Banishing it all. Everything...

Gone.

Both the phantasms of the delicious dream that hovered on the fringes, just out of grasp...

Out of grasp, also, was any semblance of wood. Of firmness. His fingers now squeezed about pliable flesh. Weak flesh that suddenly sickened him as he released his disappointing prick and rubbed the flat of his hand over his chest where the firm muscles and crisp hairs didn't disappoint and disgust.

Damn. He'd imagined it. Hadn't been stiff and stout at all.

And what was with the beat of song elevating his heart? The lift of spirits?

Why was his body in such a fine mood? Especially when his muscles ached as though he'd gone rounds blindfolded with Gentleman Jackson—and lost handily. Especially when he needed to piss with such urgency he feared soiling his sheets for the first time in nearly two years?

A guttural moan tore from his throat as he rolled, bracing himself with one hand gripped about the edge of the mattress, his other reaching for the chamber pot—

Only to stop. As he trembled anew. Felt a tiny, unmistakable flutter in his groin.

A pounding in his garret.

Because *all* of his things were gathered. In neat array. All his clothing *folded*. The ones he'd washed and strewn with haphazard care about the kitchen to dry. Transformed into tidy stacks upon the dresser.

And then the voice of an angel—his angel—reached through the shock and dismay. Zapped along his body…

Endangered the flame of mortification. Raised the flare of red-hot desire.

"Hush now, Mercury. We have already been out twice." The soft, melodic sounds caressed his ears. "No, you may not wake him. Lord Warrick, *Richard*, needs his sleep. Nay—do you not grumble and growl at me, young man."

A bark. A playful snarl.

Light, feminine laughter that threatened to claim his ballocks right then. "All right. I concede. *Old* man. But one still spry and naughty…much like the *man* sleeping yon."

He fell over to his back with a flop. A silent growl of his own.

Holy hell. 'Twas real? All of it?

His "dream" came rushing forth.

She's here? His earth-bound angel was truly here? Had caressed his face? Sparred with him? Traded quips and seen him in all his brazen-ballocks and phallic-swinging glory?

"By damn, Aphrodite Primrose..."

It hadn't been a dream? None of it? He hadn't imagined it? The kitchen full of his body's filth? Swooning nearly at her feet? Crawling off, arse-naked, before her avid gaze? His fingers clenched tight within the sheet.

Gad, snaffle me now.

25

COMING CLEAN

The faint, disappearing waft of things better left unsmelled greeted his nose when he braved venturing beyond his room. His legs, which should have strengthened overnight, trembled like a newborn foal's as he shuffled toward the kitchen. His enfeebled steps given to staggery, made possible only by the strength of his outstretched arms bracing his weight on either furnishings or betwixt narrow walls.

Her back to him, hands busy at the sink, she pretended not to hear his reeling, noisome steps as he clutched one hand on the back of a pulled-out chair (one he'd previously placed in its current position expressly for that purpose—and she'd left it alone, bless her) and hauled himself around to sit in the next nearest.

"You cleaned. You scrubbed *everything*." He sat there, stunned, craning his neck and taking in what all she had done—and it was substantial. He barely wavered in place, more steady than he would have been four months ago.

Hell, even two months ago. How easily he recalled the disaster that had bedecked the kitchen mere hours ago. He whistled as his gaze flicked from gleaming counter to sparkling floor. "And you are *here*. In truth."

She'd turned at his low whistle. "I am."

"So 'twas not my imaginings. None of it." How did he feel about that?

"Nay, it was not."

How did he feel about her? Aphrodite Primrose, so close he could almost touch.

And for the first time ever, not wearing heavy dark bombazine better suited to mourning than morning. Instead of the thick, ugly fabrics he had always associated with her form, softer attire adorned her now. The simple day dress she wore might have been years out of style, noticeably older and slightly worn, but upon her, 'twas so very fetching. In truth, the pastel blue—a much thinner fabric than he associated with her—tempted his touch. So much so that he gripped his thighs under the table and out of sight, to occupy his hands. His trembling, tingling hands...

As he stared at her, her eyes bright and cheeks flushed, gilded hair pulled back close to her scalp and tied up tighter than he might wish, more cinnamon-copper today instead of the fiery hue he longed to sink his fingers into.

Her hair. That and the flare of her hips he'd discerned in the past despite the brown abominations she had worn, the least angelic things about her.

Part of their past floated to him, unbidden.

Many evenings into the house party, when it was closer to ending than not, after the hours of dancing and revelry he had watched but not participated in, easily overlooked in his quiet spot between two curtained French windows, the loneliness of his situation had struck hard. Long after everyone else was abed, he remained in the now silent, empty and dark room, staring into the shadows.

The outside shadows, no candles nor other lamps burning behind him to distract how his attention sought out the inky blackness of night. A cold night, not a hint of clouds to blanket any warmth over the land.

The moon but a sliver, the crescent beaming stark and pale through the barren branches of a tree. Had that been the tree where his earth-bound angel had greeted him when thoughts of Albuera hounded and cast their own shadows over his mind? Was that near the bench where Redford had caught them? Or more precisely, caught Warrick reaching for what he craved...

And told him to keep his hands, and his yearnings, to himself.

As though his mental wanderings had conjured the presence of the prickly, perplexing female, her silent-but-nevertheless-sensed incursion into the ballroom had him, already reduced to utter stillness, watching her reflection as she loosed a loud sigh and walked the edges around the floor. Wistfully? At least he thought it was so, and could not stop himself from spinning his chair away from the cold window and toward the hoped-for heat and light of Miss Prim.

"Is it true," he'd mused, hoping she would stay and engage and only feeling a slight sliver of guilt when his voice caused her to startle and skid to a halt. "What Ed claims? That before your governing talents were hired to tame the firebrand, that Lady Harriet used to change governesses as frequently as most ladies do dancing slippers?"

Her inhale was audible. The hand she wound within the fabric of her skirt—and nerves it bespoke of—discernible only because he was attuned to the night. To nuances, it seemed, where she was concerned. "As to that, my lord, I would not know."

Her tightly bound hair had fallen, the strict knot she began each day with slackened until it sagged, releasing blazing strands to waft about her face. Strands that tempted more than they should.

Would he have held her upon the dance floor, he knew of a certainty his fingertips would have claimed a place within that hair. Destroyed the knot completely, and likely landed him an invitation to leave. And her? Likely on her way as well and without a reference. He could not do that to her. Would not, no matter how his nails now gouged his palms, so rigid did he hold his fists.

He would pretend that others had not danced joyfully just hours past where she stood and he now sat. He would pretend that he was not wistful over the lack—of dancing. Of laughing. Of female companionship.

He released his fists and wheeled his chair as close to her slippered feet as he dared.

Then rolled some more, as she began backing away from him. Angled only once, to keep her heading toward the windowed wall, and not the exit. *Step. Step. Step.*

Creaky wheel. *Creak. Creak. Creak.*

She retreated and he advanced.

He wanted to bump into her legs. Knock her askew. Haul her over the arm of the ambulatory chair and capture her.

Capture her lips with his own.

Capture her in his lap.

Capture her ripe arse against his thighs. His *dead* thighs. Dead lap. Buried prick.

Lost to war and regret and—

"You're very adept at operating that." Her words had

wrenched him away from the familiar maudlin turn of thought.

Thank God for poignant distractions. *Turning too deathly mawkish, Rich.* "Thanks only to more practice than one might wish."

"Have you any hope of walking again?"

Did he? "It rather depends on what day you ask *me*. Or *who* you ask."

While she pondered that, and debated another query—he could tell because her lightly freckled face, sans bonnet and shadows—now that he had maneuvered her closer to the window—was very expressive. So he added, "The surgeon on the battlefield wanted to leave me for dead." Over her gasp, he continued. "Based on his prognosis, I think I'm doing rather well."

"Something to be heartened by, I'm sure."

"I know what would hearten me."

This time, over her definite gasp, he also heard her reluctant laughter. "Not that familiar refrain, again, my lord. I am most certainly not jumping upon your lap."

"Ah, something which, I am sure, we will both regret."

Had that occurred? That dark night so long ago when bitterness and regret swamped, but her unexpected light threatened to dig him out before misery could bury him whole? Or was it more of his fevered imaginings? Such as now... When his body burned with the recollections of her touch, her willing touch. Cradling his head upon *her* lap?

Her delicate hands feathering *all over his body* making his skin dance, if not his feet...

THE CLANG OF A POT HITTING another wrenched him back to the present.

How long had his mind drifted, awash in memories?

He sought her face. Her lips were pinched. Gaze somewhat uncertain... So a while, then.

He grinned. "Did you bang two lids together to gain my attention?"

"No." She bit down on both her lips, then released them. "Mayhap."

His gaze took in the entire kitchen. "I cannot believe you cleaned everything, every stench-filled, disgusting inch to such glittering perfection. Thank you. Sincerely." She inclined her head in acknowledgment, but naught else. "Thank you also for my things folded so neatly and returned to my chamber." Another silent nod.

This was unusual. Her reticence. If anything, he should be the one mortified—by all she had seen and done for him. From beholding his weakened state, without a scrap of clothing to shield his shame, to scrubbing his mess, his bodily filth...

But despite the ease, the overly casual, overtly flirtatious tone their letters had taken a few months ago, he had not seen her in two years. Last evening didn't count, given how, in his exhausted state, he had thought it naught but a figment.

But now that he knew the truth? He wanted the fun, emboldened Aphrodite returned to his presence. He liked it when she fought words with him. Brought him out of his thoughts, and challenged him.

"So," he began, hoping to rile her—if just a bit. "Satan's spawn is your uncle?"

She frowned at him again, plucked an invisible nothing from her skirt and avoided his gaze and just like that—*boom!*—memories from their first meeting conveyed instantly to him. When he was seated at the edge of the Ballenger gardens, grumbling about how he got there, spying her within the trees, covered in—

Covered in...

He got tickled. Started laughing.

"Really, Prim, after all you have done for me in the last day, I should be heartily too embarrassed to remain here holding your gaze but instead... Instead, I cannot help but recall how the very first time I saw you, you were blushing and besmeared with pig skit."

He wanted to say *shit*. To shock her as he had so often in the past. But at the last moment, harnessed the temptation, aimed for a slightly—if only—more acceptable version. And was glad, when a small smile finally began to flit about her lips.

"Thank you for that reminder." Again, her fingers plucked at her skirt, but this time, she continued to meet his gaze. Standing there, back pressed against the sink, long skirts swaying with what had to be the motion of her feet or legs.

"My pleasure. I also cannot help but note you are no longer trussed quite so tightly and not bound in brown." Instead, she was attired in that soft-looking blue gown, more suited to spring than winter. Something that put a smile on his face—and then a full one on hers, finally.

Stop smiling at him. Encouraging him. You should not be here!

Of course she should. *This is home, is it not?*

And Aphrodite could not help but notice how very enlivening it was, at this particular moment, in the home she'd always associated with warmth and welcome, with steadiness. But now instead with eagerness, and mayhap a touch more excitement than was wise.

Not with an unmarried man residing here, it isn't! Sleeping not far from you...

She ignored the thought. For was he not wide awake now? And engaging with her—in the kitchen? The sort of place a titled man such as he would never venture.

Your uncle gave him little choice.

True. And during the hours Richard had slept, both late yesterday evening and early this morning, while she applied herself to straightening things after scouring the sordid spillage, she had ample time to think, to recall, to ponder possibilities...

Possibilities? Aphrodite, you harlot!

The protest was a snicker. Because she was anything but, and every part of her knew it. Else she would have responded differently to his governess offer this past summer. Would have known by now if she had the will to resist him.

"Your sisters. What became of their governess situation? Did you find the right person to care for them?"

And if she held her breath, selfishly in dread of learning he'd found the perfect woman?

"I did not." His next words set her instantly at ease. "But nor have I looked, not since receiving your letter counseling to the contrary."

He had listened. Actually listened and taken her advice? The knowledge warmed her—that relief knowing another did not share his abode. No wife, nor governess.

"Your dress?" he prompted. "You did not explain why it is so different from the abominations you prefer in the country."

"Ah. Um." Her gaze fixed upon a point just beyond his ear. How much did she want to tell him? She had already, long ago, hinted at the reasons. "Only to dissuade attention away from myself. Servants are not to be seen nor heard, if we can help it."

And because he shifted, until his face replaced the

nothing at which she stared, and looked as though he was about to inquire further, she rattled off, "What did you do for Christmas? Were you still at home? When did you get here? And *where* is Uncle Silas? I have known him to travel, often to London, but certainly not in December."

Now that she was no longer avoiding his gaze, his body angled upright again, fingers tapped upon the tabletop. Strong fingers, she couldn't help but note. Beautiful hands. She could stare at for—

"Oh, so many questions you pose."

She ripped her attention back up to his face. "So many answers you do not disclose."

He chuckled. "I love how you make me laugh."

She inclined her head. "And I would love it if answers ventured from your mouth."

His mouth. That was beautiful as well, his lips—

"For Christmas?" Those beautiful lips spoke. "Made sure the Thieving Beast was watered, fed and pissed, then finished off your uncle's best bottle of brandy and snored till dawn. Until noon, if I'm to be honest." A far cry different from the boisterous joy he had anticipated with the twins and girls. Money might be in evaporative supply, but he had still managed to procure a special gift for each of them. Gifts he'd decided to leave hidden away in his room, until he could see them delivered in person.

"Frown at me all you want, Aphrodite Primrose, but 'tis the truth. It was my second full day here and after the deceit the spawn of Satan wielded to attain my presence? I was due one night of pity and near puking.

"If it matters to your delicate sensibilities"—not that he needed to justify any of his actions to the softly alluring governess (aside from the change in attire, *what* was it about her that made her seem *more* approachable than ever before?)—"I have not imbibed to excess since, nor is it something I make a habit of doing at home. Not anymore."

Not since well before his mother's funeral.

"Glad, I am, to hear it." The smile she gave him was full of understanding. "But for your sake, not my own."

Silence thrummed between them for several heartbeats.

"Soap, though." Drying her hands on a towel, she left her station at the sink and took a chair at the table opposite him. "You have a penchant for collecting it?"

He frowned at her. "Soap? Not particularly. Why would you— Ahh." His expression cleared. "You spied my pyramid? When you delivered my clothes?"

The triangular mound of precisely placed and stacked soap he'd made in one corner of his room, blocked by his trunk on a diagonal so not yet destroyed by the dog. "I did indeed." Though she pretended to find the towel she folded into precise quarters fascinating, he saw the gentle lift of her cheeks before she smoothed the expression and lifted her lashes to meet his gaze. "Do you care to explain? Or do you always travel with *fifty* cakes or more?"

Once again, laughter beckoned. "If you must know…" His tone boasted, even if his words did not. "I explored the house after Arbuckle decamped. First in my chair, idly rolling where I could manage—"

"Wait." The folded towel forgotten, her hand snapped across the space between them to squeeze his forearm. "The house. So that *is* Uncle's supply? The one stored *upstairs*? I thought it looked like Mrs. Dobson's work. However did you manage…"

"To gain the second landing? Mastered the stairs with these." Definitely boasting now, he raised his arms overhead, clasped his hands together and tightened every muscle. It mattered not that his shirt sleeves hid his impressive shoulders from view. What mattered was how strong they were, for after crawl-climbing the stairs following Sophia that day to the third-floor nursery to rescue Julia, he continued to make the same upward journey long after dismissing the wretch Trugmoldy.

He'd gained strength and muscle because of the effort. Gained, of vastly more importance, the solid trust of both his sisters (and a bit of their awe, too).

What mattered, as he lowered his arms and grinned at Prim, was the incredulous—definitely impressed—look writ upon her face. "You managed the *stairs*? With your *arms*?"

"Aye." And now felt the fool for voluntarily dislodging her touch, for he still felt the slight pressure of her hand where it had gripped his forearm.

"Drag— Uh, hauled— Um..."

"You can say it. Dragging my somewhat dead legs behind me? Aye, I did. Rested a bit, but ventured a survey into every room. Found his *and* a newly delivered supply of soap upon his bed.

"Didn't know what was in it until I opened the already-torn corner of paper and yanked the heavy package to the floor. Rotten of me, I'm sure, but I was near seething at the time. Didn't much care. Counted out fifty-two cakes— What manner of man needs *fifty-two* cakes of soap, I ask you?"

Did she realize she had edged her hand back across the table? Approached his sleeve again...

"So I unwrapped the lot. Tossed them each from the room. Down the hallway. Threw them fiercely down the stairs, ahead of my slow descent, taking perverse pleasure in every corner that chipped and went flying."

As though she had been the one to hurl soap hither

and yon, with every sentence, the renewed grip on his forearm squeezed again, encouraging him to continue.

"Then, with Mercury's help, I scuttled the lot into my room and—without his help—piled them up. Kept me—and the dog—occupied a good two hours if I include nosing about upstairs."

Color stained her cheeks. Her *rounded* cheeks, for she smiled at him. No censure there at all. "I cannot decide whether to commend you or call you cracked."

"Both, perhaps?"

As though finally realizing where her hands had come to rest, to squeeze and stay, they flew backward and she grappled with the towel, snapping it in the air between them. "Definitely, you wretch. Because I used the last of the soap this morn, cleaning myself and Mercury. And will have need of part of your pyramid, posthaste, if you please."

"You may claim every stone should you have need of it."

"Generous, are you, with Uncle's supply."

Warrick sat back on a satisfied inhale, enjoying the morning immensely. "I can afford to be; he paid for it."

She was laughing in earnest now. "And fifty-two because he buys them from a neighbor who makes it for her family twice a year. Twenty-six weeks and he uses two bars a week."

"Two bars a week when they have not chipped corners from traveling down the staircase."

"Aye, that."

"And if you're wondering, I did not explore *your* room. Once I identified 'twas the sphere of a female, I assumed it was the niece he had mentioned, and I did not venture past the doorway. Not that you have any reason to believe me."

"I do believe you. Although I am curious what your reasoning was behind exploring *everywhere* else."

"You mean into his domain? Every shred of it I could reach? His deceit. The trickery he called upon, convincing me I needed to be here both for the waters and his constant attention. It was naught but a ploy. One that sacrificed both his dog and my time with my girls."

Her smile drifted away. "I can only imagine your frustration, with him, then. Have you seen gains? Since you arrived?"

He gestured to his legs. "You mean these? In all honesty, nothing has changed. Save for that difficult crumple into the floor upon your arrival."

"But why are you not using your chair if you still need it so? Surely you brought it?"

"Assuredly, I did. And used it in my first days here. I jest not when I say it disappeared one night recent. Not to be found inside nor out. So either we have ourselves an unusual thief about Bath or that dog hides it with my drawers and other absconded sundries."

And finally, Warrick realized with regret hitting him hard at the look of disbelief she now wore, after everything else that had been exchanged between them, with that most recent revelation, he had managed to make her doubt his sanity.

26

ABUSE MY EARDRUMS, PLEASE

The Merlin's chair, currently unused and unoccupied, did, however, occupy a prominent place both in the room and in the thoughts, and conversation, of the two whom it loomed before.

"I think, mayhap, we should not have taken it." Despite the irresolution of the statement, the female's voice was as strong as her personality.

The man beside her twitched his smallest finger until it touched hers, where they stood, and sighed. "Perhaps you are in the right."

An exaggerated gasp met his ears and she used her grip on his hand to swing about and face him, no longer fixated upon the wheeled chair, her eyes alit. "What? What manner of trickery is this? Did my ears hear the high-and-mighty, renowned surgeon and healer Silas Arbuckle admit aloud to entertaining second thoughts?"

He smiled, somewhat abashed—not a common occurrence. "I do, indeed, Viola, but only with you."

He used their intertwined fingers to haul her to him. Wrapped his arms about her and breathed in her fascinating scent, a mixture of the expensive perfume she had imported from Italy and sex—and the recipe of oils he'd blended together to make things comfortable for them both. Then he spun her, held her spine and fine arse against his front as they each beheld the fanglement that presently caused such angst.

"I truly believe he needs to be on his own," he told her, his arms now wrapped about her in a hug, resting beneath the gentle weight of her breasts, "without assistance from servants or siblings to take those much-needed first steps. The most troublous part is I know not whether he's fully capable of even taking them. Or if he's only hesitated until now because he's fearful of falling in front of the children. Is he not confident enough?"

"Hence, you stole his chair, taking his confidence or lack thereof out of consideration. Forcing him to stumble about or starve."

A deep groan scratched its way up through Silas's chest. "Oh, Vi, how you pierce a man unexpectedly."

Trusting him with her full weight, she leaned into him and reached up to dance her fingers over the back of his neck. "That was not my intent. I can express myself with you, say things I never would have done before, not with…"

"I know." And he did. Her husband of many years, lout for most of them, had perished only months before he'd met her.

After a formally proper beginning to their acquaintance, it had continued with expected stiff politeness whenever they happened to come into contact, and then, over time, had become more intimate as interactions centered around a mutual friend. It wasn't long after that they each discovered first like for the other and then—surprisingly, to both of them—lust blossoming between them. 'Twas soon followed by love, and now they held no more secrets, save their relationship from others.

For the time being.

"Not to be overly persnickety, Vi, but we *both* stole his chair."

She snickered. For it had not proved an easy task, drag-carrying the heavy device out the bedroom, through the house and over the threshold at nearly 3:00 a.m. one morning, after bribing Mercury for his silence with pets and finely cut, bloodied beef flank. The bottle of port on the dresser, a full third of it missing, had made Silas frown, but at least his "guest" slumbered deeply for the consuming of it.

"'Tis going on three days," he admitted. "We have yet to see him walk."

"I know."

"Pity neither of us can pop round to check on him."

"Aye. Would give up the whole of our dupery. Mayhap not give him the time he needs..."

A few silent seconds and then inspiration! "I could send the butcher. Have known Lowe for years. He can fadge a weekly delivery, cite the holidays for running behind and check on things. Ensure Warrick comes to the door, at the very least."

"And if all is not well? Then either we return his chair or end the farce?"

Unwarranted—as of yet—regret stomped through him. He had sincerely hoped to see substantial progress from his patient. *You had wished for a miracle.* "Aye, that."

———⊃○⊂———

Warrick's thoughts vacillated between flush and barren. His mind flush with thoughts of his illicit companion, barren of anything else.

There were no London friends dropping by to check on him. No estate correspondence to read and reply to. No servants to order about or to dismiss

No evil steward to curse.

No invoices to ignore.

No sisters to entertain.

No brothers to write—and bemoan their lack of response.

Nothing and no one to interrupt the drills and exercises he continued to do, in the privacy of his room, each morning after waking and each evening before bed.

Now that Aphrodite Primrose occupied the space—and his thoughts—nor did he have meals to prepare for himself and the dog.

In short, Warrick didn't know what to do with himself.

He knew what he *wanted* to do. Several things, in fact. All having to do with her body—and his.

He still yearned to dance with her. Yearned to have her in his lap. To kiss along her nape, up the side of her neck and over her jaw until his lips met hers again.

He longed to map the swells and curves her yielding dresses revealed to his eyes—and with so much more clarity than he'd been granted to surmise with her previously coarse clothing.

How long are you going to pretend that living in this cottage with an unmarried, yet marriageable-age female is not going to ruin either yourself or her?

As to that, he was almost ready to ruin them both, and to the devil with the consequences.

You would wed a pauper, no matter how refined, condemning your sisters to no possibility of making an advan-

tageous match when they are of an age? With no way to bestow upon them the dowry in your heart you know they deserve?

Ough.

While she bustled about the kitchen, seeing their dinner dishes and food remains were cleared, cleaned or sorted, he'd shuffled to the doorway, whistled for the dog and now sat, twine wrapped about his fist, dog romping in the night while Warrick tried not to shiver. "Apologies for the open door."

"Think nothing of it." Her words sailed forth.

"I'm letting the cold in."

"Nay, you're letting Merc *out*."

He smiled. She was so easy to be with.

If you think not of how you both shouldn't be here, alone, together.

"How was your journey? To Bath from Ed's?" Why had he not thought to ask sooner?

"Unremarkable." Her voice was muffled and he glanced over his shoulder to see her reaching to put away the pot she'd used to boil the last of the carrots and potatoes.

"The weather?"

"Fine. If cold."

Eh. Like right now.

The twine slackened and he began winding it so the unseeing dog wouldn't become tangled. "No difficulties due to the holidays?"

She came closer. Awareness barreled through him. So easily could he snake out his arm and curl it about her hips. Haul her to him. No pesky chair arms in his way, the simple chair upon which he sat having none.

"No difficulties whatsoever. I did not leave until the twenty-eighth."

"Ah. Are you not cold?"

"Not excessively, no." They both should be chilled, given the weather. Did the mere thought of him warm her as she did him?

Nay, hardy stock,'tis all.

So stilted. *So much unsaid.*

A%%ER SHE EXCUSED HERSELF to go upstairs, as she often did when she thought he'd like to move from one room to another, Warrick reeled Mercury in and made his halting way to the smaller sitting room, which was closer than the drawing room that housed the harpsichord.

Did she crave him even one fraction as much as he did her? Was that why, when she returned, wearing her scarf and bringing his as well (and from tidying herself, he suspected, given the fresh glow of her skin and damp hair about her face), things had been uncharacteristically awkward between them?

As she had every evening the past few, upon joining him, she lit sufficient candles and lamps, enough to see clearly. A far piece different from the darkness that had surrounded him his first week there. But tonight, unlike some of the others, she did not bring a book with her and offer to read. She did not broach a safe topic and chatter about.

Nay, she sat across the small room and appeared at sixes and sevens. He caught her fidgeting more than once. Seizing quick glances toward him, only to suddenly find the empty wall behind him, the ceiling above, or her fingernails of immense interest?

"Thank you again for dinner. Mercury and I both value your efforts."

But instead of seeming to please her, the compliment only made her squirm more.

While he cast about for another comment, undecided whether to calm her unusual fluster—or try to deepen it—she gave yet another uncharacteristic twitch. Met his gaze, held it with a soft smile, then found fascination with something that didn't exist upon his shoulder.

You could leave. She will care for the dog. Why do you stay?
I came here for a reason. And have not yet satisfied it.
You wish to dance across a ballroom once more? Never likely, Rich. Best to return home, now that her presence affords the option sooner than expected.

But...

His siblings were cared for. And, hell's blazes, he had never slept so deeply in his life as he had the past handful of days. Once he'd managed to trick out the lead Arbuckle left him with, and give the dog the roaming space he needed? That, combined with his own determination to see the exercises completed ensured that he was tired enough each eve.

Given the days that started at dawn and kept him busy until past dusk, the lack of ability to do anything about the estate or the mounting debts had granted his mind freedom it had lacked since the night before Albuera: over 900 days since he hadn't been tasked with the strain of battle or the angst over responsibilities.

Fact was, horribly wrong or not, part of him *wanted* to be ruined. With her. Be forced by circumstances to wed her.

Would that not take the choice from him? Mitigate the guilt over not saving the estate, the title...

He wanted her. And the longer he spent in her company away from others, and society's expectations, the longer he wondered if it might...just...be possible.

But you still cannot father a child. Have no hope of intimacy. Would you condemn her to that? Condemn her to your still—and likely forever—seated self?

What of the erection he'd woken with that first morning after she arrived?

Will-o'-the-wisp.

Because it had not happened since. And he'd tried. Embarrassingly, frustratingly, in the scant days since, he'd tried more than once to bring himself back to rousing stiffness. Only to be disappointed, if not devastated by the lack of any noticeable response.

His throat growled. He jerked his attention to the slumbering dog at his feet. Pretended the noise hadn't come from him at all. Bent to stir the snuffling dog to wakefulness with the order to, "Shush now, you cur. Mind your manners, lady present and all that."

The dog swung his blind eyes upward, as though to glare at the preposterous accusation.

"He smells better," said by way of diversion. "His fur is softer as well. You bathed him."

"I did."

"And now I think of you bathing me." Miraculously, he kept his eyes on his fingers, as they brushed through the clean fur, didn't challenge her with a look—as well as his words.

"And you speak thus to shock me into leaving?"

Damn. So he wasn't the only one contemplating the inappropriateness of their proximity?

"'Tis who I am." Abandoning the shield of the dog, he straightened and mocked her with a salute of his fingers. "Here is to being me."

"Nay." Her voice was soft, eyes sad. With a jerk of his snout and a decided sniff—accurately blaming Warrick for the decline in her mood—the mongrel abandoned his place by Warrick and trotted over to his mistress.

"Might have once been who you *were*," she continued, slipping off one slipper to run the bottom of her foot over the dog's coat once he reached her side, "but no longer. So shock and startle away."

She glanced down where her fingers pinched and pleated the loose folds of her pretty gown, this one a lightly embroidered soft white with pretty blue trim about the edges. Then her lids swept upward and she snared him. "It matters not. For I *know* 'tis not the real you, not any longer. And aye, I choose to stay. Knowingly."

And there it was again. Heavy silence between them. With much going unsaid.

"Lord Frostwood!" she exclaimed, as though she, too, was desperate to speak of something other than the heat that simmered silently between them. "He woos Lady Isabella Spier."

"Frost?" He could not believe it. "Thawed that fence-rail up his arse sufficient to make his bow and court a lady?"

"'Tis what we all witnessed," she assured, the polite mask slipping as she smiled. "Instantly enamored, or so I heard. Even saw for myself."

"Tell me of her? Is she a flighty young flit out to snare herself an earl and naught else?" he asked, though he knew —a little. The woman Aphrodite spoke of was the daughter of Lord Spier, owner of the Spierton property that abutted Warrick's. A horrid crank of a fellow if one awoke on his bad side. But he knew naught else of the reclusive daughter.

"Nothing of the sort! Lady Isabella— Pardon, *Lady* Spier is a true delight. Much the age of Lord Redford's Lady Anne. Her closest friend, in fact—did you know?

Blind, also." The toes of her stockinged foot stroked over the now-exposed belly of the dog who had lost all sense of decorum—*much like yourself?* "I told her of Mercury, here."

"You spoke with her?" The governess and the lady... Seemed he was not the only one compelled by Miss Primrose to leap across boundaries.

"Aye. She came weeks ahead of the others. To learn the house and how to traverse through it. Harri took to her right away. Now battles Lord Frostwood for her attention."

"I'll be..." Frost and a blind recluse? One who conversed sufficiently with Prim to learn of Mercury?

Suddenly, the impossible almost seemed...somehow... with a miracle or three...mayhap not so unimaginable after all.

You would abandon your responsibilities, your hope of saving the estate? Of providing for your sisters and choose instead to subsist on what...? Leaves? Because without an heiress, that's what you will be dining on and heating rooms with.

"Sing for me," he commanded before frustration made him growl again. "Your favored song."

Distract me from dreams I ought not be having. Not seated here. In the cold. When I should have started fires, warmed us both. When I should be in a position to take care of you.

"I DO NOT BELIEVE I SHALL." Aphrodite managed a confident tone—startling, given how disordered her insides. "I do not appreciate being *ordered* about as your servant. Or your dog."

Mercury's tail *whomped* against her now-slippered and still foot upon hearing "dog".

"My servant? My dog?" Richard's dark voice was too

inviting by half. "If you were mine, I would not order you about. But I would bid you to be at my side."

"I am not very biddable." Especially to one who was *not* her employer. Especially not to one who tempted so...

"Think you I do not know that by now? Do not revel in it?"

She gave his perplexing self a serene smile, one that belied the furious pattering of her heart. Sitting so close to him, even with half the room in between, breathing in his scent, seeing the bristle that shaded his cheeks and jaw, *and* recalling with vivid clarity exactly how he looked unclothed, did not make her feel the least bit tranquil. No matter how being near him brought wicked, wanton urges to the fore. Urges she was in no place to acknowledge.

So she would pretend. Pretend his trifling words did not thrill. Would hold tight to the least vexation, magnify it a thousandfold. Pray her ire toward him grew.

What ire? All you feel for him of late is a tendre.

"Sing for me, would you, Prim? I turned away carolers who sought to entertain me on Christmas Day. But I would be entertained now."

"Ordering me about is the least likely way to obtain my cooperation."

She held his gaze, watched his eyes narrow, his jaw flex. He gave an abrupt nod. "Then would you, my dear Aphrodite, my love, my peacock in hiding, would you *please* see your way to entertaining my dreadfully beset-with-ennui ears with the lilt of your voice?"

"How you ask so very sweetly." His love? She quashed the pang that it wasn't so. "And yet so insincerely." So she would reply just as. "How I so regret..." This current demand notwithstanding, he never treated her as a servant; she would not call him *my lord* again, certainly not *Richard*—far too temptatious!—(save in her thoughts).

"How I regret, dear sir, dear *difficult* man, not doing as you plead, but I will not because I *can*not. Because the 'lilt' of my voice is more of a screech; one—please believe my words and heed them well—you do *not* want to hear have you any desire whatsoever for a restful evening."

"Mayhap a *restful* evening is the last thing I want." And there he went again, speaking with that boldness that never failed to alight her insides and flitter about her middle. "The very last thing…"

His voice had turned sultry. Wretchedly intriguing. Not anything she needed to hear right now, already battling her own desires as she was.

So she mimicked Lord Frostwood—how well she remembered the friend of Warrick's and her employer's son-in-law—and gave a deep, guttural grunt. There. That ought to dissuade him.

In that, she was sorely misguided. For he only laughed. "Then, if not your voice, *play* me something. Please. *Anything* to enliven this quiet evening that makes one wonder what loved ones are partaking of, listening to, longing for, doing…pondering…"

The hint of ruefulness threaded through his words made her realize how dreadfully he must miss his siblings.

His mother. Of a sudden, she recalled this was his first Christmas without his parent. Though Aphrodite had expressed sorrow during their correspondence, and thought to touch upon it again, she refrained. He sought a lighter tone to their evening?

No matter how she might yearn to dislodge any hint of loneliness, she must remain staunch in her refusal, for both their sakes. "You actually asked that with a modicum of sincerity, so you are to be commended. And, if I could, *if* the harpsichord, ancient though it is, would manage to stay in tune longer than a minute"—or if she could, even at all—"I would be more than pleased to entertain us both. But alas, Uncle's harpsichord is likely older than King George's carved ivories. And, alas again, I do not possess the talent to make it—or my voice—sing."

"You speak truth?"

"Unvarnished."

His gaze dared. "Go tap out a few notes?"

So he did not believe her? Challenged her to "play" the harpsichord in the other room?

This was one instance that she could easily prove the accuracy of both statements: lack of singing ability and lack of playing talent. She rose, flashing him a grin over her shoulder. "Do not blame me if your ears hurt the rest of the evening."

How he loved her spirit, sparring with her; how he hated her playing.

Warrick hadn't known a female existed who claimed England as home and yet, when put fingers to keys, managed to make such noise, such horrid noise. It wasn't that, aye, the notes *were* out of tune more often than not. It wasn't how hard she plunked down her fingers and struck the venerable keys that should have been cherished not whipped with such callosity.

Mercury woke from his doze, whined and made his way to Warrick's side, flopped down and buried his ears between outstretched paws.

Warrick laughed. "Stop, I say," he called out, aiming his voice to carry to the other room. "You are paining the dog!"

Though he was tempted to follow suit, slap palms over his own ears to mitigate the misery.

But in truth, it wasn't his ears that bothered him. Nay, it was his head.

For these screeches, the shrieks and squalls she somehow managed to pull from that beautiful old instrument languishing alone in the drawing room were what one might expect from a mythological beast come from the shades, now inhabiting their realm, one roaring with hunger. And having indigestion and flatulency in addition.

When the pounding in his head grew more intense, he knew she had won.

"Stop! Halt, I beg of you," he yelled again, only to the melodic sound of her giggles as she kept going, killing that poor machine with chops and slams and *whollops* of her fingers. He raised his voice. "I beg of you. Please, stop. I believe you! You are wretched, utterly so, I grant that!"

The song of her laughter only increased.

But the distraction, the abuse of his ears was so very welcome, given the stiffness of how their evening exchange had begun. Her mirth danced through the lovely cottage, caressed his ears and fluttered his belly.

It was then that Warrick realized he would suffer any number of pains to bring such laughter and delight to her spirit, and by association, his.

Uncomfortable with that notion, he yelled again, "Stop, woman, else no sane parent will ever engage your services again to train their daughters to be ladies!"

By now, she was laughing harder. Brought her full hands (or so it sounded) down in an ear-splitting, head-curdling crescendo of *plunk-plunk-plunk*, before she finally ceased punishing the instrument. Heavy seconds echoed with the torturous sounds before silence descended. Additional moments passed before she returned to the room.

His beleaguered head still heard the strident sounds following on her heels as she came in, calm as ever—as though she hadn't just murdered music and that poor, innocent harpsichord—and took her seat, smoothing nonexistent flecks from her skirt.

"How I wish I could have seen you play. Pardon, I mean, *massacre* that ill-treated instrument."

Her renewed laughter brightened the air between them.

"If you do not think your uncle would mind, I will take a look at it tomorrow, see what I can do to improve upon the notes."

She looked as surprised as he felt the moment the words were out. Both the request itself and that, for the first time, he referred to The Tyrant as something as benign as "her uncle." Then her expression warmed, making his chest do another odd thump, perhaps impressed—dare he hope?—that he would make such an offer. An effort.

But then chagrin invaded her mien. "Even were the notes true, I could not produce anything worthwhile."

He sputtered. "As if I would ever doubt your word again. Henceforth, trust that I believe you with all my abused eardrums and aching head." He brought his palm up to the side of his temple and attempted to look as pitiful and beleaguered as he could, only now realizing the last few minutes had easily been some of the most entertaining, fun and relaxed moments he'd experienced with another since his spine took the brunt of some enemy canister shot and he'd been left for dead in Spain.

Mayhap, since ever.

HERE, HAVE SOME MEAT (PART 1)

Music?

What a tepid word for the bounty of notes that blessed her hearing when Aphrodite returned from her errands late the following morning.

She placed the basket of vegetables, one of bread, upon the first empty space along with the cherished muff that warmed her hands and tiptoed toward the riveting sounds emanating from the drawing room.

The beauty, the majesty...

Though she knew its source, she refused to believe it. Utterly refused. Until she saw for herself. Yet even as she halted in the doorway... Even as she stood there watching his shoulders and back stretch and move as he reached and played, applied deft pressure one second, a whisper the next, and then followed both with force, depending upon the sounds he sought... Even as his overlong inky hair bounced, danced against his shoulders, her mind denied acceptance.

Never before had she heard such musicalness, such a variety come from a harpsichord.

'Twas nigh impossible to believe the man that she'd come to know, the mettlesome contrariant who had bade her to entertain him last eve *could do this*.

Yet the evidence was before her, but twelve feet away.

How was it this particular man, with so many facets, could wring such heavenly sounds from such an old-fangled instrument?

Matches his character, does it not?

It did, how it did. Brash, magnetically appealing... Yet with dark undercurrents. Secrets. Sadness that shadowed his soul...

She bit her lips against the sigh that shuddered from her lungs, unwilling to make a sound that might alert him to her presence and stop the magnificence.

Every second he played with such passion, such abandon swept her further under his spell. So much of him was wrong. Certainly wrong for *her*, for her never-to-be-admitted yearnings. This overly flirtatious, sometimes foul-mouthed earl. Here was a man born into the peerage. Someone used to all of the rights and privileges that came with the chance of his birth. Yet someone who willingly fought against tyranny—and had paid a severe price for that effort.

Yet now someone who sought to better himself, even if it was—to an uncomfortable degree—at her expense. At the expense of her heart, certainly, given how part of her was starting to think she wanted to experience anything and *everything* knowing him might allow for.

Even if that means turning tart in the process?
Aye, even if.

. . .

The sounds. The notes, in perfect tune or not. The melody and rhythm. The utter exhaustion of playing for over an hour after not touching a similar instrument for an age... The memories it wrought, rolling forth like a stampede. So, so damn many memories...intertwined with his childhood, his parents...school rollicks with his mates.

Dancing in Portugal with Ed amidst the conflicts... Soused, and with riotous laughter, not long before both their lives would be inverted.

Everything ceased to be, the dog dozing on the floor alongside the instrument, the anticipated return of Prim—and the fresh food she would bring with her.

His shoulders ached. Fingers throbbed. Soul rejoiced.

Warrick couldn't remember the last time he engendered sweat upon his brow through efforts not having to do with his blasted legs. Couldn't remember the last time his heart had soared at anything—save bantering about with the tight-laced governess who so easily held him in thrall, did she but know it. How she'd been gone these last two hours or more.

Had he ever before so fervently recalled the past—with pleasure, no less?—while basking in the present and hoping, praying for a different future?

Playing this instrument, his mother's favorite, even his own, in spite of the three pianofortes they had between their townhouse and country residences when he'd been young, had helped him remember not only the past, but *himself*. Everything he'd denied since Spain.

Exhilaration hastened his fingers, quickened his lungs as he felt pride in accomplishing something he hadn't since that last battle. Playing, and impressively so, even if no one was here to enjoy it save him and the dog.

For it was an *accomplishment*, his skill at the keyboard. Something he and his mother had honed together, with determined effort, to surprise his father one Christmas with the most beautiful of recitals; Mama with her spectacular voice and Richard her only accompaniment, she sought to grant her spouse a surprise. But the surprise had been upon them both, when Father and a friend had chanced upon them while practicing a few days before their planned performance.

That friend had been aghast that a young male and future peer would dare spend so much time at the aging instrument better suited for females. Warrick's father had chided his friend for such a beetle-brained stance, immediately come over and hugged them both, heaping praise upon their heads, and more than a little astonishment toward his son of six—at how well he played after only a few lessons.

His father had recognized talent and had encouraged his son's time at the instrument, saying it was good for such a boisterous lad to have *some* claim to refinement.

But now? With his breath gusting forth, his muscles beginning to tire, he felt anything but refined. Anything but practiced. His play turned wild.

All the disappointments and angst, the sorrows and sadness, the fear and anger—both directed inward and not—that he had stifled these last two and a half years came tumbling out as he played. Ripped from his aching fingers not only pieces from memory of the great composers he favored, but as he mingled things together, made a hash of professional compositions, he also mixed in some measures he and Mama had created, and simply played.

Uncontrolled.

Loud and untamed. Balancing on the edge of what the harpsichord could handle and what he *needed* to release.

He played for himself. He played for his broken body.

His healing body. He played for his mother. From the heart, everything he had, everything he could give her.

But then his right hand cramped. Convulsed in on itself, pain shooting up his arm.

Three fingers kinked, flexing against his palm. Unresponsive. He wrenched both arms from the keyboards. Tried not to rain down the curses blistering his lips. Tried—

"That was stunning. Utterly magnificent."

Her voice surprised him. Jerked the rest of him around.

Forgetting that his legs wouldn't follow, his face and torso turned toward the interruption. He lost his balance, fumbled to regain it. And fell. Ended up on the floor with a hard thump. Another curse upon his lips. His right hand crooked and crumped, curling up into itself; embarrassment making his shoulders want to curl in as well.

Cannot even keep your seat? And you thought just last night to consider wooing the woman? Tut, Richard.

Fallen, are you, his vicious, doubtsome thoughts continued—and using the Bard to do it—*and in a dark, uneven way.*

Startled awake, not by the intense music but by its cessation—more likely by his heavy arse hitting the floor—the dog yawned to his feet and ambled over, snuffling first Warrick's unresponsive legs and up to his shoulder. Then licked his chin. Warrick yanked his lips from the unwanted slather of wet tongue.

Anger—at himself, the weakness of his body—made him lash out. "Leave me. I did not invite you here."

She ignored him. Ignored his shout.

But refused to ignore his feeble, fallen self. Instead, rushing forward, she shoved Mercury aside and reached for his hand. His cramping, on-fire hand.

Damn her.

"Leave off, I said." Aphrodite's recalcitrant patient gritted the words out through his tightly held jaw. She spared but a glance to see it was so, her attention focused on the misshapen coil of his hand, despite his continued grutchings. "I do not want your attention. I do not want you to—" To *see*, she surmised. "Go. I am not one of your charges to order about at will."

"Nay, you are not. For they would not be so incredibly stubborn as to refuse my help."

That halted his grumbling. But not the tension brimming from every clenched part of his body. "I know you are in pain. More importantly, I know how to help you." Kneeling, she reached for his kinked hands. Needed to determine where to begin. "Lest you forget, I assisted my uncle when I was younger. I have seen this before."

"Oh?" He fought her hold. "You have seen a grown man *thwap* onto his arse after butchering an innocent harpsichord?"

"Stop that. Both the complaints and struggling against me. We both know you did no such thing. And I speak of the spasmatic muscles, you difficult, difficult man. Shush. Let me concentrate." *And not salivate.*

Now that she nestled the one that cramped the worst within hers, his hand seemed immense. The palm and fingers so much *stronger*, larger than they might have been, given all he did with his arms, hauling his body about. His fingers resisted her efforts, were clasped tight toward his palm.

So she dropped to her seat upon the floor and crossed her legs, shoved her cloak behind her shoulders and drew his arm across her lap until his hand rested between hers.

Supporting the back of it with one of hers, she used the other to tend each individual muscle.

"What were you playing?" The remembered splendor of it caught her breath high in her chest. "'Twas beautiful and yet stark, too. Never have I heard it before."

She had started at the base of his palm and now worked her thumbs from the bottom into the soft center, over and over, slow, repetitive strokes of her thumb she took higher with each stroke. Her half gloves doing naught to protect her from the nuances of touching his *skin*.

"A hash," he responded, the words rough. "A bit of everything. Some Schubert, some Handel, a little Martinson."

Swiftly did she grasp his meaning. "You wrote some of that yourself? It all blended together superbly." After a time, little by little, his fingers began to unfurl. "Once again, you astonish me."

Another clench, a tightening against her efforts, as an unexpected, ragged confession met her ears. "Mine was the raging parts."

Quite without meaning to, she paused in her efforts, rose up on her knees and hugged her arms about his shoulders.

Before she could get lost in him, in his strength and scent, she hauled back, away from the temptation he presented using the action of standing to unfasten her cloak and sweep it from her, as well as the untying of her bonnet, to swallow that breath that still lodged in her chest. "My, 'tis warm in here, is it not? My walk this morning must have left me overhot. Here, let me finish."

Not giving him a chance to agree nor argue, she sat back down and caught his hand back up in hers, working her touch as deep as she could.

After he asked of her morning and she shared about

her errands, he told her of a surprise delivery from the butcher, something about her uncle's regular weekly order being delayed because of the holidays, Aphrodite responded appropriately—she hoped, for her mind was consumed with her task: relieving his pain.

To that end, she continued rubbing along the middle and then the upper parts of his palm, pressing in between the beds of each finger, until feeling the muscles loosen.

She worked his thumb by itself but it was the others that gave him the most trouble. The last three fingers more than the first. So that was where she focused. Concentrated her efforts.

Told herself she didn't notice how much his scent drew her. Not quite readily identifiable... A hint of the plain lye soap Uncle favored, but so much more. Whispers of musk and spice. His shaving soap, perhaps?

Richard's scent and no other's.

She told her ears to stop hearing every sharp inhale he made, every subtlety of his breathing, as it slowed, deepened as the seconds and then minutes passed.

Minutes that grew heavier with every pained breath, with want. With the heat that invaded her limbs. That flushed her skin and brought sweat dotting her brow.

Gracious. How did nurse-tenders ever manage to wear anything at all, if this was how very hot touching a man made them feel?

Each second passed as a weight. Every moment she eased the constricted muscles burdened with silence. With intensifying want—hers. With increasing irritation and grumbling—his.

As the clock ticked and awareness grew, she brushed her fingers, her hand, over his again and again. Until the tense, tightly held muscles released completely and allowed his hand to lie flat. Spread wide, the back supported no longer by her opposite hand, but against her inner thigh.

About the same moment that realization sank in, a quivering that pierced her belly, he flexed his other hand in the air between them, the one that hadn't cramped nearly as bad, and ran it up her shoulder, paused with it just beneath her nape and tensed—as though to support her efforts?

Time froze. Tendrils from his grip on her neck flowed like fireflies dancing along her veins.

Her touch slowed even more. Languid now. Stottered. But it didn't stop. She *couldn't* stop.

Just kept touching and touching him. Her breathing turned ragged. The thumping of her heart jagged. She refused to look away from his big, masculine hand. He had pushed up the sleeves of his shirt, looked as though one had ripped at some point. Because, easier than should have been possible, she was now stroking upward, past his wrist and to his forearm—and the more tender flesh approaching the bend of his elbow.

He caught his breath. On a gasp. A groan.

Dare she hope, his was as uneven as hers? But when she started to turn, to check and see if he was ready to rise, his hand at her neck tightened and he shoved her forward.

He pushed off the middle of her back, rising swiftly and clumsily, climbing back upon the bench. "Get out." He forcefully jerked his knees around until he faced the instrument once again, giving her his back. "I didn't ask you to come in. I did not ask for your help."

Stunned to numbness at the sudden rejection, hurt beyond reason, she scrambled to standing. "Why do you do that? Make me like you, *care* for you, and then—"

"Aphrodite." His hard voice could have broken boulders.

The prickling, tingling in her feet punished her as she straightened, swept one arm across her damp forehead. Still feeling the imprint of his hand upon her spine, her nape, she could not move.

"I said get out!" The anger toward her hastened her feet. Fired her temper.

"Fine, then. You can make your own dinner. I shall be feeding myself and Mercury and going upstairs—where the company is, no doubt, far superior!"

With a swirl of skirts and a stiffening of her spine, she left the big, unfriendly, perplexing lump of harpsichord talent and frustrating male behind her.

Only to be hauled back into his orbit not three seconds later.

"Aphrodite!"

For no other reason than because he rarely *asked* her for anything (orders to entertain him notwithstanding)... Only because until today he'd certainly never yelled at her or even *for* her, did she turn, make her hesitant way back to the sitting room.

"What?" Having him hear the hurt in her soft voice wouldn't do. So she firmed it. "Have your say, for *I* am retreating upstairs. You may fend for yourself."

"'Tis only what I deserve." A low murmur that weakened her resolve. Then still facing the instrument and away from her, but louder, "My humblest apologies. I should not have shouted at you, whipped you with voice nor words."

He remained seated upon the bench, giving her his back but naught else. "I wish to be alone. But I do thank you. My...hands...*are* better."

HERE, HAVE SOME MEAT (PART 2)

Her slippered feet racing away were all he heard of her retreat.

Warrick stared at the harpsichord where he'd refisted his hands in front of him—likely not the best of ideas for his newly soothed muscles, but good God.

Trembling, he dared to glance down, past the keyboards, to the area between his falls. Where his penis rose, stiff and proud as a pike, thrusting noticeably against his loose-fitting trousers.

What the deuce just happened?

He'd been lost in playing. Surrounded, enthralled... Then utter chaos had rained down.

Minutes Prior...

Prim, back so suddenly.

Questioning him about the music. Touching him. Confusing him. Prompting his confession about the raging parts. Then she'd thrown her arms about his neck and hugged him to her? Fiercely so.

The overt affection startled him. Comforted him. Aroused him.

He pulled back, attempting distance between them. Not easy when his lower half—none of it—wanted to cooperate.

Every second of the past few minutes pummeled him higgledy-piggledy, his spiraling thoughts too overset to even remember the order in which everything had occurred.

Confused and desperate, his mind still hearing the echo of angry notes, his body foreign to him given her sudden proximity and ministrations tending his hands, he'd sought distraction. "You were gone a while."

"It's brisk but calm out. I enjoyed a stroll before venturing to the market. Crossed paths with a friend I haven't seen in an age. We found a sunny bench and rambled."

Rambled? Despite the gnawing in his hands and forearms, the uncomfortable pressure growing in his groin—did he feel the approaching need to piss?—he bit down on both lips to prevent a chuckle.

But when she stroked over a particularly painful spot, a groan loosened them. Freed his lips and the chuckle.

Her motions paused. Then resumed. "What about that amuses you? That I would have friends?"

"Nothing of the sort. A *ramble*."

She peeked at him from beneath her bonnet, then released his hand to stand, looking rather flushed. He watched as she removed both it and her cloak. Dropping back down to his side, she picked his arm up and drew it even closer, her actions happening as though she touched him every day of the week. "Why would you laugh at the notion of me enjoying a coze with a friend?"

"Mayhap because you do not know what else 'rambling' entails." His teeth clamped against his tongue when a moan threatened. Her deliberate touch? Threw him in alt.

"Enlighten me? I would share in the jest."

"Ah...any randy young Englishman knows to 'ramble' about when he's...mmm..."

He wanted to kiss her cheek. And so, so much more.

'Tis a foolhardy notion. She is comfortable with you now, would you change that? Now that you are stranded together, currently reliant upon her for food and canine care?

The reminder grated.

When he remained silent, she ventured, "For a gentleman to go *rambling* means looking for a light-skirt?"

"Aye. Yes." *Yes*, another groan, when part of his palm unclenched. As though to counter it, his stomach contracted. She didn't seem upset. If anything, found the new meaning as humorous as he, given her dimpled smile as she kept her gaze rapt upon his hand.

She'd worn a soft sage-colored dress today, revealed to him once she removed her cloak. And that wasn't all he saw for the first time. *Really*, truly saw, he realized.

Her breasts.

Good God Almighty! Her breasts...

This close, with his arm dragged into her lap, his other clasped tight around one leg of the bench, to keep himself from toppling full-on into her? This close, by damn, the woman had a magnificent pair of breasts. Where had she kept them in the country? In a trunk?

How had he not fastened his attention *there* before now?

Blazes, but he'd always been drawn more to a woman's

sass and spirit than the handfuls—or mouthfuls—of flesh upon their chest. But now?

The tip of his tongue swept over his top lip. He quickly ordered it back in. Couldn't be salivating over Prim's nipples while staying at her uncle's home.

Aphrodite Primrose. Aphrodite...

Goddess of love. Of lust too, mayhap?

His, certainly. Lust threatened to swamp him.

Saliva gathered in his mouth and he swallowed hard.

Hard. Like another part of him, by blazes.

At some point during her tending, the scent of her hair filled his nostrils. Some light floral thing, combined with *her*. Aphrodite, prim and stubborn and beautiful and vexing and more alluring than any female he had ever known.

He heeded the urge to caress the fine hairs on the back of her nape. But then the need to move his hand and place his lips there bolted through him.

Once, and only once—disregarding dream-induced mania of the morn several prior—had he felt a similar stirring. And that sensation had departed as soon as it arrived, leaving him startled. And hopeful. And doubtful it had even existed.

But during the intervening months—three, if one were counting—no other interest, or movement, from the limp, lackadaisical area.

Until this week, with *her*. Until *now*.

And it wasn't *departing*.

Not even close.

"The fingers have stopped contracting," he babbled, needing her to leave. Needing to release her nape, draw his hand back where it belonged, but unable to do so. "Thank you. You may go now, see to your groceries and the butcher's delivery."

"If your hands are feeling better, then I can help you get situated in the kitchen. I will—"

"Nay, take your leave now."

"Not quite yet."

"I said *leave*."

On and on, until he ended up near growling at her, with everything in him. If she saw what had happened, spied his stand? She would be gone before he could catch her.

"Get out!" Sensing her exasperation, seeing her attention falter from his arm and glance toward his lap, panic assailed. He shoved her forward, head toward her crossed legs, and climbed atop the bench, cursing silently at the clumsy effort, until finally, finally being quit of her.

Gad. Alone now, balanced upon the bench, still staring at the offensively tantalizing area, he scratched his sore fingers through his hair, pressed palms to his eye sockets.

Are you not overjoyed? That erection you woke to was *every bit as real as she is.*

Maybe this shouldn't be such a surprise; he'd always been drawn to her.

But what continued to surprise is how his groin stayed stirred—and not the stirring of an impending piss. Nay, most definitely the *mating* sort of stirring. The urge to frisk an attractive female. Though since her abrupt and irked departure (albeit, deservedly so), his prick had started to soften.

Yet even now, the outline was discernible as more than a pile of useless flesh taking up space within his trousers.

When Mercury whined and placed his grey-tipped muzzle next to Warrick's seat on the bench, 'twas an easy thing to lower his hands and stroke the back of the dog's head. "I know, Mercury. I am as full of wonder as you.

Now? *Now* it comes back? When I am not in any position to make use of it?"

Of course, this couldn't have happened in London where hiring a dove would be the work of a minute.

'Tis not some nameless doxy you want wrapped round—

Nay, he had to be on the quaint, quiet environs outside of popular Bath, surrounded by neighbors of Arbuckle's who would no doubt report any nefarious infractions he might dare commit. Why could they not be in one of the sought-after crescents in town center? Where he could find a venturesome widow, could easily hire or pay a lass for the use of her body—

You wouldn't anyway, knave, and you know it. Not wanting anyone but—

He snarled, roused Mercury to growl back and almost laughed at his predicament.

Her presence had made his cock stand and salute; thoughts of her kept it near waving.

Something he should be rejoicing over, shouting his thanks to the heavens, only instead, the realization wrought agonizing worry. Because if Prim knew he had a *working* pizzle, given the shadows of her past, how wary she was of men—titled men, in particular—doubtless she'd flee back to the Ballenger estate.

And he didn't want her to go.

Needed to spend time with her. 'Twas a compulsion. Like walking again.

So with her gone from the room, his troublesome thoughts and the dog for company, Warrick set himself to "standing from sitting". Two hundred or more ought to suffice for tiring his twanger. Rather than return to his room, risk "stumbling" into her on the way, given his uncomfortably roused condition, he used the harpsichord as both brace and balance.

Beautiful old instrument. Wasted on Satan's spawn.

Somewhere around 137, long after she had called the dog to her side and pounded up the stairs, he realized that mayhap he rejoiced prematurely. Perhaps he needed to give things a trial, to discern if all parts really were, in fact, working again.

As if you would pay a whore for the privilege of riding your cock? When you have never paid before. No, but neither had he gone two and a half years without. Without knowing if he ever would—or *could*—again.

And now that he was closer than ever before? The thought of testing intimate "things" with anyone other than the proper governess under his roof—*do you not mean her uncle's roof?*—seemed unpalatable in the extreme.

Blast it.

"That was no help at all." Frustration goading his ire, Silas shut the front door after answering the knock.

After staying out of sight, Viola now joined him. "What did you learn? I could not hear beyond murmuring."

"Let us return to the food; never pays to leave things boiling when one isn't about, and I will share." Silas placed one hand about her waist and guided her toward the kitchen where they had been jointly preparing their dinner. What a marvel, that: a lady doing without servants *and* without complaint. Definitely didn't remind him of a certain complaintive lordling still occupying his house, and quite likely, to no avail or success at all.

Once they reached the kitchen, Silas resumed slicing the potatoes and pork that would soon be joining the carrots in the pot. Vi busied herself choosing the herbs she would add.

"Well? What did your butcher friend tell you?"

And thank goodness they *were* friends, having known each other for decades, and the other man circumspect enough not to inquire why Silas now hid in another home, not his own. Though likely Lowe had his suspicions, given the wide grin and raised eyebrows when he pointed toward the opaque door before taking his leave with an apology for not having more information to share. An apology—and a decided wink.

"Nothing usable, I'm afraid. Claimed Warrick was already at the open kitchen door, twine leashed about Mercury and saw the man approach. Hailed him over, accepted the delivery with his thanks, but not much else. Did not stand nor move to place the package inside, only held it while they blathered a few moments more. Lowe said he was hesitant to delay leaving lest it rouse 'the gent's' suspicions."

Damn it all. He had anticipated learning more—especially after paying to feed the vexatious interloper. At least Mercury would enjoy the fresh meat, he knew, and damn his disordered thoughts for not thinking of that sooner. Likely by now, supplies had been running disconcertingly low.

"*Is* he walking, do you think?" Vi asked over her shoulder, liberally applying salt to the bubbling water before she came to get the platter of chopped pieces from him. "Perhaps overly tired from his efforts? Or...lazy?" She whispered the last, as though even considering the man might be labeled such was a blade to the heart.

He laughed. "Whatever he might have been two years ago upon our initial acquaintance, he is not lazy now. Not for the better part of this year, by my reckoning. I had hoped pushing him through circumstances would allow me to see, to know for certain what progress he might yet gain, but I am now thoroughly questioning that decision."

Coming back to where he still sat at the table, Viola placed her arms about his shoulders and a kiss to his cheek. "As to questioning decisions, that is something I, too, have been given much thought."

"Do you seek to distract me from my onerous thoughts?"

"Not intentionally, but I do have an idea to propose... A potential change to our own current circumstances."

Given how much joy playing at house and hearth with her afforded him, he could not decide if a surprise—a change of any sort—warranted glee or dread.

29

HARDNESS. SOFTNESS. CONTRARINESS.

HE MIGHT HAVE BEEN ROTTEN to her earlier—when all she sought was to grant relief from his aching, contracting muscles—but Aphrodite could not imagine being rotten right back. So, after a retreat of a couple hours, with energetic dog and restful book, she busied herself in the kitchen that afternoon, her efforts eased by the bounty she had procured that morning as well as the surprising extent of the butcher's delivery Richard had told her about.

Nay, not Richard. *Lord Warrick.* If he was going to yell at her for no apparent reason, then she refused to have any warm feelings toward him.

But he did bid you to return and apologize.

She snorted, as though to stifle the small voice of reason.

Mercury shuffled closer, his nose—determined to know what she was about—bringing his mouth closer than she wished.

"Move aside, young man." She used her lower leg to

nudge him away from where she sliced a good-sized roast before adding it to the already waiting vegetables. "You shall get yours when we get ours."

~~Richar~~ *Lord Warrick.*

She hadn't seen him for hours.

You mean not since you touched him and stroked him and your insides became all heavy and damp and—

She picked up the remaining hunk of roast and slammed it back on the counter. Glanced at the vegetables already cubed and sitting in the kettle, above the fire she'd blazed in the firebox.

No matter that they did not need another, she foraged a parsnip and two more carrots—the biggest ones she could find—rinsed off any dirt and retrieved a fresh knife.

Chop. Chop. Chop-chop-chopchopchop!

The rough actions might not be making her feel any better, but the sound of the blade *thwacking* into the block beneath was satisfying indeed.

She wanted to stay hurt. Frustrated with him. She wanted not to care how hard, how painfully he had landed on the floor beside the music bench. She wanted to stop lov—*liking* him.

Needed to stop liking him. Because doing so made her forget herself.

But she could not seem to forget anything about him... Nor about the letters she had glimpsed so recently.

> *Mistress? Good God, man...to suggest I gain a mistress for my dagger? And as a treatment to heal that portion of my anatomy?*
>
> *I can scarce believe you would put that notion so plainly onto the page and into my head. For shame!*

What would your lady wife think should she know you had written thus?

Bidding me to find a mistress to handle—my handle?

There had been more. Enough for Aphrodite to grasp the suggestion hadn't been as tawdry as it seemed.

For her uncle's prescripts *were* helping. According to the overheard conversation between Lord Redford and his wife (a rare one of hers and not one conveyed by Harri), Lord Warrick had managed to regain some sensation in his lower limbs and now worked to increase their strength. Something she now had her own, visible, confirmation of.

But a lord needed to produce an heir. Some might say 'twas their reason for existing.

And without a working "dagger", a man couldn't very well sire such.

Since spying that wretched, thought-provoking letter, she had wavered like the wind: ought she wash her eyes out with soap *or* pen and post a response posthaste, daring to offer *her* hands to handle his handle?

And now she was here, with him and no one had any inkling.

You could offer to help him now.

Help... How?

Rub his legs. And things in between.

The knife clattered from her fingers and the back of her hand hit her lips.

Shush!

Tempting, is it not?

Vastly so. But not something she could, despite desires to the contrary, offer so very blatantly.

But when he shuffled in moments later, surprising her with both his presence as well as, "Miss Primrose, I am gladdened to see you downstairs again, and after my unpardonable overboiling. My sincere apologies for that. May I assist your efforts with dinner?"

"What of the waters?" The question was out before she thought it through.

He gained the nearest chair and took his seat with a thump and a frown. "What of them?"

"You mentioned taking them upon my arrival. Did you find them beneficial?"

"I would not know. I have not taken them."

"Why ever not? You've been here over a sennight. I would have thought…" She allowed her words to falter when he stiffened, glowered.

"Have you forgotten? Abandoned by your dear uncle to mind his bitc—his *dog*. And after he dismissed my servants too. Not exactly in a position to escort myself from here full into town."

"I'm sure we could manage it together." As though to mock the very notion, the fire burning behind her shot sparks when one log crumpled. She jumped forward, ignoring the slow-to-boil kettle behind her as his dark brows flew skyward, then lowered, the skin of his brow pinching. "Do you hear what you are proposing? To be seen with me?" Asked as though the very notion wasn't to be borne. "*Unchaperoned*"—as though only a dolt would not have realized—"*and in public?*"

"Really!" she huffed, as she gave him her back and knelt to poke at the fire. Once she had it back to rousing, she stood, turned and snapped the kitchen towel she'd grabbed between them. "You need not sound as though the idea is so unpalatable."

"Prim. Think, woman."

She was, and she only wanted to help him. "You're

already here. I can help you get *there*." Though how, without his chair?

And offering to escort him to the Bathing House had to be monstrously better than offering to handle his—

When his frown only grew, embarrassment flamed her cheeks. "If you suspect I seek to *trap* you into matrimony, that had not crossed my mind until *this* very instant. With you seeming so abhorrent of the idea of being seen together."

OF COURSE THE NOTION OF SNARING herself a husband had not occurred to her. Why would it? He was not exactly catch-match.

"If not me," she said, her exasperation with him plain, "we could hire someone else to escort—"

"With what funds?" Warrick asked. "I would not be in this difficulty now if I did not owe your uncle for the past several months."

She bit down on her lips. Pinched those plump beauties his tongue wanted to trace until they flattened. The color that already flared across her cheeks blazed to cover her forehead and down her neck. *What* was she thinking of now? What would cause her blush to deepen so?

And how far did it descend? Did that deep hue reach between her breasts? Color her nipples?

Now he feared he slathered like a starving dog faced with a juicy steak. "What?" he all but barked when she glared at him in disappointment, her skin heated to such a state he wanted to devour her whole.

"What...of the other?" Voice suddenly subdued, her gaze drifted from his face, down his torso, to center about his groin. Remembering what he looked like earlier? Standing before her in his birthday gear?

His skin tingled. "What other?"

And why did she insist upon staring at his loins? He glanced down, made certain his falls were secured. Then faced her with narrowed eyes. "What *other*, Prim?"

When she remained stubbornly silent, he goaded, "You stare at my lap. Comparing me to past lovers?"

She wheezed. Sucked in her cheeks before blowing out a breath that *whooshed* the sunset hair from her forehead and danced strands past her cheeks. She stepped closer, lowered her voice. "I saw letters." He had to strain to make sense of the whisper. "Inadvertently. Open letters in Lord Redford's desk when Lady Ballenger bid me to find paper for lines to punish Harri. Lord Redford offered some in his top drawer." Her arm waved between them, gestured toward his groin. "Do you still need assistance working... um, *those* muscles?"

By the time she finished, 'twas near a squeak.

He struggled. Mightily. To comprehend what she was saying, but more—her meaning.

The letters he had composed late at night after the girls were abed? The ones he and Ed had bantered about the last month or more, mentioning mistresses and who remembered exactly what else?

But her fast gasps and the darker pink upon her face made the hinge of it clear enough. "Primrose. Do my ears deceive me or are you offering to fondle my bauble and pair in the guise of exercise?"

"You need a wife. An heir."

Heir?

Air was absent. For both of them, it seemed.

"An heir*ess*," she emphasized, ensuring neither forgot his destined fate.

He couldn't breathe. His chest was tight, as though trampling elephants perched upon him in a squat with no intent to move. As to Prim? Despite her bold words, if she panted any faster, he feared shortwindiness would soon see her horizontal on the floor.

How could he think, even remotely so, of wedding another, when *she* had just suggested stroking him to a stand? "So you read of his suggestion I find a doctor to work my phallus? Or, failing that, a mistress to do the same? Are you offering?"

And did he want her to say yay or nay?

Would he be disappointed either way? Or beyond gleeful?

You really ought to tell her 'tis no longer necessary. You have managed a stand on your own, twice now—

Blast it. Silence!

Too entranced, not so much with the notion itself—although, aye, that could certainly snare a man's attention—but with the very thought that his prim Aphrodite would offer such.

Her mouth worked, but no sound emerged.

Matched how he felt: shocked. Nonplussed. Both exalted at the very idea, yet disappointed in himself...

Shamed that he would even consider such. Especially given the events of the last few hours...

From her throat, a single squeak emerged.

"Sounds as though you have swallowed a mouse. I suppose that tells us both."

"Tells what?"

"That despite whatever nonsense you have just sputtered, you mean not a single word."

"I do!" That came shriekingly. "I very much do. I know I could help."

"*You?*" Disdain dripped from his voice. Only because he dredged it up from somewhere. Trying to halt the madness.

"Yes, me. Just what do you think I did before becoming a governess?"

"How in blazes would I be privy to that?" He bit down on his lips. Refused to allow what hovered there freedom. But damned if it didn't escape on its own. "What would you have me know? That before you excelled at assigning young Harri lines, you offered to palm pricks?"

"When I wasn't away at the Young Ladies Improving Academy, gathering knowledge and 'town polish', I was here, helping Uncle Silas."

"He let *you* put your innocent, dainty hands on rough-hewn soldiers?"

"Not everyone he helps is a virile soldier. Or male. Or young and careless enough to be inappropriate and intentionally crass about the idea."

"The idea of what? You *touching* me? Intimately?"

Heart pounding with illicit excitement for once, and not frustration or exhaustion, he couldn't help but grin. "Did you just call me *virile*? Again?"

"If I did..." She surprised him by grinning back, grumbling beneath her breath as she turned to the firebox and checked the boil. "I was obviously deranged. Delirious. Decisively wrong—"

"Wrong?" He barely contained his mirth. "Do you not mean decisively *dunder*headed? Flows much better, do you not think, my proper, anything-but-prudish Prim?"

Rising to her feet, she whirled toward him, the added heat from the fire deepening the flush already pinkening her face. A fine sheen of sweat dampened her forehead. "Dunderheaded, the both of us, I am sure. Let us never speak of *that* again."

"That?"

"You know full well what I refer to, you fiend of a philander."

He laughed. "Thank you."

"'Twas not a compliment," she growled at him, such that Mercury awoke from his doze in the corner and growled back.

They both laughed at that.

"Compliment or no, conversation to be blotted from memory or not, I do not know what to make of this new and brazen Aphrodite Primrose. One I like very much."

He startled her with that. For she took a nervous step backward, toward flame and danger.

"Your skirts," he explained when he braced himself on the table, gained his feet by leaning forward over it and grabbed hold with one hand to tug her closer to him and away from the cooking fire. Sitting back down, relieved that was where his arse landed—and not the floor, the small ache in his back niggling at him since that morning's harpsichord-and-hand calamity, he debated whether to continue conversation down the provocatory direction or guide them into something safer. Something less likely to rouse that part of him that had been slumbering for months, suddenly wakened now that Prim was near.

"I'm surprised I have had no word, no letters from neither brothers nor sisters. I expected surely they would have written by now." Especially the girls.

"Do not forget the mind of a youngling." Like him, she seemed grateful to grasp on to the neutral topic. "Away from home and what they know, whatever is right in front of them will command their attention to the exclusion of all else. Particularly if they are happy and playing with other equally excitable and distractible children." She paused, her expression turning thoughtful. "What of yourself? How many times have you written them since you arrived?"

"That is not a clear answer. As your hound made off

with both a completed letter and another only half begun, neither of which made it to the post." The dog in question received a meaningful glower. Too bad the cur remained oblivious.

"Well now. Perhaps they have a letter-hungry canine thief in their midst as well?" So nearly had she regained her composure, as she gave him a small smile, he could almost imagine she had not just offered to fondle his phallus. Almost. Doubtful it was something he would ever forget.

"You seem different than you did two years ago. More assured."

Did she? "I do?"

And how could he say such a thing, given what she had just proposed? How, *how* in the world had her thoughts of escorting him to take the waters ended with her offering to rub...

His...penis?

Oh glory. Her hands came up to slap her cheeks. She still gripped the towel? Fine, then. She blotted the fire's sweat from her face. Even the sound of that word in her mind was naught but a whisper.

Penis?

Aye, that.

Penis. Penis. Penis! P-E-N-I-S!

Heavens. Stop it!

But now that the thought was there, 'twas lodged. Secure as certain, in her garret and not leaving. Not so much the idea of touching Richard, and more than just his hands and wrists, but the idea of *touching* what she had seen mere days before.

He sat, with a relaxed posture, at the table. Held

himself with ease, she was pleased to note. Had only frowned twice, something she noticed he did when tired or hurting. Was that from the effort to come in here from his room, where he had occupied himself when she came down earlier? Or had he injured something when he fell?

"Exactly so."

Exactly so... What? Her thoughts were a complete muddle.

You. Different. Assured, that is what he said.

Oh. Right. "I *am* two years older."

"Are not we all? Nay, 'tis something more than four and twenty months." He brought one of those strong-fingered hands up to cup his jaw, his thumb and index finger grazing along the curve of his chin as though how she behaved now versus previously was a troublesome quandary he sought to solve.

You are beautiful to me. More stunning tonight than ever before. What happened to make it so?

In the scant days since, she still hadn't discerned quite whether what he'd said that first night had been an insult or high praise indeed. So she asked. "Right before you claimed I was a vision and crawled off to your room, you asked me what happened, why I was more attractive to you than before. What did you mean?"

He groaned. The contemplative gesture changed to a slap upon his forehead before he rested his chin upon his palm, elbow so very casual upon the table. "Please tell me I did not ask you 'What happened?'"

"You did."

"Do you remember everything I said?"

If she confessed to how very much she did, he would think her a loon. "The pertinent parts, I admit."

A stirring Mercury drew his attention, and he abandoned his stance to snap his fingers, drawing the dog to him before he responded.

"You are...not as rigid as you were at the Larchmonts'," he explained. It was then that she realized, since the summer before last, she had left off binding her breasts as she used to, simply let her stays do their job, keeping her waist trim and bosom from bouncing overly much. Nor had she thought to bind them once since her arrival, even whilst under the same roof with a *man*. A peer. "Mmm... *softer*."

Softer, indeed.

But then he continued, not commenting on her physical charms at all.

"It is...not so much how you *look*." He kept one hand on the table as he gave Mercury a vigorous side scratch with the other, but his midnight gaze stayed on her. "'Tis how you...comport yourself now. Your *manner*. It's more...I do not know... Confidence, perhaps?"

"I was courted, you know." *Why are you telling him this?* "Since I saw you last."

30

FALLING FOR YOU

Why was she telling him this?

Why did a red-green, irritated-envious, utterly disordered haze suddenly color everything in the room?

Warrick strove not to let his instinctive, inexplicable reaction show. "Aye?"

Inexplicable? Mate, you know why—

"Mmm. He was an amiable gentleman, music tutor to Lady Harriet. He stayed all summer."

All summer?

Warrick had to swallow before asking, "At the Ballenger estate?"

"In the village. But he visited frequently."

Visited *frequently*. His posture stiffened to stone, hand lifted from its relaxed perch upon the dog's head as he spread hands before him upon the table. Locked them in place. "Visited for Harri's lessons."

"Certainly, those, and to see me as well. To escort me out—"

"Out? Where? Was Lady Ballenger apprised of this?" And why the devil did he sound so jealously *angry* about the notion?

"If anything, I think she encouraged it."

Was his Prim *gloating*? Being braggartry toward him? His ire must have shown, because she immediately added, "Well...if not *encouraged*, Lady Ballenger didn't censure our activities in any way."

"Did you fall for him?"

Not like I have for you.

Did her eyes convey that? Or did he only wish it were so?

"Not sufficiently to leave with him when he asked."

"Asked? As in *marriage*?"

She gave a slow nod.

"Are you *trying* to make me jealous?" And why did he both yearn to hear every detail of their moments together and, at the same time, want to quash them from her memory forever more?

"Jealous?" She laughed, but did not sound at all amused. "Would you not have to care about more than stolen lap kisses to be jealous? Of course I know better. Know better than to suspect you harbor any feelings toward me. Certainly know better than to aim so far above my station." As though what she blathered could be nothing but the truth—however distant in reality—she slapped her hands together, the sound and action muffled by the towel—before retrieving a spoon, avoiding his gaze as she trifled with the stew, scooping vegetables and meat to test for readiness. He could already tell by the lack of smell things were not finished boiling.

Nay, naught boiled but his ludicrous jealousy.

"I am only attempting to explain what you inquired

about. Any newfound confidence, I trust, likely came from the summer I spent with him."

An entire summer. Days and days. "Did he grant kisses? Your music tutor."

Warrick bit the edges of his tongue the moment the words were out. *Too late, Rich.*

Abandoning the spoon with the partially cooked chunks with a *plop* back into the kettle, she spun to face him, hands upon her hips. "He didn't *steal* them, if that is what you ask."

Didn't steal them. Didn't steal kisses—as *he* had. Not giving her a choice.

And bit upon or not, his traitorous mouth kept going. "So you *gave* them?"

Gave kisses to this unnamed bastard of a music tutor he felt the strong urge to pummel.

"A few."

And what else? What else did you freely give? He clamped his lips at the roar that sought to escape. Clenched his toes —or at least tried to—and squashed the urge to stomp from the snug kitchen which had grown overwarm. He knew better. Falling on his face first and arse second was no way to impress his prickly Prim.

She didn't marry the fellow.

He sought to console himself. The dog sought to console him as well, giving a light whine as Mercury rubbed his snout against Warrick's thigh. He stared at the action, no clue whether he felt it, his thoughts in a turmoil. *She did not leave her job as governess for the man.*

Did *not* accept an offer. One that, from what he could glean, had come from a very suitable suitor.

Or—

Or...

Had she accepted the man's kisses and found him wanting?

At the new thought, joy bubbled up through the jealousy.

Mayhap there had been something wrong with him. *Like you?*

"Was he aged? Infirm?" *Like you?* "Ugly as a troll?" he all but spat, his personal control floundering worse than a hooked fish upon the shore.

She did not laugh at his absurdity.

Did not answer, either. Only twitched in place, brow puckered and lips pursed, staring at him as though *he* had green skin, warts upon warts, not a strand of hair upon his head but copious tufts of it protruding from his ears and nose.

"Forgive me." The apology tasted like ash. "I did not mean to imply only an aged, ugly old fool would find you worthy of courting. I..." He faltered.

Faltered more when she slapped the towel in front of him upon the table and glared at him as she took her leave without saying another word.

The baleful look cast once over her shoulder after she called Mercury from his side enough to make him feel about toenail tall.

Prim. Courted.

Hours later and the notion still plagued.

The fear, the very real fear, of how close she had come to being lost to him forever.

The jealousy did not sit well with him. In fact, it had set up camp at the base of his spine, not just the niggling ache he had the last hours or so—since tumbling off the harpsichord bench pell-mell—but fiery. Sharper. More intense than anything he had experienced since those first months of healing.

He strove to ignore it.

Both the physical pain as well as the emotional. Wasn't about to let something as insignificant as envy—for a paltry music teacher, no less—or the wringing in his back, sensation he should be grateful he could feel, dissuade him from whatever he chose to do. However he chose to act.

And just what is it that you are contemplating?

He was of multiple minds on that...

Seduction. Friendship. Desperation?

Desperate longing, of a certainty.

He had yet to decide which course to pursue.

Because circumstances—his infirmities, familial responsibilities, necessity of a sinfully wealthy wife—bid him to pursue nothing at all.

No matter that his envious heart ached at the notion of remaining idle.

THINGS REMAINED RUINOUSLY STRAINED between them all the rest of that evening, and deep into the next day.

Between ordering her evacuation from the drawing room and harpsichord, and ruining the calm so recently restored between them by insinuating the only man who might offer for her was akin to an ancient troll, Warrick had cause to regret every second.

If only he could confide the reasons *why* he acted the surly brute: out of respect for her concerning the former, attempting to preserve her delicate sensibilities by not shocking her—not with words (for once) but with the evidence of his visibly growing desire; and as to the latter, his own buffle-headed jealousy.

Neither of which he was at liberty to convey.

After a strained nuncheon, Aphrodite retreated to Arbuckle's front two rooms, the ones she claimed he entertained patients in. No surprise, that, given the unusual furnishings Warrick had glimpsed in one and the supplies laid out within easy reach in the other. Seeing those meticulously sharpened supplies had made him realize when the man wasn't performing Tyrannical Duties, Arbuckle must have been an accomplished surgeon in his day. Likely still was. He might think of the man as an ancient annoyer, but he couldn't be much more than Warrick's own father would have been, had he lived.

He knew she went in there not only to escape the tenseness surrounding them, but because she planned a thorough cleaning of something. When he'd wondered aloud at the bucket of rags, the water she heated, she'd mentioned "a good scrubbing to keep myself busy".

Determined to set things right between them, and feeling strong after the early night and deep sleep—if still plagued with the nagging, growing pain low in his back—he used one of the kitchen chairs as a crutch to traverse the distance and upon reaching the doorway where she had seated herself on the floor, both she and the soapy bucket in front of her surrounded by towels and drying implements, he greeted her more cheerfully than he felt.

"What may I do to assist?" Not giving her time to protest, he swung the chair into the room and settled in it. "Please. Let me help however you need. Mercury has already romped this afternoon and snoozes—quite loudly, mind—alongside the kitchen firebox."

One good-sized window provided ample light, and though this day continued as cold as the one prior, they had both taken to wearing scarves—and for her a shawl as well—which mitigated the chill.

With less hesitation than he might have expected, she nodded toward one of the clean, unused rags. "I am checking his older tools for rust, cleaning what I can. Something I did often after coming to live here." She gave him a small smile, burdened with more reserve than he liked, and handed him what she had been working on. "From the looks of some of these, they haven't been cleaned since I left. It will save me a step if you will dry."

'Twas an easy thing to grab his own cloth and apply it to the dripping metal. She wore again the soft blue dress she had upon her arrival. He found it very fetching, but knew better than to mention that. The freckles dancing over her nose were visible as she sat facing the window. For once, her hair was not constrained in a tight knot near her neck, but instead bound in a loose braid that marched several inches past her shoulders.

He had to yank his attention from the yearning to free every bit of that braid and focus on the sharp steel she handed him next.

Did Aphrodite know she tidied the stage of so much torture? His job of drying took much less time than hers of washing and scrubbing. It had taken not a moment to determine how close a match this room was, with certain tools and odd furnishings visible, to the one where he'd worked with The Tyrant those early months in London.

"So." After several quiet moments, he ventured, "How musically accomplished is Harri, now, after your young Adonis of a music tutor tutored her thus?"

All must be forgiven, he hoped, given the loud laugh that bellowed from her then. "Not accomplished at all. I claim more talent."

"Oh horrors." He exaggerated his gasp. "Please say it is not so."

"All right, I may embellish. Only a modicum, I vow. He tried an abundance of instruments with her when she did not take to the pianoforte. All, I fear, were less than stellar. Although she has now announced her intention to master the cello."

At the thought of the delicate if vibrant Lady Harri, seated, skirts raised, the big body of that instrument—one only intended for men—resting between her legs, his howl of laughter matched her own.

But thoughts of Harri brought others to the fore...

"That night, when we kissed." His hands paused in their task. "What became..."

"You mean the night you dragged me onto your lap and practically proposed—after kissing me most lewdly?"

"You thought it lewd?" He grunted. "I thought it rather chaste."

"If *that* was chaste"—the instrument she now scrubbed made a loud *plop* when it fell into the bucket of soapy water—"I cannot dare contemplate what you consider salacious."

"Did you suffer ill consequence?" he asked, the drying cloth wound tight within his fist.

Her arm splashed into the bucket as she sought what she'd dropped. She avoided his gaze. "From our actions?"

"From mine, yes." That brought her eyes back to him.

"You take responsibility, then? Do not plead inebriation as your excuse?"

"I may have claimed being soused at the time, but nay, I was not. I knew full well what I did, and with whom. Might have ker-*plunked*—jumping being out of the question—in with both dead feet, fearing I would never again be granted such an opportunity."

"Opportunity? To seize a kiss beneath the mistletoe?"

"To seize one with you."

Would there be? Another opportunity? he wanted to ask, needed to know. But knew better than to risk the accord that had developed between them again. "What happened afterward? To you? I have always wondered."

"After that disaster of a kiss?"

"Nay, the kiss was anything but a disaster. Everything *after* it was rather disastrous."

THAT SURPRISED HER. That he would confess such a thing.

He and Lord Frostwood hadn't waited until morning to depart, instead had sent round for Lord Frostwood's carriage and left as soon as it drew up—at Lady Ballenger's urging, no doubt.

Aphrodite only knew because she had seen it brought around as she climbed the stairs, faint-hearted after the reprimand received moments prior from her employer. "I thought I would be dismissed posthaste."

"But you weren't."

"Nay. Though I did receive a stern talking-to. Was threatened with several thousand lines myself."

"No, you weren't."

"It felt like it. I expect *you* had something to do with my retaining my position within their household." Suspected, but had never known for certain, being unwilling to do anything other than reply *Yes, my lady* to everything Lady Ballenger had sought to shrill, shriek or scream at her that woeful evening. Lord Ballenger watching on, silently, a grim frown—of commiseration or condemnation, she never knew which—flat upon his features.

"I may have persuaded an ally or two to make certain

the Larchmonts knew *you* had no choice, faced with the compelling antics of men solidly in their cups."

"And you?" she asked archly. "Repercussions?" Though she knew there hadn't been any.

"Why do you think we left off that night? Did not wait until morning? Dangerous, it was, traveling with so little light; the moon not yet up and much of the sky blanketed by winter clouds. Ed was quite overset with me, I tell you, when he learned of the entire contretemps." Shifting one foot with his hands, to balance his weight, he leaned forward and tugged on her arm, pulling a rusted scalpel from her unresisting hold, as well as the stiff-bristled brush she had been scrubbing at it with. "Here, let me attend to that one."

His offer surprised her. But not enough to halt what she needed to ask. "And what would he think if he knew you were here with me now? Your close friend, *Lord* Redford?"

She made sure to emphasize the title, because that was the pertinent part of her question. No matter how interactions betwixt the two of them continued to defy expectation and amaze her down to her core, they could not forget who they each were. What worlds they—separately—inhabited.

He opened his mouth, closed it. Made a murmur of consideration as his thumb nail scratched over the bristles. So he was actually thinking it through? Not just prattling off some drivel to curtail her valid concern? That heartened her.

"Likely, he would care naught. For by now he knows more of Harriet and what value you provide. More than that, he would be insanely grateful for any assistance or improvement you could bring to...my situation."

He turned his attention downward, to the brush in his

hand, but not before she saw the frown deepening the grooves on either side of his lips.

His situation...

He spoke of his desperate bid to find an excessively rich wife. The one she could not help but be aware of based on conversations Harri relayed between her sister and brother-in-law, Lord Redford. Not to mention Richard's own mutterings at times both distant and recent.

How easy it was, remarkably so, to forget Richard was even a part of the strata of the titled, elevated few. So easy that, given how he made her feel despite her determination to the contrary, she could no longer think of him as a condescending, pompous peer—even on the rare occasions he might behave like one. Not since opening the door and finding him standing and naked and so hauntingly, temptingly close.

Every time he startled her with something complimentary ("Prim, you beauty, where did you learn to make stew so divine? Tell me it wasn't The Tyrant..."); every time he gracefully acknowledged something she did for him ("You spoil me, sweet Aphrodite. Clean clothes, again?"); something she did for the dog ("You are remarkably patient combing through those damp, tangly knots each time he comes in."), his deep voice rolled through her both unexpectedly and familiarly. His tone and words a balm that soothed every hurt she'd endured over the years.

From her parents' demise, to being shuffled from one relative to the next, to the virtue-threatening actions of peers that scared a young, new governess into more sleepless nights than she wanted to admit... Lord Warrick's, *Richard's* words and actions bolstered her confidence. His very presence buffered her against the storms of life.

He was the only man to affect her thus. Certainly the only one to ever voice his appreciation so readily.

Being acknowledged, having a lord treat her like a person 'twas such a novel experience. And yet one she had quickly come to revere. As she did the man himself. How would she get on when they left and each went back from whence they came?

When she had no news of him? Could no longer see his comforting smile or devastating, wicked grin? Could no longer delight in his forthright humor and sometimes naughty conversations?

When at night, instead of conjuring him sleeping snug in the bed below hers, she would have no notion of his whereabouts? Of who else he might spend time with. Of what challenges and travails he might face—without her there to assist?

The thought of the years looming, with unimaginable, never-ending loneliness, the years without him lumped a tangle of its own in her throat.

As though privy to her turbulent thoughts, he shook his head, his features brightening. "Come now, you have been in here an age. I hear Mercury stirring and am sure your limbs"—he raised his eyebrows at her, ensuring she noticed he did not say *legs*—"could use a good stretching. Take a pause, as long as you like." He tugged the lip of the bucket closer to his chair, until he could lean over and lift the entire thing—with only a single tightening of his frown. "Leave that whole batch." He gestured to the bottom drawer she had just opened, the one with the most, and most rusted, items revealed thus far. "I can work on those this afternoon. You are doing more than enough with food and fires."

Drat him, he proved again his thoughtfulness? Now? When she already struggled so? Was weak to everything about him?

"Pardon me." Before he caught a glance of her shimmering lashes—before he could ask about her precipitous flight—she raced from Uncle's treatment room and Richard's balmy presence.

Stormed up the stairs and escaped into the privacy of her bedroom, her heart lashing the inside of her chest like sails thundering in a gale.

Oh, falling stars and fallen hearts. There was no denying it, not any longer.

She had fallen in love with the man.

Drat him. And damn her silly widgeon of a heart.

THAT MOONLIT KISS

THE LOUD CLANGING didn't wake Aphrodite. She would have had to have been asleep for that.

Staring at the ceiling, restless and languoring, scowling the past hour or more at the bright moonlight coming in despite the curtains she'd pulled across the window panes. Courtesy of the early evening patter of first rainfall and then snow flurries, the white-coated ground reflected everything and made the light a true annoyance for someone desperate for the allure of sleep.

The rattling *Clang! Bang-a-lang-lang!!* proved welcome, if heart-jerkingly startling. A reason to rise, to wrap a shawl around her shoulders, slip her already stockinged feet into her slippers and storm downstairs.

"Mercury," she said on a loud whisper, seeking the four-legged culprit. "Mercury, what have you gotten into?"

"It isn't the dog." The low rumble made her start. She swung round to find Richard, half-standing in the kitchen, coated but not scarved nor hatted, one hand on the table as though he'd just gathered the energy to rise. He had a lamp on the table burning low. At his side, Mercury panted and jumped about, tongue lolling forth.

"I apologize if we woke you." Richard sat back down, attempted to calm the excited dog. "He was eager to go out and I'm afraid I fumbled retrieving the rope. Did a bit of damage, knocking that off the sideboard." Her gaze followed his. The containers that held both the lard and the flour had suffered in the mishap. "Only one of the crocks shattered, but the mess is rather splendid."

"Oh dear." She rushed forward, only to be stopped when his arm shot out in front of her. "Let me clean it."

"No need." His voice brimmed with confidence. "I will tend to it after he romps outside."

As the air thickened between them, she stepped back, away from the arm that had so briefly, so solidly, been across her middle, near her hips. Attempted to concentrate on something other than the flare of heat that sparked at the contact. "But what if Mercury cuts his—"

"He won't. I tossed a blanket over the broken crockery. And with the temperatures, we need not worry about ants invading before I have a chance to tidy things upon our return."

"Our?"

He gestured with the rope he had fixed into a harness around the dog's chest and front legs. "We were heading out, not in."

"May I join you?"

"It's cold. Your attire isn't made—"

"Lying in bed is tedious. A few minutes won't freeze me through."

"By all means, then." Using his arms for the bulk of the effort, he pushed to standing. The back of the chair he had been in and then the one he had stationed near the door each supporting part of his weight until he turned the knob, opened the door and let her precede him, after the frolicky dog winged ahead.

Warrick saw Aphrodite cross her arms against the cold the moment she moved beyond the threshold, from within to without. But instead of withdrawing, she flashed him a grin over her shoulder, so easily seen with the full moon beaming bright on one side of her face.

Though Mercury gamboled ahead of them both, his lead a light and now familiar tug upon Warrick's wrist, she paused just beyond the door. The hair that escaped her sleep-mussed braid shimmered in the stillness, while he braced himself against the jambs of the open door content just to breathe her in.

"I love nights like this," she whispered. "So crisp. Fresh. They're my favorite."

Something to note about her. To remember. She revealed so little, at times, that he cherished every new revelation.

Mercury had darted to his favorite pissing corner, as Warrick had come to think of the far section of walled-off property, making use of the long lead he'd become adept at navigating about, even without his sight. The dog dug his paws through the light layer of snowy frost that had fallen earlier that evening, making dirt and ice crystals fly. Warrick knew from experience that the weather would not drive the thief back in until he nosed about a good several minutes.

Now that he had a companion, wasn't sitting on the chair in the open doorway, nor sitting in his still-missing Merlin's chair as he had his first days here, Warrick gauged the distance to the stone wall about five feet hence. That was the part he could sit on. For though someone had long-ago stacked the stones high closer to the house, creating a shield from the wind, for most of the yard it was not quite waist high. A suitable perch, were it not for the icy coating—and his inability to walk with ease.

"What may I do to assist?" she asked, noticing where his attention had landed, her body already turned, primed.

He wanted her touch more than he wanted his next breath.

But the disaster on the harpsichord, his ill-timed jealousy over Prim's suitor and how things had ended between them earlier—with her continued monishments of his need to hunt for an heiress (and thereby stop entertaining foolish fantasies about taking her to wife)... Given how she'd avoided him ever since that unwanted but warranted reminder, did he dare take what she now offered?

Do not be too proud to accept her help, whatever may have gone before. You aren't an imbecile. Do you dare waste an opportunity to touch *her?*

His throat thickened. He swallowed hard. "Do you see where that horizontal stone sits, somewhat wider than the others and just past that jutting one?" He released his grip on the frame long enough to point with one finger. "Can you knock the snow free? Confirm it isn't iced beneath? If not, that's where I aim to sit." Because he could not imagine confining her to the doorway, as he would have himself, not after learning how she basked in the cold night.

"Oh? Is that why you had a blanket at the ready?" She did as bade, no hesitation at brushing the wet cold with her bare hands. "You were going to sit upon it?"

"Mmm." Certainly, let her think that. When in truth he intended to wrap it about his shoulders and huddle in the chair like a youngling. Nay, much better to let her think he, too, had planned on enjoying the beautiful winter evening.

"Not icy," she pronounced, after testing the flat surface with both her palms, as though she'd heated the rock herself. "Definitely frigid, but I daresay it will warm fast enough."

"Thanks to my hot arse, you mean?"

With a laugh that carried easily on the quiet night, she came to his side and ducked beneath the arm not holding the rope. Snugged her arm around his waist. While that threatened to snaffle his wits, she gripped his other hand, and pulled it over her shoulders, anchoring it just above her breast. "How is this? Steady enough?"

How was it? *Humiliating.* But...mayhap not. Mayhap this is what he had needed to do all along: accept assistance with grace and humility instead of focusing on his embarrassment. "I fear I may be too heavy for you."

"I fear I may be too strong for you," she boasted and it was all he could do not to kiss her right then.

"Two strides, long ones, and I may slip. Three or four and I think we can make it."

"When you are ready," she encouraged. Her hold about his waist tightened.

He was careful not to put too much weight upon her shoulders, but almost as though Mercury were trying to assist as well, the dog strained against the lead, pulling on his hand and wrist where it was wound, and Warrick shuffle-stepped as fast as he dared but without panic until he was close enough to the wall to lunge for it, slipping from her grip to catch the top.

"Look at that," he muttered, turning his hips and sliding into place to confirm his buttocks now rested firmly upon the horizontal stone. "I am all that is graceful."

"Stop that. I know this is not easy. You need not mock yourself in front of me, ever."

He gave a grunt, wound the rope a couple more times about his wrist. "Haven't been watching the dog. Has he done his business yet?" he asked, even though he already knew.

"Does it matter?" Her voice breezed against his forehead. "We just got here. Rest."

"Oh aye, because everyone wants to *rest* on a frozen night against frozen stone."

"My oh my. Since when did you turn so curmudgeonly?"

"I could mutter something about French canister shot, but let us not go there. Not tonight."

He used his hands to check behind him, ensure his seat was secure. He already had his legs straightened and feet planted. *Falling not allowed,* he could practically hear Sophia encourage. With the wall supporting the bulk of his weight and his feet somewhat dug in to the frost-hardened ground, he actually felt stable.

But he saw Aphrodite's shiver, the one she tried to hide. Against his better judgment, giving in to what he wanted, he used his hands above his knee and whatever strength he could muster from his leg to move one foot outward a couple of inches, and then did the same with the other.

"Come here." She had hovered this whole time, no longer touching him yet remaining close. He easily snared her wrist and tugged her in front of him. Hands just above her hips, he spun her until she faced the yard, pulled her down, against him, in between his legs. When she didn't immediately jump back up, he wound his arms about her torso and clasped his hands lightly around her waist, without touching anything he should not. But that didn't mean he wasn't thinking about it.

She remained stiff for but a moment, then relaxed. But not completely, he could tell.

Mercury barked at the rustle of a brave, unslumbering bird flitting overhead.

Warrick waited. Rested his chin upon her shoulder, sensed her every inhale. Still, she did not yield. "I won't bite, unless you ask me to."

A soft squeak escaped her lips.

And I said you weren't an imbecile? Probably not the thing to goad her with.

Her hands fluttered and then landed over his wrists. Icy, indeed. They had both failed to don gloves.

At least he had his coat on. But her wrap was thin. He released one hand and brought it up to brush her wild hair away from his mouth, to tuck it between them, letting his fingers rest on the side of her neck.

Could she feel how furious his chest pounded? Hear how haggard his breath?

The innocent touch of her skin, of *her*, affecting him as nothing he could remember. Nothing wholly unique about the moment either, nothing truly special—not anything that he could put into words, except it was *her*. Prim. Whom he wanted to school in passion.

Whom perplexed him beyond reckoning. Holding her, being with her seemed as familiar to him as staring at his signet ring; as chest-drummingly exciting as his first time.

He inhaled near the delicate skin of her neck he longed to taste. She smelled like home and happiness.

First time? Be honest. You want her to be your "last" time. You want her—forever.

He damn well did. And he had absolutely no clue how

to go about making it happen. Not given the state of his pockets—and estate—and uncertain, but definitely wankly future.

Aphrodite's stomach tumbled like an acrobat. Being so close to him, being in his arms, her temperature had soared like that bird full of foolery flapping about the yard. She stared at the white-blue frosty scape, looked overhead where she knew the stars should be, their presence blotted out by the moon's brilliance. Noticed where fast-moving clouds approached from the south.

The misadvised bird taunted Mercury again, courting danger. Silly thing should be abed. *Like you?*

Richard's breath warmed her one ear. His hand, still resting lightly, thumb upon her nape, fingers toward the front of her neck heated more than mere skin. Those acrobats? Now jumped around her middle like Harriet impatient with news to share.

They remained that way for heartbeats. Heartbeats that turned into minutes. Mercury bounded back and forth barking at the bird and chasing its chirrupy, taunting flight, ignoring the rope, content to be outside in a familiar, safe space.

But she felt anything but safe. She felt threatened. Exhilaratingly so.

Though danger loomed…her next actions potentially a peril to everything she held dear, more than anything, she wanted to turn and place her lips against his.

"Why did you order me from the room yesterday? After you played?" she braved asking instead, the whisper freezing in front of her, loud enough she hoped he heard. Both prayed and yet feared he would answer.

Had that only been yesterday? Given how it was closer

to midnight than morning, and earlier *today*, they had cleaned and dried tools, until her bewildering feelings precipitated her flight from his presence...

"I could tell you a lie or three, or I could confess I would rather not reveal the truth. For I am certain that, curiosity aside, you would rather not know."

Peculiar.

But honest. A comfort, that, surely. "Then do not say more. I would rather you stay silent than treat me to surfacy responses we both know mean naught."

More silence. More hard and thumping heartbeats. More twisting and turning within her stomach. A twitch of his fingers, a caress over the front of her throat, up behind her ear. A settling of his touch. A harsh gust of breath past her ear, then a low murmur. One felt more than heard. "Do you want to return inside?"

Did she think it or did he ask? She wasn't sure. Hushed as he, she answered, "Nay. Not yet."

More minutes. More moonlight and advancing clouds as the earth slowly rotated a degree or so with every hundred breaths.

A silent gasp—hers—accompanied by an audible sigh —also hers—when he shifted behind her, brought her deep against his chest, snug within his hold, and arranged his coat to enfold them both. More, when she felt that unprepared-for yet definite part of him, stiff and sure, pressed insistently along her bottom and low back.

Another degree and the frantic knot in her belly turned to liquid heat that sank deep, promised to drip lower.

"I want to kiss you." He startled her with those words. "May I?"

She pushed away from his embracement and turned, feeling wobbly and very uncertain as she stood before him, his hands now gentle upon her hips. His head much on the same level as hers. "You...ask? *You?* He who takes whatever he wants whenever he wants it?"

"I do not." Though accented with shadows, the harsh planes of his face were visible in the moonlight, which meant her dumbfounded expression was hidden. But he had to feel her quivering, her nervous excitation. "I *certainly* do not take whatever I want," he insisted with a slight pinch between his brow. "For if I did, I would have crushed you against me yesterday as well as this afternoon and dared to lift your skirts."

She slapped her hand against her mouth at that answer. At that image. Then slowly freed her lips. "Yet you did not. Why?"

And why do you not run from him now? You know what you just felt. What he's capable of.

"Mayhap I am not that man any longer." Which echoed her own thoughts. "The man who doesn't give a farthing for the consequences and takes what he wants. Tumbles intriguing governesses into his lap and *steals* kisses." He dragged one fingertip along her trembling bottom lip. "Perhaps, in four and twenty months, I have matured as well."

"Then...if not he, what man are you?"

He hesitated answering. Debating truth or evasion? "The man who wants your kiss, freely given this time. Desperately so."

"Desperately?"

"Aye." The syllable was yanked from him.

"I do not believe anyone has ever desperately wanted me."

"*Needed.*"

"Needed *anything* from me desperately. And neither

am I the same as before, for unlike your claim, I *no longer* give a farthing for any consequences."

She curved her hands about his shoulders, braced the back of his head within her palms and lowered her lips to his.

This. This is what he had craved since first seeing her walk away, oblivious to his presence after bargaining with her charge in the corridor outside his room so long ago. What he had yearned for after laughing over pins on paintings and stealing a taste of her beneath the mistletoe.

What he had ached for after mocking her so thoroughly in front of everyone and regretting it—yet not... After dooming Frost and himself to a hasty departure, *this* is what he had craved in the empty months since.

Was he shaking? At a mere kiss? An innocent kiss upon another's mouth? With clothing on? It wasn't as though he licked her bare nipples or applied his lips lower, upon lips of another sort, dripping with honey, with want...

Time enough for all of that later. Please, God, let it be so.

So that could not be him trembling, could it? Not at so tame an action. A simple and light kiss.

One you do not want to blunder.

32

MORE FALLING

AFTER ONLY A SECOND OR TWO, Warrick angled his head to the side, evading the light pressure of her mouth. "I don't want to hold back, not with this kiss," he rasped against her skin. "Nor do I want you to take alarm and cause you to tremble and trot."

If he scared her with his ardor, scared her at all, and caused her to run? 'Twould cut like—

Gentle, if determined, fingers upon his jaw turned him back. "I might be trembling, but not trotting away from you. From us. Please."

With that, he released all the restraint and yearning he'd stifled every time he'd been near her. His strong hands splayed across her back, his tongue delved within her mouth, licking against hers. Her ardent moan and eager response fired his own. His groin twitched—or did it?—as her tongue reciprocated, following into his mouth, surging against him, drinking in his taste as he consumed hers.

His hands roamed up and down her spine, found the plumped flesh of her arse and squeezed once, twice. She squirmed toward him, not away, and he tugged her forward, released her buttocks to draw her higher against his chest. She scrambled ever closer, bringing her legs up and over his.

The persistent bird swooped nearby, Mercury's blind but tenacious chase tightening the rope about his wrist. He firmed his balance, his hold on the delightful bundle now, somehow, in his lap at long last.

Breath ragged, tongues active, the cold air heating around them, they kissed and kissed. Her legs wrapped around his waist, feet locked behind his back—thank heavens for low stone walls—as she rubbed against him, both firing his blood and soothing his soul.

His hands mapped across her back, stroked up from her waist, fingertips nearing her spine while his thumbs—torturous, traitorous bastards that they were—edged over the sides of her lush breasts. Her hands petted his jaw, his cheeks, fingers threaded through his hair, tips scratching along his scalp.

A couple of excited barks and the rope on his wrist tugged, but not painfully. Nay, the only harsh and painful thing between them was desire. Hitting hard, hot and fast. After so many long months without his prim Aphrodite—who was anything but, he had come to learn—he should have anticipated the conflagration.

Though his past injuries still deadened much feeling, and the cold stone deadened the rest, he imagined she rocked her loins against his. Imagined he felt her slippered heels snug about his hips, his sitting place through the weathered-dampness of his trousers. Imagined *he* was hard as a result. But wasn't sure. Wasn't thinking that far below, concentrating instead upon her mouth. The sweetly swollen lips that sighed against his when they broke apart before surging back together.

Capturing her top lip with his teeth, he exulted in her moan. Released her to swipe his tongue back into her mouth, only to retreat after a few strokes and nibble her lower lip until he enticed yet another sweetly seductive groan. She continued stroking fingers over his head and neck, nails engaged over his scalp until all he wanted was to kiss her till sunrise. Until forever.

She rested her breasts against his chest, the big mounds that he felt for certain. He skimmed one greedy hand beneath the edge of her night-rail, grazed his fingers up the surprisingly warm flesh of her leg and thigh. Groaned against her lips. Could not help but venture delicately farther...

Her heat. Her warmth. The liquid desire from her body greeted his questing fingers the moment he reached her core. And shockingly—he *was* erect. His prick pressed against his thumb even as he sought to turn his hand, to caress her more fully. Breathing as though her chest were made of bellows, she leaned back, touched his cheeks, placed fingers on either side of his mouth. "Yes," she breathed between them, "aye, please...more."

He brought his thumb up, through her moist petals, edging deeper and higher, until she wiggled against his forays, and then he did it again. Her slick heat coating his thumb. His breath came swiftly and lightheadedness hit out of nowhere. Had he forgotten to breathe? His lips still devoured hers. His heart thundered against his ribs.

Prim. Aphrodite—the woman he needed beyond all others—was in his arms, not afraid but eager and responsive, the motion of her hips encouraging—

With a sharp cry, the bird flit inches above their heads. Mercury gave chase, attempting to scale Warrick's legs, threatening to destroy his tenuous balance.

They broke apart. Abandoning his naughty play, he

wrapped his arms fast around her back, holding her secure. Harsh, staggered breathing shared betwixt them on a ragged chuckle.

"Oh, my."

"Indeed."

But he'd relaxed his guard too soon, for the bird chattered hauntingly and the dog responded. The rope pulled hard against his arm, jerked him to the side, and in his efforts to combat the motion, he lost. Fell backward, brought her with him, and toppled, hitting the ground on the other side of the wall in a blaze of embarrassment, aye, but more one of pain.

Pain that burst through his low back like a raging wall of fire. Slammed into his forehead as he held on to consciousness with a thread...

It took Aphrodite seconds, seconds that seemed like an eternity, to make sense of what happened. They had been kissing. Touching. The wild thrill of riding his fingers, of experiencing such an intimate, slick touch, one felt so much deeper than any of her own. And then she had been flying, soaring, seeking the elusive goal his tantalizing touch promised, arching her hips, groaning, kissing...kissing... Oh his taste, his tongue. She could not get enough of him. And then she flew faster. But instead of soaring, she crashed. Landed with a jolt that stunned. Hitting the ground with a staggering thump that jarred every bone in her invigorated, now thoroughly disordered, body.

Behind them, claws scrabbled against the wall, Mercury barked like a madling.

Against the echo of Richard's teeth knocking together at their hard landing, she aimed to make sense of the insensible. Her woman's flesh fluttered around nothing, seeking the return of his touch, so hungry for him—for all of him—yet empty, barren... Her brain grappled against her body's cravings. *Not the time!*

Nay, not the time at all. She shoved away the disquieting urges, the emptiness now taunting her.

"Are you injured?"

"Did you hurt yourself?"

They both asked at once.

"Back." Anguish propelled his sharp response. "Something's...bad. Ahh, *different*," he gritted out from tightly held teeth. "Give me but a moment. I shall rise and—"

"You shall *wait*. Let me see."

"*See?*" he snorted as she untangled off him as awkwardly as she felt—what they had been doing!—and as carefully as she could without jarring him further. "Prim, 'tis not sunlight but moonlight"—a harsh whimper, one he instantly subdued—"that surrounds as now. Doubt you will be seeing much of anything till morn. Return inside where—"

"Pah. As if you think I'm leaving you to freeze here until the cock crows." Quickly did she explore every inch of him she could reach. His legs, one upright still resting on the wall; the other had slid wide, down the side. Perspiration dotted his brow, and above his lip, where she cupped the side of his face. He lay in shadow. She moved to the side so she could see him better, with the nearly full moon at her back.

Moisture thickened the air. *Are you sure it isn't just coming from betwixt your legs?* She shook off that naughty thought. Heavy clouds marched forth, heralding more weather. "Talk to me. You said your back. Where else?"

"Head. Did I split it open?" The question was more ragged gasp than clear speech. "That and my spine?"

"May I turn you on your side?"

He didn't answer, just kept breathing in a deep, harsh pattern.

She brought his legs together, lowered them both down this side of the wall. Sensing her movements, Mercury bounded near, jumping against the other side of the stone wall, small yips of delight, thinking this was a new game. His front paws scraped across the top, spilling frost down upon them as he sought a way over.

"Cocks crowing... You remarked upon..." Even as the rock fence kept them shadowed, his speech, though slow, gained in clarity and volume.

That had to be good, right? "What of them?"

Kneeling at his side, she lifted and heaved the shoulder closest to her so she could roll him to his side.

"Have to ask now, Prim. If I freeze tonight or Old Winter pilfers my ballocks, might not get another chance. Did you...notice? *My* cock crowed—for you."

Her frantic motions stilled. "I...ahm..."

"First time, Aphrodite. Second or third if I count dreams and music, but all for you. Ay!" Another burst of pain he quickly stifled. "Growing darker. If I falter and swoon, needed you to know. You're my angel, sweet Prim."

"'Tis growing darker because of the clouds. Can you smell the snow?"

His *angel*? Would angels have participated in what she had just been doing?

Oh glory and goodness—what was he spouting? Admitting to spectral fancies? "I need to check your garret for bumps and bruises."

"Aye. You need to..." His volume wavered. "Check me *all* over, I'm sure."

The rake. He might be in severe pain and close to sweltering into a faint in truth, but his wits were intact, that was assured.

As soon as she had him turned, she brought fingers to his back. He did not react. But a thorough, explorative pat over him and the ground "showed" her much, especially what caused the pain. "You landed on a large stone. A jagged-edged, pointy one. And with your full weight, and mine as well. Can you move? Can you still move your toes?"

He laughed at that. A pained chuckle. "I nearly fainted to naught, still might, and all we care about is can I wiggle a toe. I do not know. The thought of trying is agonizing."

Mercury barked, no longer playful, but now howls of distress, his efforts frenzied as the dog tried to leap over. "Let me settle him and we shall get you inside."

That he didn't answer nor protest worried her. Even weakened and upon his back, he was a force: humor, wit, determination. The thought of hauling all two hundred pounds of him by herself, if he sweltered to naught, chilled more than the air.

After unwinding the rope circling his wrist, she climbed over the wall and urged Mercury inside.

She secured the dog in her uncle's bedroom, a place he was comfortable with, but still had to battle Mercury's efforts to slip out the door before she could shut it. Of course, howling plaintively all the while.

"Stop whining, boy. I shall let you out as soon as can be."

She returned outside with a blanket to see that fat, puffy flakes had begun to fall, the moon's light shuddered by thick clouds. "Still awake?"

An unmistakable grunt her answer.

"All right. I do not want you to try and walk, not now.

Let's get you on this and I will drag you around to the front."

He barked another laugh, reached out and grasped her ankle. "No. Nay." He took several breaths, less ragged than before. "The pain. It's faded, partially. Grant me a few more moments and I want to stand. You'll not be dragging me around this cottage and the next to get back to your uncle's. Who knows how many stickers, rocks and brambles you might embed into my noggin?"

It took longer than one might wish, but less time than she had expected, and they were no longer battling the cold and falling flakes. Just Richard's flagging energy and the constant noise from Mercury's hearty lungs.

First was a brief rest in the kitchen, where they removed his greatcoat and she brought a chamber pot per his request and made herself absent, but only after his, "Ah, damn me. Apologies, Prim. Appears you'll also be cleaning the broken crock and flour after all." And her, "As if that bothers me any. Summon me when you're done."

And then 'twas time they made for his room, pausing in between "steps" while she raced around him, dragging two chairs from the kitchen forth and back, to give him handholds and a "seat" when needed, both of them cursing *his* mysteriously "missing" chair.

"Should have brought the lamp." Thought of only after she bumped into a table and knocked something off with a *thump*.

"Cannot do it all, even as talented as you are."

His room was in shadows. No curtains on his window, but only muted moonlight now that snow fell. She eased him onto the mattress. "On your stomach," she directed. "I need to inspect—"

"No, thank you." He remained sitting. Naught but a dark, gasping-for-breath shadow. "Now that I'm here, I will be fine, just return to bed."

"Oh, you sparking imbecile. If you think I am going to run craven *now*." She bent to lift his feet, tugging on the bottom of his trousers until they, too, were situated atop the bed. "After I retrieve the kitchen lamp, I shall see if there is any damage *visible*, make you some tea to help you sleep, and remain downstairs in case you call out."

His hand shot out and snared her sleeve through the gloom. "If you expect to stay downstairs? Near? Waiting for me to call out, then you can damn well sleep next to me in this bed. It isn't as though I will be doing anything untoward. Not tonight." Definitely stronger now. No chance of losing consciousness now, not with how forceful he sounded.

"Not tonight? So mayhap I can look forward to something *tomorrow* night?"

"Do not make me laugh. It hurts too much, you wicked woman."

She left his room with a naughty smile, glad he could not see it. How quickly she had come to both an awareness of him as well as an acceptance of their closeness. Granted, the unexpected proximity still spun her thoughts into disorder—as he did her body—but despite their joint flirting, the earth-shaking kisses of earlier, she could not deny the ease she felt in his company.

Moments later, she bustled back in, placed the lamp near his bed and turned it up. "Can you take off your shirt? Trousers?"

"You just want to get your greedy hands on my body."

"How could I aspire to anything else?"

He snorted at that. "It's not pretty, what you're going to see."

"That's all right. Your face makes up for it."

He laughed and groaned. "Told you *not* to be amusing."

Well, he needed to stop being so deuced appealing. "Let us remove your shirt and loosen your falls. We may not need to take the trousers off—"

"Pity."

Ignoring that, they worked together—or she worked and he rolled, maneuvering from one side to the other, face-and-stomach down as he was, the clothing practically trapped beneath the bulk of his body. When she helped him tug the shirt over his head, saw the expanse of his naked back, she bit the inside of her cheek to keep from exclaiming.

Though she'd seen *all* of him the day of her arrival, the whole—the *standing* whole—had proved so mesmerizing, she hadn't studied, at length, his spine. But seeing the torn and once-shredded skin, healed but severely twisted, scars upon scars, had her stomach and throat rebelling.

She slapped one hand over her mouth. Swallowed down the sick nausea that churned like the ocean in storm. She refused to turn away. To blink or demure. He *lived* it. The least she could do was learn the extent. To understand, if only a fraction.

"You did not believe me, did you?" A bleak whisper. "Told you to leave off, that I—"

"It could be worse." *He could be dead.*

And she was so very, very thankful he was not. *That* cleared her throat, calmed her stomach. Made her heed the urge to lean down and press her lips to the worst of it —whether he could feel her or not.

"I'm glad it's not."

"That makes both of us." Of course, she'd seen worse injuries. Living with her uncle, a trained surgeon, and assisting him, meant she was no stranger to gruesome injuries. 'Twas that this wasn't simply a patient to help. This was the man she lo—

None of that, now, missy. Love is for ladies; lust is for affection-starved governesses who know their lot in life.

Another light kiss and she straightened. Now that she had gotten over the shock of things, it wasn't as awful. "I believe, for all that it looks quite wretched, you healed rather well." She probed the area, tugged down the waistband of his trousers. "Goodness. You did land on that rock. Your skin is torn." She feathered around the area. He hissed, stiffened, then held still. "You felt that, then?"

Something to celebrate? Or to deepen concern?

"Every brush of your fingers. Please. Continue."

She did, exploring the gash that had ripped through the surface of his skin in a series of jagged tears. Since he could not see, she became his eyes. Described things as Uncle had demonstrated time and again while her younger self had hidden nearby. "Everything around the gash is red and swollen. Likely to bruise, I am sure. 'Tis not quite a three-inch rent upon your skin. And not just one, but a small series, it appears." Her weight crashing down on top of his hadn't helped.

"Bleeding?" he asked.

"Not *drip* bleeding," she said, lightly circling the area. "Scrape bleeding, yes. I don't know that there's anything to clean *from* it, as it didn't rip through your clothing. Wait, let me make sure." She climbed over his legs and reached down from the side of the bed, where she'd tossed his shirt. Lifting it, she sought the bottom hem, then searched upward. "No. No loose threads, no tears in your garments, so there is that, at least."

When she pushed off the edge of the mattress, he shackled her wrist and tugged until she toppled onto her side, facing him. His head was turned, hair mussed and damp. "It doesn't need cleaned, then," he concluded, deep blue eyes sparkling as much as ever, she was pleased to note. "Stay. After you let out the barking alarm."

Stay? Stay on a bed, *in* a bed, with a man she knew was in no position to take any sort of liberties—even should she want him to? Drat.

She gave a deep sigh. "Let me turn down the lamp. In truth, there is nowhere I would rather be. Are you cold? Shall I retrieve more blankets? Build up the fire?"

The ones she'd started after her arrival and he'd helped maintain. He shook his head, the action muffled by the mattress. "Dog. Lamp. Naught else unless *you* are cold."

"After lugging your ranklesome self through the cottage? Not cold at all."

He gave her a sleepy smile and a squeeze on her arm before she slipped from his hold and went to release Merc to a suitable number of murmurs, pets and apologies for his brief and unexpected confinement. Then she returned, the canine snuffling at her night-rail. Her frost-dampened night-rail. Extinguishing the lamp, she removed the wet, dirtied garment, illicitly drew *his* discarded shirt over her head and climbed atop the bedclothes. Pausing. Uncertain.

Was he still awake?

"I hear your dithering. Lie down, Prim. The dog shall chaperone."

A small smile grew upon her face when Mercury sniffed atop the bed, made his way around and jumped up behind Richard. The dog dug into the coverlet and settled with a loud sigh that ruffled his long lips.

Gingerly she followed suit, lying stiffly on her back until a big arm hauled her closer, followed by a grunt of discomfort. "Relax," he coaxed, drawing her back to his front. "Become comfortable, remain at ease, and sleep."

Was he telling her—or himself?

"*You* cannot be comfortable," she said, "sardined between us."

"Of course not. Feels like a damn horse stomped on me and left his shoe embedded in my spine. I confess, though, I have grown accustomed to the dog's heat. 'Twill likely soothe my tight muscles if naught else."

The arm he'd wrapped about her remained neutrally at her waist. She grabbed his hand and brought it up to her heart, held it there. Every bit as much as she held him inside that very organ as well. "Can *you* sleep? Should I bring you some wine? Port?"

"Likely so, but no. Just let me breathe you in."

And so it was, that cold and snowy night that progressed so very differently from whence it began, Aphrodite Primrose knew three things with utter certainty:

1. Sleeping with a man brought about extreme awareness of herself as a woman.

2. 'Twas significantly warmer lying alongside him without any coverings than it was sleeping bundled up alone.

And...

3. She would never, ever, *ever* be able to forget the handsome rake after this.

Her brain was doomed. Heart stolen and lost forevermore.

Vivid memories embedding themselves with every second, every breath that gusted over her shoulder and across her cheek...

33

CUTS LIKE A KNIFE

DREAMS. So very many of them.

Warrick dreamed of his father, the big, laughing man, long hair pulled back in a queue, chasing him round the dining room, exclaiming that pranky little boys who played tricks on the cook shouldn't be allowed to giggle so much... Remembering Mama's face when she bit into the stew, seasoned with sugar. Not salt.

He dreamed of his mother, stern-faced yet eyes twinkling with love—and glistening from the tears she refused to let fall—ordering him to return safely and posthaste when he announced his intention to join the dragoons alongside his two closest friends, Ed and Frost.

He dreamed of a feisty governess who didn't moderate her words when they spoke in a frozen garden. A shadowed nook. An empty ballroom. Nor anywhere else. He dreamed of her sun-blazed hair, her saucy wit, of tasting her breasts...

He dreamed of King and Knight, growing strong and

tall, growing muscles and confidence and arguing over the merits of Oxford versus Cambridge.

He dreamed of Sophia, a mischievous prankster herself, and her antics entertaining their maid, their cook, the stable boy they no longer had...

He dreamed of Julia. Sweet, silent Julia who would let him hold her, but who still wouldn't speak.

He awoke on fire. His entire body blazing with heat.

He woke with watering eyes, the moisture beneath dashed aside with a rough swipe of his finger because the knife tearing through his back commanded every ounce of his control.

"Prim? Some-something's happening."

Sleep-fogged, her every limb weighted, head heavy and thoughts sluggish, Aphrodite dozed on.

"Aphrodi-teeee!"

It took the aching whisper of her name to yank her awake.

She pried open eyelids, blinked into darkness. *Richard.* Bed. No longer holding her, but thrashing—

At the jagged note in his voice, the restless buckle of his body, she burst into sitting. "What is it?"

"Knife. Back. That or flame. Cut-cutting me. From the inside."

She was up in a moment, lighting the lamp and scurrying around the bed. The whining dog, already on his feet, jumped down at her approach. "Shhh. Not now, Merc. Settle."

She rolled Richard onto his stomach and brought the light close to his back.

A fine sheen of perspiration covered every inch. She couldn't see much beyond the ragged, torn flaps of skin that greeted her, the area worse than before, the redness deeper and swelling more inflamed. She laid her fingers alongside the gash and felt the muscles twitching, jumping against her light touch. Confirming the confusing blur. "Hold on. Bite the sheet if you need to. Don't let your teeth break."

"Good God, Prim." A harsh chuckle. "I'm in pain, not a sniveling weakling."

"I know, I know… Give me but a moment. You have the right of it—something *is* happening, though I don't know what. It's as though your muscles riot."

With Mercury having lost interest and wandered away, she placed the lamp on the floor and shut the door. Returned to place both hands, fingers barely connecting with his quivering skin, over the fresh wound. Smoothing her flattened fingers outward, she observed, "Your muscles. They move chaotically. Like a spasm…but not."

As she watched, the convulsions strengthened, rippling through him, arching his hips off the bed before dropping them back down. He moaned against the bedding. No idea whether he bit down or not. "It cannot last," she told them both, as panic amplified. "Not at this intensity."

Another two forceful contractions that buckled his body. "Have you—" Then she saw something that made her squeal. "Have you tweezers?"

Another moan, then he lifted his head, spat out the sheet. "Certainly. Let me reach into my pocket and pull them out for you. Hell no, I don't carry *tweezers* on my person." A pause when his body convulsed again. "Not my house."

"Right. 'Tis Uncle's. One second…"

"Don't leave," he protested when her weight lifted off the mattress.

"I'll be but an instant." She ran from the room, knowing exactly where her uncle stored his supplies—where they had cleaned and sorted many of them so recently. She came back carrying gauze and cotton; a wrung-out, not quite drenched cloth to rinse the sweat; clean towel to dry him; and a small pair of steel forceps.

For she had seen a tiny gleam poking out from his skin; had felt the sharp edge when she dared tap it with one finger. *That* was not skin, nor rock, and it had definitely not been there before.

APHRODITE WORRIED. He perspired more every moment, even a long while later. Breathed out in exhales so harsh, she could only imagine how great his pain. All through gaining his feet outside and helping him traverse over the stone wall and then return indoors, she'd held out hope that the injury wasn't dire.

But now?

What if she wasn't enough, if together they could not—

"I must marry an heiress." His startling pronouncement halted her fingers as she waited for the gleam to reappear. Heart thumping painfully, both at the way his body would start to expel the...thing, and then how it would sink back into his skin, into oblivion.

"You must marry an heiress," she repeated dully. Why would he state such a blunt, uncourted fact? Something they already acknowledged, knew with certainty between them. The lout!

And after you have shared a bed for an hour or two!

She blinked away from the terrifying, stomach-unsettling sight of his sweating, shuddering back—*because you cannot blink away the hurt from his words?* Painful determination had her fixing her gaze upon the clean forceps—not yet used. "And you tell me this…why?"

"It seemed vital."

Vital? "For you?"

He shuffled his arms, as though restless, and came up on his elbows, tangling the bedclothes around one hand. "For you."

S*plat*.

The wet washing cloth landed cold upon the fire blazing within Warrick's back.

She huffed off the bed and to her feet. Despite the dripping chill, his back burned with the heat of her glare. "As I have not expressed any desire to marry—much less marry *you*—I see not why 'tis appropriate to utter such."

Despite the effort, the pain, he rolled over to his side, dislodging the icy cloth.

Only to face the pain in her gaze.

Despite her claim, his statement was founded. Was necessary. "A reminder. To us both. For if I had a choice, I believe I would put forth the effort to make you express such desire."

Her eyes heated with the passion shared between them earlier, a bright beam that doused the anger. "You would have me claim a desire to marry you?"

With all the anguish his sore body and tired mind could muster, he spat the words her direction. "I would have you claim any desire at all, were it toward any part of me."

Fighting his muscles, his prescribed future, he wrenched to his stomach, flinching at the wet cloth now freezing his middle and soaking through to the bedclothes. "Be gone with you. Out. Upstairs. Or, sick body or not I might try to claim that which I have no right to and make you mine—wretched, wilted penis or not."

And wasn't that a lie? The wilted part. For the remembered hardness of his prick reached his tormented awareness even now. His healing body mocking him.

Mocking his reckless, irrational desires.

The ones that made him yearn for a forthright governess with no money but more sense than he could ever possess.

Because every moment spent with her, with every day they played at house, he wanted a hundred, a thousand more.

Another tremor ripped through his muscles, taunting forth a scream he refused to utter. Abandoning any pretense of conversation, he shoved his face toward the mattress again. Damn desires.

He wanted forever. And he needed it with her.

If only he lived through the night...

"I STILL CANNOT COUNTENANCE that some...*thing* is coming out of your body."

Warrick knew not how long it had been. Her soothing voice had lulled him to slumber—that or the wretched, unrelenting buck of bone and sinew, his rebellious body having a mind of its own.

His mind? Drifting beyond these walls more than remaining firmly within. But he heard her now, heard her whispered gasp. "It...defies...everything..."

The dismay in her tone, the worry conveyed as well, surfaced him from the depths.

To find his face squashed into the mattress. He turned his head to the side and responded, despite the Herculean effort it took. "One of the physicians, after we made it back to England..." A swallow against the pain and he continued. "Not the field hack that wanted to leave me for dead but another, told me he hadn't removed everything. 'Twas more risk than...boon to...do so."

As he faltered toward the end, her palm met his exposed cheek. Fingers brushed down the side of his neck, swept back sweat-dampened hair from the side of his face until coming to rest upon his shoulder.

Where he needed her to stay. To keep touching him. Providing such a marvelous distraction. Focusing on those fingers—hers, on the bare skin of his body—strengthened his voice. "Claimed he had seen pieces of shot appear weeks or months after battle. But no one mentioned years."

"Well, something jarred it loose."

"Loose? Doesn't feel anything of the sort."

"Something happened to cause this." Her fingers flexed over his burning skin.

"Right. One of those dastard falls. My arse meeting the ground... What? Three times since you arrived."

"*Me?* So 'tis all *my* fault?" The gentle chide in her voice was obvious. "You suffer now because of my presence here?"

"Nay." His salvation, more like.

She took him away from his body, his long-standing troubles, his non-standing legs. "You free me."

Her hand abandoned his shoulder, returned to the inflamed area low on his back. The one that still seared like a brand. "I would like to free this stubborn, blighted piece of..."

Curse away, he wanted to encourage.

White light blazed across his eyes. Even with them closed. But no troop of angels swept down to carry him off this time.

They did not need to.

For he had his own personal, swearing angel caring for him through the night. Watching his back—on so many levels.

That comforting thought uppermost in mind, he lost the battle to remain awake as the next clash of pain took him under.

LATER, DISTURBINGLY, AGONIZINGLY LATER, Aphrodite suspected the worst had passed.

Richard's breathing had calmed though he still felt entirely too flushed to her. But the copious sweating had subsided. Or mayhap she only convinced herself of that given how frequently she blotted his skin with the towel.

Overriding his weak protests, she pushed a tumbler of gin against his lips and made him drink. Aye, she'd known where Uncle kept *those* sorts of supplies too, and from what she'd seen, Richard needed the oblivion of sleep. *Healing* sleep, she hoped.

After the gut-churning chore of assisting the metal sliver in its exit during the harrowing while that Richard's mind tranced, she refilled the tumbler, likely higher than she ought, and drank it down herself before cleansing the area and trimming the torn skin surrounding it in preparation of applying a sticking plaster.

Now that she no longer explained her every action and sight to him, given his slumberous state, she no longer forestalled her astonished gaze from glancing over at the blackened shard his body had expelled.

Not quite half an inch long, only a sliver thick yet sharp as a blade, the curved fragment loomed like a spectre of death. *This* had been in his body since Albuera? That was over thirty months ago. She couldn't imagine.

Well yes, she could, after the last anguishing hour.

The tumble off the stone wall and into the rock had seen fit to jar this loose?

Were there others? She could only pray not.

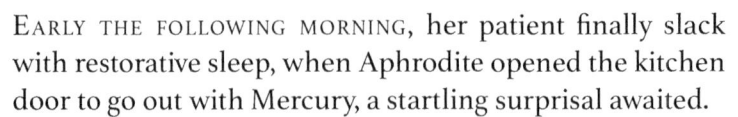

EARLY THE FOLLOWING MORNING, her patient finally slack with restorative sleep, when Aphrodite opened the kitchen door to go out with Mercury, a startling surprisal awaited.

For not only had a thick snowfall blanketed them during the night, pushed up close to the cottage, a monstrously large delivery blocked her path.

With more than a bit of trepidation, she lifted the oilskin tarp, covered in an inch or more of snow, to discover Richard's Merlin's chair.

She assumed it was his, for it was not the same one she'd seen him use two Christmases prior, but it could belong to no one else.

Richard's missing chair.

Returned under the cover of night, the snow concealing any evidence of footprints: theirs from the moonlit kiss folly and fall *and* those of the perplexing pixies who, it appeared, possessed an affinity for ambulatory chairs and frolics of their own.

Even more of a marvel, was the second tarp beside it, keeping a copious amount of logs, split and readied, dry and within easy reach. Oh my.

"THERE NOW. It still looks heinous, but the bleeding has stopped." Prim probed about and he let her.

She had bustled in as soon as he'd stirred, brandishing

more wet rags and drying cloths, and ordering him to use the chamber pot, wash and she'd be back with plaster in hand. She'd also mentioned about washing his hair in the kitchen after he roused fully. What a stirring promise, that.

"It's only seeping a bit. Shouldn't come through the bandage if you want to rise"—ahem—"and dress. As long as we can keep you from a fevered infection, I think you go down the right path."

Warrick wasn't sure he agreed. Felt as though his body had been the turf for a dozen horse races. Everything hurt. Even his eyelashes.

"Please forgive me," he told her, once she finished her inspection and he rose from his prone position on the mattress into sitting, "practically whined like a baby last eve." He made no mention of the other conversation. The other thoughts that made him want to cry like a babe. Had he really—stupidly—attempted to shove her away? To deny the feelings that kept burgeoning between them?

Slapped his need of a bloody heiress in her caring face?

She rounded on him. "You did *not* whine. You did not complain. Thank heavens that is gone from your flesh. Not another word." She swooped past the fingers he coiled into a fist to keep from drawing her closer, swept the bandaging supplies up and left with the direction, "Attire yourself and I shall see you in the kitchen to break your fast."

She shut his door with a snap, but not before flashing him the secretive, seductive smile flitting about her lips. Likely berating him in silence, given how it was approaching if not past noon.

Managing Prim. How he adored her.

Once washed and clothed, leaning heavily against the wall, his ill-used muscles trembly, he opened the door.

To be greeted by wonderment.

APHRODITE HAD BUSIED HERSELF, breathless, anticipating his arrival.

Hearing the slight creak of turning wheels, alerting to his approach, she put the chopping knife on the counter next to the ambitious pile of sliced carrots and spun, waiting for his entrance.

The second he met her gaze, the bottom of one palm hit the arm of his rolling chair. "Where, Prim? Where in the world...?"

She pointed. "Right out there, beneath an oilskin and next to a copious stack of dry, split wood."

His bewilderment grew. "You are bamming me."

"God's truth."

He stared at her. "Did I ever tell you I have angels?"

Beyond his muttering last night? She thought back to their encounter long ago in a frozen garden. "You might have mentioned such, but never explained."

His teeth sunk into both lips before he released them on a sigh. His hair really was longer than it ought to be. Was lank at the moment, flattened from the hours of sweat and toil he'd endured. After she fed him, she couldn't wait to wash it.

How considerate of you. How very... Not prim. To give yourself a chance to stroke your fingers through his hair, washing and rinsing? And I wager you shall offer to comb it through once finished? Continue the effort until it's dry?

She would. And savor every second.

Oh, how her heart was going to ache once they parted. How the empty nights loomed—

"Angels," she prompted, pulling herself from the notion of future pain. Time enough for that later. When he wasn't within reach. "Yours?"

"A legion," he admitted, more serious than she could remember seeing him. "Thought to take me off in Spain. Rattled as much to Frost. Not sure he heard me."

She swallowed against the notion of him dying there—on the battlefield. "I am heartened they did not. Take you from us, that is."

Still staring at her, still more solemn than she was used to, he said, "As am I."

More disordered than she could admit, needing to touch him so fiercely she ached with it, she approached where he had brought the ambulatory chair to a halt. "May I?"

He nodded.

She braced one arm on his shoulder and the other above his knee, and knelt before him. With a light touch, she reached for one thigh. Then lifted her hand away. "Close your eyes."

He did so without protest.

She put two fingers upon his thigh about three inches apart. "Do you feel anything?"

"I do." He blinked his eyes open and smiled when he saw her hand on his leg.

"Tsk. *Keep* them closed."

"Yes, milady."

"*Pfft.*" She lifted her hand and took her index finger and ran it up from his knee toward his groin.

"That I feel." He whistled, gave her a slitted-eye, heavy look, his attention focused on her face. "Atop the bruised hash is your light and wickedly wandering attention, I do believe."

"No peeking, now," she ordered through the answering smile she could not dim. Withdrawing her hand from where, admittedly, it wanted to wander farther, she kept her motions silent and touched his opposite leg.

"Yes," he hissed—in wonder? "Left leg now. Ankle. Top of right thigh—again, Prim? Naughtier than I'd expected. Left...calf? Or is that the dog?"

"Open your eyes." When he did, the first thing he sought out was Mercury—still curled up across the room. His gaze found hers again, pleased, she thought, but not in alt. Not expressing any supreme surprise, which caused disappointment to tighten her chest.

Had you expected a miracle?

Mayhap not, but she had wished for one. For *him*, for Richard's sake.

"Is that any more or less than what you have felt previously? With Uncle or on your own?"

His hands, which had been resting, open, on the outside of each leg just above his bent knees, flexed, then fisted. "In all honesty, I would say about the same as the last two or so months."

"Why then, if this is no different than recent weeks, did you start to appear so elated?"

"Aphrodite." The deep syllables of her name rolling over her brought tingles in their wake. "Think, woman. Where were *your* hands just now? Why would that not delight me?"

Familiar heat flushed her cheeks. She granted him a delighted smile of her own, rising to her feet. "Be that as it may, perhaps we should not expect anything different so soon? The swelling no doubt still needs to recede. Landing upon that rock may have done the favor of freeing that wicked piece, but it certainly didn't do your back any good. I will need to check the wrappings later before—"

"You do, though. You do me very good."

"Thank you for that."

"Truth told, *tu me imprimis in profundis entis meae.*"

She impressed him down to the depths of his soul?

Oh my. "Richard."

That's all she could manage in that moment. His name. The sound of it aching with every bit of caring and longing from *her* depths.

"I mean it, Aphrodite. Every ounce of you is beautiful and competent and much, *much* more amiable than surly Arbuckle. Are you certain you are related? Other than eye color, I see no resemblance at all. Well, that"—he gave her a smile full of confidence, mayhap even pride—"and how you could be a physician yourself."

"*Pfft.* As if women could do such a thing."

"*You* could."

Unused to such praise, she took one step away. "Thank you for that, but no. I am too content with my job as governess."

"'Content'? Not in alt? Not thrilled to your lovely toes?"

"Lovely?" Not used to being under discussion, her toes stretched in her slippers, dug in to the solid floor beneath. "You will embarrass them. For all you know, they sprout warts and hairs."

"Ah. Troll toes, then? Worry not. Mine are much the same." She knew they weren't. Had seen his toes—*and every other part of him too, lest you forget!* "Will you? Can... you?" His brow furrowed, but the crooked smile boded for outlandish. "May you, please?"

"Will I, can I, may I... What? You are one perplexing fellow."

"May I entice you to sit upon my lap?" Hands now

wide, on either side of his wheeled chair, he wiggled his fingers toward his groin—then wiggled his eyebrows as well.

She couldn't help it. She came closer, bent and kissed his cheek. Leaned over and kissed the other, then placed one hand upon the back of his neck, her thumb delving up through the long strands while her fingers took note of the temperature of his skin. Finally, no longer fiery. "You wicked, wicked fellow. There will be *no* lap sitting today. Ask me again in a week."

It wasn't until after she picked up the knife again that he said, "A week, hmm? *If* I can tolerate you for that long."

He caught the uncooked carrot that sailed toward his nose. The smile on his lips devilishly inviting indeed.

34

TIME FOR A BATH

The Following Morning...

"I still cannot scarce believe I allowed you to coerce me into this."

Aphrodite's fingers trailed over Richard's strong shoulder as she walked unhurriedly by his side after releasing the hack that conveyed them to the center of town, the Corinthian columns alongside escorting them to where they were bound.

"Me?" She dared to laugh—at them both, nervous delight making the sound a bit sharper than she might have wished. "You are every bit as much to blame as I."

They neared the pump-room. The pump-room! In Bath. Where the fashionable went to see and be seen.

Though cold, the day 'twas warm enough to have melted the recent snows. The sun shone, as bright as the light his earlier words had blazed upon her breast, after she suggested he brave the day now that his pixie-begotten chair had been returned to him. "Time for you to take the waters," she had proposed while they broke their fast.

"Come with. Walk with me, Prim," he'd responded. "In public. Let us ruin each other and find a parson."

Those exact words: "*Find a parson.*"

And no mention of his lap or his twanger this time, either.

Her heart hadn't stopped galloping since the utterance. Nor had her thoughts stopped spinning. Round and round, like the wheels on his chair...

"'Tis not too late, Rich—Lord Warrick." Mindful of others nearby, seeking the same destination they approached, she amended. No sense being overheard. What if he came to his right mind? Thought better of the reckless statement he'd made that morning? "I can wait outside. Or enter before you. Or minutes after. Pretend—"

He lurched to a halt, his hands leaving the controls to grapple for and capture one of hers. A solid squeeze of her fingers. "Aphrodite Primrose. *You* be brave now. Be foolhardy with me. Be in love as well."

While her eyes flew wide and her heart threatened to soar to Mars, he released her and turned his chair. "Get the door, would you, Miss Primrose? For the cold now biteth at my nose."

BE IN LOVE AS WELL? That is how you tell the woman you want to marry that you love her?

Warrick leaned forward to grasp one edge of the door as soon as it came within reach. He might be seated, might have endured the hired coach ride from The Tyrant's to the center of Bath society before stumbling down and into his chair the man readied—the chair that had been tied on the roof of all humiliating things—but he'd be damned if he didn't hold the door open for her. "Miss Primrose. After you."

He wanted to rib her over the pinkened hue of her cheeks. Wasn't sure if it was the early January weather or if she was feeling as dazed as he...

Had she really agreed to wed him? Even if only tacitly?

Nay, you bufflehead, she did not. For you did not ask. Just told.

Well, certainly. No risk of her saying no that way.

You haven't even gifted the woman a posy, a book, a fan. Only your dubious wit, tweaking over her name, and your doubtable body, contorting all over the bed whilst you squeal into the sheets. You offer her naught but your questionable future—

"Richard, mmm, Lord Warrick—" There went her skin again, tomato red, nearly obliterating that smattering of freckles he wanted to kiss.

After he maneuvered his chair over the entrance (for once, he wasn't the only infirm seated atop wheels), he paused until she joined him, his thoughtful Prim holding the door open for an older couple, had to be nearing ninety, approaching hand in hand, before she returned to his side.

"Richard is fine, Prim," he said in his regular voice, no moderating or subduing at all. "Richard. Always. And *anywhere*." There. Let her not be afraid to claim him. Because that's what he planned on doing to her—if she let him.

"Mmm." Her cheeks still blazed, but she couldn't hide the flush of pleasure entering her dark eyes. "The book." She pointed to one wall, wasn't gawping at the size of the place as he did—so somewhere her uncle had brought her before. "Mayhap you should inscribe yourself there?" she suggested. "Announce your presence here in town before you take the waters?"

The pump-room was vast. Much noisier than he'd prepared for; even this early in the day, an orchestra played from a laddered gallery. His gaze swept from one side of the immense place to the other.

Had to be five men high and twice as long. At one end, water bubbled and flowed, collected by a big fountain, steam edging off the dripping cascade where attendants filled glasses and handed them off to waiting patrons.

At the other end, sat the huge clock he'd heard of, a pair of fireplaces burning on either side. And in the middle, along yet another elongated wall (everywhere in the midst, crammed with milling, standing folk or those seated and yammering) was *the book* she indicated. The one that loomed as if she spoke in capitals: The Book.

Not the Good Book, as in Bible; nay this was one of man's inventions. Compliments of Beau Nash who had run this town for decades, the book was in place awaiting the names of all those who visited Bath. Because what good did it do to travel to town if one's presence was not noted by others?

With a barely muffled grunt, he nodded and aimed his chair. "Were it up to me," he told her softly, intending no one overheard and, gah, the place was crowded. Like a London crush the first week of the Season, only there were more children and more aged.

More of them in Merlin's chairs than he had expected, as well. One old roué saw Aphrodite and leered, giving Warrick a lascivious wink, one he refused to dignify. "Were it up to me, I would ignore the custom, for I have no desire to spend time with anyone but you. However..."

He paused about eight feet ahead of the book that currently had three young ladies tittering around it. He angled toward the wall, not wanting to be recognized nor interrupted until he got the rest out.

She came round and knelt in front of him, the wall behind her. "What is it? Your back?"

"Is sore," he admitted, taking up her gloved fingers from where she'd started to rest them upon his knee but pulled back out of propriety before they could connect, "but not screaming at me. Worry not, Prim. Aphrodite." He blew out a breath, clutched at her fingers and met her honeyed gaze. "I gave you no time to consider. Failed to *ask*. If I commit my name to that book, I'm having you write—"

Because he couldn't reach it from sitting and didn't want to risk standing and being jostled, chance missing his chair on the way down. Wasn't willing to suffer another hard landing. Wasn't sure his back could take anymore right now. "Having *you* pen 'Warrick and betrothed, Miss Aphrodite Primrose'," he finished fiercely. "There will be no turning back, no retraction lest you wish to be labeled a jilt."

"Oh, the horrors." She smiled but her eyes glistened.

"Prim. Damn it, do not cry. Not here." Not ever, if he could help it.

"I am not. I'm sure." Giving proof to her clanker, she swept her fingertips beneath her watering eyes, then gave him a smile that quavered. "Neither am I sure you are thinking with all your wits. You'll be ostracized. A poor governess for your c-countess?"

He gripped both her wrists. "Stop it, Prim. Right now. Your eyes are flowing over more than that fountain of hot water I'm supposed to be drinking from. Heard it's ghastly. Ah, good. You smile. I want to sweep you into my arms— and lap, if I'm to be honest—and retreat back to The Tyrant's. Wish now we'd never left. Want—"

"Miss Prim*rose*? Why, that is you!" The astonished gasp was loud enough to jerk them apart—and her to her feet. Whereupon she paled to a sheet.

Warrick whipped his head around, followed with his chair and body and immediately recoiled on her behalf.

Verdell. One of the men she'd mentioned so long ago, upon their first meeting, as not befitting the titles they held. Tate, Paulson and Verdell.

"Verdell," he acknowledged with a tight nod, his body now straining in the chair.

"Warrick." Verdell's attention jerked from Aphrodite to him and back. After delivering a disdainful glance and a mutter of *conceited governesses*, he addressed Warrick. "Any by-blows you became recently aware of? Is that why you associate with an unreliable, light-fingered governess?" Warrick's spine stiffened to steel. The man would dare call her a thief? No wonder she hadn't trusted peers. "Or is she now plying those light fingers in a different manner?"

The man's insolent gaze dropped to Warrick's feet, then rose, settling near his groin. Nothing twitched but the fire of anger growing in his chest. He positioned himself directly in front of her and glared at Verdell. So much for mentally giving the man neutral status when she'd first lodged her complaint toward the grub.

Warrick flipped one hand to his shoulder, palm upward, imminently gratified when her trembling fingers met his. His, he hoped, soothing grasp. "No by-blows, recent or otherwise," he drawled. "You?"

Not expecting the challenge, Verdell grimaced. "None I'll admit to." His eyes narrowed at their clasped hands. "What are you doing with *her*? I know from experience she's a cold bitch. Won't thaw your pego if that's what you—"

One moment, Warrick sat in his chair, posture

perfectly erect, her comforting presence behind him, trembling touch within his. The next?

The next second, he'd launched himself at Verdell's legs, nabbed the scourge to the ground. With a roar and one powered thrust of his arm, Warrick's fist connected with jowls. Flabby jowls and the sickening lips above them rippled. Verdell's eyelids fluttered, and *whoosh-thunk*. The man wilted. Folded right into the floor.

Then silence. Silence as his ears rang. As his blood rushed like a river through his head. The music screeched to a halt as a collective gasp circled the cavernous room. A gasp that grew in volume. Accompanied by mounting whispers. Growing gossip.

He shifted—also relegated to the floor—as he comprehended the attention he'd drawn, despite his desire for none of it.

Then, as though his mind had held everything suspended while he catalogued each aghast face and the censure directed his way, *bang!* Like a pistol shot, it all hit at once. *Whump.*

Individual voices cracked across his ears.

"Did you see that?"

"Who is—"

"Earl of Warrick, I believe."

"Inappropriate, I say!"

"What is the world coming to?"

"Richard!" Aphrodite shoved his abandoned chair aside with a *thump* and raced to where he lay.

The hacking cough of Verdell accompanied her arrival. Another man came to his aid, near dragging the oaf from the melee. Warrick only had eyes for her.

But then a new and louder voice joined the others...

"Damn me!" A familiar voice. Masculine and strident. "Lord War*rick*?"

Beside him, Aphrodite paled anew.

"Aphrodite!"

"Arbuckle?"

"Uncle?"

Mary Viola Snowden Redford, widowed not quite three years past, had found happiness—finally—surpassing her wildest imaginings these last few months. But the woman known to most as *Lady Redford, the elder* had suffered several deep and abiding hurts in her decades-long life.

The first, when a new bride of seventeen realized not long after the vows she took so seriously that her rather dashing spouse—the fifth Viscount Redford—preferred dashing off to the beds of many others rather than staying in hers.

The second, when she realized he'd seasoned their oldest son to behave just like him, with a single-minded pursuit of physical pleasure that discarded any care for the feelings of others.

The third hurt, not quite three years ago, when her middle son perished in a foolhardy duel over *another* man's wife.

The fourth and fifth, and by far the most troublous, the ones that had cut the deepest were seeing her youngest son, Ward, injured to within an inch of his life and the recent death of her dear friend Elizabeth Martinson Feldon.

Mrs. Feldon—though still recognized as *Lady Warrick* at the time of her passing—had become the closest friend of Viola's life. No surprise, really, after their bond forged to steel when both their boys had been devastatingly injured at Albuera.

Aye, these were the life-altering wounds that now shaped the strong and resourceful woman she'd become.

Not that she hadn't already been strong—that seventeen-year-old had quickly determined the only way to salvage any sense of worth was to behave with every ounce of propriety and consideration she could call upon, to treat others kindly while still guarding the remnants of her broken heart. But in the last years? Witnessing the wasting away of her friend, well over a dozen years Vi's junior, made Viola determined to eke out happiness wherever she might find it.

When her Ward had arrived in London two and a half years ago, fighting infection, the bones in one hand crumpled beyond recognition—and his other hand *gone*, his lower arm sliced clear off? Well, now. Seeing her thoughtful Ward near destroyed, her sole remaining son —now the viscount—fighting for his life?

Standing with Elizabeth as the other woman quaked with worry over *her* unmoving, unresponsive son, Rich? Watching as Elizabeth hid her own declining health while giving every ounce of fight she could to *her* son, *willing* his recovery. Praying he did not lose hope nor give up on life, whether he walked again or not...

Being there with them, through each and every step— or complaint, curse word and reluctant rotation of a wheel —of the way, Viola had remained strong for them all, because that is what a properly reared Englishwoman did.

She persevered. In silence, if need be.

She grieved. In private—never in public.

She endured, found solace in Sunday services, in the staccato whistle of a warbler, the bud of a flower about to bloom, the rhythmic patter of a light rain.

And then...when Fortune and God smiled down upon her? She found an unexpected attraction to the surgeon she'd accompanied her friend to visit. An attraction that, over time—and as her son Ward slowly reclaimed his health and independence, even while her friend's health declined—deepened first into love, an emotional closeness beyond anything Viola had previously experienced. And finally into a physical expression of that love.

And with a younger man! Who would have thought?

That at four and sixty Viola would be clandestinely courted by a man in possession of only seven and fifty years? My, her body heated at the very thought.

But in truth, it was likely the sweltering surroundings in the pump-room.

'Twas absurdly hot, the waters heating the very atmosphere. The orchestra in the gallery and the dancing they prompted encouraging the flame. The crowd, those who were not seated and sipping, busy promenading in a near march, from one side of the immense room across to the other.

And now, an unexpected (and secretly satisfying) fight.

Satisfying because she knew Lord Verdell to be both piggish and priggish when it came to getting his way, pious in public but—according to others she trusted—overly grabsome when it came to groping females, of any station. Seeing the squib downed with a single clout proved an unexpected boon to this already exhilarating morning.

But mostly, if she were honest, the temperature rose because tempers flared.

The surgeon beside her near strangling on his outraged, "Niece! What are you doing here—with *him*?"

"What in blazes are *you* doing here? In town!" The fallen man, his upper body so recently proving beyond doubt how strong he was, glared fire-tipped daggers toward her companion—until Rich's gaze faltered to her, grappled with comprehension. "L-Lady Redford?"

She could not miss how Miss Primrose remained beside him, knees to the floor, hands upon his shoulders, fingers whitened, equal measures of dismay and addlement writ upon her face.

Rich struggled to swallow. "You..." He spoke to Viola. "*You* are...with Arbuckle?"

The poor man blinked as though she slept with Satan.

Egad. Perish the thought.

At her side, Silas bristled. "What have you done to my niece? You rotten piece of—"

"Silas." Viola snagged his sleeve and drew him to her side. "They know each other. Have for years." She might be exaggerating, but only a wee bit.

For of course she knew of that scandalous kiss beneath the mistletoe betwixt a randy returning soldier and—formerly—reserved governess; had been with her son and his Anne when Anne's mother, Lady Ballenger, screeched, shrilled and shrieked the event to one and all. "Do you forget your niece is governess to Ward's sister-in-law, young Lady Harri?"

That reminder didn't stop his grumblings.

He was already on edge, she knew, the two of them only having *just* decided—and committed to that decision with their joint presence here—to make their relationship public.

"But *here*?" Silas spat toward Rich. "By God, is that why you attacked Lord Verdell? Because the man knows you are making a trollop of my niece?"

"Uncle!"

"Silas!"

"Arbuckle." Glowering, Rich sat up straighter, his legs

out to the side in a haphazard fashion, arms keeping him balanced. He shifted, put more weight on one so he could cover the feminine hand on his shoulder with the other and spoke with decisive intent. "Do not speak of my future wife that way."

Silas hissed. Sputtered. Nearly turned purple.

Miss Primrose looked as though she'd swallowed a lemon dipped in brine and laced with spines. But she didn't contradict Rich, only held tight to his hand. Leaned toward his ear and whispered, "Let me get your chair?"

He gave her a nod, his glare not leaving Silas.

"No need," Viola trilled, indicating Miss Primrose should remain where she was, determined to repair what she could—she wasn't Lady Redford for naught. She snapped her fingers toward one of the many hoverers, their eyes—some gloating, some with avarice, others only considered—gleaming over every word of gossip they gathered. "Lord Munson." She addressed one of the kinder expressions in the crowd. "Will you see to the chair?"

"Immediately." With a respectful nod, he retreated from their spectacle to do her bidding. He had been an easy choice, though she didn't know him exceptionally well. The duke was easily the highest-ranking peer in the tight circle that now surrounded them. A decent man, from what she knew. And now that she had singled him out, he would realize she expected him to squash whatever rumors or murmurings he could.

Gratifying, it was, how years of redeeming the remnants of her former spouse's reputation had given her the ability to measure others and gauge their worthiness. Was that not how she had managed to secure her dear Ward such a valuable and commendable wife in Lady Anne?

"We need to pause until we are outside," she told the trio close to her after Silas and Miss Primrose—along with his own significant effort—saw Rich seated in his chair, "before we make more of a ruffle than we already have."

Rich and Silas's niece... Wonder of wonders.

The Vi of twenty years ago would have been aghast; would have done everything possible to—gasp!—mitigate the horror of being *discussed*. Fortunately, time had mellowed her severe stance on much. Now? The news near titillated.

Her deceased, dear friend Lady Warrick would have been thrilled. Completely uncaring at the lack of official pedigree Rich sought to woo. Had Elizabeth not found happiness both with her earl, as well as her humble, country baronet?

It boggled! Elizabeth's son and Silas's niece!

Well, niece of a sort, Viola corrected her mental meanderings as she followed the three of them out the door and they made for a shaded spot between columns, away from others. Niece of a sort...given the surprisal waiting for her.

A wave of perverse satisfaction rolled over Viola. She could use this to her advantage—and to theirs, she knew; to Rich's and his future wife's. If only she could secure Silas's assent.

Fret not, Viola, you have ways to convince him...

She did, she thought with a tiny flutter that tingled her insides. Had she not learned that to her amazement the last handful of months, their union allowing a discovery, and exploration, of herself that proved joyous to them both?

Aye...should Silas prove resistant to supporting the union of Rich and his niece? Viola would relish convincing him of how very *suitable* their match would prove to be.

35

DUTY CALLS (ER, WRITES)

"Mr. Arbuckle! Mr. Arbuckle!" The young lad's cry reached Silas before he could find his feet, much less his way, after the last few seconds.

Before reaching the full shade of the colonnade, he turned, recognizing the lad who brought the mail. The postmaster's son, always willing to deliver on behalf of his father, hopeful for any additional custom that might come his way.

The youth skipped to a breathless stop before diving into the shade with the others. Reeling from the hard scrabble of the last moments, Silas followed.

Lungs panting, the lad grinned. "Lucky I saw you, eh? On my way back after deliveries. 'Ave a post for you. Not the one you been expecting, I don't think. But no one answered either place."

Either place. Gah. The lad had knocked on Marigold Cottage after not finding him at the residence Viola rented where he'd been the last two weeks? Silas feared his silence—and potential sins—were about to come crashing down about his ears.

Wasn't quite sure what he thought about that. Wasn't sure what he thought about anything nor anyone. Not after the last few minutes.

Aphrodite? The dear girl he loved like a daughter, with the near reprobate Warrick? She had come home for the holidays, after all? Had been *here*—and with *him*? The complaintive lordling Silas considered naught but an annoyance—despite Viola's claims to the contrary.

Why would Silas hold any soft feelings toward the crank of a conceited lord?

Oh, mayhap because your "niece" might be marrying the fellow?

His brains jumbled at the thought. Jumped about and jangled in his garret. Gave him a right aggravating headaching.

Overhearing the boy, Viola stepped to his side and reached for her reticule, to pay for the letter. He stayed her with a hand to her wrist.

"I have it." She might command more money at her disposal than he could ever dream of, but he could pay for a blighted letter. One he both anticipated and dreaded. But when the letter was delivered into his safekeeping after the exchange of a coin, it was not addressed to him, but to *Lord Warrick, of the Ah-bom-in-abel Tyrant's Abode*, followed by his direction. And definitely not in the hand of an adult.

Instead of being insulted, Silas chuckled. Could not manage to keep the quirk off his face as he silently handed the letter over.

Though he was gratified at the flush that reddened the seated man's cheeks upon seeing how his lack of respect had rubbed off on the impressible youth, the look of alarm as Warrick began reading the missive halted any satisfaction Silas might have savored. "What is it?" he asked with true concern. "Is your family well?"

Are you? the healer in him wanted to inquire, after hearing the voices raised in the pump-room, mocking at first and then in anger. After hearing the decisive pronouncement—regarding his niece's future—and seeing his patient dive toward the floor and take Lord Verdell down with him? Despite the unprecipitated nature of his insides, he could not help but yearn to take Warrick aside, talk to him, measure his strength and monitor any injury his precipitous actions might have caused.

But none of that was to be. For instead of answering him, Warrick turned to Aphrodite, who, up until then, had remained at his shoulder, like an avenging angel, alternatively frowning at Silas and sending what he could only describe as looks of adoration toward Warrick. "The girls. Sophia. Julia. I need to go to them," Warrick said abruptly, giving no hint as to the letter's contents. "Now. Will you come with me? I know I should not ask, but—"

"Of course I will."

And while Silas sputtered about the *absurdity* of such action—Warrick taking off with his niece (Unmarried! Totally inappropriate!)—Viola silenced any further complaints by standing on her toes to whisper, "We shall *all* go. Straighten everything out in due time."

THE CARRIAGE RIDE NORTH proved…interesting. As various pairs traveled together, with and without a dog delighted with all the new things to sniff, in two equipages: the travel carriage that Warrick had borrowed from Lord Redford and the fine conveyance Lady Redford called her own.

"Miss Primrose. Aphrodite."

The words Lady Redford spoke to her from the opposite side of the carriage possessed a warmth Aphrodite had not anticipated once it was agreed she and the older woman would travel together in her elegant carriage, leaving Richard with Uncle in the other.

Though she had no doubts how *that* conversation must be progressing (badly) she had significant ones about how the next few miles might go...

"Yes, my lady," said with all the deference due someone this intimidating woman's position warranted. Aye, that *was* her name, and it wasn't the least bit gauche and doltish and awkward in the extreme to agree thus.

Once the words were out, though, Lady Redford frowned and, to Aphrodite's dismay, reached across the carriage and took up Aphrodite's fretting fingers—gloves certainly hadn't disguised her agitation—and gave a gentle smile. "Aphrodite, please. I cannot fathom how awhirl your thoughts must be, but as we shall be, for all intents and purposes, *family*, in the coming months, I would bid you to dispense with any formality. You may address me as *Lady Redford*, but you do not need to. I will very comfortably answer to Viola, if you wish and can bring yourself to address me thus."

"Vi-o-la?" Scratched out as though 'twas Aphrodite—and her horrid lack of musical talent—that scraped a horsehair bow across the strings, producing a wretched sound indeed. She swallowed the pebbles in her throat and tried again. "F-family? Has Uncle proposed?"

With a light squeeze, Lady Redford—definitely not a Viola as of yet—released Aphrodite's fingers and leaned back against the squabs. Here was a woman in full possession of her composure, exhibiting nowhere near the swirling morass that threatened to beggar Aphrodite's brains at the moment. "Oh, you are darling. To think thus. Nay, and I do not anticipate one in the coming weeks. A proposal, that is." The woman pursed her lips, not in frustration or anger, but in contemplation it seemed, before releasing them. "Not that a proposal would be amiss. I *could* bring myself to take delight in the thought, but nay. After wretched years of marriage endured in stoic resolve, returning back to that state is not something I am eager to embrace so soon, so not what I intended to imply.

"After how close I grew to Rich's mama, Lady Warrick, dear Elizabeth"—the way Lady Redford near sighed the name, the grief of loss was still fresh—"after how I watched *him* suffer along with my dear Ward, why, he's become like another son to me. That is what I refer to. For his claim that you were his future wife rang unmistakably, both stout and sure, through the pump-room for all to hear.

"And unless I have lost all ability to judge matters—which I doubt—that is something you are inclined to be amenable toward?"

As though Lady Redford's supportive attitude released Aphrodite from hesitation, her words poured forth. "Oh yes, very much agreeable, amenable, thrilled toward. Although now that I hear myself, I do sound rather juvenile in my exuberance, do I not?"

Lady Redford granted her a light laugh. "As exuberant as your charge, Lady Harriet, perhaps?"

And there it went, the flush that had been absent for minutes, flaring heat into her cheeks and bringing her palms up to slap them as it went. Her eyes flew wide, aghastment hitting her as well, as the reality of that situation slammed into her for the first time. "Harriet! Oh my word. Lady Ballenger will be fit to faint if I leave their employ. Whatever will—"

"Tut-tut. Dear, refrain from spanking your cheeks, if you will? That will never do for a future countess." With a single slide of her gloved index finger, Lady Redford indicated Aphrodite needed to lower her arms and fold them in her lap, which she did, almost without thought.

Nay, for her thoughts were now fixated upon C-O-U-N-T-E-S-S. Lap bound, her fingers threatened to strangle the life out of each other.

"There now. See how much more composed you look? One may not control how the body responds—and you do have a tendency to blush beyond that of reason"—said with another of those indulgent smiles—"but you are very intelligent. Lovely in an unusual way, once one gets beyond the shock of your hair color—I have known of courtesans to rely upon henna and prayer to get anything approaching that shade. And your background—"

Aphrodite groaned. A deep-throated gargle that was in no way ladylike. She kept her fingers clenched amongst each other, to keep them from flying upward. "I know. 'Tis completely inappropriate for Richard—I mean Lord Warrick—my background, that is. For him to even conceive such..."

Another smile. A decisive twinkle in her expression, telling Aphrodite that Lady Redford found this entire situation highly amusing and much to her liking.

At least one of them did.

"We shall return to that in a moment. As to Lady Ballenger? How she will react upon learning you are leaving their household? We both know should the sun shine, she will complain about it. Should a cloud pass over and grant shade? Why, the very outrage! Should the temperature be mild and warm? 'Oh, 'tis a horrid, *horrid* day full of flies and sundry buzzing beasts!'" The portrayal now had Aphrodite, if not outright giggling, then definitely smiling, for Lady Redford could mimic her employer down to every nuance of her shriek and mannerisms. "If the outside weather deigns to be cold? 'Harri*et!* Fetch my bonnet! My shawl! My cloak! No, wait. I want my pelisse first! The one with fur trim. Nay, not *that* bonnet, you silly girl, the one with the *two* peacock feathers, not the single *broken* one.'"

By now, the two of them were howling with laughter, the sort that quickly drowned one's eyes with mirth.

Aphrodite knew Lady Ballenger loved her daughter, in her own way, for there had been touching—if infrequent—moments of true affection between them. Lady Ballenger was much like other mothers of the *ton* Aphrodite had encountered. Even if she was—at times—more involved than some, the woman left the rearing of her child, and the curbing of that child's rumbustious behavior, to the governess.

"You portray her startlingly well," Aphrodite complimented when she managed to mute her gales of mirth some moments later. "But Lady Harriet will no doubt be distraught. She and I have grown quite close in the nearly three years I have been with them."

"I did not know the exuberant miss, not excessively so, before my Ward came to his senses after a mental delay and applied himself to courting her sister, but Lady Anne impressed me from the moment we met through letters she wrote, condolences upon the death of my other sons and spouse. No matter how forthright and inappropriate Lady Harriet might be at times, take heart. For there could be no one more appropriately behaved than her elder sister. I have every faith that with time and additional years in her cup, Lady Harriet will mature as well, whether you are there to guide her in that or not.

"As to how Lady Ballenger will take the news?" Lady Redford drew herself up and conformed her features into that of haughty expectation, a stark contrast to the amusement and friendly mien of moments before. "That is no longer your concern, and something you must remind yourself as often as necessary. For you, my dear, will be *Lady Warrick*, and you will be her equal in every way except in intellect and manners. For I am not hesitant to state that you exceed her in both. I do believe Anne and Harriet get their wits from their father."

Be her equal in every way... Exceed her in intellect and manner... Get their wits from their father... "You also have no hesitations being forthright with me."

A deep breath that lifted her chest and firmed her posture before Lady Redford admitted, "I stifled my personality, stifled my words for years. Gazing back, I now realize I married an emotionally stunted man and was forced to depend upon myself for every ounce of affection and company I might wish. It makes one very independent. Very observant, those years of watching without responding."

Enrapt by the revelations Lady Redford continued to divulge, mayhap Aphrodite *could* begin to think of the woman as Viola...

Even though she had not yet spared a moment to begin to appreciate the grandeur of the carriage within which they rode. For who would have *ever* dreamt Lady Redford, Viola, the exceedingly polite, if somewhat reserved mother-in-law Aphrodite had witnessed interacting at times with Lady Anne and the other Larchmonts could have this...nearly maternal, caring aspect to her?

"During the second half of my unpalatable marriage,

when Redford no longer made any attempt to appear anything but the scoundreling wastrel that he was, I slowly started, resisting his demands, countering his opinions—only in private, you see, never in public. Because I had been taught that appearances were everything. In our society, they are.

"But, perhaps fortunately for all four of us—you and I and the two men we care for—after suffering so many losses the last three years, I have decided I am quite beyond all of that. I will speak my mind when it suits me and go about my life however I wish. My sole goal is to not harm others, but beyond that?" Lady Redford gave a dismissive flick of her hand. "I care not what anyone else thinks. If I did, do you think I would have convinced your uncle to take me promenading today? And are we not thankful I did?"

After those startling revelations, Aphrodite could do naught but nod.

"Be advised—and this is not something I shall admit to my daughter-in-law, cherish her though I do—I worry what Ward will think when he learns of my, now public and obviously intimate association with a surgeon. Think you it does not occur to me that if I support you and Rich, *he* might be willing to lend his support toward me and Silas? Temper any resistance my son might hold?"

Aphrodite's heart sank. "Then you might be speaking in my defense for naught. Richard does not like my uncle. Not at all. Refers to him as The Tyrant. Well"—Aphrodite had to clutch her fingers even tighter, press them firmly against her thighs, to not raise them to her lips—"that is no longer any secret, not given how his sister's letter was addressed."

Which had Lady Redford laughing anew. At least one of them thought it funny. Aphrodite didn't. The only two men in her life hated each other? How did that bode for her future?

And what of the second letter, the one that came just as they were leaving Marigold Cottage? The one also addressed to Richard—but much more formally. The one he'd had no time to read and share with her, as he had the first? That first letter, penned by young Sophia, a heart-rending combination of childishness and maturity that even now sat, read and refolded, within the confines of Aphrodite's reticule.

"Come now, child. I see your worry. Do not fret. For there are things Silas must explain to you, things that will give you leverage to gain his cooperation." And with that inexplicable hint flitting about the air between them, Lady Redford concluded with, "Fret not about any of it. Richard cares nothing for society, not since the accident. While his outrageous charm may not have been extinguished, his desire to live only for himself died a swift death with his mother's. I have seen how he now thinks of the future, and more for his brothers and sisters than himself.

"And, lest you wonder, my primary motive for assisting you is not to gain his cooperation. Nay, that is simply a lovely benefit I thought of and aired betwixt us. Be at ease and exhibit confidence." Another pointed finger circled Aphrodite where she sat, reminding her to appear serene whether she felt it or not. "Together, we shall see things set to rights, somehow. Starting with your employers. Your *former* employers."

"Despite the constant challenge she presents, I will miss her, very much. Lady Harriet..."

"As it should be, for someone who cares."

A change of scenery as the carriage jostled merrily—and swiftly—along drew her attention beyond the window. Staring at nothing as the view blurred past, she spoke. "It was very kind of you to lend your carriage to our journey homeward. Very competent and admirable, how quickly you summoned back Lord Redford's servants and had his carriage made ready as well."

In truth, the last two hours had been a blur—every bit as disorienting as the view. Once Richard determined he was returning to his siblings, and with an attitude that made it clear nothing would dissuade him, Lady Redford, operating with a quiet firmness Aphrodite could only admire and commit to memory, said, "Silas, see to locating my son's servants, if you would?" (Explaining that he had already remarked during the past days seeing them outside a stabling house, so he knew where to start.) "Command they see their employer's carriage made ready posthaste."

Between that and hers, despite the lack of household servants, the four of them trunked up travel belongings, saw them loaded with the help of the groomsmen and coachmen, and were on their way in less time than Aphrodite ever knew nobility to move.

Uncle had stopped Richard when he pushed up from his chair and started to alight—with the help of Lady Redford's coachman—into her carriage, had suggested—in a way that everyone knew was *not* a request—the men ride together while the ladies had a "coze" to themselves.

"I can scarce believe it." The words were but a whisper, reflected back to her as she had edged closer to the window, finally releasing her nervous clutch and lifting gloved fingers to slide against the glass. Glass that had chilled the farther north they traveled. "Even now, think I must be dreaming. That we will stop, change horses, and I will learn he has been but toying with me. To think? Imagine? Even the notion of a life with him..."

"You do realize that he may never walk fully again? Silas confided to me his doubts and uncertainties on that."

"I know." Her whisper grew even softer, now that her eyes brimmed with moisture of a different sort, no longer that of mirth but misery. The edges of her upper teeth scraped over her lower lip as she turned to Lady Redford, met her gaze and held it. "I know he may never walk. I know if he does, it will not be with ease, and likely not for long. I do not care. It is not his legs that make me love him."

There. She had finally admitted it, and out loud. Seeing no censure at her words, if anything even more understanding on the features that she would have—previously—labeled imposingly regal, but that now seemed comforting, her voice strengthened. "I love his wit, however inappropriate. I admire his strength—and I'm not talking about that of his arms. I know he's been hurt, but the way he speaks of his sisters? His brothers? Why, they could have been of his loins, the way he cares for them. Seeks only to provide the best home possible."

"What of *your* children? If he cannot give you those? Babes of your own."

And for once, when her face should have flamed, when embarrassment should have heated her skin to a boil, it did not. She remained in confident control—what a marvel. "I would consider myself the most fortunate of women to bear his children, but more for him than even myself. Nurturing his siblings will succor any yearning I might have toward a child of my own. I can imagine growing old with him without any other children to bless our lives. But—but—" A sigh shuddered through her chest. "I cannot imagine how barren my existence if I must grow old *without* him."

"If he does not heal beyond where he is now, you will

have many years of hard work ahead of you, seeing to his comfort."

"I am aware of that. And are you aware of how many years I will also have being dismayed to frowns and startled to laughter by his bawdy wit?"

Lady Redford released her own composure long enough to laugh until she coughed. "Well said. I see you do know him well. Well enough to love him." Then the woman shocked her silly, when she rose and joined Aphrodite on her side of the carriage, bringing arms about her and granting her the most comforting and welcome of hugs.

Some moments later, when Lady Redford had retaken her own bench, she ordered, "Tell me what you know of your family. What you remember of your parents."

36

SPEEDING TOWARD THE END

Warry,

You must come get us. Julia will not stop crying. It made me sad at first. But now I am quite ready to pull her hair out. Mayhap then she will fight me back and the tears will stop.

She keeps crying for Papa. I do not know if she means our real papa or if she cries for you. We have all wanted her to talk for so long but if I hear PA-PA-PA-PA-PA-PA-PA-PA-PA-PA-PA-PA-PA-PA-PA-PA-PA-PA-PA one more time, I vow I will pull <u>my</u> hair out—see if I do not. And we both know I will assuredly not look agree-a-ball balding. (I never thought I would miss having lessons, but it is beyond frustrating having words I want to write and not knowing how to spell them. I cannot reach the dictionary here. It is not like the one at home you keep on your desk.)

As to that, I am not allowed to go into <u>any</u> room by myself. I cannot choose a book to read nor have a moment's quiet. I thought Knight and King were loud? And Julia's silence saddening? 'Tis nothing like living with more children than chickens.

I am miserable. Julia is more so.

We both want to come home. Will you come get us?

Now that the antisipashun of Christmas is over, and everyone consoomed with thoughts of the new baby (overly loud and full of hickups, very red in the face also, not nearly as pretty as I remember thinking a bald Julia was when Mama had her), that dreadful play is <u>all</u> anyone wants to talk about.

Warry, I know your doctoring is important and truly hope you are able to walk, but I do not care if you ever stand up again. I am dreadfully leaning toward sorrow, with every hour I go by without you to barter with.

Come home? Nay, <u>come get us</u>! And then we shall all go home. I vow, I will behave for a ~~month~~. A week! I promise! Empekabel behavior shall be yours, if you will just please come get us.

When I asked Julia if she wanted me to write anything for her, she only cried harder.

Mr. and Mrs. Shieldings said with word from you they would return us home with haste, but without knowing your wishes, could not go against what you had agreed upon or some such drivel that continues to mire us here.

Please.

The elegant and wonderful, Sophia
(Your loving sister who misses you too.)

AFTER JUMPING ABOUT LIKE A CRAZED BANSHEE once everyone returned to Marigold Cottage and being banished to the yard whilst the humans sought the gathering of possessions and wits that had gone begging, Mercury now slept like the dead beside Silas.

His dog. On the seat, and not the narrow confines of the floor between him and the ragged-breathing, seething peer studying the letter in his hands. The *seat*. Nothing Silas would have allowed if they had been in Vi's carriage but this one? Borrowed from her son, *Lord* Redford? A man imbecilic enough to *befriend* the troublous lordling?

Did Mercury have fleas this time of year? Mayhap he could drop a few? Leave something irritating behind they could blame on the vexatious lord who continued to ignore his presence. Had since settling inside, trunks and chair strapped atop.

At the moment, about the only thing Silas could think to be grateful for was the steady rise and fall of his pup's side as he allowed one hand to rest lightly on his dog while he waited interminable minutes to even be acknowledged by the man across from him. Given the canine boy's age, Silas appreciated every light snore and snuffle to be heard, or felt.

And the longer the man across from him remained mute, eyes downcast and forehead pinched, the more Silas sought gratitude for his dog—and the women in the other carriage.

Warrick Estate, January 3, 1814

Lord Warrick,

Forgive me for interrupting your healing efforts in Bath with the following news, but I believe in my soul it is information you would rather have than remain ignorant of.

Your brothers, Lords Beaufort and Buford, were returned home to us here at the estate unexpectedly. It appears they perpetrated some sort of pranks, <u>along with</u> the friend whose home they visited during Christmas vacation. Yet they are now being blamed for the instigation of it (though they assure me it was <u>not</u> their idea at all).

Regardless, the parents of that youngster has informed their school of their actions and they arrived at Warrick Estate last eve with a note from their headmaster saying they were not being permitted to return to school next term either, after winter vacation.

And in effect, both boys are now running rampant over your estate, the one you and I seek to salvage? Rescue from ruin?

(Forgive me. Being so new to your employ, I am in a state of extreme unease sharing such news. But also doubtful you would want two such lively lads gadding about without any sort of discipline or accountability. Given how I had not met them until they arrived at the

door—in a hack I was required to pay myself—they have no reason to respect anything I say nor give me any semblance of obedience.)

To the best of my ability, I will endeavor to keep them from harming themselves—or lighting any part of your estate on fire—until your return.

But I do bid you to make that return sooner than you might have otherwise planned.

I remain, sincerely,

William Delaney
Steward, Warrick Estate

Egad and damn and damn and damn!

Warrick lifted his gaze from the page that shuddered before him, given the carriage's speed out of Bath.

He faced Arbuckle. "I know you have things to say. I can see them ready to burst forth from your pinched lips. Give me but a moment, please. A moment to gather myself and then you can rail at me to your heart's content."

The man seated across from him, riding backward out of deference to Warrick's title (or possibly his infirmity—he knew not which and was not about to ask nor decline the consideration), gave a single nod of agreement, even as a muscle in his tightly held jaw twitched.

Arbuckle—Satan's spawn—was the new man in Lady Redford's life? The one her son suspected of bringing her such joy these last months? Gah. Warrick choked on his own spit.

His fist crumpled the page in his hand as he leaned back until his head hit the padded wall above the squab.

He didn't care that the swiftly moving vehicle rumbled his body about. He closed his eyes and tried not to think. Tried to give his mind a rest.

Meadows. *Think naught but of meadows.* Green meadows. Majestic mountains. Flowers. Beautiful flowers in bloom. Petals unfurling. Prim's lips. *Nay, not that, not now.* Clouds. Bulbous white clouds. Soft clouds. Prim's bosom.

Ack. The effort proved fruitless.

Not even thoughts of his beloved could mitigate the horror tearing through his chest.

Julia cried without ceasing.

Sophia—smart, insightful Sophia—remained intellectually unchallenged, and emotionally hurt by her sister's increasing sadness. Likely by his abandonment as well.

Foolish, foolish man! To think any of his siblings could do on their own—no matter how insistent they had been. To think any one of them were strong enough to do without the other. They, who had lost first a father and then a mother and then their home. He, who had lost his mother and gained an entire family.

He, who had fallen deeply in love over the course of the last week, if not the last two years, and now doubted everything.

As the seconds turned into minutes, the minutes into miles, and his eyes remained closed, Warrick shifted one foot. A good sign, was it, perhaps? A good sign that one of his thighs clenched, his calf followed suit, sufficient to edge his foot, even a fraction of an inch. A good sign that restlessness assailed him now. Mainly in spirit, though. A troubled spirit that now caused his body to want to break free of this carriage, race to the other, and hold Aphrodite against his thundering heart.

It did not matter what trouble lay ahead, what difficulties these two letters so recently received promised. It did not matter that his future was in shambles, he wanted to share it with her.

His eyes popped open, gaze fixed on the carriage ceiling. He brought his head down, clashed eyes with Arbuckle. "I won't apologize for loving your niece. Nothing untoward has happened between us." Heated kisses and his fingers basking in the honeyed heat of her aside, which Arbuckle certainly didn't need any hint of, nothing untoward had happened. "But I will apologize for how Sophia addressed her letter. That was inappropriate, having been visible to others, and I will educate her of the nuances of insults at the earliest of opportunities. Say what you will. I am ready."

Silas grunted. He heard himself and wanted to slap his chest. His throat for letting the sound emerge. Since when was that how he responded to conversational sallies?

But Warrick had caught him unaware. The first words out of his mouth: *Won't apologize for loving your niece.* Certainly not what he had expected.

Denials. Excuses. Those he had expected.

Nothing untoward has happened between us. Did he speak truly? "So, if I were to give my consent for marriage, requiring you wait nine months from now?"

"To ensure my bastard doesn't grow within her belly?"

"There he is. I knew you could not remain civil for long."

"I only responded in kind. Neither of us wish to wait that long; I can confidently assure you she will agree with me there. But if it is what you require—in order not to disparage her, which I will not allow, then aye. We can wait, and it will change nothing."

And there he went, this annoying, plaguesome lord

surprising him yet again. "I would never disparage her. *You* are another matter altogether."

"Will you withhold your censure? Should we choose not to wait? Or will it blast forth at every opportunity? I would not have her feel your wrath nor your undisguised displeasure, for both would cause her pain."

"Then I will say my piece, share things of which you, and she for the moment, are unaware of. And if you can tell me, upon the completion of it, that you truly believe—in your heart and in your head—that she is not better off without you, then aye, my blessing you will both have."

"That is a bold statement. What could you tell me that would make me withdraw my avowal of love? My determination to see her my countess?"

"Do you hear yourself? An earl, even one…"

"Damaged? Infirm? Unable to walk?"

"Even one who might not be in the most prime condition of his life would *never* take a governess to wife."

"Oh no? I beg to differ." Warrick then proceeded to name two dukes and a viscount, all off the tip of his tongue and all of whom had married either actresses or known courtesans. "Would you not agree Aphrodite's personal reputation is far superior to those three women? I would. Doubtful even marrying me would cause a hint of the scandals those three weathered with success."

Not thrilled with the other man's even replies, but unable to deny the facts presented before him, Silas made an effort, a significant one, to set aside his bias toward the lordling who had somehow—when God must have been napping—managed to secure his niece's affections.

"Your sister has admirable penmanship," he said by way of an olive branch. "Even included Marigold Cottage in her direction."

"She possesses a keen intellect, much like her brother."

Silas suppressed a guffaw—barely. "You aren't lacking in confidence, I will say that for you."

Lord Warrick accepted the compliment with a dignified nod willing, it seemed, to continue the truce. "Aphrodite told me how you planted seeds together, her first weeks with you. How your abode gained its name; that you promised her she would not be sent off again, but would remain until they bloomed. Did you choose marigolds because they flower quickly?"

"Had no idea," Silas confided. "I chose them because they were the only seeds at hand. By the time I noticed how frequently she glanced toward the door, as though fearful of being pushed right back out, I was in a scrabble to find anything the tearful lass might latch on to, anything to give her any measure of security."

Which softened Warrick toward the old rat. A modicum, but still. Lest the doctor get the wrong idea, he said, "I'm still disinclined to like you."

Arbuckle grinned at him. Grinned! "Grand. Seems we are in accord." But then, after the two of them had reached an agreement to continue their dislike of each other, the older man sobered, his smile turning flat. "What do you know of Aphrodite's parents? What has she told you?"

Warrick cast his mind back to one of the many spirited discussions of the past few days...

"As the youngest of seven sons of a country solicitor blessed by family and burdened by bills"—she had given a gentle laugh upon the telling of it, as though they were words she had heard many a time—"there were few resources for Papa. He was left to make his way and had a love of literature and learning. He worked as a tutor before coming to London and then as a bookseller after."

"Ah. Now I finally learn the source of your unique name."

She couldn't stop her grin. "Yes. Uncle loved to tell me the story of how they met over an illustrated volume of Greek mythology."

"And your mother?"

"Dishonored her parents' wishes when she ran off with my father instead of marrying who they had chosen. Created quite the scandal, or so I gathered."

"How did they die? Was it together?"

At the question, her smile had faltered. "Footpads," said succinctly and his heart cramped. "A wealthy patron of the shop where Papa worked recognized him as the man who once tutored his now grown boys. He gave Papa use of his theater box one night, him and Mama. They had walked, no family carriage, you see, and...and I never saw them alive after that."

Instead of offering a humorous, pithy remark to see the smile returned to her cheeks, he had reached across the keyboards, where he was entertaining them both—before ordering her out because he still had a duty to a hundred or more drills that evening—and extended his hand, waiting until she placed hers in it. Giving her fingers a hug, he remained uncharacteristically silent, allowing her time with her thoughts, as he had with his.

Thinking of his mother, his stepfather, even himself—all lone children without a sibling one, compared to Aphrodite's parents with many... Yet no one had wanted to raise this lovely young woman—except a crotchety old uncle? (He kept those thoughts to himself, of a certainty.)

She had squeezed his hand back and suggested he "Play me something lively, if you would. Something by Martinson".

Grateful that was one of the many conversations they

had had over the last few days, Warrick shared what he knew with Arbuckle, inside the confines of Ed's carriage. Keeping his gloat to a minim when the waking dog stretched, sniffed and ambled down, off the opposite bench, to lean against *his* legs. Let Warrick's extended arm and outstretched fingers scratch over the top of his head, behind his lolling ears.

"That is not quite accurate, for all that it is what she was told." Arbuckle surprised him with that, drew his gaze from the dog. "The truth is both better and worse. And something I had been intending to educate her of as gently as possible, given the recent changes, but now…" Arbuckle frowned at Warrick as though he were to blame for altering the man's intentions. "Now I see there is no help for it. She must be told."

"Told what? Explain that. That and why in blazes *you* stole my chair, inflicted such adversity on me." Why had he started to sweat? "And what do you mean by 'recent changes'? What are you keeping from her?"

What was his body telling him? Because his ears—and cryptic Arbuckle—told him naught.

You sweat because you fear.

Deep inside, Warrick started to shake. For he did fear—

That whatever Arbuckle was about to reveal might bring his own plans—and hers—crashing to a halt.

37

THE LIST

―――――>○<―――――

APHRODITE, NOW SEATED across from Uncle, listened with growing horror and numbness.

The words, which she saw his mouth forming, the ones swirling about her like a tempest that refused to land, did however explain the stricken look from the window Richard had not been able to conceal, when they had stopped for a swift change of horses and a change of occupants. Uncle having joined her in Lady Redford's carriage while the lady herself had bustled over to ride with Richard and Mercury.

"Seems several of your mother's siblings never took to how *their* father refused them contact once she fled her planned marriage, choosing to run off with your father instead. Refused to even let them speak of her as he still had three more daughters to marry off and railed how the scandal would jeopardize those efforts.

"When the baron died, leaving his wealth to the eldest son—one of her three brothers—your uncles—the new title holder, unlike many, chose to portion some resources out for each of his siblings. More than that, once he was made aware of how severely his father had extinguished any mention of his missing sister, had refused any of the siblings contact with her and rebuffed her efforts at reconciliation once she was back in London, he made efforts to seek her out. His long-lost sister, your mother."

Her mother. Who had siblings in abundance, it seemed. More uncles, her sole reliable relative claimed... aunts...*family* who wanted to know her, per Uncle Silas. Who had written to him of their impatience. Wanting him to tell her so she would be part of their lives.

The storm refused to abate. 'Twas like hail hitting her every exposed inch, every startling, unfathomable word he spoke drilling dismay deep. Threatening to destroy everything in its path. Now, when she should be floating with happiness, fragility peltered.

"But by then," Uncle continued, "they knew not where she'd gone. It took time before they learned of the tragedies of their deaths, your mother and father's, for the old baron had kept that news to himself. By then, they knew not where *you* had gone.

"In recent months, the new baron's solicitor, who had inherited the brother's custom from his father, chanced across mention of their direction, of your father's family. Knowing of his client's search for his missing relation, a series of letters began.

"Letters that traced you to me, and...well." He sucked in a lungful of air. "Aphrodite, not only do they seek to renew acquaintance with you, but the siblings who disagreed with their father—your grandfather, the old baron... The ones who never countenanced his banishment of your mother? They put portions aside for her, never losing hope they would see her again and she would one day rejoin the family. Portions as their only child that are now yours. Portions that have grown these last fifteen years or more, and while you might not be considered an heiress possessing a *fortune*, you now have, at your disposal, the means to live, and quite comfortably, mind, the rest of your years *without ever having to work again.*"

Numb.

Money?

But Richard! The ephemeral life he'd alluded to. The joy being with him promised. The—

"But"—Richard!—"Harriet…"

Never before had a carriage ride made her bilious. But news that should have delighted instead devastated. Threatened to destroy—

"I know," Uncle said. "You have commitments. Commitments to Lord and Lady Ballenger, to young Lady Harriet." Uncle leaned forward, took up her lax fingers. Gave a squeeze. "Do you hear me, child? You are now a woman of means. You could travel. Own a townhouse outright in London, should you wish. Or a modest property in the country. Hire a trio of servants to tend it. To care for the grounds. To cook. To clean…"

With every word he uttered, the future he painted, all she could think was *But I want the life Richard's owdacious boldness made me think was possible…*

"There is more, sweet Aphrodite, daughter of my heart."

More? Could she take any more? Would Richard still want—

Will he still want you? Now that you have funds? And Viola just complimented your intellect? Come now!

"Things I must confess…"

LOST. She was lost to him.

Numbness threatened to assail more than Warrick's lower limbs.

A wealthy woman *in her own right*, Satan's spawn had claimed. Great-grandfather was a viscount; rotten grandfather a baron.

Warrick had no hold over her.

Thundering hooves trampled homeward, scattering his thoughts, stomping the breath from his lungs. Froze him in place every bit as much as he'd been upon the battlefield.

Paralyzed.

He couldn't move. Couldn't think.

Could only *feel*. Gut-deep remorse that he wasn't another. Someone full of limb and accounts, able to court and woo her properly. Able to win *her*. Her, and not this blasted bank account she was only now learning of in the other carriage. With the wretched man who'd *pretended* to be her uncle, a relationship forged with naught but a note pinned to a child's chest and handed over into his care.

Lady Redford, trusted confidant, Mercury's dozing head perched upon the lady's dress, the rest of the dog sprawled next to her, continued to answer questions and fill in whatever gaps Arbuckle's distressing news had left.

Arbuckle. Who had been given the "gift" of Aphrodite by one of his former *patients*. A grateful mother who showed her "appreciation" by foisting off an unwanted child onto the helpful surgeon. Assuming he'd find her an apprenticeship or toss her into a foundling workhouse. He had never been expected to keep the "weeping, mournful chit" as she'd been described.

And are you not indebted that he did?

Thankful down to your booted, occasionally feeling toes that Arbuckle—the man you have failed to appreciate, to thank—altered the course of his *life and gave hers a chance? Gave her a home?*

Even sought out her family? Only to be told through the old baron's solicitor he had *no granddaughter to speak of*?

Warrick's eyes watered; nose stung. That anyone could have cast aside such a bright light.

So easily could the joyful spirit he had come to cherish have been extinguished on the streets had Arbuckle not had the kindness, the generosity to care for and nurture her. So easily—

Stop the mawkish turn, Rich. You need an heiress. Is she not perfect? Now that her purse is plump?

She had already been perfect, by damn. He could not *use* her like that.

His Aphrodite Primrose, whom his heart had already chosen.

Was that not the truth?

Had he not, ever since the injury and even before, rejected each and every female suggested to him as a potential countess?

Had his skin not crawled, tongue near spat and shudders wracked his frame at the notion of wooing a single one?

Yet had he not, from the humiliating moments of their very first meeting upon the Ballenger estate, sought her out? *Her* company. Her intriguing conversation. Her lips and taste?

Aphrodite Primrose, the Latin-speaking, alluring governess who made him ridiculously verbose? Who brought forth lyrical words and longing thoughts that he'd never had about, nor spoken to another?

Breath gusted audibly from between his lips.

By God. That was it. *Not* because of her newfound funds. But because he was utterly lost without her.

Aphrodite Primrose, the lass to whom he must *propose*.

Secure her willing allegiance to him forevermore, as she had his.

"Burn the list," was what he said into the weighted silence between himself and Lady Redford.

No need for the list his mother had composed. The one of suitable, wealthy candidates. He had never intended to use it. *And if Aphrodite has doubts about their future together, now that she has options?* It mattered not.

Because he was fighting for the woman he loved.

"I care not if she has funds that could grant her another life. An easier life. It will not be a *better* life," shared with utter conviction. "For no one else will love her as I do. Burn the bloody list."

"Oh, dear Rich, there never was any list. Your mother fabricated that, fooled us both I daresay. She placed a folded scrap into my safekeeping and told me to hold on to it until you were ready. When you declined, and understandably so, after we buried her and grief was so fresh, I unfolded it—for it wasn't sealed—vastly curious as to the females she might have thought worthy of you and her other children. Only to find naught but a brief note and a solicitor's direction."

No list?

"The man holds on to some schoolbook of Mr. Feldon's," she continued, "one he wanted passed down to Beaufort and Bertram, where she has tucked in letters for you all—*all* of her children—but didn't want them delivered until everyone had gained a few years.

"Now that you have finally mentioned it, I shall see it returned to you so you can ensure the children receive what letters she has for them when you deem it appropriate. From what I can gather, she invented *the list*, hoping to encourage you to select your own wife. It took longer than she might have wished, but I believe it all worked out in the end, don't you?"

No list?

His chest hurt, but a chuckle emerged anyway. No damn list.

"She would approve of your choice," Lady Redford said. "Your mother. Not that you need to hear that, but 'tis true."

"I may not need to hear it, but it will mean the world to Aphrodite. I may tell her you said so."

"I will tell your future bride myself. In the two years Elizabeth and I traveled together, stayed in London together, fought for both you and Ward; in the years I was blessed by her friendship, I daresay I came to know her as well as any.

"Did you know I accompanied her on her travels to Bath, once she learned of Silas? Sought to convince him to see you? It took more than one effort, I will share."

Knowing now what he did of his family's finances—of his mother's and what all she had faced alone, without his help—he had no doubt that Lady Redford had likely funded much of those efforts. The travel. Had helped keep his mother safe, as well as comforted by the presence of a friend.

"Thank you. For everything. For myself. And for Mama."

Her lips wobbled before she firmed them and continued. "Other than her death, other than you boys both being hurt so severely, I would not change any of it. For it brought me to Silas. It has brought both you and Ward strong women, happiness. Comforting futures for one and all, would you not say?"

He would say. He would shout to the heavens. If only he could hold Aphrodite in his arms, see how she got on. If her uncle's revelations had stunned Warrick, how was she bearing up to the news?

He glanced out the window but without taking it down and sticking his head completely out—something he would not do to the lady he traveled with, not given how cold seeped in from the edges—he could not see the other carriage. But he knew how close they were. Close yet far, given the ache in his palms and his chest. How he needed to hold her close.

"And you will speak on my behalf?" Lady Redford inquired after he resumed his seat, settled after straining his yearning gaze out the window. "You will tell Ward you approve?"

"What? Of you and Arbuckle?"

"Just so."

He remained silent. Let the jingle of harnesses and galloping hooves fill the air.

"Rich..."

"I'm thinking."

"Rich!" A startled cry.

"Trying to decide."

"That isn't at all humorous." But he saw her lips twitch.

"I beg to differ." A satisfied grin crawled across his face. "After all the ordering me about over the last months, the harping on accounts, the deceptions? He's due a bit of squirming."

"Rich." A sigh this time.

"But I promise not to leave him dangling on the hook for too overly long. For without his machinations which stranded us together, Aphrodite and I might not have made our way to each other."

Aye, you would have. Eventually.

He made a fist and banged on the ceiling, signaling to the coachman to stop.

Alarm flared in Lady Redford's eyes. "What is wrong?"

"Nothing is wrong." Nothing except the woman he loved was in the wrong carriage. "I would like to stretch my legs."

It wouldn't occur to him until later, much later, how that might be a good sign. It occurred to Silas instantly, the moment the horses were reined to a halt and everyone climbed down.

Even if they left the ambulatory chair tied in place and Silas and one of the groomsmen assisted Warrick finding a spot of privacy, just the fact that his patient used the phrase *stretch my legs*, the acknowledgment of restlessness, he hoped, was a positive sign indeed.

But after a few moments, when it came time to return to the seats inside, after Mercury had romped about until whistle-commanded to come back and the longing glances his niece kept casting after Lord Warrick made Silas as nauseous as if he sailed aboard a ship, he was beyond ready to see the journey ended. For only after this journey ended could he contemplate his return trip to Bath.

Glory. His patients!

At the realization he had abandoned everything in Bath, to jaunt north, he near slapped his forehead. Still hadn't remembered to bring his blasted favorite hat. Cold nipped at his ears every bit as much as the last agonizing minutes had battered his heart.

Holding the gently crying Aphrodite as she learned he wasn't her uncle in truth had threatened to break him. But with honesty shared, with feelings that could never be extinguished and an acknowledgment of the solid relationship forged over years between them, he hoped the woman he thought of as a daughter would continue to want him in her life.

"I will ride with Aphrodite," Lord Warrick announced before ascending into his borrowed carriage.

"Not unchaperoned, you won't!" blustered from his lips.

"Silas."

"Uncle!"

The women's soothing tones clashed with Lord Warrick's contempt.

"Good God, man, do you think I am crass enough to try and tup her in a carriage?" *With you only a length away* didn't need expressed. His scowl made it clear enough.

"Very well," Silas finally agreed.

But watching his niece climb in after the lordling did nothing to calm the seas battering his insides.

38

THE BEWIGGED HERMIT

"Thank you for being insistent," Aphrodite said after the groomsman handed her up and she nodded for the servant to stow away the steps and secure the door, "about us riding together."

"My pleasure." His words were simple; the glittering promise in his eyes was anything but as she untied her bonnet and removed it, too exhausted to care for proprieties. To feel anything but relief at how hungrily he stared at her, as though the past hours had starved him as well.

The moment the carriage was off, she flew into his open arms, no further persuasion necessary. For the miles without him had proved wretched; the news Uncle imparted so unexpected. Distressing, really.

"Your embrace." His heat warmed as the chilled breath she'd been holding through the past two posting stops and even before shuddered from her lungs. Richard's strength, his very presence, soothed the flayed edges so recently exposed. "This is what I have n-needed."

"Tears, sweet Prim? The bastard made you cry."

She pulled back, brushed gloved fingers beneath her eyes as a tremulous smile greeted that accusation. "You ought not curse Uncle so. He gave…" But then her lips trembled anew. Eyes fair swam. "Gave me a home—his love—when I had no right to either."

"Ah, Aphrodite. You had, *have* every right to both. And a whole new family who wants you as well, aye? Not just me.

"Before I apply myself convincing you *I* am the better bargain, which we both know to be false, tell me of Verdell? The rot he spewed. What maggot crawled into his garret?"

Now wasn't the time to ask but Warrick could not bear her sadness a moment more. Would rather see her ire. Toward Verdell and how the knave spoke of her or toward *him* for making such a spectacle at the pump-house, he cared not which.

"Verdell," spat as though the name soured her tongue. But it also stiffened her posture, prompted her to ease from his hold and regain the seat across from him. "Aye, you deserve to know. It is not true, what he said about light fingers."

As if there were any doubt. "Of course not. You worked for him? As governess?"

"I did, to his two daughters. At first all was well. Then his wife became pregnant and his eyes started to wander. Then his hands. Until one night, after she grew heavy with the babe, I awoke…awoke…" Panic suffused her features. Before he could tell her to halt, she finished in a rush. "Awoke-to-find-him-on-top-of-me-forcing-his-tongue-and-grabbing-breasts—"

"Shh now." He pulled her unresisting form back over, tugged her against his chest, brought her legs up beside him on the bench and stroked his palm over her head.

"The lamp. Next to the bed. I hit him with it. Ran screaming from the room while he roared. He was incensed, shouted to everyone we awoke how I'd stolen from his wife. A ring or something."

Did she realize how fretful her fingers had become? How she'd yanked off gloves, now wound her hands in his neckcloth?

"The other female servants? They knew the truth. I could see it before they looked away. Scuttled off. But the damage had been done. He put rumors about the next day, I learned, that I had been dismissed and without character, but it mattered not because I had left during the night. Sought refuge with a friend and then Uncle until finding another position, closer to his London practice."

"Tate?"

A nod beneath his chin, those hands mangling the knot he'd taken pains to fashion to impeccable precision before they'd left the cottage so, so many happenings ago. "And Lord Paulson's brother as well. Both proved unpalatable. It wasn't until an instructor from the improving academy, upon hearing that I was back home in Bath, wrote telling me of Lady Harriet and the Larchmonts' desperate need for a governess who would not cry off due to their youngest daughter's exuberance and excitability that I found my place among those I could respect."

"I hope you did damage to his noggin. Verdell's. Bashed him hard enough with that lamp that his crown ached for a month."

"Doubtful." A sniffled laugh. A light kiss to the skin of his neck, unearthed by her industrious fingers. "You did that for me. Today." Another kiss, one that lingered. "Thank you."

"My *vast* pleasure." His arms tightened about her. "What wasn't my pleasure was those first two hours confined with Arbuckle. He tried to convince me to withdraw my suit now that you have greater options to further your future. He likes me not."

She pulled back to frown at him. "You have been vocal about the same."

"Deservedly so."

"How did you respond?" she asked with serious intent, no more plying fingers or playful kisses.

"About letting you go? Rescinding my offer?"

A nod.

You still have not, with any sincerity, offered for her.

"Told him to stubble it. That I was the best man you could hope for—thought he might challenge me to swords at dawn over that. Truth told, Prim? I remain selfish in the extreme.

"Were I a better man, I would tell you to run. To lift up your skirts and race like the wind as far away from me and mine as you can go. Grant yourself some semblance of the future you deserve.

"Yet the thought of you turning from me and bounding off? Fills my chest with a nagging sort of sadness I doubt I would ever be able to dispense with, no matter how many other Latin-speaking, blushing, audacious governesses stumble across my halting path..."

"Richard, please. Do not belittle yourself."

"Why would you ever, ever agree to wed me now?" He spoke over her protest. "When the news shared by Arbuckle, your new-found startlings give rise to options beyond compare? Especially when I cannot offer you anything but a broken body and beggared estate?"

"Meekness does not suit you, my lord," she mocked, her frown growing. "You know better than to disparage your worth, walking or wealthy or neither.

"We both know trials exist ahead. Challenges I fear you may not have considered," she said, the frown now reaching her eyes. "Regardless of what Lady Redford may think, I doubt that her son and Lady Anne will be so quick to accept me, not as anything other than Harri's governess. I would hate to come between you and such a close friend."

"I believe they may surprise you." He soothed her agitation with the press of his fingers feathering over her lips. "But for good or ill, I care not. As close as we are, as much as I would never forsake him, I can live without Ed by my side. You? Not even for my next breath.

"Will you have me, despite the plentiful reasons not to?" Her lips opened and her tongue teased his fingers until he withdrew his touch and coiled his hand by his side. *Courage, Rich.* "Will you bind your life with mine and what, *who* comes with—my sisters and brothers? Will you live with me and our dearth of servants, in a rambling, somewhat desolate abode that needs your light and laughter above all else?

"I lay myself bare before you. I adore you, Aphrodite Primrose. Your sunset hair. Your enlivening nature. Your intellect. Your heart." His now thumped faster than a runaway team. "I know not what the future holds. I know not whether I will *ever* walk with ease. But I do not want to take steps if you are not by my side."

"I cannot imagine not being there, for steps. For hopes. For laughter. Cannot imagine the misery of being apart from you. And after those last sentences? Did my uncle and Lady Redford not travel so near, I would remove my dress and fan my skin, for I feel well-warmed indeed."

But he could not smile along with her, not yet. "I am no longer certain I can save the estate. Were it just myself? I would take to wearing a wig and hide from debt collectors." He heaved a sigh of regret. "'Tis really not the most well-conceived notion, to tie your future with mine."

"You goosecap." She tilted her head, evaluating him as though he were a featherhead in truth. "Should you keep blathering, I doubt you will manage to shove me aside, especially after those touching avowals of admiration I have no intention of forgetting. So cease making an idiot of yourself, hmm?

"I do not want the easy way of things. Did I, doubtless I would have fled your presence the moment you made me hither from the woods. Richard, part of me still baffles that we are here, now. The other part of me? Just wants to wrap hands about your shoulders, climb fingers up the back of your head to tug on those silky black strands and bring your mouth to mine. Put it to better use than all that buffoonery, trying to make me doubt. A useless endeavor, that."

Daylight waned as evening approached. At the last horse change, he had lit the lantern. Now, he chose to turn it down, for with less light came more privacy.

"Everything I have or that may come to me," she said, the moment he finished, "however much it might be, I want it to be yours."

His forehead pinched in a scowl. "So many ways that is wrong."

"Then use what you need to keep the creditors at bay. The rest? If there is enough, we shall maintain what we can of the estate, your birthright, keep the roof over our head, mayhap furnish dowries for the girls..."

His hands found their way to her hips, clenched tight.

"And if I fail? If the debts cannot be appeased sufficiently that I avoid debtors' prison—"

"*We* will not fail." Her faith staggered him.

"But if the worst does happen, will you guard the children? Visit me in—"

"Oh, pish and poh! Do you hear yourself? Debtors' prison is out of the question! Nay, from what you have shared, Sophia and the twins would no doubt plan a jail-breaking and then where would Julia and I be? We shall order you that wig, a long beard as well. That and a grey cloak, let you hide away in the hermitage before we allow you to be taken from us," said as though she were a general commanding troops.

Her words, her very insistence snaffled his wits. "I...I... The estate doesn't have a hermitage, I do not think." He'd been absent for so many years, who knew anymore?

"And you call yourself an *Englishman*? An *earl*?" How appalling she made both sound. And once again, in her presence, he was fighting not hopelessness but laughter. "That should be our highest priority, then," she asserted, "once you are reunited with your siblings—"

"And you with *your* family."

She beamed at that but did not let it stop her. "We shall build—"

"You mean dig out, I believe. Are not hermitages dug out from rock, from the earth? Certainly nothing so fanciful to be *built* above ground."

Despite his interruptions, his gentle needling, nothing dampened her enthusiasm for the project she had just conceived. Nay, she blasted any hesitations, any concerns he might have dared voice and continued planning out his life. His entire family's life, and with every word shared, every idea described, he fell more and more in love.

"Shall we have Sophia supervise?" Aphrodite

pondered aloud. "From what you have shared of her, she would relish putting the twins to work. Part of their punishment, mayhap?"

"She would thrive in that role. And they would chafe."

"Wonderful choices all around, then."

"Looking wonderfully satisfied with yourself, Prim. And Julia? What part shall she have in building—"

"You mean digging?"

"This hermitage of yours?"

"Mine? Perish the thought! Do not expect me to join you there, not without warm water but instead addled by insects? Nay, I shall maintain my happiness within *walls*— ones that are *built*; you may visit me at night, every night if you please. But only after you bathe."

"Of a certainty. When I am not hiding from creditors."

"Exactly! As to Julia..." So easily did she include his fragile youngest sister. Included her in a way that touched him anew. "I shall work with her on the recordation of it all. That will give us time to evaluate her vocabulary, spelling, penmanship and even math. But without any sort of formal schooling. She and I, with Sophia's assistance I am sure, will monitor and record the hours spent, tools used, mayhap add drawings and lists... We shall communicate without requiring spoken sentences until she is ready for more. She will not be left out."

"I adore you, Prim. Love you more than you can fathom."

"Grand. So no more annoying talk of foisting me off on unknown family?"

"None."

"No more ridiculous notions of not using whatever monies might come my way to help your estate? No more preposterous consideration of debtors' prisons?"

"Mmmm." He could not help but dither, knowing the possibility, however distasteful, existed.

"Only notions of wigs and hermitages?" she proposed, all saucy determination again.

"Aye. I concur. I shall be your bewigged hermit and you shall see to running the household."

"Brilliant. I concur as well."

"And…" He allowed his voice to become as deep and low as he could make it. "You shall sit upon my lap. Starting now?"

"You really are a bufflehead."

"Is that any way to speak to your lord and master?"

The sound of her hilarity rang loud and true—until he convinced her to put her mouth to better use.

So, all through the night, the carriage creaked, harnesses jingled as the wheels sped onward, taking both of them into a future that neither would have envisioned even two weeks ago, much less two years, but a future that now tantalized, beckoned more with every breath and heartbeat shared between them.

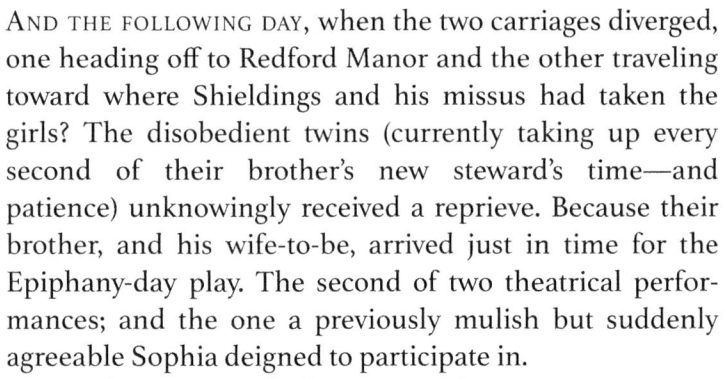

AND THE FOLLOWING DAY, when the two carriages diverged, one heading off to Redford Manor and the other traveling toward where Shieldings and his missus had taken the girls? The disobedient twins (currently taking up every second of their brother's new steward's time—and patience) unknowingly received a reprieve. Because their brother, and his wife-to-be, arrived just in time for the Epiphany-day play. The second of two theatrical performances; and the one a previously mulish but suddenly agreeable Sophia deigned to participate in.

For the bartering had commenced.

In exchange for her cooperation that evening and the next while they resided within the burgeoning walls of the extended Shieldings' family's home, even though she had vowed to behave for a sennight, Warry concurred that she could ease from her vigilant perfection after *five* days. She had haggled for four but relaxed her stance when she saw how much difficulty he had maintaining his—physically, that was.

When the curiously pretty Aphrodite (what a burdensome name!) knelt and whispered to Sophia how vastly worried he had been, said something about *another* injury, Sophia decided to be the bigger personage. See if she didn't! (Because if Warry could take the blushing, freckly, orange-haired governess to wife? If someone found *Aphrodite* appealing, then mayhap there existed hope for Sophia, too. With her thick brows and commanding nose, her even more commanding manner...)

And that evening, after tears had been dried (Julia could still be *such* a baby at times) and applause suitably rendered?

While looking out over the crowd of gathered, cheering adults, Sophia took more satisfaction than she might have expected upon spying a sleeping Julia, coiled tight in Warry's arms, head on his shoulder, her baby arm outstretched and clinging to some of that fascinatingly ugly hair of the smiling woman by his side.

A step-mama? Hmm. Another adult to bargain with?

One more "parent" to punish King and Knight once they returned home two days hence?

For, aye, Sophia had overheard plenty about her brothers' antics since Warry arrived. She chuckled. The twins were going to be in *so much trouble!*

She couldn't wait.

EPILOGUE I - APRIL 1814

THE TWINS RETURNED TO SCHOOL in a week.

Thanks to groveling—Warrick's and thoroughly touching letters each boy had penned (with Aphrodite's guidance)—*and* sizable donations—these, thanks to Ed and Frost—King and Knight had only suffered only missing one full term.

Which meant they would all be here for Easter services tomorrow. But more than that, what caused Warrick measures of both sadness and anticipation, as he checked his cravat in the hand mirror before placing it on the table beside his bed and reaching for his boot, was this morning's family jaunt.

'Twas April 9th. One year since Mama's passing.

He blinked fast as one boot blurred, tugging it on after dismissing Shieldings' help for the morn. He needed to do this himself. For his family.

His eyes glanced around the chamber he shared with his wife of two and a half months, the bed, dresser and bedside tables crowded by the addition of his upstairs ambulatory chair and a couple of other wooden ones strong enough to support his weight.

It was the feminine touches that helped dry his eyes and buffet his aching heart. The marigolds she'd coaxed to an early bloom in a vase beside his shaving kit. The prime fan he'd given her as a wedding gift. The ornate hairbrush from her (still favored) "uncle" Silas sitting beside the old scribbled-in Bible one of her "new" aunts had sent her, it having belonged to her mother. That handkerchief, long ago snaffled during a mistletoe kiss, folded neatly and tucked inside; the other having been returned to Ed's wife, Lady Anne (who had taken surprisingly well to the news that her sister's governess would soon outrank her, aided likely by Harri's jubilance).

Married since the end of January, thanks to the simple ceremony conducted as soon the banns had been read, enough to bind them for life.

The banns. Suffering them to be called out each Sunday for three weeks? Casting glances over his shoulder, not quite certain whether Satan's spawn would make an unexpected appearance and protest...

But Arbuckle remained silent, as far as any complaints or grievances toward Warrick. As to his niece? He remained close, all that was complimentary, had even turned his disparaging remarks toward Warrick aside—after sweet Prim started engaging in some glaring of her own.

Now that the surgeon stepped out with Lady Redford, no more hiding in Bath, he was frequently seen at gatherings when they went to Redford Hall.

And if Lady Ballenger had sniffed her disapproval on the rare occasions they crossed paths? Then the joy conveyed by Harriet's continual, bounding enthusiasm over the "romance of the ages" along with her father's clap on Warrick's shoulder (and the whispered "Found yourself a good woman, congratulations.") far surpassed any hurts the other woman's negativity thought to aim their way.

His second boot bumped into place over his heel with a slight jerk. Placing both feet solidly in front of him, Warrick leaned forward to retrieve his chair, his eyes landing on the small package delivered yesterday, not yet opened but something to look forward to.

For, according to the note attached, Mercury had finally revealed his hiding spot, and not only had Arbuckle's favorite hat been found (though why that had been included in the note, Warrick wasn't sure) but (and these were the parts he smiled over) Warrick would soon be reunited with his missing neckcloth, a lone sock, his drawers (unrepentantly ripped), portions of two unposted letters (also ripped) and three canine-chewed pencils. (Oh, joy.)

He rolled the chair into place and made sure it was secure before shifting his weight. He knew better than to "walk" much today, not if he had any hope of making it, with cane and Aphrodite's assistance, from the carriage to Mama's headstone.

Just as he gained his seat, Aphrodite swept in, looking uncharacteristically frayed. "Oh," she exclaimed. "I thought you were already downstairs. In the carriage and waiting for me."

He gave her an indulgent smile. "You know better than that. Who— Ah. Sophia?"

Nodding, she approached, retrieved his cane from beside the bed and then moved to tug on her gloves, her features smoothing into their more customary sereneness as she realized she wasn't delaying anyone. "Indeed. Is still more than a little miffed we didn't let her go with Cook and son to the coast."

Ridiculous. He didn't care how divine the woman cooked nor how well behaved her son, his sister was not about to be apart from the family today. Not about to travel willy-nilly without Aphrodite or himself. "So she told you I was outside?"

"Not...explicitly. But implied you and the boys were both waiting, impatient for me in the carriage."

"The minx. Lines for her! And Julia?" Who still wasn't talking—much. As in, if she gave him a two-word sentence in a week, 'twas cause for celebration.

"Awaits by the door, eager to go outside and bobbing in place." Aphrodite came near his ear, lowered her voice. "But she left her blanket on her bed again."

"Progress!" He laughed. "But, Prim, she's not about to hear you. No need to whisper."

"I just want to take care." She gave the open door behind her a guilty look, then anointed his recently shaved cheek with a kiss. "Are you ready?"

"With you by my side? Always."

EPILOGUE II - EIGHT YEARS LATER

APHRODITE PRIMROSE MARTINSON, Lady Warrick, knew three things with utter and complete certainty:

1. Her husband loved her with every beat of his heart and showed her frequently a thousand different ways.

2. She could not love him, or their family, any more than she already did—no matter how big it might grow.

3. Unfortunately, no matter how much healing he might do, her husband would never dance again. Never run. Most days might barely walk, but with every step he took—or didn't—and with every word he spoke, she would always be grateful he still possessed the *in*ability to fully moderate his speech to a manner becoming someone of his station. ("Do I need to assign you lines?" she would ask once they were alone, after a particularly ribald remark made before others. "By all means," he would reply, that unholy light glinting in his midnight eyes. "Assign away. I will draw them upon your skin with my tongue.")

EPILOGUE II - EIGHT YEARS LATER

THE LIGHT TWINKLING OF NOTES, melodic and uplifting, drew Aphrodite toward the harpsichord in the study. An unusual domain for such an instrument, mayhap—for any instrument, really—but it had a place of pride at the Warrick estate, in its master's domain.

She smiled upon entering, seeing the two backs, side by side. One strong, tall and broad—comfortably attired in shirt sleeves—the other a miniature, feminine version, dressed in a white muslin gown with a midnight-blue sash, small feet kicking in the air beside her papa on the bench as she chattered away. The uplifting notes continued, as Richard reached around his youngest daughter and played over her shoulder, laughing when she *plonked* several fingers in the middle of his hands, nodding even though the discordant sound made Aphrodite wince.

She had just seen their seven-month-old son consoled until he finally nodded off. Teething could be such a trial; fortunately, the music seemed to help.

Never would she forget the first time she heard her husband play. Saw the raging intensity, witnessed the raw power of both man and music turmoiled together unlike anything she could have imagined. Not that she didn't still love it when he played fiercely, which he did on occasion. If frustration got him down. Often after his quarterly meeting with his solicitor, noting debits (always so many) and credits (never enough).

When Sophia expressed irritation with her position, assisting a visiting scientist, or a local lad dared to call on Julia. ("She's too young for that nonsense!") If he didn't hear from Knight or King as regularly as he thought they ought to write. If he had a specially rough day. But those times were farther and fewer between.

Though he still tested his boundaries, maintained

EPILOGUE II - EIGHT YEARS LATER

repetitions of the dreaded seat-to-stands, his newest Merlin's chair, delivered just last month after his other was rolled to within an inch of its life, was but a foot away—within reach as it would always need to be.

Yet it was moments like these, when the shared laughter between family members, when his quiet notes filtered through the rooms, luring her in from another part of the intermittently furnished manor house, that nourished her soul to overflowing.

Times like these, when he laughed, stopped playing to pull his three-year-old daughter upon his lap and let her make merry with mangled music, without a word of complaint upon his lips that tugged at heartstrings.

"You take after your mother, little one," he told the child after a flinch-worthy *bang-bang-bang* upon the dear instrument they had relocated from Marigold Cottage, with Uncle's blessing.

"Her mother is standing right here."

"I know," said with his back still to her. "I always know. One of my angels, my favorite one, lest you forget. I always know when you are close and watching over me."

"Mama! Listen!" *Bang-bang-plonk!*

"Utterly brilliant, sweetheart," Aphrodite said, working hard to conceal smiles and stifle laughter.

Richard had no such difficulty, laughing outright and glancing over his shoulder. "You know what happens to liars."

"They get lines?" she asked, heart near to bursting.

"They do indeed!" He wiggled his eyebrows at her before facing forward once more, ere he lost his balance. "They do indeed. How soon is bedtime?"

THE END

NOTE FROM LARISSA—INCLUDING A PLEA

Dare I admit I had a *really* difficult time saying goodbye to these characters? I thought Daniel and Thea, of my other loooong novel, *Mistress in the Making*, would forever remain my favorite pairing. I must say they now have some competition…

Wrapping up this story has been a challenge. I don't work well with deadlines, but I knew I could not put off releasing it *another* year! As both my husband and house can attest, the last few months finishing *Moonlit* has been my sole focus. I truly hope you have enjoyed reading both the challenges and triumphs presented within. ❤

Interested in a bonus, potentially intimate scene between Aphrodite and Richard? If that's something you're clamoring for *and* I receive enough requests for it, I'll get that done. Email me at larissa@larissalyons.com.

Still craving more Christmas Kisses? Catch up with Ed and Anne in **A Snowlit Christmas Kiss** and Frost and Isabella in

A Frosty Christmas Kiss. Other goodies and snarky cats (*Rescued by a Christmas Kiss*) abound at my website.

Laugh, love and dance whenever you can!

>^..^< Larissa

P.S. **Please take a moment and leave a review.** Even just a sentence or two helps authors. And for some reason, reviews with pictures—yes, just a picture of your ereader with *Moonlit*'s cover or you holding the paperback—may get those highlighted over other reviews. Snap a pic and share your thoughts…

AND NOW FOR THE "PLEA" PART…

Please assist me in finding more fans.

I've been hearing grumblings from other authors for a while about the lack of new readers to historical romance. All those avid book lovers hanging out on TikTok? Regency romance has not sparked near the interest many other genres command.

As it is, I'm debating switching my focus to writing contemporary because **my historicals are not selling enough to cover my costs of writing, much less provide any sort of profit.** 🐱

If you enjoy my stories, pretty please with sugar on top, *write those reviews, post online (anywhere…FB, Reddit, etc.), share with friends—or your friendly librarian* ;-)—and help find more readers looking for fun, Regency-esque escapes. Thanks gobs!

ABOUT LARISSA

HUMOR. HEARTFELT EMOTION. & HUNKS.

Writing strong men with a weakness for the right woman, Larissa blends heartfelt emotion with doses of laugh-out-loud humor. Her goal is to give readers an escape from their everyday stressors.

Larissa lives in Texas with her husband and their menagerie of bossy cats and big dogs in one cluttered abode she's constantly hoping to clear out. She avoids housework one word at a time listening to the voices in her head clamoring to reach the page…

Creatively working around some health challenges and computer limitations, it's a while between releases, but stick with her—she's working on the next one.

Learn more at LarissaLyons.com.

LARISSA'S COMPLETE BOOKLIST

AS OF WINTER 2024

Historicals by Larissa Lyons

FUN & SEXY REGENCY ROMANCE

Lady Scandal

Lady Imposter

Lady Reckless

REGENCY CHRISTMAS KISSES

A Snowlit Christmas Kiss

*A Frosty Christmas Kiss**

A Moonlit Christmas Kiss

(Also available - FREE 40K Preview of A Moonlit Christmas Kiss)

*(expanded version of *Miss Isabella Thaws a Frosty Lord*)

MORE REGENCY CHRISTMAS KISSES

Rescued by a Christmas Kiss

ROARING ROGUES REGENCY SHIFTERS

Ensnared by Innocence

Deceived by Desire

Tamed by Temptation (forthcoming)

MISTRESS IN THE MAKING (Complete)

Seductive Silence (free ebook)

Lusty Letters

Daring Declarations

Mistress in the Making - Bundle

Contemporaries by Larissa Lynx

SEXY CONTEMPORARY ROMANCE

Renegade Kisses

Starlight Seduction

SHORT 'N' SUPER STEAMY

A Heart for Adam...& Rick!

Braving Donovan's

No Guts, No 'Gasms

POWER PLAYERS HOCKEY series

*My Two-Stud Stand**

*Her Three Studs**

The Stud Takes a Stand (forthcoming)

**Her Hockey Studs - print version*

Literary Madness!

Printed in Great Britain
by Amazon